KINGDOM COME

KINGDOM COME

Shane Wesley Shelton

Believing Magic Books

First U.S. edition 2014

ISBN 978-1-941570-11-1

Printed by Amazon CreateSpace

Artwork for all covers in the Believing Magic series purchased on Shutterstock.com

Grammatical and line editing for all books in the Believing Magic Series by:
Karen Robinson – Freelance copy editor and proofreader
Bachelors, English & Masters, English | Texas A&M University, Doctorate, English | Perdue University, Faculty Fellow | Ivy Tech Community College teaching English and Composition

Second Editing and Final Read Through Proofing for all books in the BM series:
Sherri McDougald – English major at University of North Florida
Artist: acrylics, ink, pencil/charcoal, and glass etching
Contact for any work requests at: sherrir30@yahoo.com

Interior book design and ebook conversion by:
Jimmy Sevilleno – professional interior book designer and ebook conversion specialist

Cover artwork tweaked and adjusted and prepped for print by:
Jeesun Hwang – Graphic artist and designer

Believing Magic Books
13 Kingfish Avenue
Ponte Vedra Beach, Florida 32082
visit us at **www.believingmagic.com**

Also by the Author

Contents

Amen Hale

Book of Shadows

Read, before you choose to hate
Read, before you give your love
Hate me if you must,
Love me if you desire it…

This is what I am.

A desperate young girl in the motherly way
Spoke to herself on one horrible day.
Too weak and too scared to do the dread deed
She created a friend in her hour of need.

I need you to help me, she whispered to me
I made you to help me, to help set me free.
Free from the shame of the life I now hold.
Free from the shame of the lies that I've told.

Please! I begged her. *Don't ask this of me!*
Please! Oh please! I begged Rain Marie.
She would not listen, though I begged and I cried.
I MADE YOU! she yelled. *My will now abide!*

You go now, and kill the child, I can't do it myself!
I've tried and I've tried and each time I have failed.
My heart cries out and I run from the room,
but my time is short and I'll have to leave soon!

Why do it at all! Oh please, let's just go!
But no matter my tears she firmly said, *"NO!"*
I made you myself from the dark of my heart,
Now take up my body and go let them start!

The nurse said kind words, her voice filled with lies
Don't worry my child, there's no need to cry.
I wept as I entered the room filled with blades
Where the doctor was waiting to end Brendon's days.

As soon as it started she spoke once again.
I lay on the table, cold steel still within
Jabbing and stabbing up into our womb
Turning a safe place into a tomb.

Thank you for helping, but I need you again
And I know it's not fair and I know it's a sin,
But I want you to kill me, to kill once again.
I don't want my life. I want it to end.

You bitch! I shouted, *You go straight to hell!*
You made me kill Brendon, but that's all! I yelled.
The murdering hands then slipped with the blade,
I laughed and I laughed at the pain that cut made.

The doctor and nurses then strapped me down
They stitched and they worked as they bustled around.
This one's gone crazy, I heard the nurse say.
I laughed and laughed and said, *It's my birthday!*

Born from the shadows of Rain Marie's heart
Born to kill, right from the start.
Shaped by her mind to help her to kill.
I did the damn deed but I hated it still.

If you don't take this body from me,
I'll kill myself. Just wait. You'll see.
You know I'll do it. It will kill Mom and Dad.
It's your choice, if you don't want them to be sad.

Please! Oh please! I begged once again.
But Rain Marie said, *I'm sorry, my friend.*
If you want to keep our body alive
You'll have to kill me to make it survive.

How do I do it? I asked in defeat.
You just push me out and then take my seat.
This body will be all yours and not mine.
I'm through with this life, now it's your time.

I'm scared, Rain Marie. What will I do?
How will I act when I walk in your shoes?
Don't worry, you'll remember the life that we shared
And you'll be with our family, and you know that they care.

So I pushed as I cried and shoved Rain Marie out
And taking her place, I stood and walked out.
The bastard who brought her stopped at the store.
Give me some money! NO! Give me some more!

I walked into Wal-Mart and filled up my bag
with things that were black, no white but the tag.
I arrived at the trailer at a quarter past noon.
I cleaned out my closet and emptied my room.

No yellow. No white. No pink and no blue.
I bagged it all up and I threw it out too.
I sat on my bed wearing nothing but black
When her mother came in, carrying a sack.

Rain Marie, why are your clothes in the trash?
She opened the bag and I started to laugh.
Mother, my name is not Rain Marie.
She gave me a look, she stared right at me.

You're not Rain Marie, then who are you instead
You sure look a lot like the child that I bred.
No tears stung my eyes but that ended my mirth
As I looked in the face of the one from our birth.

She did not murder the child that she made,
She birthed it, and loved it, from then to this day.
I, myself, had killed Rain Marie
The very child she swore me to be.

Mother, my name is not Rain Marie.
I'm sorry. But I'm afraid. She died. You see.
I hope you don't mind if I live here instead
And sleep in this room, and lie in this bed.

She looked alarmed when she heard what I said
And sat down beside me on Rain Marie's bed.
She asked what had happened and if I felt well.
I gave no reply though she begged me to tell.

So on that day, that's how I was born
Not from a womb, but from her heart was I torn
A scrap of her soul she left here behind
To live out her life. A life, that's now mine.

I would say "God, forgive me" but He does not hear my words.
I would forgive myself, but that seems blasphemous, even to me.
It is enough to say I am what I am.
Let the Black Witch now live in me. So mote it be.

As above so below, as within so without.

Journal Entry

IT IS THE third day of the Kingdom, 1/3/1. The date is Friday, the 5th of August, 2016 in the world outside these walls.

This morning when I entered the Cathedral Hall I found these words. Some time during the night *she* wrote them. The smudges and stains are not from my tears but from the one who wrote these words.

I am shocked. I have read it through many times. Though I had heard the story from others it is altogether different to see it told here by her hand. She is not willing to forgive herself, and I think I can understand why that is. I am the least of the servants of the Hall. My voice the quietest. The smallest. But I forgive her. And I love her.

Calvin Leonard Pyle, bond slave of Amen Hale.
Keeper of the Book of Shadows.
A brick in the wall.

Thursday, the 4th of August, 2016

K.C. 1-2-1

Penny

Welcome Home

PENNY WAS A pretty little black girl, almost thirteen years old, with big brown eyes and a bright happy smile. Penny lived in Alma, Georgia. It was nothing but a quick flash of structures lining a painfully boring stretch of state highway passed in an easily forgotten blur. And yet, if you did drive right by it, without realizing that you passed it, you would definitely remember it, but not fondly, because you would get a ticket, stimulate the local economy, and be sent on your way.

Alma, a.k.a. "The Armpit of Georgia," was located in the middle of the least populated part of the state. The number one industry in the quiet area was trees. Pine trees. Sometimes Penny thought pine trees were taking over the whole world.

Row upon organized row of perfectly aligned pines in various stages of growth filled every available tract of land for miles around in every direction.

It made Penny appreciate the small stand of oaks, cypresses, and other hardwoods nestled behind her grandmother's old house. She loved walking in those woods with their twisted, unpredictable limbs reaching this way and that. It was like her own little magical island, so different from the plain, straight world that surrounded her.

Her mother had abandoned her at her Gran's dilapidated shack in the middle of nowhere three years ago, but Penny was happy there. She liked living with her grandmother and enjoyed curling up with a book on their comfy old couch to read the day away or watching scary movies with Gran that they borrowed from Alma's tiny library. Most of her life was just as plain as the pines. Straight and normal and plain and ordinary. But there was a part of her life that wasn't straight and normal at all. Penny was a witch, just like her Gran.

It was Wednesday night. Penny had just drifted off into a deep dreamless sleep when her grandmother's ice cold hands shook her awake and forced a black garbage bag into her hands.

"Get up, girl! Get some clothes and get in the car!"

She was still half asleep as the old wood-paneled Buick RoadMaster rumbled to life and pulled out of the drive at ten fifteen. When Penny asked where they were going, Gran told her that they were headed to a place down in Florida called Amen Hale that was a two-hour drive straight south. Penny's grandmother admitted up front that they might be on a wild goose chase and that everything she'd heard might be nothing but bunk, but she said she just had to see it for herself!

Penny had never seen Gran so excited. She was almost like a little girl, laughing and giddy and smiling her biggest smiles as she jabbered away. Gran had been watching the news on TV and she'd called a few of her "witch" friends who had internet. They'd told her what the TV hadn't. It seemed that "Amen Hale" had somehow become its own tiny little country and that they had a real, live, honest-to-goodness King and Queen, just like in the old days.

Penny listened wide eyed as Gran told her about the King of Amen Hale and how he'd been murdered yesterday and that a Red Witch had raised him up from the dead with a human sacrifice! To Penny it sounded like one of those stories straight out of the Bible, and Gran said that it was *all true!* or at least she meant to go and find out for herself if it was true or not. Gran also told her that the land of Amen Hale was filled with real magic, witches, and even monsters and real live dragons!

Penny fought with the old radio as Gran drove, turning the knob this way and that to keep it tuned to the news as the miles passed and stations came and went. Gran didn't know what they'd find when they got to Amen Hale, or if they'd let her or Penny in, but she just kept saying, "*I's got to see it for m-self!*" The two of them had a fantastic time driving down the dark freeway in the middle of the night trying to imagine what wonders and magic they would see when they got there.

It was like walking into a war zone when they arrived at the gates of Amen Hale. There were hundreds, no, thousands of soldiers. Some stood opposite a concrete half wall barrier that was still under construction, others rushed about moving trucks, tanks, and other equipment while yet more soldiers were busy keeping the growing crowds under tight control. A loud continual hum of noise and movement vibrated the air. Planes and helicopters buzzed overhead and news crews were everywhere with their cameras and bright lights, turning night into day as they did their interviews and news stories.

Penny and her grandmother joined the others who wanted in to Amen Hale, taking their place in the impossibly long line that led to the gates. There were people who looked like witches standing in line with them, but there were also many others who didn't. Church groups and angry protestors were there too, crowded around the gate and ranged up and down the line, shouting and preaching at those waiting to get in and handing them so many flyers and tracts that the ground was absolutely littered with discarded materials.

Penny and one other very strange girl named Angel made a game of it and went around collecting the discarded literature. Once they had amassed two full garbage bags, they began to tile the flyers out on the ground like flooring material so their feet wouldn't get all muddy. Soon after they started, all the younger children of those in line joined them, and Penny and Angel assumed management roles, organizing and directing the operation like a couple of generals directing their troops. The parents were happy because it kept the children entertained and out of trouble, and everyone agreed that not walking on mud was also nice, but not everyone appreciated the use of soul-saving literature as flooring material.

As soon as the church groups noticed what the children were doing they started shouting and crying out even louder, and more soldiers had to step in to keep the peace between the two groups. One preacher with a sound system started a new shouted out sermon that he directed at the waiting line of petitioners seeking entry into Amen Hale. "The road to Hell is paved with good intentions!" his voice cried out.

It went on for hours and hours as they waited to be seen. The preachers "preached," the protestors waved their signs, and the mocking crowd made jokes and laughed at all the "fools" that wanted in, waiting in the endless line.

It did seem hopeless.

They watched people far in front of them in line reach a big green tent where they were spoken to by someone from Amen Hale. Almost everyone was being turned away, some leaving peacefully, but some were being carried away by soldiers as they cried like babies or yelled, loud and angry.

After hours of waiting, Penny and her grandmother finally reached the tent where a very tall older man who introduced himself as "Byron the House Steward" asked them all kinds of questions once he found out that Penny was a Red Witch. He said Penny would be allowed into Amen Hale and they would see *if* she could serve as Princess Bethany's maid.

Penny's grandmother was sad not to get in herself, but she was very happy for Penny. Gran asked her if she wanted to go and try. Penny was scared, but she still said yes. She was too curious to even dream of saying no. She wanted to see for herself if the magic was real or if all of it was just made up stories. Penny hefted her bag of clothes onto her shoulder, kissed her grandmother goodbye, and went with Byron the Steward.

Penny, her strange friend Angel, and a dozen others who were fortunate enough to be chosen climbed into a long black van and headed down the road, past all the soldiers and through the metal gates. Byron rode in the back with everyone else and spoke to Penny on the short trip to the house. He told her that Princess Bethany was also a Red Witch. Penny knew that meant blood, but blood wasn't all that scary to her. Penny had been helping Gran for past three years now, so she was used to animal sacrifice. But she'd also heard the stories while she waited outside with the others. There were lots and lots of stories being passed around and all the ones about Princess Bethany were very scary.

As Byron guided their little group into Amen Hall, Penny couldn't stop herself from looking up at the high ceiling in the Entry Hall that was sprayed with millions of little drops of blood. Everyone who entered did the same, looking up at the high ceiling. A chill went down Penny's spine as she remembered the stories she'd heard about *how* the blood got onto the ceiling. The blood was from someone that the Princess had killed with just one word *and a look*. Penny thought that if this story was true, then the ones about her raising King Cornelius from the dead with a human sacrifice must also be true.

Penny was scared but she was also happy. Happy and excited to be chosen when so many others had been turned away. Byron led them though the house and out to a building they called the Guest Hall where everyone had their luggage checked for cameras, weapons, and other things that were forbidden. It didn't take long to search Penny's one bag of clothes. Soon she and Angel were taken to the showers to get clean before being led to a long room that held ten beds. It was early in the morning, barely two hours remained before the sun would rise and a new day began. Penny and Angel were careful not to wake the other girls who were already sleeping. Angel was in the bed right beside Penny but the two girls didn't talk to each other; the second they crawled into their beds and got settled between the warm clean sheets they fell fast asleep.

In the morning all the "newcomers," which was what they were being called, were roused and brought outside to a beautiful garden where the King and Queen came out to meet with them. Everyone dropped down onto their knees and Penny copied them and did the same as the King and Queen of Amen Hale stepped up onto a metal table so everyone could see them.

The King was a tall, older man. He wore a nice grey suit with a white shirt but no tie. His long silver gray hair hung down to the middle of his back. He had a kind smile and his voice was warm and friendly as he spoke to everyone gathered in the garden. Penny thought he looked like he would be a very nice King and the beautiful blonde lady standing beside him looked exactly how Penny imagined a real Queen would look.

Kind, but serious, as she studied the newcomers. Tall and slim, the Queen still held the posture and look of youth, which made her age hard to guess from a distance. Her hair was blonde and she wore an elegant white and blue dress with metal clasps at the shoulders and back that shone like gold in the morning light.

They weren't able to speak long, just enough to say hello and welcome before they were interrupted and forced to go deal with some other important problem. Byron the Steward took over and spoke to the newcomers himself. Byron said that all those not already given a place of service would be summoned before the King and Queen later that day to see *if* there was a place for them in Amen Hale and *if* they would be allowed to stay.

Next, Byron told everyone about the Royal Family. King Cornelius, Queen Cathryn, the four Princesses (Black Rain, Mary Fae, Bethany Grave, and Emma Hale), and the other Lords and Ladies of Hale. Byron explained that Amen Hale was its own Kingdom now, and that the laws of the United States of America ended the moment you passed the gates and entered the Kingdom. In Amen Hale, he said, the King and Queen's word was the only law. He said that those who chose to stay here would live and serve exactly how the King and Queen wanted them to and anyone who didn't like that really should leave immediately.

Byron talked for a long while about what it would be like to live in Amen Hale and what it meant to live in a land with a King and Queen. He explained how everyone was supposed to act and talk and bow and serve the Royal Family. Then Byron talked about how he loved the King and Queen and the royal family and said that everyone here should love them too.

"Why would you want to bind yourself to serve someone that you do not love?" Byron said.

He encouraged all the newcomers to take some time this morning to seriously think over their decision and consider whether this life was what they wanted. He said it would be magical and fantastic but that it was still a life of service. As he finished, Byron told the newcomers to wait in the guest house until they were called to present themselves before the King and Queen, but right before he released everyone he called a few people aside to meet with the Queen personally. "Penny Haig" was the first name he called.

Queen Cathryn herself asked her to be Bethany's maid. Penny said she would try, but she also told the Queen she was very scared. The Queen told her all about the Princess as she led her up to Bethany's bedroom. Queen Cathryn said that Bethany was very attached to her witch dress and that she would probably stay in it most of the time. Part of her job would be to wash the dress as quickly as she could whenever Bethany took her bath or her shower.

The Queen told her to watch the Princess and let her know if Bethany needed anything or if she was unhappy or angry, and most importantly, if she seemed dazed or out of control. She explained how Penny would have to be careful when she talked about blood with the Princess. She didn't say that she shouldn't talk about it, but to be careful if they did.

Then Queen Cathryn told her about Bethany's home life so she would know a little about how the Princess had grown up and all the things that she'd gone through. That was horrible to hear. It made Penny appreciate her grandmother a lot more. And then Queen Cathryn showed her a box that held the most beautiful sacrificial blade she had ever seen.

"This is Bethany's blade," Cathryn said. The Queen took a few minutes to tell her how to care for it. Clean it. And she told her which of the kitchen staff to take the blade to after it was used so they could sharpen it for her. Then she handed it to Penny. Penny's eyes were huge as she gazed at the magical blade that had started the Kingdom of Amen Hale and raised the King from the dead.

"Keep it safe, keep it sharp, and keep it ready for the Princess. I have a feeling she will need it soon."

"Yes, Queen Cathryn," Penny said as she placed the blade back into the wooden box.

Emma and Mary

Snooze Alarm

"FOR CRAP'S SAKE, Mary, it's time to get up!" Emma growled as she tried to untangle herself from Mary's arms and legs.

"UhUuu," Mary mumbled and tried to grab her again, like Emma was a bad pillow that wanted to run away from home where she belonged. She'd already drug her back into bed twice, but this time Emma slipped down to the foot of the bed out of her reach.

"Nooo! Not yet, Emms—just a little longer. Cuddle with meeeee!" Mary begged. Her eyes stayed closed, but she switched to using her feet, slipping one foot around each side of Emma and squeezing, trying to reel her back in with her legs.

"Get up Mary! It's gotta be late. Let's go see what's happening."

Mary gave up, but she didn't move. She lay there, talking with her eyes closed. "Emma."

"Yeah?" Emma replied as she looked around the big empty room. The pallet that Cathryn and Cornelius had used as their bed sat empty beside theirs. Last night had been weird. Emma was still trying to make sense of it, and she wasn't getting anywhere. What had happened? Was she an employee now? A household servant? Was she already late for her first day of work? God she hoped not. She didn't want to be in trouble already. And she didn't want Cathryn to think she was lazy and was the kind of person who would just sleep the day away.

Maybe she had just dreamed what she thought had happened last night. Her brow crinkled in foggy morning contemplation. Mary sat up in the bed. Her arms encircled her from behind. Emma didn't fight it. Why bother? She felt like a puppy that was owned by a little kid that had to squeeze the life out of it. She just sighed.

Mary schooched up behind where she sat on the end of the bed, resting her chin on top of Emma's shoulder.

"Emma," Mary said again.

"Yeah?" Emma's cheek was right next to Mary's, but for some reason it wasn't wigging her out. Being this close to someone normally would have made her go totally nuts. She usually didn't let anyone touch her. Emma guarded her "personal space" like a demon from hell, but for some reason Mary's touching her didn't seem to bother her anymore. Even Mary's arms wrapped around her middle didn't make her start to sweat and squirm and fight to be free.

Maybe it was because she knew that Mary was "handicapped" and "had to touch people." She really wasn't able to help herself. Being mad at her for it would be wrong. Like being mad at a crippled person in a wheelchair because they couldn't walk. They couldn't help it and neither could Mary. Or maybe it was because she was just too tired to fight her off anymore, but it definitely wasn't because she actually wanted to be hugged by her. At least that was what she was telling herself.

Emma had struggled with her personal space "issues" along with a bunch of other "issues" since she was a small child. Mary hugging her made her think of her parents. Emma couldn't remember a single time her mother or her father had ever hugged her. She'd been picked up, held, washed, cleaned, but not hugged. There was a difference. A hug was something you did because you wanted to and because you needed it, not because you had to or to get someone to shut up. Emma couldn't remember having been hugged by either of them. To say that her mother and father were not affectionate people wouldn't quite cover it. Emma didn't know if her own issues were an inherited antisocial phobia buried deep in her genes or if it was something else. She'd given up on trying to figure it out.

Something wet was on her check. Emma turned her head to the side and looked at Mary. She was crying, but she also had a dazed, unfocused look on her face that Emma recognized. Mary was doing magic.

"Are you doing witch stuff to me right now?" Emma asked as she looked at Mary, giving her her best disapproving squinty-eyed glare. Mary's tears were getting her all wet. Her long, snow white hair with its one green stripe was all over the place; some was caught in her mouth and plastered to the side of her head, getting wet in the tears.

"Yeah, I'm doing magic," Mary confessed quietly. "But it's nothing bad, Emms. I love you."

Emma gave that some thought. She knew Mary couldn't lie. *Love?* For some strange reason Mary loved her, which was weird, but okay. So if she loved her, then whatever she was doing was probably nothing bad, like she said.

"I know it's not bad, but what is it, Mary?" Emma asked, still doling out the squinty eye. "What *exactly* are you doing to me?"

"I'm getting to know you—with my magic."

Emma looked into Mary's pretty green eyes. Yesterday was the first time they'd ever met, but Mary was looking at her as if she already knew all about her. Maybe she did. Emma had heard and seen enough yesterday at the wedding and dinner to know that Mary knew things by touching people. She wondered how much Mary knew about her as she looked at the green-eyed girl whose face was so close to hers. Mary probably knew everything there was to know by now. And she was still hugging her. Like there was still something there, inside her, that she actually wanted to hug. She relaxed, ending her squinty-eyed gaze and sat there just looking back at Mary.

"Okay," Emma said.

Mary smiled. "Really?"

Emma nodded. For a few minutes she didn't say anything, she just sat there on the edge of the bed enjoying the hug. Mary didn't say anything either.

"Maybe fifteen more minutes," Emma said. She gave Mary a small smile.

Mary's smile was huge, but she answered in a whispered, "Okay, let's cuddle."

The girls crawled back into the bed and held each other.

Sky

<hr>

Not Just a White Dress

"HEY, WE'RE NOT dressed in here!" Ryan squealed as the bedroom door opened. He'd just climbed out of our bed and was peeking out the front window—*completely naked*—as the maid entered our room. Ryan dashed back to the bed and snatched a blanket up to cover himself then looked down at me and realized he'd uncovered parts of me that were naked. His face went so red!

"Oh! Sorry!" he said and quickly covered me back up, exposing himself completely, and I laughed as the blanket settled back over me.

"Ryan! It's just the maid!" I shouted from under the blanket as I listened to his feet run across the room toward the bathroom. I was still laughing as I dug my way out from under the blanket and looked at the little blonde maid who stood by the door. She had her head down and looked worried that she'd stepped in on us.

"I'm so sorry, m'Lady. Sorry to disturb you and your husband, but you have guests that would like to see you when you're ready to receive them. And if you would like anything for breakfast I would be glad to bring it for you. My name is Julie." She curtsied toward me again, really deep and formal. "My Lady Sky," she said with her head down again, looking at the floor.

She was nice. I hadn't had a nice maid in a long, long time. The bathroom door opened a crack and Ryan's head popped out.

"Did someone say breakfast?" he asked, all chipper and happy. I laughed and the little maid looked up and smiled.

"Yes, m'Lord. Breakfast or an early lunch if you prefer. It's almost ten now."

I stepped out of bed, and Ryan's eyes got huge as he looked at me naked.

"Sky!" he whispered to me and darted back into the bathroom only to emerge a second later with a towel that he launched at me from the safety of the bathroom where he was hiding. I watched its flight as it landed on the bed. "Quick! Wrap yourself up!" he whispered urgently.

"Why?" I asked, totally confused.

It looked like his eyes would pop out of his head. "Because you're NAKED! And the maid is right there!" He pointed at the little maid.

I didn't get it. Why was he pointing at her? I already knew she was there. She and I looked at each other. I shrugged. She smiled.

"I don't think your husband is used to being attended by servants, m'Lady," supplied the maid helpfully. "And I think he may be a little shy," she added with a quick glance in his direction.

"Oh!" I said, finally getting it. I looked back at Ryan. He was still hiding behind the door. "Ryan, she's the maid. It's okay if she sees us naked."

He just grunted and shut the door, going back inside the bathroom.

I looked back at the maid. "Shy?" I asked.

"I think so, m'Lady." She stepped on into the room and started to strip the bed.

"Sorry about the blood," I said, embarrassed as she got down to the stained bedding.

There was blood on the sheets. I was sore from being with Ryan but I was also very happy. I wasn't worried about the blood. I knew that it was normal to bleed some on my wedding night. And I had.

Julie smiled at me and talked as she worked on the bed. "I seen some of the wedding on the telly. There was a bunch of us together in the Guest Hall watching it on the news last night. They've been showing little clips of all of the weddings. You looked so beautiful in white. And if I may say so, m'Lady, it makes me proud to know that it wasn't just the dress you was wearin' that was white," she said this as she lifted the stained sheet from the bed and carefully folded it. "I just can't believe that two people as beautiful as you and Lord Ryan waited to get married afore goin' at it." She gave me a big grin. "That's almost more impressive than you flying about or even making people out of clouds. It's magical, is what it is. It makes me glad to serve you, m'Lady."

She took the folded sheet and placed it in an empty dresser drawer instead of putting it in the laundry basket with the other bedding. I guessed that I was supposed to save it. I didn't know. I couldn't imagine why but I didn't want to ask and sound silly. The maid continued to talk as she worked.

"They talked about you on the news, m'Lady. How even when you was little you always knew you could fly. They even showed some psychiatrist bloke that went on and on about how he used to be your doctor and how he tried to convince you that you couldn't fly but you just kept believin' it. You sure showed him. And they talked about your parents, how they kept you locked up for all these years because they thought you'd hurt yourself, trying to fly." Julie paused in her mile a minute chatter as she stretched across the bed to tuck in the new sheets.

"It's just like a fairy tale, isn't it? And now you're the Lady Sky and your husband is Lord Ryan." Julie sighed happily.

"Julie, why are you calling me 'Lady'?" I said. "And Ryan's not a lord."

Julie nodded. "You are now m'Lady. We was all told this morning at the gathering that you and Lord Ryan were to be treated as royalty of Amen Hale. And for as long as you're here I am to be m'Lady's maid." Julie's face went red then too, like she'd said something she shouldn't have. "I mean, if it pleases you, I'm to be your maid. There was lots of girls who wanted to be your maid. Yours and Lord Ryan's."

"There were?" I asked, surprised again.

Julie nodded. "Dozens. We've none of us slept a wink all night. We've been too excited about everything that's going on, and then, first thing this morning, some of us were given our places of service. Lots of girls wanted you and Lord Ryan." Her eyes glanced toward the closed bathroom door and she came closer to me, speaking quietly so Ryan wouldn't hear. "Queen Cathryn said I was to wait to speak to you alone and ask you if you wanted me to take care of both you and Lord Ryan or if you wanted to pick his servant out yourself. The Queen said that a wife should always be the one in charge of her husband's servants so she told me to ask you. What would you prefer m'Lady?"

I thought that was very nice of Queen Cathryn, but I felt weird making a decision like that. I was still getting used to making decisions for myself, let alone for other people. My whole life, every single little decision had been made by my mother and now that I was making my own decisions they all felt so important. Even the small stupid ones. But this wasn't a small one, this was a big one. But I was Ryan's wife. He was my husband so this was my decision. I thought about it some. Ryan sure seemed nervous about servants. Hmm.

"You've already seen him naked. So just you for now, okay?"

Julie seemed surprised by that, and I didn't know if I'd said something strange.

"Yes, my Lady Sky." She curtsied again. "I'll let the Queen know."

"Did you say that someone was waiting to see me?" I asked her.

"Yes m'Lady. It's your mother and father."

"WHAT!" I shouted.

A half second later Ryan burst out of the bathroom door in a white bathrobe with a toothbrush sticking out of his mouth. He came running to my side. "What is it! What's happened!?" he mumbled around the toothbrush, getting toothpaste all over himself as he wrapped his arms around me, looking at my shocked face. "What is it, Sky!?" he mumbled again, then reached up took the toothbrush out of his mouth and asked again, "What is it, Sky!?"

"My parents are here!" I said.

His eyes opened wide like mine. "Are they downstairs now?" he asked the little maid as he wiped toothpaste onto the sleeve of his bathrobe.

She was frightened by our reaction to the news. Her eyes were wide like ours as she answered. "Only m'Lady's mother is down below waiting to see you both. Her father is at the roadblock the soldiers have made, beyond the edge of the property. Lucius would not allow him to enter the Kingdom till tomorrow morning."

"Why?" I asked. "Why just my mom?"

"Lucius said that Princess Rain banned your father from her sight for two days. I think it was when she was angry with him, after he and Lord Ryan got in a fight."

"Oh God!" Ryan groaned. "Does everyone in the whole castle know I got the crap beat out of me yesterday by your dad?"

The maid giggled. Ryan groaned. Then I giggled. Ryan groaned some more but then it seemed he got distracted watching my boobs as I giggled; his eyes focused on my chest. Then he noticed us noticing him noticing *me* and his face went red.

"Woman! Go get some clothes on!" he ordered and pointed to the bathroom.

I giggled again. Ryan really didn't know how it worked. He didn't know what he just asked. He didn't know that the maid was going to help me get dressed. But we needed to get cleaned up first.

"Ryan, we need a shower before we get dressed."

Ryan arched one eyebrow as he thought that through. "We," he considered that word. "need a shower. Like the two of us. You and me." His other eyebrow went up. "Both of us. Together in the shower."

I nodded and smiled, then turned to the maid. "Julie, we'll take a shower first. Could you find some clothes for us and have them ready when we get out?"

"Yes, m'Lady. And should I bring up breakfast or will you be going down to eat with your mother?" she asked.

I looked at Ryan. I didn't know what he wanted to do. I watched as he thought for a minute before speaking.

"We need to talk to them, but I'd rather talk to your father and mother at the same time, in person, and get it all out in the open. After we get dressed I'll go talk to Rain and see if she'll let your dad come to breakfast with us."

"Okay," I said and hugged him. I was still mad at my father, but I didn't want him left outside.

"Let Sky's mother know that we'll be down soon and that we'll have breakfast with her," he told Julie. "Or actually make it an early lunch. I'll need to talk to my sister before I go down," Ryan said. "And please find my mother and father and invite then to join us for lunch also. They need to meet Sky's parents and it might as well be today."

"Yes, Lord Ryan," Julie said. She curtsied, turned and left, closing the door behind her.

I looked up at Ryan; he was thinking hard about something, his brow wrinkled, his jaw clenched tight as he thought.

"What's wrong, Ryan?" I asked.

"Sky. Before we meet your mom I need to tell you something important." He looked so serious all of a sudden. It scared me.

"Wait," I said as I reached up and untied his bath robe. "Wait, wait, wait, not yet." I slipped inside the robe with him and wrapped my arms around him, pressing my naked flesh up against his, and rested my head on his shoulder. "Okay. I'm ready. Now tell me." Now I was ready for bad news if I had to hear it.

Ryan ran his hands up and down my back, holding me. "Don't worry. It's nothing bad, my Sky. I just wanted you to know that your mother has quit drinking and quit using drugs."

I pulled back and looked at him. I wasn't sure I had heard him correctly. "What?" I asked.

"Your mother. She quit drinking and using drugs, Sky," he said it again, then continued on. "Hopefully she won't be so mean any more now that she's off all that junk, but some people are mean just because they're mean. I guess we won't know till we see her downstairs at lunch. If she attacks me again at least it won't be because of the drugs. But I guess she still has plenty of reason to attack me, since I ran off and married her daughter yesterday." He thought about that as he wiped the last of the toothpaste off his face. "You know, maybe we could bring Sky Dragon with us, you know—for protection. I don't want everyone in the castle to see me get beat up by your mom. I'd have to hide under the bed the rest of my time here."

I pulled away and stepped out of his robe and looked at him like he was totally crazy and he laughed.

"You don't believe me, do you?"

"No way!" I said with a frown stuck on my face. He didn't know my mother. "She would never stop taking her pills. She doesn't think life works without pills."

Ryan's big smile faded into a sad little smile as I watched. I didn't want to disagree with him, but he didn't know my mother! He didn't know she couldn't stop.

"Come on, let's go get in the shower," he said, his voice calm, changing the subject.

We walked together into the bathroom, but now I felt bad. I wanted to believe him, but what he said was just plain impossible. My mother wasn't going to stop taking her pills. She liked her pills. I hated them but she actually liked them. I watched as he took off his robe and hung it on the hook then reached into the shower and turned on the water and adjusted the temperature. I kept thinking about what he had said. And what I had said back.

"It's ready, Sky."

Again, his voice was funny. Too calm. Too sad.

We stepped into the shower together. I felt like I'd messed up somehow. My stomach hurt. But it was crazy to even think that she would quit her pills. Why did he even say that! Was he joking about it? Ryan did like to make jokes. He couldn't be joking about something like that though, so why did he even say it!?

"Okay! Why!?" I yelled. Ryan jumped and almost slipped and fell. "You don't know her like I do! Just tell me why, Ryan! Why would she quit taking her pills and how do you know she did? Why would you say that to me!?" I shouted and shouted at him as we stood together in the hot, steamy shower until I ran out of breath.

I stood there panting on one side of the shower as he stared at me with concern on his face on his side, his hands held up in a calming gesture. I felt bad because I didn't believe him. I felt like I had called him a liar, but I didn't, but in a way I think I did. And now we were having our first fight and I didn't like that. And I think I started it.

Oh no! I'm acting crazy. I'm acting like my mother!

"Sorry!" I said and started to cry. Ryan stepped closer and hugged me and we both slid down to sit on the floor of the shower together. I cried as the hot water rained down on us. Why did I yell at him? I shouldn't have yelled at him.

"Sorry, Ryan. I just get crazy sometimes. I've been crazy all my life. Everyone has always told me I was crazy so, I must be crazy." I looked at my husband. At his worried face. "You married a crazy girl. I hope you know that. I'm gonna need a lot of help," I told him. I hoped he didn't run away. I needed him. I didn't want him to run away but I should have told him I was crazy before I married him. "I should have told you that I was crazy before we got married, but I just didn't have the chance. I'm sorry." I cried as he held me.

"Sky. I don't blame you for not believing me about your mom," Ryan said. "Actually, if you did believe me I'd be more worried about you being crazy. It's my fault. I should have explained it better. Don't cry, my Sky." He held me and rocked me where we sat on the shower floor.

"I could tell your mom was messed up even on that first day of the drug study. I'm sure everyone in the whole waiting room could tell. She just kept going on and on and on, she couldn't stop talking. And she was completely bombed out of her mind when you two had your fight on Tuesday. Every time I've seen her she's been wasted. I can't imagine what it must have been like living with her and your dad all these years. And your dad has issues too. And them keeping you like a prisoner, all drugged up, for years." He hugged me tight.

"I still shouldn't have yelled at you though," I said as he held me. "Yelling at you is crazy. Like my mother."

Ryan kissed me on the tip of my nose. "Sky, don't feel bad about yelling at me. Yelling at me doesn't make you crazy. Actually, that makes you normal. Yesterday, I think everyone I know that loves me yelled at me. My mom yelled at me, my dad yelled at me, and I know you saw Rain yell at me." He said seriously, "I probably should have told you, before we got married, that I'm a very annoying person… sometimes. And I should have told you the 'why' and the 'how' of it before just laying the 'what' on you. I think that's what set you off."

I had understood everything up until that last part, but now I was totally lost again. "RYAN! Whys, hows, and whats—what are you saying? You're making me crazy!"

"See! I was right!" he said, all happy again. He quickly added, "Sorry. I told you I was annoying." His smile was back. I liked his smile; I was glad it was back and it made mine come back too.

"That's okay. I love you anyway," I said. "Even if you're annoying."

His smile was back, but it didn't last long, as I watched it faded out again. "My Sky. You need to know. I have powers. Just like you." He closed his eyes, leaned his head back against the shower wall and added, "Or at least I had powers yesterday. I don't know if I do anymore."

I blinked. Had I heard him right? "You have—"

"Powers. Because of the pills," he finished.

"Really?" Yesterday he had told me he didn't have any powers at all. He'd even complained about it. "You told me you didn't have any powers." Had he lied to me? Great! Now we were lying to each other. This sucked!

"Did you lie to me?" I asked, angry again. His eyes flew open at that, and he looked at me. "Is it something horrible like Jane and Dan's stuff or something scary like Bethany?" I was angry as I shouted at him, "Why didn't you tell me you had powers!?"

He examined my face for a moment, studying my hurt expression carefully before he answered me. "I didn't know I had any powers when I told you that. I didn't find out myself until a few minutes before the wedding. I just didn't know." He sounded upset now. He didn't yell or raise his voice any, but he didn't sound happy. "And no, I did not lie to you, Sky. I would never lie to you. I love you." He closed his eyes and leaned his head back, bumping it against the rough tile wall. He kept bumping his head as he talked.

"It doesn't matter anyway. I don't have my powers anymore. I think I lost them."

"You lost them!?" I said, surprised.

Ryan kept his eyes closed. He just nodded and kept bumping his head. Harder now.

"How?" I asked, scared that I might lose my powers too, but I was also scared for Ryan. I didn't want him to hurt himself; he was acting strange. The tile was rough and sharp in places like natural stone. "How did you lose your powers, Ryan?"

"I stopped believing," Ryan said, hitting his head even harder. I saw blood on the wall behind his head.

"Ryan! Stop! Stop your hurting yourself!" I shouted.

His face crumbled into something horrible, and he fell over onto his side on the shower floor, crying. Not just little tears, he was really crying! I'd never seen a man cry before. It was scary. I didn't know what to do other than hold him. So I held my husband while he cried. I wanted to ask a hundred questions. But I didn't. I just let him cry.

Black Rain

Pleasure and Pain

"AAOOO," I MOANED. I felt Believer squeeze me, a warm wave of pressure from my toes up to my head, inside and out drawing me out of the most wonderful deep sleep I'd ever had in my life.

"My wife. Your mother, the Queen, and the maid are at the door. They wish to speak with you." Believer's deep, rumbling voice came from all around me before heading up to his head and out of his body.

"Mmomm" was what came out of my mouth. Not quite what I had intended to say, but most of my vocabulary had been reduced down to moans, sighs, groans, laughing, shouts and occasionally even cussing. I tried again to use my mouth for words.

"Mmy mother," I said. "And the maid." I felt so loose and lightheaded from everything we'd done last night before I had passed out. As I floated here inside him I almost felt like I had become a piece of cloud, just another part of Believer's body. But it was like my solid body gave us both something to hold onto here inside him. Thousands of his ghostlike little nerves were burrowed down inside me, filling me and holding me tight, connecting me to him while I floated inside him.

"Yes. Your mother and the maid. She says that it's time for you to come out. There's much work to be done and you are needed. And your body needs to eat and rest and recover from all we have shared. I'm a little worried I may have damaged you some." His voice certainly sounded worried.

"Damaged?" I asked. I didn't feel damaged. I felt kinda high and spineless like a limp noodle, and sore from having sex, but not hurt. Definitely not hurt. I felt around nearby inside Believer, searching for him, for his "heart" as we liked to call it. He could move it around, anywhere inside his body, and last night he had put it in exactly the right places and totally blew my mind. What was left of me seemed to be a numb, groggy jellyfish that just wanted more sex or more sleep.

"Stop looking for it, my love. It's time to get up and recover and spend time with your family."

"Oh," I said. "Hmmm." I closed my eyes again, relaxing in his hold on me. I felt so safe. So safe. So happy. Squeeze. "Aaaooo," I moaned.

"My love. It's time to wake and help your mother."

"Hhhmmm" was my comment. "I don't wannaaa—"

I felt movement and I knew that Believer was walking but I kept my eyes closed and happy.

"Please come in." Pause. "She is still within me." Pause. "She is somewhat disoriented. Once she is out it will take her a while to get acclimated to her own body again. And she is reluctant to come out. She knows she needs to, but she seems unwilling to be able to make herself think. She's very, very—relaxed." He seemed at a loss for words to describe what he'd done to me. I laughed. Was that what I was? Relaxed? But then I felt Believer's little connecting nerves start to pull out of me, and I almost cried.

"She can hear my words as I speak to you but not yours as you speak to me." Pause. "Yes, Queen Cathryn. That may work." Pause. "Yes, please, thank you." Pause. "When I bring her out, she may not be able to walk, you will need to assist her."

I felt him pushing me forward, out of his body. I couldn't move my arms but somehow Believer got them to come out first just with the clouds inside his body and I felt hands close on my hands as soon as they were outside and then those hands started to pull me out. I closed my eyes before my head and shoulders came out followed by the rest of me. I was soaking wet and seemed unable to use any of my limbs; even my head was all loose, like a newborn child rolling around on top of my shoulders. I tried to open my eyes but my long wet hair was wrapped all around my head hiding the world from my sight. I gave up and just closed my eyes. I felt two people, one on each arm carrying me.

"Mom," I said.

"Yes, Rain?" Cathryn said.

"I'm naked."

"Yes, we know." Cathryn laughed.

"Oh," I said. I felt warm flesh on my flesh. "Are you naked too?" I asked.

"Yes, my child and so is Beth, your maid. We're taking you into the shower."

"Oh," I said. "But I'm already wet, Mom, and you're going to wash off all my good Believer smell."

"Yes, we know you're wet, Rain, and I'm sorry about washing off his smell but we need to get your body working again. A nice hot shower and a good rub down will get your blood flowing back where it needs to be."

"You're getting in with me? Is that why you're naked? That's nice." I'd never taken a shower with someone else before.

"My, she does smell lovely, like spring rain," said the other girl, the maid.

"Hmmm. He tastes like a summer storm," I said in a dreamy slur.

"I'll hold her, get the water ready, Beth." Cathryn took my whole weight. I tried to get my legs under me to help but nothing seemed connected anymore.

"Mom. I'm all loose and floppy."

"Yes, child. I can see that."

Right then my body started shaking, muscles contracting between my legs and a familiar pressure began to build—I sucked in a gasp of air as a spasm hit, like an echo from last night. Was I having another orgasm?! I hung in Cathryn's arms, pulling in shallow little breaths, completely helpless, as my body twitched and danced all on its own. Parts of my brain seemed to be stuck, reliving what had happened last night, unable to let it go. I stopped thinking about anything other than the tingling warm chills that gripped my body and just let it take me—

After a few minutes in the steaming hot shower, it stopped, and few minutes later I started to feel my legs again. I was in the biggest shower I'd ever seen, lying on some kind of fancy table while they worked on me. Four hands were rubbing me and touching me at the same time, while hot water from the overhead shower beat down onto me. It felt so wonderful. In a way it reminded me of being inside Believer—warm, safe, and held by people who love me. My mom and Beth washed my hair and rubbed me down with expensive bath soaps and cleaned me up (every inch of me!).

When they finally turned off the shower I was able to stand, wobbly, on my own feet. I hadn't said anything while they worked on me. I didn't really know what to say. This was one for my list of weird things.

"Thanks, Mom. Thanks, Beth," I said.

"Good to have you back, Princess Rain," Beth said and I looked over at her.

She was a middle-aged lady, with red hair, freckles, and a kind face. Actually, Beth had freckles everywhere, on every inch of her. She was naked just like me. And I saw that Cathryn's tattoos went all the way from her arms down her body. They were beautiful. We were dripping wet, but with a thought, I dried us and our hair.

That done, I willed strength to flow into my own body so I could stand without help. Enough was enough. I'd enjoyed all of it, even the weird, out of it, euphoric haze, but it was time to get going. I released some of my magic and felt its strange warmth slide out of my skin. My hair flailed about my shoulders like a gust of wind had just blown through the bathroom as I stepped toward the enormous, ceiling-high vanity mirror.

"Rain, help!" Cathryn called out.

I turned to find her kneeling beside Beth, who was lying in a heap on the tile floor of the bathroom, out cold. I willed strength to flow into her, and then lifted her up and set her on her feet with another thought. Cathryn started to check on her as I turned back to the mirror.

I floated up into the air, level with the vanity and walked on air toward the mirror. I imagined in the mirror the reflection of an arch, like the one that I'd made in Dan and Jane's crypt. There before me in the mirror it took shape. It looked just like a reflection.

"Be careful, Rain," Cathryn called out from behind me.

"I won't be long. I just need to check on them," I answered as I stepped into the mirror and out into the crypt of the vampires.

As soon as I stepped through the mirror I gasped! It was everywhere, almost overpowering. I stilled my own magic, my hair lying flat, so I could take it all in. The smell of a *million* beautiful roses. I laughed, and the noise seemed loud in the quiet of the crypt, echoing off the walls.

"Jane," I whispered out into the darkness. There was no answer. No one appeared out of thin air.

I remembered with a little start of surprise that I was still naked! I hadn't thought to get dressed before I came through the mirror. I looked down at myself, embarrassed for a moment, but then I relaxed. So I was naked. So what? I did not summon my black dress. Maybe it was part of being a witch or maybe being naked with two other women for the past thirty minutes in a shower had left me completely shameless, but I felt fine. Better than fine—it felt right. And I'd been naked with Believer all night. So far, being naked was working out great, and the magic all around me felt so wonderful on my skin. I didn't want clothes to get in the way.

Absent the rustle of clothing or the "tap-tap" of shoes, I pressed on. My bare feet were silent on the cold, red glass floor as I walked down the hall and stopped at the entrance of the bed chamber and looked in. They were there, together, on the bed.

I took a couple of steps inside to get a better look at them. They were naked, holding each other, looking into each other's eyes like they always did. I could tell they were dead. I could feel death, here in the room with us, wrapping all around them. They were dead, but Jane's magic wasn't dead. It was alive and it was absolutely amazing! I closed my eyes and breathed it in deep as I stood there, naked in the near darkness. It felt like I could even smell it with my skin it was so powerful. Roses. I stayed there for a few quiet minutes, breathing in her lovely magic.

I needed to go. Before I left I gathered the wedding clothes from the floor around the bed and willed them to change to red for Jane and black for Dan. The time for white was over. I shaped and formed a little alcove and even made a bar and some hangers to put the clothes on. At least they would know I had been here when they rose.

"I love you. See you soon," I whispered to them then walked back to the archway and willed it to open back to the mirror, and I stepped through and back out into my mother's bathroom, standing in air above the vanity top.

"How are they?" Cathryn asked. She'd gotten dressed and was holding my black dress in her hands.

I smiled at her. "Dead," I said. "But I have a surprise for you." I floated down to the floor and walked over to her and grabbed a handful of my long black hair and held it up to her. "Here, see if you can smell it, Mother," I said.

Cathryn leaned forward and sniffed my hair and a smile sprang onto her face. "I see what you mean about the smell," she said with feeling. She reached down and got a good handful and buried her face into it. "Mmm, it's wonderful, isn't it?" she said, buried in my hair.

"Yes, it is. It's Jane's magic. It's very much alive," I said with a happy smile.

"I didn't think a human was able to smell her magic?" Cathryn said.

I shrugged. "It's so much stronger now. Or maybe I did it." I shrugged again. "All it takes from me is an idle thought to change the world, so it could have been me. Or just being close to me this morning may have rubbed off on you some, I'm letting a little more of me out than what I usually do." I looked over to the doorway, fifteen feet away, where Beth was standing. "Sorry I knocked you out this morning, Beth."

"No harm done, Princess. I'll get used to it." She sounded scared; I could hear it right there in her voice.

"Will they will be rising soon?" Cathryn asked. I nodded. "Good. Now get dressed, we have work to do, child. And your mother and father wanted to see you before they leave for home."

I hugged her. "Yes, Mother." While I was still hugging her I added, "And thanks for helping us this morning. We were kinda stuck. My brain wasn't working for a while there."

Cathryn laughed. "You were—as Believer put it—very relaxed."

"But you didn't freak out or run screaming or anything. I'm so glad you're my mother now," I said as I held onto her.

"So am I, Rain. So am I."

"My lady," Believer's deep rumble called from the bathroom doorway.

I looked over and smiled at him. "Yes, my love?"

His worried face broke into a big grin, happy to see that I was feeling better. Not that I was feeling bad before, but still—he was happy to see me on my feet again.

"Your brother is at the door. He said he must speak with you."

"Go ahead and let him in."

The clouds around Believer's eyes darkened as he looked down at me. "You are not dressed," he complained.

"Oh!" I said, abashed. I had totally forgotten about clothes again! I willed the dress in my mother's hands to appear on my body and it did. It would have taken forever to do all the buttons if I hadn't used magic. "Better?" I asked him.

"Yes," Believer said before turning to let Ryan in.

Beside me Cathryn laughed. "Sometimes I'm amazed at how human your husband is. You should have seen his face when Beth and I got undressed."

"Did he get embarrassed?" I asked, surprised and delighted.

"Very." Cathryn said, giving me a playfully wicked smile. "I think the whole situation this morning embarrassed him almost to death. He was so worried he'd hurt you."

"Oh, he definitely didn't hurt me," I said with feeling. "Although I may need help tomorrow morning relearning how to walk—again." The thought of tonight, with Believer, of doing IT, *again!* It was exciting and firghtening at the same time. "I don't think I'll ever get used to that," I said with my eyes as wide as they could go and Cathryn laughed.

"I should think not. Even the little bit of what I saw in the shower was amazing, just the leftovers of what you experienced, I guess. I don't know what he did to you but you did seem to enjoy it."

"Oh God, did I!" I said as I walked out of the bathroom with Cathryn.

Ryan was standing in the middle of the bedroom. He looked like shit.

"What the hell happened to you?" I blurted out. His hair was all over the place, like he hadn't bothered combing it once he got out of the shower and he held a towel to the back of his head. He was bleeding and had bled on his shirt; a big red stain ran up the sleeve. He looked upset. As I got closer I got even more worried; it looked like he'd been crying!

"Is Sky all right? Are you hurt? What's happened!?" I spat out, panicked as I ran over to him.

"Don't freak out!" he shouted angrily.

I slid to a stop just a couple of steps away from him. That was *not* like Ryan. Something was wrong. On the other side of the room I saw Believer's eyes grow to a brighter red, like a banked fire. He said nothing and remained motionless, simply watching. Cathryn and Beth did the same. They stood against the far wall quietly, watching. We had our quiet audience for whatever drama was about to play out.

"Sky is fine!" Ryan said in an agitated growl. "I hit my head in the shower. It's no big deal. But that's not why I'm here. You told Lucius that Sky's father can't be around you for two days. He's outside at the gate right now." He pointed with a quick, angry jerk of his thumb, back toward the gate. "I need you to let him back in here. We're planning on having lunch together—me, Sky, her mom and dad, and our mom and dad."

I nodded. I willed my words to carry to Lucius, wherever he was, and spoke out loud so Ryan could hear me. "Lucius. Ryan has spoken with me. Mr. Han is to be allowed to come into the house. He will be having lunch with Ryan and Sky. Thank you, Lucius." I looked over to my brother who appeared to be somewhat mollified. "So mote it be. Now what's wrong with you?" I demanded.

He looked at my face for a moment, studying me. "Did you know, Sis? All this time. Did you know that I had powers?"

"What?" I barked back in confusion. He studied my clueless expression, looking at me for some answer he wanted.

"You! Have powers? From the pills?" I stuttered out, still trying to think what power he might possibly possess. I was coming up blank. If he had any powers at all he wouldn't have let Sky's father beat the crap out of him. His face relaxed; I watched the anger drain out of him as he came closer and took my shocked face in his hands and kissed me on the forehead, right on my mark.

"I guess you didn't know, did you?" he said.

I was confused. "What's to know? What powers?"

Ryan laughed; it was one of those humorless laughs that was more cry than laugh and it made me worry even more that something was really, truly wrong with him. He stepped away from me back toward the door, but I followed him.

"I *had* powers, Rain. They're gone. I think I lost them the moment I knew I had them."

"You lost them?" I asked as I followed him. "But you can't *lose* your powers, Ryan. I don't think it works that way."

He turned and faced me. His sad, knowing smile was scary. "You can lose them, if you *believe* you can lose them, Rain. If I believe it, it can happen."

I blinked. I never really thought about it quite that way, but I guess he was right. "What did you believe that made your powers go away?" I asked.

"I believe that there is only one God. And His name is not Ryan Bryant."

"Oh," I said. I was still lost and confused about most of what he was talking about, but it seemed like my brother had figured out his situation and thought he knew what was happening, even if I didn't. He thought he'd lost whatever powers he'd had. He believed that he'd lost them. So, just like that, they were lost.

"What are you going to do now?" I asked.

He laughed his sad laugh again. "Go downstairs, have lunch with my wife and family, and enjoy my last miracle."

"What miracle?" I asked.

"Sky's mother. I prayed that she would stop using drugs and drinking."

"Oh," I said. It was making more sense to me now. I thought about some of the other times Ryan had prayed. "So when we all prayed for Williams to get better—"

"Yeah. That was me."

"And when bullhorn guy was shouting and—"

"Yeah. Me," Ryan said again. He shook his head. "Tuesday night I prayed that Jane, Sky, and Dr. Burgis would come to our church on Wednesday. And somehow, they all came, didn't they?" He laughed again. "But they didn't come for church, they came for a wedding. Who knows, maybe I made us all get married just so my prayer would get answered. I don't know. Only God knows, and that's not me." He ran his hand through his hair and it came away bloody. He gave his hand a disgusted glare and wiped the blood off with the towel he carried in his other hand then pressed the bloody towel back to his head again.

"I also prayed for Mr. Denton. He's cured now. No cancer. You may not have noticed, but he was in church on Wednesday watching the weddings. He was one of the loud ones shouting to throw you out." Again with the mirthless laugh. "Should have just let him die, I guess." He stared to walk away again.

"Ryan, wait," I called and he stopped at the door. I willed his head to heal and fixed his hair, making it shorter. Then I styled it, spiking it up. I thought he looked best like that. I changed the blood stained top he had on into something nicer. The ruined top became a button-up long-sleeved white shirt made from magic fabric. I made the buttons at the cuffs and up the front solid, shining gold and I took all the wrinkles out of his pants too and changed his shoes into fancy black boots and added a black belt to finish his look.

Ryan stood still until I was finished, then asked. "Why'd you do that?"

I shrugged. "Because you looked like shit, Bro. And Sky will want you to look good for her parents."

"Thanks, Sis," he said and left.

Cathryn came up from behind and slipped her arms around me. "Sorry, my child. I know it hurts you to see your brother suffer. I wish there was something we could do for him, but it sounds difficult. I'm afraid he may be right about his powers."

I nodded. I thought about Ryan's powers. His prayers were all answered. But that was when he thought God was the one answering his prayers. Now that he knew he was doing everything with his own power, he was—"broken." It was the only way I could think to describe him. He was broken.

I thought about myself. I was cut off, apart from God and everything else. And I remembered everyone talking about me when I fainted in the garden. I lay there in Believer's arms and listened as he told my parents that I wasn't human anymore. Mary touched me with her magic, feeling me, trying to find out what I was, and she said that I wasn't human either. She said that I felt like God. Mary called me God. Not the God that created all things, but she didn't know what else to call me. And then there was what I did last night, before I went up to the bedroom with Believer.

"Mom."

"Yes, Rain."

"Sometimes I pray to myself." I whispered guiltily, like I'd confessed a sin.

"But you still pray to God as well. I've heard you. You still use his name. You still love him," Cathryn said.

I nodded. "I know. And this is his world. I do love him, but—but last night I prayed to myself."

"Did you get what you prayed for?" she asked.

I looked over at Believer's red eyes. He was looking at me. I knew he would be. "Yes," I said. "Oh, yes. A thousand times yes."

"So mote it be," my mother said.

"So mote it be," I agreed.

Bethany and Penny

———◆———

A Penny for Your Thoughts

P ENNY'S HEAD WAS spinning as she tried to remember which door was the right one. After their time together, Queen Cathryn had given Penny into the care of one of the household servants who took her on a quick tour of the house and introduced her to the people she needed to know. She briefly explained what they expected of her "in addition" to keeping an eye on the Princess and caring for her dress and blade.

One of her jobs was to take care of Princess Bethany's breakfast, and that was what she was trying to do right now—*if* she had the right door. The Princess had spent the night with her (other) mother and father and had slept in their room. Penny held her breath and knocked on the door.

A smiling man with a stubbly face in need of a shave answered the door. Inside the room she caught her first glimpse of the Princess. She sat on the bed with her eyes closed while her other mother ran a comb through her long, beautiful hair.

"Hello. I'm Penny. I'm supposed to ask you if you want breakfast brought up to your room or if you want to go downstairs and eat with the others." She delivered the message she'd been saying over and over with what she hoped was good diction. She was mindful and embarrassed of her country accent in this home where everyone spoke so properly.

They chose to come down. Penny watched Bethany as she came out into the hall with her mom and dad. She didn't look well. Face drawn and pale. She seemed sad or sick or both. Penny had to focus on remembering where she was going as she led the way downstairs to the dining hall. The Princess and Mr. and Mrs. Bryant sat at the big table, joining the others already seated there. David, Dana, and Dr. Burgis were already seated, happily eating breakfast, talking away, and they gladly welcomed the Bryants and Bethany to the table. Shortly after the Bryants were seated Jane's parents came down to breakfast and joined them.

Penny backed away from the table and went to the far side of the room and sat on a little bench that was set into the side of the wall for the servants to sit on. She was surprised and happy to see Angel already sitting on the bench. Angel scooted over to make room.

"Hey, Angel," Penny greeted her, in a whispered voice.

"Hey, Penny," Angel greeted her back in her own whisper.

"Who's yours?" Penny asked.

"Lady Dana and Lord David," she answered and pointed discretely with her bony finger.

"Did your mom get in?" Penny asked.

Angel nodded, then pointed with her chin back to the table, directing their attention back to the group eating breakfast, ending the reunion and the talking. Penny wasn't surprised. Angel didn't talk if she didn't have to.

The girls watched silently and waited there on the bench. The crisply dressed serving staff stood about the table, ready to hand anyone a napkin, fill a glass, or take care of any other need the group may have while an entirely different set of servants brought in the food.

Everyone was happily eating poached eggs or fancy French soufflés, talking away while Bethany looked down at her plate. She looked ill as she pushed the eggs around with her silver fork. Bethany took a microscopic nibble off the end of a crispy piece of bacon and ended up spitting it out in a napkin, fighting off the urge to vomit. The bacon didn't taste right on her tongue. She took one small sip of her orange juice that her mom ordered for her but ended up spitting it back into the glass and wiping her tongue with a napkin to get the taste off.

"Do you want something else, Bethany?" asked Mr. Bryant. "Would you like them to bring you something different?"

Mrs. Bryant watched her play with her food for another minute before she started in as well. "You must be hungry, honey. You didn't eat anything last night, only a bite or two at most."

"I am hungry," she said in her quiet little voice.

"What do you want to eat, Bethany?" her mother asked.

"I don't want to say." Bethany pushed her plate away with a frustrated shove.

"Bethany honey. What's wrong?" Mrs. Bryant got out of her chair and came over to Bethany and hugged her.

"I need to talk to Byron. Or Lucius," Bethany said, looking down, not meeting the eyes of the others around the table.

"Why, Bethany?" asked Mr. Bryant.

"I just need to." She pushed her mother's clinging arms off and slid out of her chair and took a few unsteady steps away from the table. She looked horrible, as if she were moments from fainting or vomiting.

"Honey, what's wrong?" Mrs. Bryant asked again, truly worried now. Everyone was watching Bethany now. No one noticed the little black servant girl who ran from the room. No one asked where she was going or why she left.

"I'm a doctor, Bethany, perhaps I can help," encouraged Dr. Burgis. "Just tell us what's troubling you." He had joined in with the others, everyone trying to find some way to help her or encourage her to at least talk and share what was bothering her. Why she wouldn't eat. Or couldn't.

"Bethany, please tell us what's wrong!" Mrs. Bryant begged for what seemed like the hundredth time.

"I'm STARVING!" Bethany shouted like a monster, her little face contorted in frustrated rage. Her terrifying magic set teeth on edge and hearts to racing as it rolled across the room for just a second before Bethany squelched it. She stood there beside the table, both hands covering her face, eyes squeezed tightly shut, breathing hard as she swayed on her feet. Mrs. Bryant rushed over and wrapped her arms around her before she dropped to the floor.

"Holy shit," said Dana, not loudly. David shushed her to keep her quiet as they watched.

Byron the Steward entered the dinning hall and paused to assess the situation, but then Mrs. Bryant noticed him standing there and waved him over urgently to where she held Bethany in her arms.

"What do you need, Princess?" he asked, voice gravely serious as he studied her pale, sickly, tearstained face. "You can tell us. This is your home and we are your family. You can tell us, no matter what it is."

Cornelius entered the room on the heals of the little, servant girl. Penny continued into the room and sat back down on the servants bench beside Angel, but Cornelius held back and remained at the entryway, silent as he studied what was happening with Bethany and the others.

"Princess, this is your home. We are your people." Byron pulled out the handkerchief that was always peeking out of his lapel pocket and used it to gently wipe at Bethany's tears. "You can tell me anything, my child." his voice putting a darker emphasis on just what those things may be.

Bethany's guilty eyes darted around the room, looking at everyone watching her. She pressed a hand to her stomach and grimaced, swallowed down the pain, then looked back to Byron. "I think—I can only eat—" and she stopped, shaking her head. "It's so horrible!" Her little voice shook, at the trembling edge of a crying breakdown. She looked at Mrs. Bryant who stood close by and said, "I'm sorry Mom." She reached up, roughly wiping fresh tears from her eyes with the palm of her hand. "If you don't want me anymore I understand."

"We want you, Bethany, no matter what," said Mr. Bryant firmly. "We love you."

"Don't worry about hurting our feelings, Bethany. We will still love you," said a very confused Mrs. Bryant. "I know that you're a Red Witch and that you need blood now. It's okay. I understand that now."

Jane's father, Mr. Miller spoke, "I'm sure they can get you blood just like they did for Dan and Jane."

Byron spoke, "Princess, is it blood that you need?"

"No. That's not it Byron. I'm not a vampire." She didn't sound angry, just sad and resigned. "I'm way worse than a vampire. If blood was all I needed I wouldn't be so scared."

Mrs. Bryant was confused. "But what happened, Bethany? I don't understand. You were able to eat regular food yesterday morning at the trailer. You ate breakfast and lunch with us. I cooked it myself. We all ate it."

Bethany started crying. Cornelius came over and joined everyone trying to comfort her and find out what was happening. Why she couldn't eat. What she needed but wouldn't tell or couldn't bring herself to say. After ten minutes of combined pleading from all those gathered around Bethany started talking again. Mr. Bryant cradled her in his arms like a little child as everyone crowded in, grim expressions forced into compassionate masks normally found at a hospice patients bedside.

"I don't want to die." she'd said this before, but her voice was different this time, as if she'd reached the end of her tears, and perhaps more. "If I don't eat soon, I think I'll die, and I don't want to die. I really, really don't want to die. Especially not after what I did yesterday to Yanosh and Fiona. I didn't just kill them. I did more than kill them." Bethany shivered, as if chilled by the thought of whatever it was that she'd done. Cornelius quickly took off his jacket and covered her with it.

"You said you did more than kill them. What else did you do to them, Bethany?" Cornelius asked.

"I took the magic from their blood, Father. But there were other things in their blood too. Bad things. When they died, the stains on their soul came out in their blood. Evil, filthy, disgusting things." Bethany shivered again. "It all happened so fast. I didn't even think about what I was doing when I was doing it. Only after. Later, when it was all over and we had you back."

Questioning looks were shared around as everyone tried to guess at what Bethany was hinting. Cornelius decided to go with the direct approach. They weren't getting anywhere and Bethany was weakening fast.

"Blessed Be, my child, trust me when I say this. *I don't want you to die and I love you.* Speak to me, Bethany. You are my daughter and I am your father and I command it of you. Tell me. Tell me right now." Cornelius stared right at her, waiting for her answer.

Bethany started to speak, her voice small and weak. "Last night I killed the pretty moth Mary was using as a hair bow. I asked her for him first and she gave him to me, I didn't steal him." Her dark eyes darted around the faces staring at her, meeting each set of eyes as if she expected someone to accuse her of something.

"I remember, Bethany," Mrs. Bryant said gently. "You took it to the bathroom and threw it away after you killed it."

"No, Mom. I took it to the bathroom but I didn't throw it away or flush it down the toilet. I tore its wings off and I ate it. I ate a *yucky bug* and it tasted good to me!" She sounded mad and disgusted and grossed out at the same time.

"Maybe that moth was poisonous, Bethany—maybe you—"

"It wasn't the moth, Mom. I tried to eat other stuff last night before I ate the bug and I tried again this morning. I can't eat regular food anymore. I can't eat what I haven't killed. I have to see it die—and watch it die—and feel it happen with my own hands. But I don't want bugs, I want blood on my skin again, I want it in my hair and on my blade." Her face was all grim determination as she pushed out the last of it looking at Cornelius. "I didn't just kill Fiona and Yanosh, Father. What I did was worse. I think I ate them. Sort of. Somehow I turned their life into death, but to me, death tasted like life, like I'm all upside down on the inside now." She looked confused by what she was saying herself but continued anyway. "Their pain made me feel good. It was weird. I could even taste Fiona's fear, it was really sweet. Sweeter than red wine. And the ugly things in their blood—tasted—good. Sin is my candy." She confessed with a quiet sigh. "I'm a monster, but I still don't want to die. I'm scared." Bethany closed her eyes and leaned back in Mr. Bryant's arms, exhausted.

Before anyone could react or say a word, Cornelius spoke, his voice loud and commanding. "Penny! Bring Bethany's blade!" The little black girl took off from her seat on the bench, running down the hall at a full sprint. "Byron, gather the red witches we have among the newcomers and have them prepare an animal sacrifice in the Cathedral Room. Let's feed my daughter!"

"Gladly, my King," Byron answered. "But will an animal sacrifice suffice? She may need a human sacrifice."

"We will *never* sacrifice an innocent life in Amen Hale," Cornelius said firmly. Mr. Bryant nodded, openly pleased with this statement while Mrs. Bryant busied herself with patting Bethany's brow with a damp cloth as Cornelius continued. "If an animal doesn't work then I will be her human sacrifice. Bethany can take my life back if she must."

Instantly, Byron and the others started to voice their objections but Cornelius cut them off soundly. "Enough!" he shouted. "What kind of father would I be if I were not willing to die for one I claim as my own child? I died trying to protect her yesterday, and if the animal sacrifice does not work I will die for her today as well!" Cornelius drew a deep calming breath. "Summon the red witches, Byron, and prepare an animal sacrifice. My child is hungry and I will see her fed and happy again, even if it kills me."

Bethany

—◆—

Eating Death

THIRTY MINUTES LATER.

They'd gathered six red witches, three young and three that were very old. They all wore red or black and red robes, each with different patterns and markings. It was obvious that they came from different covens. Set into the floor of the Cathedral Room was a beautiful pentagram mosaic made from thousands of brilliantly colored pieces of tile. The witches stood around the circle, one at each point of the pentagram and one in the center, inside the circle holding the sacrifice. A goat.

The red witches tried to school Cornelius on how to properly prepare the sacrifice, the need to burn incense or herbs and prepare the circle; they argued about the need to invoke the circle and cast some spells before they started, but Cornelius rejected all their advice. He told them to do nothing but form the circle and hold the animal and be ready to help with whatever Bethany needed. Penny squatted on the floor, just outside the circle, ready with Princes Bethany's blade. The tall and beautiful blond witch in the center of the circle held the goat by a rope tied to its head. She stroked the animal, murmuring to it soothingly, keeping it calm. The witches had rushed to answer the Kings urgent call, sifting through their belongings and into their robes and rushing to get the animal ready and the candles in place, but now everyone was waiting.

Princess Bethany was sick, throwing up in the bathroom. Almost three hundred newcomers had crowded into the room. They stood off to the side, having to stand almost shoulder to shoulder to fit into the room without getting in the way. The children were not up front sitting on the floor so those behind could see, but were hidden behind the adults so they could not see. Cornelius had ordered every newcomer not already given a position of service to be here and witness the sacrifice but the parents of those children were still doing what they could to shield them from what they could all see was about to happen. They were a silent wide-eyed crowd; most of them had never even seen any of the Princes or Princesses or the Lords and Ladies of Amen Hale. The ones with magic. And most of them had never seen an animal sacrifice before. Other than the soothing, cooing noises from the witch with the animal the only other steady noise in the room was the "clack clack clack" that came from King Cornelius's boots as he paced back and forth beside the circle and waited.

Finally, there was an excited murmur from the crowd which quickly went silent as Mrs. Bryant came in with Bethany leaning on her side. The Princess looked absolutely horrible. Her olive skin was pale and sickly shade of green and she was barely able to stand on her own as she was helped to the edge of the circle. Mrs. Bryant looked very uncomfortable and out of place as she glanced down at the pentagram set in the floor and at the red robed women that stood around the circle and at the goat. She gave Bethany a hug and stepped away with small shuffling steps. She seemed on the edge of a mental breakdown as her husband collected her, pulling her along, guiding her a short distance away where they stopped to watch.

"We are ready for you, Princess Bethany," said the young blond witch holding the animal.

Bethany drug her feet as she stepped into the circle; she looked so tiny and different from the tall women in their red robes who surrounded her. Bethany wore her witch dress that Rain had made for her, dark blood red on the bottom fading to stone grey on the top with what looked like raised little roots running down the sleeves. The women around her kept their faces free of any sign or hint of displeasure though some smiled at her encouragingly. It was wasted on the Princess however, who had eyes only for the animal.

"My blade." Bethany put her hand out to the side. Penny rose to her feet and walked into the circle and very carefully put the handle of the blade into Bethany's little hand and returned to her spot.

The Princess seemed stronger now, steadier on her feet as she slowly walked around the animal. She spoke as circled the goat, her little, innocent voice was easily heard by everyone, as if the acoustics of the high domed ceiling had magnified the sound directly below while at the same time, oddly, hushing the other small noises of the crowded hall.

"Hello goat." Bethany addressed the animal as if it were a person. "I will name you Mike. Mike. Mike. Mike. I knew a guy named Mike once. He was a bastard. Just. Like. You. I hate you Mike. If you could talk, you could ask me why I hate you, or ask me what you did to deserve this—but you can't talk. Can you, Mike?" She paused as if waiting for a reply. Bethany shook her head sadly. "So I hate you. I would say, thanks for coming today, Mike, but you can't think either. You don't know. So I hate you. I hate you because you are a goat named 'Mike' and not a man named 'Mike.' If I kill you, it won't be murder. I can't murder a stupid goat. I can only slaughter one, and for that *I hate you Mike.*" Bethany's little voice seethed with both hate and disappointment. It really did sound like she hated "Mike". "You don't have a soul, only a spirit, so there are no lies or hate or filth or shadows inside you. So I hate you."

Bethany circled the goat as she spoke to it. The other three hundred sets of eyes looking on simply did not exist for her. The opposite was true of the crowd; they couldn't look away from the child with the knife as she berated "Mike" the goat. The whole room was spellbound, drawn in like magic to the bizarre and chilling scene.

"You never hurt or raped or tortured a child. Not even once, Mike. You've never even made someone cry." Bethany looked down at the goat and shook her head, this time with disgust on her face, appalled by Mike's utter and complete failure as a villain. "And you call yourself a *goat*—what kind of fucking goat are you, Mike!?" she seethed. "You've never even made a little girl cry! AND I HATE YOU FOR IT!"

Everyone felt the dark wave of dread magic that filled the room, pouring out of Bethany's little body, including the goat. The terrified animal bleated, kicked, and struggled wildly against the rope, trying to get away from Bethany and the young witch who was struggling to hold him still. Bethany's hands tightened around the blade as she closed in on Mike, her snarling face lost in blood lust and rage as her magic grew and poured through the room, through the house, and through all of

Amen Hale. The Hall itself seemed to seethe with the power of her dark magic as she screamed at the terrified animal.

The girl holding the goat fought to lift its head and give Bethany a clean stroke with the blade, which she did. The razor sharp edge sliced deep into Mike's neck. The animal let out one final surprised noise before going silent. Its feet still kicked but the young witch held him in place, holding the head up as the Princess knelt down and let the blood flowing out of Mike's slit throat spray all over her face and hair and all down her back.

The blood kept pumping and pumping out of the wound like magic until every last drop of blood that had been inside the goat was outside, on the floor or covering Bethany Grave, the Red Witch, Princess of Amen Hale. Bethany set the blade on the floor beside her and bent down, pressing her palms flat into the sticky gore that covered the tile floor. It wasn't the blood of a man, but there was death in this blood. Sacrifice and Death and Fear and Loss and Pain.

She sighed as she pulled into her body what magic she could from the blood and then she lifted her hands to the goats face, running them over the dead staring eyes, the mouth, and slit throat, feeling the death around the animal. She pulled it all into herself, and breathed in deeply of the strong smell of blood and animal and death. The loss, the surprise, the fear, pain, shock, and the emptiness of the end—it all filled her body with warmth and filled her lungs like life giving air. Bethany ate Mike's death and sighed contentedly.

The Princess picked up her sacrificial blade and held it out to the side. Penny stepped forward and took it from her bloody hand, quickly and carefully getting the dangerous blade away from the Princess like she'd been taught. Her grandmother had told her many times that most accidents with a blade happened right after they were used, so now was the time to be the most careful. She stopped at the edge of the circle and waited to see what would happen next. She didn't bother to clean the blade yet. She held it carefully and waited. They might not be done. For all she knew there would be another animal. Who knew? Maybe even a person. She hoped not. She liked Cornelius.

Bethany's face, her beautiful hair, and her dress were covered in red blood. It had even gone down the back of her neck, under her collar, and down the front, all the warm blood cooling and drying onto her flesh.

"Thank you," Bethany said to the frightened girl still holding the goat as she rose from the bloody floor. Bethany looked like a nightmare, but her voice sounded hale once more. Stronger and happy already.

The girl holding the goat upright let the rope slip from her grasp, catching it again just before the dead goat fell flat onto the bloody floor. Her face was a mask of pain as she worked the limp animal back into an upright position with just one hand. Bethany noticed that the girls left hand was cradled up against her chest. She was hurt and bleeding badly.

"You're bleeding." Bethany's eyes went wide. "I didn't get you with my blade, did I? I'm so sorry!" The Princess came forward to help but the girl shook her head no.

"No, Princess! No, it wasn't your blade. It was my fault. I–I was careless," she stuttered out. She quickly hid her bleeding hand behind her back putting it out of Bethany's sight. "The goat bit me. It's nothing, really. It's just a scratch." She shrugged dismissively, wearing a weak, trembling smile.

"Let me see it," Bethany asked. Ordered.

The girl looked terrified as she held up her shaking hand which Bethany took in her own, turning it this way and that, looking at the bite and getting more and more glassy eyed by the second. It was a nasty bite, down into the soft meat of the palm just below the girl's thumb. The skin was torn open in a circled flap, the exact match of Mike's goat mouth, and it was bleeding badly. No one had noticed because the girl's blood had blended in with the goat's and her red dress hid the rest. Bethany lifted the hurt hand to her face and licked the girl's bloody hand like it was a completely natural thing to do.

"What are you doing, Princess?" asked the terrified girl in a breathy whisper.

Bethany didn't answer, she just kept licking her hand. Bethany licked the blood that ran down the girl's wrist and arm. After a moment the young witches face relaxed, and after another minute she seemed completely calm and even helpful, moving her arm around to give Bethany the best angle to get at the blood. Two of the other red robed women stepped into the circle and took the dead animal, carrying the goat back to the edge of the circle with them. Bethany and the young witch didn't even notice that the goat was gone, busy and happy with what they were doing. A worried murmur of whispered voices came from the on-looking crowd.

"Bethany, my child. What are you doing?" Cornelius's concerned voice called from the edge of the circle.

"Eating," Bethany said between licks and added, "She has lots of sin, Father." Bethany resumed her dark breakfast, licking away happily.

Cornelius grunted as he watched, "Don't we all, child, but it's time to let her go now."

Bethany took one or two more licks before wrapping both of her tiny bloody hands around the girl's goat bitten hand. She arched her back and looked up to the ceiling with her eyes closed as she chanted.

"By the teeth of a goat, by the edge of a blade.
Blood has been shed, the price has been paid.
I call on the power of blood now set free.
What *he* has torn, heal now for *me*.
Blood! Blood! Blood! Blood!
Magic and Death and Sacrifice made
Blood has been shed, the price has been paid."

A different kind of magic tingled through the room, not the wave of dark dread that Bethany had released earlier when she sacrificed the goat, but an eerie tingle, like thousands of little magical ants crawling all over everyone in the hall, raising hairs and goosebumps on the flesh upon which they crept. It only lasted for a minute and then it was over.

"How's your hand, Ariel?" Bethany asked the young witch, whose name she now knew.

Ariel held up her hand and flexed it, wiggling her thumb around, testing its movement. There was a faint scar but that was all. Her hand was perfect. A bright smile broke out across her face. "Oh! Blessed Be! Thank you, Princess Bethany. That really hurt like hell."

Relieved laughs rose from among the newcomers, servants, and the red witches, breaking the pent up tension that hung thick in the air like suffocating smoke. After watching Bethany with the goat, everyone had assumed that the absolute worst was about to happen to the girl. Hearts were still racing. The past few minutes had been an intense, emotional roller coaster—from the fear and horror brought on by the bloody sacrifice and Bethany's dark magic, plunging into the terrified worry for the young witch, finally to crash land (quite unexpectedly) into a happy outcome for all! Except the goat of course. He'd had a thoroughly bad day.

"I told you Mike was a bad goat." Bethany's eyes cut to the dead "villain" held by the two red robed women at the edge of the circle.

Ariel laughed. "Yes, Princess, you're right, he *was* a bad goat," she agreed happily. Ariel seemed very happy. "Thank you, my Princess. I feel so much better. I'm very glad I'm here." She went to her knees before Bethany, head bowed. Healed. Content and happy.

Bethany looked back to where Cornelius stood just outside the circle with Mr. and Mrs. Bryant. "Thank you, Father. I'm feeling better, but I'm still hungry. I need to eat his flesh now. I need to eat Mike," Bethany's happy little voice called out. Her white teeth shone brightly out of the bloody red mask that was her face. "Do you want to join me and Mike for lunch? He was a bad goat, but I bet he still tastes good."

Some of newcomers in the watching crowd laughed which drew Bethany's attention. "Oh," she said, surprised by the huge crowd, eyes going wide as she looked back at all the staring faces. She quickly combed the bloody hair out of her face and pulled her dress straight where the drying blood had glued it to her skin. "Welcome to Amen Hale," Bethany greeted the crowd of strangers in her best formal voice once she was arranged – bloody - but presentable.

They bowed to her and mumbled a hundred different greetings all at the same time. Cornelius stepped up beside Bethany and looked out over the crowd. First one, then eight, then the others like dominos all went to their knees awkwardly. They didn't know if they should or shouldn't, or even how to go about kneeling and showing the proper deference to a King or a Princess. Obeisance was new to all of them.

"Yes. Welcome to Amen Hale. This is my daughter," Cornelius presented Bethany to them with his hand, "Princess Bethany. And here in this circle is where she raised me from the dead. Made me a King. Gave me a Kingdom and Knowledge and Power. Before this day is done you will see the power of Amen Hale and the magic of her children." Cornelius gave Bethany a loving, fatherly smile before turning back to the crowd.

"I summoned you here so you could see this, now, at the beginning. Let there be no misunderstandings between us. You have been told that magic is real, and so it is. Most of my children and the Lords and Ladies of Hale have normal needs, but some are unique, like the vampires and my Bethany. Bethany must have sacrifice and death and blood to live."

Cornelius paused, eyeing the crowd for a moment before going on. "If this offends you, leave my Kingdom. And if you are offended with an animal sacrifice, what will you do when you see a human sacrifice? As you know, we have many enemies. There are many who hate us and would do us harm if they could. I have but one penalty for anyone who would harm a child of Amen Hale. Death. But death is valuable to us, and not to be wasted. We value all innocent, human life. But those who seek to kill or destroy us are not only our enemies, to my children they are food."

Cornelius gave the mass of quiet, and very nervous people a reassuring smile. "We would like you to stay and be a part of the Kingdom, but you are free to leave if that is your desire. If the thought of human sacrifice, no matter how justified, offends you, I understand. This is not your place. Byron has arranged transportation to carry you back to the gate. But be careful. Harm nothing as you depart and go in peace." Cornelius pointed toward the door, "Go now, out the back, and gather the possessions you have brought with you."

And about thirty people did exactly that, walking toward the back door where Lucius and Byron waited. The house steward and the ex-soldier stepped outside with the departing crowd and a servant shut the door behind them with a quiet thud.

As soon as they left, the room filled with busy activity as house servants prepared for the King and Queen of Amen Hale to hold court for the first time. The crowd of newcomers had been standing but now servants brought out folding chairs for them to seat themselves in while others got busy assembling a two-foot-high raised platform for Cathryn and Cornelius to place their chairs on.

"Father, did you want to come to lunch with me and Mike?" Bethany asked again, her eyes begging him to join her. "I've never ate goat before," she added. Dried blood cracked and flaked off as her brow furrowed in thought.

Cornelius voice was encouraging and happy as he replied, "But of course! I would be delighted to join you and 'Mike' for lunch my child. Andre has a few excellent recipes for goat that we can try together. I'll see if your sisters can join us as well."

"That sounds great!" Bethany answered with a happy smile of her own. She was alive again, filled with happy energy, completely revived and ready to have fun. Cornelius told a servant to take the goat to the kitchen and have it prepared for a late lunch for the Royal Family. And he told them to let the other Princesses know that they were invited to lunch.

"Mom, Dad," Bethany asked Mr. and Mrs. Bryant, "do you want to join us for lunch too?"

Mrs. Bryant laughed. "Honey, I'm sorry, but we've already promised Ryan and Sky that we'd go to lunch with them and meet Sky's mother and father. We have a lot to talk about. I'm sure they'll want to talk about Ryan running off and marrying their daughter without their permission."

Bethany nodded. "Oh. Okay." She made a face. "Yeah, they're probably gonna yell at you. Ryan told me Sky's parents are kinda rough. Let me know when you're ready to go home and I'll use magic to open the door for you to get back to the trailer. Could I come over tonight?" she asked shyly. "Maybe we could sit on the couch and watch some TV together." Bethany's innocent eyes stared out of her bloody face as she looked at them. The sweet voice and the childlike request coming from the bloody figure seemed jarringly odd to the crowd of staring faces who did not know Bethany.

"That would be great, honey," said Mrs. Bryant with absolute calm, as if nothing were amiss or out of place with the request or the girl making it.

"That would be fantastic," said Mr. Bryant with a big smile of his own. "And I'm glad to see that you're feeling better honey, but before we get comfy on the couch," he eyed her up and down, "you're gonna need to take a shower."

"Yes," Cornelius agreed. "I do believe a shower would be needed before lunch as well." He gave Bethany a look.

"I just got all this good blood on me and now you want me to take it off," she griped even as she turned and headed in the direction of her room and her shower, leaving little bloody footprints behind as she stomped away. "That better be some good goat!" she shouted as she disappeared into the entry hall.

Bethany could hear them laughing behind her as she made her way up the broad grand stairwell, fouling its crisp white carpet with every step. She charged into her room and was surprised to see the little black girl, Penny, sitting on the floor. Penny had her blade laid out on a white sheet where she'd been cleaning it with a rag and some oil, but she must have jumped or slipped with the blade when Bethany burst into the room. A dark crimson line, that ran from side to side across her palm, was welling with blood.

Penny looked up at Bethany. Bethany looked at Penny. Penny held up her bloody hand in invitation. Bethany turned and shut her bedroom door.

Black Rain

Work Work Work

CATHRYN AND I stood on the balcony together, surveying the rutted up ruin that all the military vehicles had made of the once beautiful front lawn.

"It's so quiet and peaceful now," I said.

The view forward was damaged, but absolutely empty. No huge green trucks or tanks or soldiers were anywhere within sight of the house. There weren't even any stiff backed, silent FBI in their suits tucked away in out of the way places. They were all gone. It seemed so still after all of the chaos that filled the area yesterday. All of the military and their equipment had been pulled back almost a mile away from the house. If the noise of distant helicopters and jets didn't give it away you could almost believe that it was just another quiet, normal Thursday.

"I'm surprised Trisha or Agent White or someone from the government isn't already here to bother us."

Cathryn nodded and explained, "Cornelius told them last night that we wanted no FBI or government visitors of any kind until this afternoon at four, when we have agreed to officially meet with whoever the US government wishes to send. He told them quite firmly that their soldiers are to stay off our land unless we invite them in."

I took a deep breath and let it out slowly. It was time to get started. "What needs to be done first, Mother?" I looked at her. She looked relieved I'd asked the question first.

"There's much to do, Rain. We need more protection. We need more space for our people. We need to talk to the FBI today about Kendal. And we have to do it in person because the phones no longer work. We don't know if she's home now or stuck out at the new checkpoint they've set up or possibly detained somewhere by the government. We need to find out. And we have no money. The government has frozen our assets and seized our accounts. But even if we had money it wouldn't do us any good. We can't get out to spend it. And we'll be running out of food very soon, especially with all these new mouths to feed. The soldiers have been less than helpful with the deliveries we have tried to have brought in. We need food, and money to pay for the food, unless you can just make us what we need here."

My new mother was right, there was lots of work to do. Work, work, work. Things only I could do. "Believer," I said and looked over to my husband.

He stood nearby, but not too close, giving my mother and me some space and time together, but now he came forward and reached out a huge cloudy hand to touch my face. His red eyes looked so happy and his slit of a mouth smiled at me before he spoke. "Yes, my lady."

Just hearing his deep rumbling voice made me go weak in the knees and my mouth went dry as I remembered things that had happened last night and what might happen again tonight. Before I lost my mind again completely and just threw myself at him and chucked it all, I managed to speak one stuttering sentence. "I've–I've got to–go for a while. I'll be back soon, my love." I pressed his hand into my face, covering my mouth and nose as I breathed in his wonderful smell while I looked up into his bright red eyes, like glowing red coals, two solid fixed points inside his ever moving tempest. Two points that stared down at me. His gaze pulled me in and held me.

"I will go see my Sky and explore the house." he said suddenly. "And I may go spend some time with my brother as well. He has been keeping an eye on the doctor and helping Lucius with security. Perhaps I will help. Go and do what is needed, my lady." He pulled his hand away. And he had to *pull* it away because I wasn't able to let go or stop trying to breathe him in, like a drug I couldn't get enough of. Cathryn's arms encircled me, holding me back from following after as he stepped away. "I'll see you this afternoon, my lady." He smiled, turned, and walked away, ducking through the low balcony doorway.

Cathryn held me as I stood there looking at the doorway he'd left through for a few moments as my breathing slowly returned to normal. I hadn't even realized I had started breathing so hard.

"Are you feeling better?" Cathryn asked.

"No." I shook my head. "Yes," I said, disagreeing with myself. I didn't know to be honest. I closed my eyes trying to get my head to stop spinning and somehow get my brain to start working.

"Be quiet and breathe, Rain," Cathryn's calming voice counseled. "Everything is fine. You're fine. Be still, look at the trees and breathe."

I did what she advised. I breathed, feeling more myself after each deep breath of humid Florida air while I looked out at the oaks that lined the lawn.

I kept losing my mind around Believer. Maybe I *was* somehow damaged like he feared. I felt sure that if I willed it, if I wanted it, I could easily fix myself, but I really didn't want to. I didn't want these feelings for him to change because I forced them to change. If they ever changed, I wanted it to be a natural adjustment between two people being together and not something I forced to happen with magic. Hopefully, given some time, I could be with him and handle everything better, but I didn't want to simply wish it away. I liked the way he made me feel. But it was time to go to work now, and Believer knew it. Believer loved me enough to leave me. Right now, I needed to be away from him, and I needed to work, so he took himself away.

"I'm a mess, Mother, but I like it. It feels right," I said as I breathed in a few more deep lungfuls of air, air that did not smell like spring rain and did not taste like a summer storm— I felt myself start to drift again and shook my head back and forth like a dog with a bone to clear out the cobwebs.

"Perhaps some hot tea. Or maybe some strong coffee?" Cathryn suggested, trying to be helpful.

"Hold my hand, Mom," I said as I kept my focus on the lawn.

Cathryn took my hand and we both left the balcony and lifted up into the air. I willed us to fly up out over the ruined lawn. Cathryn floated beside me, a delighted smile on her face as we came to a stop about thirty feet above the lawn.

"This is wonderful. I've never flown before," Cathryn said.

I smiled back. "You should see Sky. She's so beautiful when she flies."

"Is she?" she asked, almost giddy as she enjoyed the feel of her first flight.

"She's amazing. Maybe we could all go flying together later tonight."

"Maybe tomorrow night, my child. Tonight we're meeting with the government, and we still have a lot to do."

"All right, let's get started fixing things right now." I looked down below us at the lawn thirty feet below. I willed the cut and rutted terrain to smooth out and level up where it was scarred, and it did, earth rippling eerily before lying flat and leveling. I willed the few weeds that marred the lawn to wither and die. Next I had the grass grow, stopping and shaping it to an exact trim height and ripening the millions of identical blades to a deep, luscious green.

Cathryn and I watched as the world beneath our feet reshaped itself to my wishes. A perfect green carpet of beautiful grass spilled outward, extended beyond its normal boundary set by the landscapers, running all the way out to the line of big oaks that edged the property in the far distance.

I looked at the long driveway that ran out to the gate and the road. Military trucks had trampled the shrubs bordering the cobbled brick drive and the decorative flowers beds which were spaced out every twenty yards or so all the way to the gate of Amen Hale. It was all flattened mush. I created a ten foot wide border on each side of the cobbled drive, willing the ruined flower beds, shrubbery and grass on each side to fade down into the soil. In those two browned and ready swaths of earth I wanted lillies. We watched as millions of little green shoots pushed their way upward, bursting open in a riot of colors running down either side of the drive.

The grass was a perfect dark green, every blade exactly the same. The flowers were so bright, the colors so outrageously vibrant, and each one was so perfectly placed the whole vista looked unreal. Staged. The land below made me think of a picture on a postcard that had been digitally enhanced with Photoshop kung fu, cloning out every little imperfection to create impossible beauty. But with postcards, once you reached the source of that impossible image you would see that reality didn't match the picture. But here in Amen Hale, the fantasy was real; the impossible was there on the ground just below us. In just seconds the scarred, mutilated landscape had been transformed into something magical.

"It's so beautiful, Rain," Cathryn said, her voice thick with emotion. "Now the gate and the wall."

"Yes, Mother," I answered as I guided our flight down the drive and toward the gate. Two military Hummers were parked nose to nose outside the gate, blocking the entrance. And the Hummers were the only vehicles in sight. No tanks, rocket launchers, or other fancy war stuff remained. All the soldiers were gone as well. Now only a dozen special forces types dressed in black stood vigil outside the gate, along with a small group of standard issue men in suits who had to be FBI or something. The men in suits had one tent set up out by the street, but that was it.

The soldiers didn't panic when they saw us floating in the air thirty feet above the driveway, looking down on them. They held their hands up, shielding their eyes from the sun, as they watched us. Some of the suited men brought phones to their ears, busily calling whoever they had to call when they saw something weird. I guess flying witches counted as call worthy.

The two lane paved road in front of the house was totally empty. No cars in sight. Constantine barb wire ran along the outside of the cast iron fence that wrapped around Amen Hale, the brightly gleaning spirals running off into the distance in both directions. On our side of the fence was the real destruction zone. The military had brought in bulldozers, running them down the property line, creating a ten foot wide swath of freshly turned and flattened earth following the fence line from the inside. On the earth they prepared they laid ten foot long sections of barricades, connecting them together like Lego blocks, forming a four foot high cement wall. As if the metal gate was insufficient protection and they wanted something more solid to stand behind. It looked terrible. And then, after everything they'd done, they just abandoned it all and moved further back.

"They left a huge ugly mess," I said as I looked at it.

Cathryn squeezed my hand and smiled at me. "Yes, but thank the goddess we don't have to leave it this way. Perhaps a better wall, Rain? I'm sure anything you do will be a huge improvement over this."

"Yes, Mother." I got to work. I used the existing raw material, the cement wall, the metal gate, even the barb wire to build the new wall. I thought about all of it coming together, and they did (gate, wire, and concrete), sliding together and joining, not with a metallic crash of stone and metal but with a wet splat of a sound. The entire fence, stretching out in both directions moved as if it were alive, a long, thin, living blob of liquid material. The "substance" rose up, thinned out, and shaped itself into a fifteen foot high wall made of something that looked like glass but was much harder and stronger.

I heard my mother laughing beside me as she watched it take form. I added the finishing touches. I spread the lilies from the ten foot flat plane of ruined earth lining the drive and filled in this new open flat space with millions of ultracolorful lilies. The wall itself almost looked like the top of a fancy fish bowl. The surface was black, reflective, and shiny, like a massive dark mirror. The oak trees and colorful flowers reflected in its surface like a beautiful painting, making the world beyond our borders look as if it went on and on.

Two worlds faced each other, a brightly lit and living world, and its dark mirror match. The wall was only an inch wide at the very top and three inches at the bottom. It was made of one solid piece, completely without seam or crack. I was worried about people digging under the wall too but I didn't want to hurt the sewer lines and water pipes. Or power lines for that matter. It was all underground. An image of toilets that didn't flush flashed in my mind. Yikes! I willed the wall to extend carefully down into the ground, wrapping around any existing pipes and wires instead of cutting them. Then I wrapped the pipes and wires in a shield to keep the rest of what I planned to do from hurting them. Satisfied with the wall, I turned to work on the gate, but the gate was gone!

"Dammit! The gate's gone!" I'd accidentally combined the gate into the wall; now it was all part of the big seamless fish bowl I'd made. The driveway ran straight into a dead end. Then I thought about it some. What the hell did we need a gate or even a driveway for anyway? I was thinking like a human. I laughed.

"Hey, Mom. I kinda like it. Let's keep it this way."

Cathryn looked over at me, puzzled. "We'll need to get out sooner or later, and others will need to get in to see us as well."

"Mother, I think I'm going to change things some."

"In what way?" asked Cathryn, not worried in the least, only curious.

"Mother, we don't need roads or gates. The days of gates are behind us." I looked off in the distance and saw a jet flying by. Even with the wall we would never be safe from rockets, missiles, or helicopters landing inside Amen Hale. I needed to change some of the rules if I meant to keep us safe.

"Let's go talk to the nice FBI guys, Mom. We can ask them about Kendal, and there are some other things I need to tell them."

"So be it." She looked down at them, her brow creased as she studied the tiny figures below. "Try to stay calm when you see them, Rain. You still have a hard time with strangers."

I nodded. "Yes ma'am." She was right. I did need to be careful.

We floated out beyond the new wall and dropped down onto the drive a few feet away from the government agents in their suits. As soon as we landed, one came forward. He was about forty, black hair, tall, and wearing a cowboy hat, which seemed odd for an FBI guy. He looked as if he'd woken on the wrong side of the bed this morning and blamed us for it. He did try to smile as he made his introductions.

"Good morning, Black Rain." He gave a quick little jerk of a nod in my direction. "Queen Cathryn." He acknowledged my mother without so much as a head bob, tip of his hat, or even the decency of a direct look to meet her eyes. "My name is Robert Osteen. FBI. How may I be of service to you this morning?" His tone wasn't all that friendly or even respectful. I felt my temper rise darkly, as if a separate part of myself that had been asleep was waking up from a long nap. I recognized it right away. The Black Witch, that wild and dangerous part of my soul was rising within me.

"Rain, stay calm. It's all right." Cathryn tried to soothe me, seeing something in my face that alarmed her. "Politely and respectfully if you please, Agent Osteen," Mother cautioned.

Everyone was staring at me. The soldiers. The other FBI men. Staring at my solid black eyes, staring at the mark on my forehead and at my hair that seemed alive as it moved about. My temper rose higher and little more of my power slipped out. Like contents under pressure finding cracks in its cramped cage, power crawled out of my skin, down my hair, pushing out of my body. Everyone except my mother backed away. I laughed darkly. The Witch within me often found other people's fear amusing. I attempted to focus on what I needed to say before things got badly out of hand. I really didn't want to kill anyone this morning.

"Threes. Three things. Three things that you'll need to remember, Mr. Osteen. Three important things. The Wall, the Way, and the Witch."

He pulled out his digital palm cam. "Just a minute. You've got a message for us, right?" Osteen clenched his jaw tightly as he forced himself to step closer. He pointed the camera at me and moved it about, looking in the little flip out screen on the side of the camera until he was happy with his angle. I laughed. He kept filming.

"I'm afraid that's not going to work, Mr. Osteen, but if it makes you feel better, please keep using it," I encouraged and gave him a wink and a grin which he ignored completely and just kept filming like a robot.

"The Wall: No metal shall come near the walls of the Kingdom. No metal shall fly over the walls of Amen Hale." I turned away from him and looked back to the wall that I had just created and held my arms out wide as I contemplated what I wanted to shape and what magic I needed. I spoke and willed my words to hold my power until such time, if ever, that I chose to release it. As I spoke, everything hushed around us. It was like the whole world was listening quietly, ready to obey my will.

"As above and so below,
I shape the world and set it so.
Around this wall I set a curse,
For things of metal dug from the earth.
That which was taken and shaped by hands,
Guns and tools for the race of man.
Taken from earth to the earth now return,
Metal first fashioned to sand now reform.
From the wall to the street and high in the air,
Like a dome o'er the Kingdom, let the spell be held there.
Around this wall now let this curse live.
By my will, by my words, by the power I give."

Lots of things happened at the same time but mixed in all of it was the sound of men cursing. Soldiers started shouting and cursing as the things they wore or held in their hands changed. Watches and rings dissolved. They watched with wide-eyed horror as their guns and all the fancy military hardware strapped all over their bodies dissolved into perfect white sand. Their weapons turned to piles of snow white sand at their feet. Two men were sitting inside one of the Hummers as the whole vehicle came apart, the metal parts turning to sand, but it was a huge mess because of the parts that remained behind. The cloth headliner, the seats, and all the plastic parts that were in the engine and inside the Hummer lay on the road like a pile of junk. The soldiers cussed and shouted as they struggled out from under the headliner like two children that found themselves trapped under a big unruly blanket. They were also wet because of the fluids, the many gallons of gasoline, antifreeze, and engine oil that soaked into the soil and ran off toward the ditch on the sides of the drive. The strong smell rose into the air.

Agent Osteen's camera quit working. "What the hell?" he said as the little viewfinder fell right off the side and dangled by a plastic wire as the tiny metal screws turned to sand, but the camera held its shape, the plastic clips holding it together where metal would have failed. But guns weren't the only thing that had turned to sand.

"Rain. A little help, please." I heard Cathryn say.

I turned to her and let out a shocked "Oh my!"

She stood there, smiling but almost naked. She still wore a bra and some very revealing black thong panties, but her dress lay on the ground at her feet. The metal clips at the shoulder and back of her beautiful dress had dissolved. I laughed and so did Cathryn as she stood there in her underwear. Cathryn was fifty years old but she looked like a super sexy thirty-something, a tall graceful blonde with beautiful tattoos running down the length of her body and arms and legs.

The soldiers and most of the FBI men smiled as they enjoyed the pleasant view and they were also put at ease by the sound of our laughter. Some of the men also laughed as they watched the two soldiers fight their way out of the Hummer rubble, slipping and sliding around in the gas, engine oil and sand. I relaxed, my anger vanishing and my power ebbing to a more endurable level for those around me. The soldiers and the FBI men were also struggling with clothing issues, shoe strings on boots held with metal clasps or hooks were gone, creating snarled mess-es, metal belt buckles, buttons, zippers, and rings for straps disappeared and left pants loose and sagging.

One of the FBI agent's eyeglass frames dissolved right off his nose and he appeared nearly blind without the lenses that were now somewhere at his feet. He knelt and began to feel the ground with his hands. His partner picked on him, telling him he was missing his one chance to see the Queen naked. He searched harder.

Cathryn gathered up her dress with a smile, and I fixed it as I laughed, fashioning some metal clips for her dress. "Rain. I thought metal would dissolve this close to the wall. Why is this staying?" my new mother asked as she looked at the new gold shoulder clasp I placed on her dress, running her hand across the shiny metal that happened to be *real* gold now.

"Remember the curse, Mother. Only metal shaped by men's hands. I used magic to make and shape the metal. And I'm not human, so I don't count."

"So mote it be," she said and smiled.

"So mote it be," I agreed.

"Dammit, Johnson, pull your pants up!" Agent Osteen fussed at one of the FBI men who was having a particularly hard time keeping things in place.

"Sir. I'm trying." The very skinny man struggled with his pants as Osteen stood there, frowning, looking put upon and embarrassed.

"Come on, Osteen, leave the poor man alone," I said, defending the guy. "It's not Johnson's fault he has no ass. All he has is a back with a crack. Just be glad and thankful you have some ass to help hold your pants up. Not everyone does," I said with a straight face.

Osteen didn't smile but Johnson and Cathryn did. They both burst out laughing and so did a few of the other FBI guys who'd overheard the exchange, which made Osteen even more upset. He turned his back on Johnson and the others and directed his attention back to me and Cathryn.

"Let's finish this up, please. We can see that metal will not be allowed near or over the wall. What else did you want to tell us?" He raised the ruined camera then realized what he was doing, muttering a curse under his breath as he pitched the thing to the side and then reached into his jacket and took out a note pad, but when he reached for his pen in his front suit pocket he made a rather yucky discovery. The pen was metal, so it had dissolved and the ink had drained out into his pocket. The expensive lining had kept it from bleeding through so far. Osteen's mouth stayed pressed tightly shut but his twitching eyes screamed a colorful barrage of cuss words as he stood there looking at his blue fingers. He took off his jacket, and set it and the notepad down and just looked at me expectantly. Waiting stone faced as he wiped ink off his finger with a napkin one of his men handed him.

I'd had just about all the Osteen "fun" I could stand. Just looking at his face irked me. He was ruining the good mood I'd managed to mount from Cathryn's dress malfunction. If he wanted to be an asshole, so be it. I was game. We could play 'who's the biggest asshole' to the death if he liked. I knew I'd win.

"The Wall, the Way, and the Witch," I said. "The Way: Answer me this if you can, Osteen. You're such an uptight, stick in the mud, self-important, anal, tight-ass you may not be able to, but work at it and try to surprise me. Kay?" I thought about how I wanted to explain this as I watched his shocked face and cursing eyes process that line of insults. Beside me, my mother smiled. It seemed she agreed with this new method of communicating with Osteen. Good. I proceeded.

"Osteen, if I told you to go to hell, could you drive there and see the sights? Perhaps do a little advanced planning and find the perfect hole to crawl into when your time's up? I'm not joking, I'm asking you, Osteen, could you be a sweetheart and do that for me? I want you to go to hell." I stood there waiting, looking at him with my solid black eyes and a blank expression on my face.

The other agents had enjoyed hearing Osteen called names, trying not to laugh loud enough to get caught as they laughed behind his back, but now the happy faces vanished and were replaced by nervous looks. It seemed they were still waiting for me to say "just kidding," but they didn't know if I was.

"Can you go to hell for me or not, Osteen?" I waited but he remained silent. "What's the problem?" I asked. "Don't know the street address? Can't get past the gate? Scared of the dog in the yard? It's not a problem, just drop my name. I'm sure they'll let you right in. So I'm asking you. Can you go to hell for me—" I took a step closer, looking up into his face, "or not?" I asked as serious as death.

His eyes stayed on mine as he answered. "I don't believe I'll be able to do that. I'm sorry."

Whatever else Osteen was, he *was* tough. He didn't look away for a second from my midnight eyes. I nodded. "Thank you for helping me make my point."

His brow wrinkled up, his face went redder, he was somewhere between embarrassment and rage as he asked, "What point?" He reached up and snatched his hat off. He turned the hat in a circle, adjusting the rim as he asked again, "What possible damn point can you make by asking me to go to hell!?"

I smiled big as I heard "*it*" there in his voice, just the thinnest trickle of fear. A little quaver in his voice. Oh how bitter it must taste to a man as proud as Osteen. He managed to keep it out of his eyes and off his face, but it was hiding in his voice. Fear. The smile stayed on my face as I explained myself. "What kind of magical land can you actually drive to, Osteen? Does Zeus call Domino's pizza and have it delivered to Mt. Olympus? Did Alice take a taxi down into the rabbit hole? Was Superman's Fortress of Solitude located in the suburbs? Shit, even the one time Harry Potter missed the train he had to drive to Hogwarts in a flying car. So I think the same should apply to us. No roads will lead into the Kingdom of Amen Hale."

I looked at the driveway and the pile of Hummer junk sitting at the front of the drive. The soldiers had already clambered out and away from the leftovers and I used the twin piles of junk and sand. I shaped them like I had the wall. The two piles of junk seemed to liquefy, rise up in two heaps and move toward each other, joining together in the middle to form an arch of black glass. It was about nine feet tall and five feet wide. I wanted it to be tall enough for Believer to walk through comfortably so I made the door "Believer sized." My man was big. In lots of ways. I sighed happily, my mind starting to drift off toward my more erotic memories of last night when Osteen's voice interrupted my mental issues.

"How are we supposed to use this thing?" He and the other agents were gathered around the beautiful arch, running hands over the solid black glass as they discussed its formation and possible use.

"How do we use this when we come back at four with the Secretary of State and her party?" asked one of the other agents. An older, serious looking fellow with a stocky build and cold focused eyes. Other than Osteen he was the only one who hadn't laughed or even smiled during Cathryn's little show.

"Way: A way to open the gate." I drew the earth right up from the ground beside the arch and shaped something that almost looked like a vanity table or a fancy podium with a mirror. I used that same black, glasslike material for its construction but the mirror itself I made of solid silver. On the little table top I shaped a wide shallow basin, almost like a sink with no drain and then I finished by adding the parts that only I could see. I took a few minutes to wrap the table in the magic I wanted before I turned back to Osteen.

"At four p.m., come make your attempt. If you have someone with you who is worthy and willing you won't have any problem opening the gate."

Osteen looked confused. He and the other agents were already gathered around the mirror table, looking it over with bewildered expressions. Osteen almost shouted. "What do you mean!? *Make the attempt?* You want us to guess? We still don't have a damn clue as to what to do!" He walked around the alien contraption beside the arch then he directed his frustrated gaze back at me. "The Secretary of State, Hillary Clinton, plans on visiting you today at four p.m. representing the President of the United States. I suggest you tell us how to open the gate, or better yet, you made it, open it yourself! Do you think you can manage that?" he growled at me angrily. His voice demeaning. He spoke to me like I was a child or in some way stupid or slow.

I understood. His feelings had gotten hurt because I scared him. He wanted to hurt mine. I was too surprised to act. I was having a hard time even remembering the last time someone spoke to me like that directly. Maybe at the church when I had tried to get married there, but even that wasn't like this. Maybe Officer Williams, when I first met him on the porch steps. But Williams didn't know what I was when he did it. This guy did.

"Smack!" I heard a loud slap and my head snapped up from my daydreaming. I was surprised to see that my mother had just slapped the hell out of Osteen. A red handprint blazed on the side of his head.

"Fool! Keep your mouth shut! Say another word and I will let her kill you!" she yelled at Osteen as she wiped her hand on the side of her dress, disgusted, like he was a worm she'd been forced to touch and she wasn't very happy about it.

Osteen stood there, stunned. He slowly raised a hand to his face and rubbed as he flexed his jaw then turned and walked away. We watched as he went and stood with the soldiers about fifty feet away.

"Sorry, Mom," I said. She'd warned me before we landed about strangers.

Cathryn turned to me, putting a hand to my forehead and another on my cheek as she looked me over. "How are you, Rain?"

"Okay, I think. Just surprised," I answered as she mothered me. "Was I bad, Mom?" I asked honestly. "Did I act poorly? I did insult him and call him names. Maybe he had a right to be ugly like that," I said, thinking through the situation. "Was I evil?" I asked, honestly wanting an answer.

"Rain. If Agent Osteen loses his temper and gets mad and yells and cusses or even thinks horrible thoughts about us, nothing is going to happen. But if you lose your temper or curse something or someone, or even think the wrong thing, even for a moment, it's bad. In a way it's unfair that he has to be more considerate. But he doesn't have to worry about his every word or thought bringing about the end of the world." Cathryn looked at the remaining FBI men who were listening to every word she said as she went on.

"We have told *these people* that you cannot tolerate rudeness. It amazes me that they are so simpleminded that they can't grasp how dangerous it is to yell at you or insult you." She stared them down for a minute more before turning back to me. "And, Rain, you're a witch. You know what that means as well as I do."

I nodded. I did know. "I'm crazy."

We both heard yelling and looked up to see two of the soldiers dashing down the road as fast as they could with their stringless and floppy shoes toward another Hummer that was driving in our direction. "Stop! Stop!" they yelled as they waved their arms. They reached the Hummer before it got close enough to get turned to dust.

The older agent with the cold eyes walked forward and addressed us now, apparently taking over negotiations for the FBI now that it was obvious we didn't want to deal with Osteen anymore.

"Queen Cathryn. Black Rain. The name's Shaw. I want to apologize for Osteen. There was absolutely no excuse for his rudeness and I do beg your forgiveness. But if I may, you mentioned wanting to tell us three things. I understand the first is the warning about the wall. And I assume the second is that we will need to use the—aaa," he glanced at the front of the drive where the alien artifacts now stood, "the arch and the mirror table as our 'way' to get into Amen Hale. But is there something else you wanted to say or are there any further instructions you can give us? We honestly have no idea how to operate the arch or use the table you've provided." He looked sincere enough as he spoke which was an improvement over Osteen. "We want to be able to do our job when we come with the Secretary at four and now it seems like part of that job is using this arch." Shaw spoke very carefully and respectfully and so did I.

"It won't work for our enemies. Thieves. Spies. The mirror table will know. Only the right person will be able to open the gate, someone who wants to come to Amen Hale for an honorable reason and is willing to pay the price. That person will be able to open the gate for himself and for others."

Shaw looked less than thrilled, his face sagging into a worried frown. "Could you please explain what you mean about paying a price? And the right person?"

"The right person will know the price, Shaw. It may take a while to find the right person. Hopefully by four you'll be able to find someone that can open the gateway. But if not," I shrugged, "then maybe tomorrow."

His only reaction was a raised eyebrow. "And the third thing you wanted to say?"

"Witch," I said and looked at Cathryn.

She spoke to Agent Shaw. "We have not heard from Kendal Flame for almost twenty-four hours now. She is one of the witches that belongs to Black Rain's coven and she is missing. She was in the video that was on YouTube and I'm sure the FBI is aware of her, knows exactly who she is and I'm sure you're looking for her even now. Have you found her?"

He grabbed his phone and got it halfway to his ear before he remembered it was useless and broken. All the metal pieces were sand. "I'll make finding her my top priority, personally. And I'll come at four with the others with a report for you or with the woman herself if we already know where she is. Will that do?"

Cathryn and I both nodded. "Thank you, Shaw," my mother said, "I will look forward to seeing Kendal this afternoon then. Or seeing you with your report."

"If you find Kendal, she can open the gate for you," I encouraged. "But one way or the other I want to see Kendal or hear what you know. If they can't open the gate then stay here and wait for me to come out and see you. I don't know when that will be but stay right here, even if you have to put up a tent and camp out. Got it?"

"Yes. Of course," he replied.

Behind Shaw I noticed the poor man who had lost his glasses; he was holding the lenses to his eyes with both his hands like a pair of binoculars so he could see. And his lenses were really thick. He was probably just about blind without them, and it made me feel sorry for him. He was watching me as I looked at him. It looked funny; the lenses he held magnified his eyes and made them look huge. I didn't speak; I just raised my hand palm up and crooked one finger, calling him over. The blind man obeyed and came forward, still holding his lenses like binoculars.

"I'm so very sorry you missed your one chance to see my mother naked. She's very beautiful."

He smiled at that. His eyes got bigger and smaller as he moved the lenses back and forth, trying to keep me in focus as I stepped over to Cathryn. "Yes. She is," he said, as his binocular gaze slid over to my mother and he added, "And, yes. I am."

My mother smiled, pleased by his heartfelt regret, and the sincere compliment. Cathryn looked at me. "Rain."

I knew she wanted me to do something for him. I nodded. My mother liked this guy's moves. So did I. He was a normal, nice looking man about forty and he'd laughed and enjoyed himself in spite of his glasses coming apart. Cathryn walked around him with a smile on her face, and he turned with her, keeping her in sight as she circled, still holding his lenses to his eyes. It felt a little weird watching my new mother circle this guy like a hungry shark, but Cathryn was a witch, and she probably had her own little set of issues that I didn't know anything about yet.

"Don't think I do you a kindness, remember, I am a witch," Cathryn said and then looked at me again.

I willed his eyes to heal, his vision to improve to crystal clarity and for his stupid lenses which he still held in front of his eyes to vanish into oblivion. The lenses vanished; he looked at me, then all around smiling as he enjoyed his first sampling of perfect vision. I watched as his eyes finally locked in on Cathryn and he blinked in surprise. My mother was a very beautiful woman.

"I see what you mean Queen Cathryn," the man said with a frown, completely serious as he looked at my mother and she laughed happily, glad he was smart enough to play her game the way she wanted it played.

"Look upon that which you shall never see naked and despair. That is now your burden to bear. So mote it be." She said it, and it sounded so hot and sexy, the other men standing around weren't even able to laugh and make jokes, they were too busy drooling—but that was when we all felt the magic coming from Amen Hale.

"Bethany!" I shouted a second before my mother did. We both looked toward the wall with alarm as we felt the rising tide of dark magic that was Bethany's power crawling across the land. Birds burst into flight from where they perched in trees around us and from inside the walls. They shrieked and cried out as they took to the air, fleeing the dread power. Squirrels and small creatures burst out of their hiding places on this side of the wall, fleeing and running from Amen Hale. Away from Bethany! Away from death!

"By the goddess! What could she possibly be doing to cause this?" Cathryn shouted.

I held up a hand for her to give me a minute. The FBI agents were wondering the same thing. Shaw and the other agents gathered together, like they feared some type of physical attack was eminent and they might find safety in numbers. The soldiers did the same, cursing the loss of their weapons as they grouped up and eyed the wall.

I closed my eyes and felt the magic, letting the dark waves of dread pass over me. I smelled and tasted the flavor of Bethany's power. The Black Witch within me knew death when she felt it. I could smell the death, the sacrifice and magic Bethany had unleashed, but the power was directionless, like she'd just called forth death itself and let it run loose across the land just for the sake of doing it, which didn't make any sense. I couldn't imagine why she would do such a thing.

But then it stopped—suddenly it all pulled in, like the ocean pulling back after a tidal wave, drawing in all the black magic that had just flooded the land with its frigid black waters. She was drawing the death and magic that she had unleashed back into herself. I felt the draw and pull as she "fed" and I laughed at my sweet little Sister's power. It was pretty damn frightening. Bethany was getting stronger.

"Don't worry, I think she's just feeding, Mother. I think she's sacrificed something. She's killed something. Or someone. And somehow she's feeding off it. I'm not totally sure." I opened my eyes.

In front of me Cathryn stood with her own eyes closed, trying to feel for herself the magic I'd described, but the FBI men were staring wide eyed, whispering among themselves as they listened to our conversation. They'd felt the dark tide along with us and they were shaken, even skittish. It looked like they were ready to get the hell out of here if they had a choice. Which they didn't.

Cathryn opened her eyes and looked at me. "Bethany's feeding?" Her brow creased as she considered that. "Feeding off the blood and death of a sacrifice?" she guessed and then shook her head, rejecting this notion. "But this was stronger than when she killed Yanosh or even when she raised Cornelius from the dead, and she used Fiona as a human sacrifice for that." She looked back toward Amen Hale with worry. "This was stronger, Rain. Much stronger."

I shrugged, unconcerned. "Bethany is changing, Mother. Her power is growing. And changing."

"Rain, I need to go check on her and see what's happened." She took an anxious step toward the wall. "And I need to see how many people she's killed." Cathryn frowned, worried about what type of carnage my sister (her daughter) had unleashed at home.

I nodded. I didn't bother telling her I thought it was only an animal. She would find that out soon enough.

"Mistress, Queen Cathryn." I was surprised as I looked over to see Lucius with Sky's father and some others still walking our way. They must have been in the Hummer the soldiers stopped before it got too close to the wall and turned into sand.

"Oh yeah," I said as I remembered. "You went to pick up Sky's dad."

Lucius nodded, "Yes, my Mistress, I received your message. But what's happened at Amen Hall, what did we just feel?" he asked, all business as he looked toward the wall and Amen Hall.

"Rain, let's go please! I want to check on Bethany," My mother was getting all worked up and flustered.

"Easy, Mom, I think it was only an animal she killed, not half the household. It's okay."

She cut me an unsure look and turned back toward the wall and crossed her arms. Cathryn was worried. I guess it was only normal for a mother to worry. She wouldn't be a good mom if she didn't.

I walked over and gave her a hug from behind. "Fly home, Mother. Go check on your daughter and my Sister. So mote it be," I willed her to fly straight home and land back on her bedroom balcony where we'd taken off from. As soon as I let her go and stepped back she started to rise into the air. We all waved but she didn't look back; she was worried, looking only forward toward the Hall as she flew up, over the wall and out of sight.

"The Queen can fly now?" said a familiar voice. I turned, surprised to see Agent White, Trisha, and one other man I didn't recognize. What the hell!? It was Sky Dragon! He was dressed like a human! He had on a cowboy hat and a long trench coat. The hat covered his dragon head nicely, and as long as he didn't extend his neck he could pass himself off as just a tall cowboy easily enough at a distance.

"Sky Dragon! Wow! Looking good, Bro," I said to him. "Looking reeeal good." I gave him my best smile which seemed to work. His dragon mouth turned up at the ends just a little, which was about all the smile he did.

"Lucius thought it would be good for me to blend in," he said, and again I was surprised at how smooth and clear his voice was. It was nothing like my Believer's deep rumbling voice, but it suited him perfectly.

"Mistress, the magic we felt. Is everyone safe? That didn't feel right," Lucius was still concerned.

"And Sky. Is she safe?" Sky Dragon asked. "I knew I should have stayed with her." His good mood darkened quickly, his smile gone.

"Relax. Believer is with Sky. He went to see her as soon as I left, so don't worry. Sky is fine. And Ryan is with her too." That seemed to make Sky Dragon feel better, but Lucius still looked like he was about to have kittens. "Calm down, Lucius. Everything is fine; what we felt was just something with Bethany. She sacrificed an animal and—well," I made a yuck face, "I think she kinda did some crazy stuff to it that made its death into some pretty nasty black magic," I made another yuck face, "and then I'm pretty sure she ate it."

Lucius raised an eyebrow in surprise. "Why would she eat something filled with black magic?" Lucius was trying hard to understand. He knew that magic was part of his life now and he wanted to comprehend what had happened, but Trisha, who was standing beside him, was too grossed out to keep quiet.

"She ate that!?" Trisha shouted, her face doing the "yuck" now too. "That horrible, nasty feeling we all just felt!?" She put a hand to her mouth like she might get sick just remembering how that magic had felt as it touched her. After a precarious second she passed the tipping point and fought her stomach back into submission without losing containment. "My God, Rain! I almost threw up and we're way out here. Who knows what it felt like up close. Why the hell would she eat something like that!?"

"Trisha, don't talk to her like that! Be respectful," Agent White scolded her.

"Shut up, White. Don't talk to her like that. Be respectful." I fed him his own words and tossed him a dark look as I answered Trisha's question. Trisha was a friend. White was an ass. "I'm not absolutely sure of the details, Trish, but I felt her draw the magic in and I'm pretty sure she ate it. I think Bethany eats death or black magic now. Or maybe even sins." I shrugged.

"Why on earth would she eat that?" asked Trisha, horrified.

"Did you say black magic?" asked agent White. "But I thought you were the Black Witch and that dark, black magic, was more or less your specialty."

I stopped everything, turned slowly, and looked right at him. The men standing with White stepped away. Even Trisha stepped farther away from him as I spoke to the pushy old man.

"White, your name is a color. You want to talk about color. Fine. Let's talk about color. Here's a color question for you that you better answer or you'll wish you had. What color is sin?"

White ran the back of his hand across his mouth and wetted his lips as he thought through his answer. "Sin is black of course." He sounded sure of himself. A few of the other agents nodded their heads in firm agreement.

I sighed loudly, not really shocked at their ignorance as I quoted the verse in the Bible I'd memorized as a child. "'*Though your sins be scarlet they shall be as white as snow, though they be red like crimson they shall be as wool.*' Isaiah 1:18. Red is the color of blood. Red is the color of sin. My sweet little Sister is the Red Witch."

In many ways Bethany's life was filled with more darkness and evil than mine ever was. My memories were of growing up in a loving home, with parents and a twin brother who took care of me and loved me, even when I was wild and rebellious. All the horrible things that had happened to me were partly my own fault, or at least Rain Marie's fault as the only childhood I had was the one I shared with her. But all the horrible things that happened to Bethany weren't her fault at all. She didn't have a choice. She'd been forced to live with it, and survive it. Her whore of a mother, constantly bringing her filthy johns home and trying to sell Bethany to them for extra drug money.

I was a Black Witch, and most people think that black is the ultimate color of evil and darkness. All those years my parents made me go to church, I'd endured it and never really believed it, but I did listen and learn. It seems strange to me, that now, when it was too late for me to do anything about it, I believed all of it. Even the parts in the Bible that talked about sin. Black is not the worst color. Red is. Because sins are red. And sweet little Bethany was the Red Witch. I hoped she was okay with what she had become.

"Rain. Rain, wake up. You were daydreaming again." Sky Dragon was waving his hand back and forth in front of my face.

"Oh." I blinked, coming out of my dark thoughts as I looked around at everyone staring at me. Concerned faces. I wondered how long—

"Are you awake now?" he asked.

"Sorry, Sky Dragon," I said. "Thanks."

Sky Dragon nodded. He knew I had problems with getting distracted. "How are we going to get through the gate with Mr. Han?" he asked.

Mr. Han was standing silently a short distance away watching me. I'm sure he still felt awkward after yesterday and almost killing my brother. I started to feel my temper rise just thinking about it while I looked at him and quickly looked down at the ground. I gave myself a shake.

"How are we going to get inside, Rain? Mr. Han and Lucius can't fly there and we're almost late as it is," Sky Dragon said impatiently. He went to look at his wrist; I guess that he'd found a watch to put on, but he growled and his eye ridges cut into an angry V as he realized that his watch was gone, turned to sand by my magic. He shook his head and rolled his eyes.

"My new watch. Gone. And you wiped out the gate and cursed it so metal can't go near it. Now we can't even drive the Hummer back home." He stared down at me, giving me a hard time. Like somehow I'd messed up. I didn't care though. I smiled at him. Thankfully, Sky Dragon's whining got my mind off hurting Mr. Han.

"Don't fret, Bro." I closed my eyes for a minute and thought about an archway forming just on the other side of the wall that was an exact match of the one that I had made out here. I even copied the mirror table so non-magic people could get out, just like they got in. If they were able pay the price. With a thought I opened the arch.

"Whoa! What the—" Trisha shouted, surprised. She'd been standing right beside it when it opened. Through the arch we could see the drive and the bordering flowers that now ran either side of the cobbled stones that lead toward the house in the distance.

"But what about the Hummer?" asked Sky Dragon. He looked back toward the truck affectionately which made me think of something.

"Hey, who was driving the Hummer?" I asked, raising my eyebrow as I looked at Sky Dragon. "That's it, isn't it? That's why you're upset! You were having fun learning how to drive and I threw off your groove, didn't I!?" I laughed as Sky Dragon's eye ridges narrowed at me.

"Come on, let's go," Sky Dragon growled and waved Mr. Han forward. Mr. Han approached the open archway slowly, cautiously putting first a hand, then a leg through, but Trisha marched right past him, giving him a bump as she went by.

"Geesh, it's just an archway. Stop being so freaked out," I overheard her saying as she stepped through. I also heard Mr. Han telling her not to shove him again. Lucius stepped through and waited for us to follow.

"Not you!" I shouted as Agent White put a foot through the arch. He stopped and looked back at me. "You know my father forbade all government visitors till this afternoon at four. If you want in, come then, and come with the group, Agent White."

He looked disappointed but nodded and stepped back. "What about Trisha?" he asked.

I walked through the arch along with Lucius and Sky Dragon and looked back to the other side where White stood looking at us. "She's a friend. No offense, White, but you're not." I willed the gate to close and it did. The scene vanished and changed. Through the arch we now saw only the black wall.

We were on the exact opposite side, right at the start of the cobbled drive with its pretty new edging of ultrabright lilies.

"Mr. Han, sir. We need to get moving or we will be late," Sky Dragon addressed him very respectfully which surprised me. But then again, he was the father of his Sky, so he probably cared about Mr. Han to some extent. He was important to Sky so he was important to Sky Dragon. They started to walk down the drive together and I called out to Sky Dragon.

"Sky Dragon, please forgive me for picking on you about driving. Don't be mad at me. Please," I asked, my voice sincere. I didn't want him to think I was being mean. It seemed like he was sensitive and tenderhearted about some things. I'd have to be careful about how I picked on him. Sky Dragon stopped walking and his head stretched out on his long neck as he looked back at me and my pleading face.

He nodded.

"Tell Sky I love her, and let my Mom and Dad know I'll be in soon to see them before they go home," I told him.

"Okay," he said. He seemed to think for a minute, then he gave me a smile. "See you soon, Sis." He and Mr. Han resumed their walk down the drive, toward the house.

"How is *she* your sister?" Mr. Han asked Sky Dragon as he walked beside him.

Sky Dragon looked at him for a second before he answered. I heard Mr. Han's question and I wanted to hear Sky Dragon's answer but they were getting farther away. I willed myself to be able to hear them, improving my hearing. I wanted to listen in for a while longer.

"Rain is my sister by marriage, Grandfather. She is married to my brother, Believer. And she is my sister by race. She is a created person like I am. And like Believer. She wasn't created by Sky but by some other human girl, but she is still a created person and not a regular human. And she is my sister because she loves Sky like I love Sky."

I listened for a minute longer; it seemed like they were done talking but then Mr. Han asked, "Did you just call me Grandfather?"

"Yes, Grandfather," Sky Dragon said. "Sky made me from a part of her soul. And Sky's soul came from you. So part of me came from you. You are my grandfather the same as if I had been born. It's exactly the same. If anything, I am even closer to you because there was no other person to blend Sky's soul with as happens with normal human reproduction. But whatever the division, I am your grandson and my name is Sky Dragon."

I felt tears sliding down my face as I listened to them. I hadn't really thought about the fact that, in a way, I was related to Mr. Han now, but apparently Sky Dragon had given it a lot of thought. They were far away now, getting closer to the house, but I still heard them clearly.

I saw Trisha and Lucius out of the corner of my eye, standing beside me. She could tell I was listening in and was giving me some time to eavesdrop. Very considerate of her. She was a friend. Lucius also could tell that the best way to serve me right now was to be still. And wait.

They walked for a minute more in silence and were almost to the front door when they spoke again. "Grandfather, could you do me a favor?" asked Sky Dragon as he put his hand on the handle of the big front door.

Mr. Han hesitated only a second before saying, "What favor?"

"Please, be kind to my Sky. And to Ryan her husband. They are together now and I want them to be happy." Sky Dragon's long neck snaked out as he looked at Mr. Han, waiting for a response.

Mr. Han thought for a silent minute as he looked into Sky Dragon's eyes and then answered him. "I will be kind, my son. I love Sky too and I also want her to be happy."

I had magically improved my eyes so I could still see them clearly. Sky Dragon dipped his head, in something almost like a bow. It seemed like an Oriental gesture and Mr. Han responded to it with his own bow.

"Thank you, my Grandfather," Sky Dragon said and then opened the door and they stepped through into the house.

I'd cried all over myself as I had listened and watched them. I let my hearing and eyes go back to their normal human settings and wiped at my tears with the sleeve of my black dress.

"What was that all about?" asked Trisha. "I thought you didn't like Sky's dad."

I shrugged. "He's difficult, but I hadn't thought it through. Now that I'm married to Believer, he's family. Sky Dragon and Believer came from Sky's soul, so he is their grandfather. And that makes him my grandfather. And Sky Dragon loves him already."

"But he's an ass!" Trisha said with feeling, shaking her head.

I nodded. "Still family though. So my grandfather's an ass. So what?" I shrugged. "I'm kinda high maintenance as far as granddaughters go, don't you think?" I gave Trisha a look.

She only needed a quick second before she conceded the point with a grudging nod. "I still think he's an ass."

"Yeah. Maybe he'll be better now." I sighed and looked over to Lucius. I studied him for a moment. He had dark circles around his eyes, and he seemed even paler than before. "Lucius. Did you sleep any last night?"

"No, Mistress. I stayed up guarding the King and Queen."

"Good," I said and willed strength and power to flow into him, enough to make him rested and ready to go another forty-eight hours without sleep if he needed to. Lots of things needed to be done and Lucius was needed. Awake. Not asleep. Awake and protecting Amen Hale. Then I willed his right hand to turn black as night.

"Lucius, give me your hand." He jumped a little in surprise when he noticed it was black. And not just black, it was black black! I took his hand in mine and raised it to my face and wiped the last of the tears away from my midnight black eyes with the back of his blackened hand. Lucius watched me, concerned and confused, as I spoke my spell and called my will into words.

"We are your family. So mote it be.
My tears, let this hand, now be a key,
My gateways and portals are yours to command,
Now open to you and to your blackened hand.
Lucius protect us, protect Amen Hale.
Our Captain we trust you to watch and not fail."

I released his hand from where I held it against my face, and Lucius slowly drew it back, eyeing it, like he wasn't sure if his hand was dangerous now or how much control he still held over the blackened hand. It definitely stood out against the rest of his pale skin.

"Thank you, Mistress," Lucius said, still sounding freaked out as he looked at the blackened appendage.

"I will make other gateways, Lucius. They'll all open for you and you may use them as you see fit and bring those you need with you to do what needs doing. You're a soldier and a planner. I trust your judgment more than my own when it comes to things like that. We need you."

Lucius looked at me a moment then nodded. I guessed he agreed with me. "The Hummer was loaded with food. We're just about out of food." He grimaced. "Most of it was cans though. Which we can't bring close enough to reach the gateway because of the spell. And my phone died." He took out his cell and then tucked it away, back into his trench coat that I'd made for him. I noticed that his fancy belt buckle and his buttons on his trench coat and pants were still here. Made by my magic so they didn't turn to sand.

"Just leave it. We don't really need it now; by this afternoon we may be getting our groceries from the other side of the world anyway. Some place where people aren't looking for us left and right and you guys can go shopping without someone watching every move you make or possibly even poisoning the food."

Lucius arched an eyebrow and looked back to the portal. "Where will you place the new arches for traveling to these new places?"

I smiled. "I don't know yet. I'll make some new place close to the Hall to hold all the gateways. Which is why I brought help!"

I looked over at Trisha. "I've got work to do, Trisha, and I could really use your imagination. Could you help me make Amen Hale into what it needs to be?"

Trisha looked a little taken aback. "You'd trust me to help you with Amen Hale? I mean—sure. I'd love to." Her eyebrows V'ed together suspiciously. "Just be careful with my brain, lady, don't damage anything while you're in there."

Trisha was worried because when we designed together I liked to use magic to lift the images she thought up right out of her head, which worked way better than her telling me what she was thinking with words. It freaked her out, having me inside her skull, but I'd done it before and she hadn't turned into a vegetable. Yet.

I laughed and grabbed her hand, and Trisha shouted out in surprise as we both floated into the air. We had work to do. I had a Kingdom to build. Below us Lucius waved with his new black hand as we flew away.

Penny

Light as a Feather

PENNY WATCHED AS Princess Bethany shut the door. She left little red footprints in the plush white carpet as she walked over and kneeled down in front of her. Penny's hand was throbbing now. Like most cuts, it hadn't hurt at first, but now it was definitely making up for its slow start. She lowered her hand. Bright red blood fell from her fingertips onto the thin white sheet she'd spread out on the floor to keep from staining the carpet while she cleaned the Princess's blade. She felt a wild surge of worry. The sheet wasn't enough to keep all her fresh blood from soaking through to the white carpet!

The blood was already soaking through the sheet as Bethany reached out and took her bloody hand in her own and pulled it to herself. Penny let her do it. She watched as the Princess looked at the cut and the blood all over her hand. Penny hadn't really looked at it herself, but as the Princess held her hand flat, palm up, she was shocked to see just how long and deep the cut was.

Her head spun. She was dizzy and lightheaded as she stared at the cut that ran from the top of her hand between her index and middle finger all the way across her palm. She could see down into her hand. She watched as Princess Bethany leaned over her hand, and felt it as she licked the blood on her palm.

Instantly, her whole body felt warm. And not just her body but down inside her body. Deep down inside. Then her skin started to tingle on the outside, like her skin was cold while inside her body she felt warm. Penny relaxed as the Princess licked her cut hand. She closed her eyes and stopped watching or worrying. She relaxed, letting it happen. She felt all the worries and sorrows of her short life seem to loosen up and float to the surface of her thoughts.

Her anger and bitterness at her mother for leaving her with Gran. Her anger at her father for not being a good father and running away from them. Her anger at herself for not being able to change any of it. The guilt she felt for the handful of times she'd disobeyed her mother and grandmother. The evil thoughts she'd thought toward the mean kids at her school that had called her "little nigger girl" and thrown sticks at her on the playground. And the curse she cast at them with her own blood and the poppet dolls she'd made of each of them and placed in the woods behind her grandmother's house in the bole of an old dead oak that Gran told her was cursed.

Dark thought, evil, regrets, sorrows. Shadows on her soul. It all lifted up, like dead rotting leaves floating up from the bottom of a pond. It came to the surface, and then it came out of her hand in her blood. Her hand tingled. She heard Princess Bethany saying something but she didn't listen; she was floating, floating and happy. She felt light as a feather. She closed her eyes.

Cathryn

A Bloody Surprise

CATHRYN DIDN'T GIVE a moment's thought to the amazing view as she glided through the air high above Amen Hale; she was sick with worry. What happened!? How was Bethany!? As soon as she landed on her balcony, she dashed into her bedroom too quickly and her hip slammed into her altar table beside her bed. She paused long enough to rub at her sore hip, wincing at the bruise she knew she'd have as she frowned down at the spilled incense and herbs strewn about on the floor.

She hadn't used her altar since last night. The night Cornelius had died. The first time in years and years that she'd gone to bed without stopping at her altar. Something new, some wild whim of a crazed thought skipped through her mind.

She went to the altar, quickly righting the incense. She gathered the herbs from the floor then dropped a handful onto the hot plate and even pricked her own finger and added a drop of her own blood before sending her desperate prayers up to the goddess.

Only this time was different. This time her goddess had a face. Her whole being wanted to run and find out what had happened, but she forced herself to stop and pray. She hoped her prayers would be answered. She hoped—and she prayed.

Cathryn blew out the candle, rose from her altar, and ran out into the hall. A servant was there, cleaning the floor at the head of the stairs.

"Savanah! Where is Bethany?" Cathryn called breathlessly. "Do you know what's happened here at the Hall?"

"Yes, Queen Cathryn. I'm cleaning up her footprints right now. She's there," the maid pointed at one of the doors down the hall, "in her bedroom."

Cathryn looked down at the floor. She could see where the maid had been trying to clean bloody footprints off the white carpet. Footprints that led to Bethany's door.

"What's happened, Savanah?" Cathryn asked.

"They say Princess Bethany was sick this morning, Queen Cathryn. Very sick."

"Sick? How? What happened?" Cathryn interrupted the maid's telling.

Savanah looked worried. "I didn't see for myself, but I heard from Ivan. He was serving at breakfast this morning when the Princess and her family came down. Princess Bethany couldn't eat, and he said she was sick. Bad sick. Shaking and shivering and throwing up. Everyone kept asking her what was wrong, and she didn't want to tell anyone, but finally she had to. She said she had to have a sacrifice, so King Cornelius had the red witches prepare a goat for her in the Cathedral Room."

Cathryn nodded. "What happened with the sacrifice?"

"I wasn't there, but I've heard." Savanah's eyes seemed to take an involuntary, frightened glance back to Bethany's bedroom door. "They said that Princess Bethany spoke to the goat like it was a real person. That she cursed it horribly before she slew it and then bathed in its blood, calling forth the dark magic we all felt."

"Yes, I felt it out by the gates," Cathryn said. "But what happened when she sacrificed the goat?"

"Oh! The Princess felt much better right away. But they were worried about one of the red witches that was helping with the sacrifice; the Princess did some magic to her. They're looking at her now."

"Thank you, Savanah," Cathryn said and walked away, following the trail of bloody little footprints to Bethany's bedroom door.

She knocked gently, but there was no answer. Cathryn opened the door and stepped inside, shutting the door behind her. Her blood went cold as she looked at the small still figure lying on the bloody white sheet that had been spread out on the floor. Lying off to the side on the sheet was Bethany's blade, also covered with blood.

"Oh my goddess, no. No, no, no." Cathryn hurried over but pulled back her shaking hands before she touched the child. She could hear the shower running in the bathroom. Bethany must be in the shower.

She looked back to the body. Someone, it must have been Bethany herself, had taken the time to stretch Penny out straight and pose her arms, laying them across her chest. The little black girl's face looked so peaceful, a small smile gracing the edges of her mouth. Cathryn knelt beside the still form and bowed her head. Her heart broke for the little girl who was lying dead before her. She'd just met her this morning and thought she was such a sweet, beautiful child. And now she was dead.

And Bethany had killed her. It made her question everything they were doing. Was any of it worth this little girl's life? Why would Bethany kill this sweet, innocent, little girl? Maybe she couldn't help herself. Perhaps Bethany had turned into a monster. A killing monster that hungered for blood and death like the worst kind of demon. Where would it end? How many would have to give their lives for Bethany to live? Cathryn's mind drifted to dark places and horrible possible futures as she wept over Penny's little body.

Penny felt something wet on her face. She opened her eyes and looked up into the face of the Queen. She had been enjoying the best sleep of her life, so peaceful and perfect. She woke, surprised to find the Queen kneeling right beside her, leaning over her. Tears rolled down the Queen's cheeks and fell right onto her face.

Queen Cathryn had her eyes closed and didn't see that Penny had opened hers. Penny blinked and wiped the tears out of her eyes and then propped herself up on her elbows and looked around. Behind the Queen she saw the Princess. She had just gotten out of the shower and was in a white bathrobe, standing behind the Queen, watching her.

Penny looked over at Bethany with a questioning look. Bethany shrugged and shook her head no. She had no idea what was up with the crying Queen either. Penny reached out and touched Cathryn's arm.

Cathryn's eyes snapped open, and she SCREAMED! "Eeeeeeeee! Eeeeee! Eeeeeee!" She scrambled back as fast as she could and screamed some more, "Eeeeeeeeeeee!" and Cathryn kept screaming, scared to death by Penny's apparent return from the dead.

But then Penny started screaming because she was scared by all the Queen's screaming. "Eeeeee! Eeeeee! Eeeeee!" Penny screamed!

"Eeeee!" the Queen screamed.

"Eeeee!" Pennny.

Both of them continued to scream for couple of seconds until they calmed down enough to notice all the giggling.

"Hehehehe, Hehehehe! Hehehe!" Bethany was rolling around on the floor, her feet kicking the air as she thrashed about in her giggling fit. She was turning blue she was laughing so hard.

Cathryn and Penny both watched Bethany roll around and giggle for a second. Then Penny started giggling too, tears all over her face as she laughed. Cathryn wiped her own tears away just as the bedroom door flew open and three servants charged in. They looked around in confusion at the two girls, rolling around, giggling. Cathryn picked herself up off the floor.

"Queen Cathryn, we heard horrible screaming just a moment ago! Are you all right!?" asked Savanah, who'd led the charge into the room.

"Oh I'm fine, Savanah. My daughter and her maid scared me to death. But I'm fine." They looked down at the two girls who were still giggling. "I think we're all fine now, Savanah."

"That's good to know because you're needed in the Cathedral Hall, Queen Cathryn. The King is ready to start receiving the oaths of service from the newcomers. I was coming to fetch you when I heard all the screaming."

"Let's leave these two to their fun," Cathryn said and they stepped out of the room and shut the door on the two giggling girls. The Queen noticed a basket of laundry in the hall that one of the servants had left behind. It was her laundry.

"Oh, thank the goddess!" Cathryn dug into the laundry basket and pulled out a pair of panties. She slipped her underwear off right there in the hall and slipped her fresh ones on and handed the "wet" pair to Savanah. "That little *monster* actually scared the pee out of me!" The queen marched off toward the Cathedral Hall, leaving behind three giggling servants and one wet pair of sexy black panties.

Dr. Burgis

<hr>

Pills and Powers

"THANKS, DR. BURGIS," David said as the doctor dropped a bunch of pills into a cup. They were seated in a nice outdoor patio area, enjoying some fresh air after all the pent up tension of watching Bethany do in "Mike" the goat.

Dana needed some air, and a cigarette. She'd been trying to quit but what she'd just seen had thrown her way off the wagon. Her nerves shouted for nicotine! Her stomach was tied in tight knots and now she had something else to worry over. Her brows were locked in a suspicious glower and she pulled hard on her menthol and watched Dr. Burgis hand the cup full of pills to David. She didn't care for the doctor. She thought he was a creep.

"Take them before you eat lunch, David," Dr. Burgis urged.

"I'll take them right now." David waved over the skeletal blond servant girl who sat on a nearby bench. She seemed to always be somewhere nearby, following discretely.

Angel rushed right over. "Yes, Lord David?"

"I need a drink to take my pills, Angel. Could you please get me a Diet Coke?"

"Me too, sweetie, Diet Coke," Dana said. "And thanks."

Angel took off without another word.

"That's still so weird, David. Having servants." Dana's eyes followed the girl as she headed back inside to get their drinks. "And they keep calling us Lord and Lady, that's just creepy." Dana cast her eyes about. "This whole freakin' place is weird! They've all gone nuts! They actually plan on making this into another country. For real. And Bethany hacking up that goat, that was fuckin' nasty! And Rain is even scarier. And who knows how scary the vampires will be once they finally crawl out of their hole. I don't know if this place is going to be safe to stay at, David."

David was giving Dana's concerns some serious thought; watching Bethany with the goat and the other girl after the goat had worried him but Dr. Burgis added his thoughts to the discussion.

"Dana. If David left this safe shelter, the government would grab him and take him away just like they tried to do at the hospital. They may even kill him because they're scared of his powers. At the very least he wouldn't be free to live as he chose anymore. It may be frightening here, but this is still the safest place for David. And for you now. You're his wife so you should be where he is." Dr. Burgis turned to David. "Speaking of powers, David, how are yours holding up? You went a day without the pills, and you were hurt for a while in the hospital. They told me you were even in a coma for part of that time. Have you tried to use your ability with fire today?"

Dana and Dr. Burgis watched as David held his hand out, palm up. A bright ball of flame appeared above his palm. The rolling ball of flame looked close enough to burn his flesh, but David didn't seem bothered in the least. While they watched, the ball of flames vanished but on top of David's head a flaming crown of fire appeared. Again his flesh was unharmed, his hair didn't catch fire or singe. This time the flames were touching his flesh, pressing like a real crown on the sides of his head. It looked magnificent and frighteningly dangerous.

"My God, David! You're gonna burn your damn head off!" Dana shouted.

"Easy, Dana! This fire won't hurt you or me. Come on. Reach over here and feel it."

David leaned toward her so she could reach his burning crown. Slowly, Dana reached over to the blue and orange flames that wreathed David's head. As she got closer, her eyes got wider until she lost her fear of the flames completely and reached out and touched the fiery crown. Dana smiled as she ran both her hands over the flaming crown.

"It's beautiful, David," Dana said softly. "It's warm but it doesn't burn."

Dr. Burgis started to reach over, but David leaned away. "Don't do that, Doc. It would burn you," he cautioned.

Dr. Burgis pulled his hand back quickly. "Why is that, David? Why doesn't it burn Dana?"

"Because she is my Dana." His voice and face made it seem like this was something the doctor should have already known.

"Well, yes. Yes, of course, David." Dr. Burgis looked at Dana who was listening, taking in every word and trying to make sense of it herself. She was just as interested by the inner workings of David's mind as the doctor was. Dana was interested because she loved him and was his wife and wanted to understand him; the doctor was interested because David was one of his more successful "experiments" and as such was the culmination of his life's work.

Dr. Burgis liked to think of all the teens from the drug study as his own "children" in a purely scientific way. Children of his lifelong scientific hopes and dreams. Even now he broke down and studied what he was seeing on a purely scientific level. David's transference of powers to Dana was absolutely fascinating. Another example of "transference." Dr. Burgis was sure that Black Rain had done the same with her sister witches, giving them powers through her power.

He knew that David was very unstable when it came to Dana. The girl had been the foundation of his existence since he fell hopelessly in love with her when he was five years old. They had been in the same daycare together, playing in the same sandbox. They were in the same school. They lived on the same street. From that day forward, David had loved Dana. He never wavered for a second. Most of those years Dana had rejected and spurned his advances horribly and David was forced to love her from a distance and stalk her like a guardian shadow on her life. It was nice to see David happy, married, smiling, and firmly in possession of his heart's one desire. The doctor liked happy endings. He didn't think they were probable or sustainable for any length of time, but he did appreciate them when he was fortunate enough to stumble upon one.

A flaming crown appeared over Dana's head, the match to David's. Again she was unharmed by the flames. Dana laughed as she felt the crown on her head.

"David, are we really going to walk around with crowns on?"

"You should have a crown," David said seriously. "You are my Queen. You always have been, Dana."

Dana seemed touched by that, but her practical side was too much a part of her nature to let the romantic gesture endure. "We can't walk around with fire on our head, David, we'll burn the whole damn place down." Dana reached over and pushed a nearby bamboo tiki torch away from David's head. It was singed and blackened a little on one side.

"You may be right," David admitted grudgingly as he eyed the scorched torch. The flaming crowns vanished about the time Angel stepped up with the drinks on a tray. They both told her thanks and David took his pills.

"I liked the crowns." David and Dana were both shocked to hear Angel actually say something that sounded like an original thought. Something that she wanted to say and didn't have to say in order to serve them.

"So did I, Angel," David pointed to the tiki torch, "but I was about to burn the house down."

"We would get used to it," Angel insisted. "I like it, Lord David. And I liked it on the Lady Dana. She deserves a crown." And that was the end of her words. Like she'd run out of her allotted letters and couldn't form more complete words, she simply stopped talking and stepped away, going back to her bench.

"She is an *odd* little girl," said Dr. Burgis as he watched her go.

"Yep. But she's very nice and she's our odd little girl," Dana said protectively. She'd grown attached to Angel quickly. This morning when Angel was helping her do her hair she had told Dana that she was in charge of her husband's servants. Queen Cathryn said that it was up to Dana herself to decide who she wanted to take care of her and David. Dana liked Angel. She was young enough to be childlike and seemed respectful enough to not make a play on her man, who was apparently a hot commodity now. Literally!

Dana had cussed out a newcomer girl just this morning over David. The girl didn't recognize Dana and she overheard her talking to another girl about the possibility of marrying into the Royal Family as she eyed David up and down like a vulture. Dana's hackles were up and her radar was on for anyone who would dare to take her man. Sexy, man stealing bitches be damned! David was hers! He'd been hers since she was five and she damn well intended to keep it that way.

It may have taken dying to bring her to her senses, but Dana was with the program now and she didn't get a sexual vibe from Angel. She knew Angel cared about her and David, but it wasn't any kind of sexual thing. She was nice. And safe. And sweet. Dana planned on keeping her. That was of course, if they stayed here. And it was starting to sound like this was going to be home now.

"Well, I should be heading off to find Rain. She needs her pills too." The doctor got up and turned to head toward the house when Dana spoke.

"Unless you plan on strappin' a rocket to your ass you ain't gonna find her. She's over there, doin' the superman." Dana pointed up in the air where Rain and another girl were flying above the Guest Hall, hand in hand.

Dr. Burgis laughed. "Guess I'll need to wait a while as I don't have any 'ass rockets' handy." He chuckled to himself as he sat back down in his chair and reached into his little satchel for his notebook. "Hopefully she'll land soon. David, don't forget, you will need to eat something as soon as possible now that you've taken your pills." The doctor pushed his reading glasses onto his face and opened his notebook.

Dana stood up, took another angry pull on her third cigarette, then threw it on the ground and stomped it out as she exhaled. "Com'on. Let's get you to the kitchen and get some food in you before those pills make you sick. And I'm grabbing a bottle of wine while we're in there. I need something to take the edge off. Then we're going to go hide in our bedroom for the rest of the day. I've seen all the weird shit I can handle for one day without becoming a chain smoker."

David took Dana's hand and they started walking toward Amen Hall. "I'd hide out in a bedroom with you any day. There's no place on earth I'd rather be, my Queen."

Dana felt the crown appear on her head again, and she stopped before she stepped through the door and turned to face David with a concerned frown on her face. "But everyone will see the crown, David. And Cathryn's the Queen here." Dana was serious, and she didn't want to throw the Queen's groove off. She didn't know how Cathryn would feel about another woman walking around Amen Hale with a crown on her head.

"She may be the Queen of the Kingdom," David said, "but you are the Queen of my heart. The absolute ruler. You have ruled it and will rule it forever." That was sappy and way over the top, but the way David said it and the fact that she knew he meant it cut right through her thick emotional hide and she started to cry.

"I know," she said and kissed him. She didn't know what else to do. After a minute they went into the house. Wearing their burning crowns. Angel, their silent, smiling shadow followed them through the door a moment later.

"Good for you, David," Dr. Burgis said. "Good for you, my boy." He lifted his book back up and started reading again. Happy for David. Enjoying the sun on his face and the wonder of life. He doubted it would last, but for right now, he was happy.

"Good for you, Doc," he said to himself as he soaked in the sun and the feeling of deep satisfaction. "Good for me."

Sky

◆

Lunch with the Family

M Y MOTHER DIDN'T say anything when we came in, she just stared at me. Then at Ryan. Back and forth. I knew she was going to start screaming soon. After all these years it was easy to see it coming. We were seated in a private dining hall, at an antique square table with room for two on each side. Believer and Sky Dragon had come with us but they didn't sit at the table; they stood right behind me, standing against the wall so they would be out of the way of the servants while they worked around the table.

The clothes the maid found for me were nice but Ryan looked absolutely amazing! When he left the room to go see his sister he was a total mess, but she really cleaned him up. He looked like a real prince now, but he was still acting weird and not like himself. I was worried about him. I could tell his parents were worried about him too. I was so used to his happy, smiling face that the serious solemn expression he now wore, combined with his new look, was a little frightening.

"Hello, Mrs. Han. Mr. Han." Ryan's voice was steady and strong as he greeted my parents. "Mom. Dad," Ryan said to his own parents who then said hello to us.

Then my father spoke to me in Cantonese, "How are you, Sky? Did he hurt you? Are you all right?"

I answered in English. "I'm fine, Father. But we should talk in English so everyone can understand what we're saying." I would have said that I was "fantastic" or "super" or "amazing" before Ryan and I had our fight this morning, but now all I felt like was "fine." I was fine.

"You look sad. What's wrong?" my mother asked. She picked up on my mood right away. Her brows went into 'angry position'. It was the only way to tell if she was mad before she started screaming. Most of the lines in my mother's face didn't give her away because of the Botox she used, but her eyebrows still worked as an early warning device. Warning delivered.

She exploded, the screaming started right on schedule. "You should have never done this, Sky! You weren't ready to do this! They should have never let you get married! He should never have touched you and he *damn! well! knows it!* He should have never laid his filthy hands on you! Everyone knows it!" She slammed her hand down on the table, making plates, silverware, and the two servants jump. "Did he hurt you? Did he force himself on you!?" She shot Ryan a nasty look across the table which he didn't return.

Ryan didn't say a word. He didn't even twitch a muscle!

Mother was breathing hard as she continued her tongue lashing. "Sky's not well and you *knew it!*" She leaned across the table and jabbed a finger at Ryan. Spit actually flew! "You're practically a child molester! She couldn't consent to marriage. She doesn't understand what she was doing or saying. Sky's crazy! She's off all her meds right now and she's mentally disturbed and you took advantage of her and raped her! You filthy, trailer park, bastard trash! Are you happy now!? Now that you've raped our daughter!?" She stopped yelling and settled for staring hatefully at Ryan, watching for his reaction.

Ryan didn't deny it or even respond. He looked at her, completely unfazed and unblinking, like he was made out of solid stone. She seemed perplexed that he didn't shout or argue or even try to defend himself. She seemed unsure what to do without someone to argue back, or to at least be offended at what she'd said. Now she just seemed silly.

Ryan's stare continued for another uncomfortable, silent minute while we all watched her squirm. Eventually she just settled back into her chair. I was impressed! And it looked as if my father was too. He seemed to be rethinking what ever it was he thought about Ryan. I'd never seen someone win an argument with my mother without even saying a word! Ryan was good with arguments; he'd made me squirm too. But I deserved the squirming I got and so did my mother.

"Nice shirt son. Are those buttons real gold?" Ryan's father attempted a blatant subject change.

"I think so, Dad," Ryan answered but didn't bother to look down at his shirt. Like it didn't even matter that it had gold all over it. "Rain made it for me so they probably are."

"You saw her this morning?"

"Yes, sir. She was fine. And happy. She plans on seeing you and Mom before you leave."

"Did she do your hair, Ryan?" his mother asked him. "Rain is good with hair. Yours turned out so nice all spiked up like that."

Ryan nodded.

"It does look good that way. I like it!" I agreed and smiled as I looked at him, which finally broke his grim, stone-faced expression as he gave me back my smile. He looked so handsome and strong and he didn't care what my mother said. I loved my happy smiling Ryan. This serious smiling Ryan was different, but he was still my Ryan. He was mine. My husband. And my mother had called him names. It was my turn to make her squirm.

"Mother."

"Yes, Sky," she answered calmly, more at ease now that she'd thrown her ugly fit.

"You don't approve of Ryan?" I asked her.

"Hell no," she shot back at me, instantly. Then she took a sip of her drink—it looked like water! I looked over to Ryan. He had noticed too. Maybe it was a clear drink, like vodka.

My mother pushed her chair back and stood up. "Come on. Let's go home, Sky. Tell everyone goodbye, let's go." She was serious. She looked at me like she expected me to obey. I didn't. Father kept silent and stayed in his seat. We both knew she had to go through this process before she could move on, so I helped her out with the "moving on" issues.

"If you don't approve of me marrying someone my own age, whom I love and want to be with, why were you willing to drug me up and give me to Cho? An old man that I don't know, don't want, and don't love. Answer me that, Mother?" I tried Ryan's trick and kept my face as cold and hard as I could while I stared at her.

Again, an uncomfortable silence settled around the table as everyone watched my mother squirm. Ryan's trick worked great! I was careful not to smile as I kept the ice cold stare pinned on her. Father was sitting too close and he squirmed some too. Good! They should both squirm! I didn't smile, I just kept staring until Father finally couldn't take it anymore.

"We were wrong, Sky! We are sorry," Father said. Then he spoke to Ryan. "Please forgive me for yesterday, Ryan. I was trying to protect my daughter."

Ryan nodded. "Of course I forgive you, Mr. Han. Yesterday was a difficult day for all of us. And I know it was hard for you, having your daughter run off and get married in the middle of all of that. But no matter how it started, this is where it ended. I love her. And we are married."

"And I love Ryan," I told him. "He is my husband. I'm happy with him. He's mine, and he wants to take care of me."

"Haa!" my mother barked out. "Take care of you! Did you tell him that you're crazy, Sky? Did you tell him he's going to have to take care of you all your life?" She looked right at me but was surprised by my big smile.

"Oh yeah! I told him all of it this morning while we were in the shower together. I told him I was crazy and that he was going to have to take care of me. He doesn't even care that I'm crazy, Mom. He still wants me."

"This can't be happening," my mother muttered. She rubbed her temples. "You've got to be kidding me." She squeezed her eyes shut like she had a headache and kept rubbing her temples as she spoke. "Sky, if you told him while you were in the shower, *naked with him, in the shower*, he would have probably said anything you wanted to hear just to make you happy."

"Ryan does not lie," I said. A frown formed on my face as I remembered I'd called him a liar just this morning.

"All men lie," Mother said coldly.

"Ryan doesn't! Not to me!" I shot back, angry.

"Yes. He does. He did. And he'll do it again." She answered with cold certainty. "Hell Sky, he's probably thinking up his next lie right now. Getting it *gooood and ready* for you. Taking off the rough edges so it fits just right into the story he wants to tell you." Mother had a small vicious smile on her face now. This was getting to be too much like an argument. Something my mother knew well and something she could control. An argument with words. So I switched to arguing with magic.

"FINE!" I yelled. I got out of my seat and marched over to the little bar in the corner of the room and grabbed a bottle of wine out of the ice bucket and marched back to the table and handed it to my father.

"What are you doing, Sky?" he asked.

"I want to see if Ryan is a liar like Mother said. Father, pour a glass of wine for her please."

He looked puzzled, but he nodded and opened the bottle and poured some wine into the glass in front of my mother. She reacted oddly, scooting farther away from the glass.

"Do you still want me to go home with you right now?" I asked her.

"Yes, Sky."

"Do you want me to leave Ryan?"

"Yes. Leave him. He's trash."

"Trash?" Ryan said. "And here I was, worried about everyone calling me Lord Ryan." He looked right at me and gave me a big smile. That was enough for me. I would trust my husband with my life.

"Okay. I'll leave him." I said as I stared at him. Ryan's smile vanished. "Let's go home, right after you drink the wine." His smile returned. Smaller, but there.

"What?" Mother asked.

My smile went as wide as it could go. This was fun! "I'll leave Ryan right now and never come back. I'll never fly again or even touch another cloud. I'll never make another friend. If you can drink that glass I'll even marry that old shriveled up man you wanted me to marry! I will start taking my crazy pills again and I won't complain. I'll be exactly what you want me to be, Mother." I pointed at the glass of wine on the table. "*If* you can drink that glass of wine."

Her eyes were huge but so were my Father's. And Ryan's parents looked like they were about to be sick all over the table. Sky Dragon and Believer took a step or two toward me. They looked so worried and hurt. I smiled at them and sent them some love straight from my soul, and they relaxed right away and went back to standing against the wall.

"What game are you playing at, Sky!?" Mother shouted. Angry now. She reached out for the glass of wine but stopped short of touching it. Her hand shook for a minute before she pulled it back. "You don't have to give up flying, Sky, but let's go home, right now. Get up. Let's go." She got up out of her chair—but I didn't move.

"I'll leave with you right now, *if* you drink that glass of wine."

"Let's go!" she shouted.

I shouted right back. "Drink the glass of wine and I'll be glad to go with you, Mother!"

"Why!? Stop being inane and childish for once! Anyway, I'm only drinking scotch on Tuesdays now, not wine! It gives me a headache and I already have one thanks to you!" She walked back to the table, picked up the wine glass, and threw it across the room where it landed with a crash right beside a serving girl who let out delicate little "eek!" as she got splashed.

Ryan's voice called out, "Quickly! Bring some scotch for my mother-in-law!" Our other server standing by the door rushed from the room.

"Ryan! What on earth are you doing, son?" Ryan's dad asked him.

"Magic," Ryan said. Which confused his mother and father, but they didn't have a chance to ask him what he meant because as soon as the server came rushing back in with a bottle of scotch, Mother gave up.

"Stop it! Just stop it! That's enough!" she roared out. "I QUIT DRINKING! I QUIT ALL OF IT!" She panted for a second, catching her breath before she staggered back to the table and dropped into her chair, like her outburst and all the emotional drama had wiped her out physically. She ran her hand through her long blond hair and leaned back in the chair, squinting her eyes a little as she regarded me. "Sky. Did you do some kind of magic to make me quit drinking and taking my pills?"

"I did it," Ryan said boldly. That surprised everyone but me.

Mother sat forward in her chair. "You. You did this to me." Her eyebrows shifting into 'angry position'. "Why?"

"Because Sky needs a mother that can love her. One that's not drunk or high all the time." Ryan looked at me and I looked at him and watched as he reached up and wiped at the tears I didn't even know I'd cried. He spoke to my mother as he looked at me. "Sky loves you. And I want my Sky to be happy. And you know I will need you. I will need help taking care of her. But not the way you were." Ryan stared at me, looking into my eyes.

It reminded me of the way Dan would stare at Jane. For some reason it didn't bother me to think about them now. I knew Ryan would never lie to me, and he was staring at me and no one else. I was his world and that made me smile.

It was quiet at the table. When Mother spoke she didn't say much. "Oh" was her only comment.

The servants started to bring in our lunch. They looked a little shaken up, wide eyed and edgy after all our family drama. One girl had red wine all over her white outfit. My mother didn't eat. She had the servants take away all her plates and laid her head down on the table with her eyes closed, but Father was talking with us and Ryan's parents like he was okay with everything now, which was great!

I reached into my pocket and took out the little baggie that held the pills the doctor had given me yesterday. I had enough pills for today and tomorrow in my baggie, but Ryan needed his pills too. I knew I could get more from Doctor Burgis so I gave Ryan his pills. Everyone stopped talking and watched as I counted out six white pills and one blue pill onto a white tablecloth in front of Ryan.

"Before we eat we need to take our pills, Ryan." He looked at me for a second then stared down at the pills in front of him on the napkin. He didn't reach for them though; he just stared at them. I counted out the same number for me and took them a couple at a time while everyone watched me. Even my mother opened her eyes and propped her head up to watch as I took my pills.

"Would the pills work for me if I took them, Sky?" my father asked.

"No, Father. You're too old. They don't work if you're too young or too old. Dr. Burgis told me all about it. He tried and tried to get them to work for him but he couldn't do it. The pills only work for people like me and Ryan. You have to be seventeen years old. And you have to have issues."

"Issues?" my mother asked. Her interest captured for the moment.

I nodded. "Umhm. The crazier you are the better the pills work for you."

"Haa!" Mom barked. "That figures. I wondered why he let you into the drug study with all your mental problems. That sick, sorry bastard. I hope he burns in hell," she said halfheartedly, then laid her head back down, too out of it even to cuss well.

Mr. Bryant frowned and shook his head. "Dr. Burgis knew from the very start that something like this would happen, didn't he? He chose girls like you and our Rain, that—" His jaw clenched tight. "That had issues."

Mr. and Mrs. Bryant looked at each other. They were both getting worked up and angry and I didn't want that.

"Well," I began uncertainly, "the doctor hoped something would happen, but I don't think he ever expected us to change the way we have." They still looked upset. "Please don't be mad. I think the doctor is a bad man too. And I know he's done bad things, but I'm glad that I took the pills. My life is so much better now than it was before. I was sooo lonely. And every time I flew I would fall and hurt myself. And I didn't have any friends at all; they never let me see anyone my own age. I only had private tutors so I never went to school with other kids. I wasn't allowed to watch TV or even listen to the music that I wanted to hear. My parents never let me out; they kept me locked up with my horrible mean maids or left me all alone, locked in my room. And the friends I made for myself so I wouldn't be all alone never came to life before I took the pills no matter how hard I tried. But now I have lots of people that really love me. Ryan loves me and Believer and my Sky Dragon love me, and I've got lots of friends now. And I have you and Mrs. Bryant now too. And my mother and father even talk to me now! They have to treat me like a real person now!"

"Oh, Sky, honey, I'm so sorry." Ryan's mother looked like she was about to cry. His father was giving mine a very angry look. I guessed he thought it was all my father's fault. My father looked down, studying his food as he squirmed.

"I'm sorry, Sky," Mother groaned. "I've been a horrible mother." Her head was still resting on the table. Her eyes were closed but apparently she was still tuned in to what we were saying.

"But I'm not crazy," Ryan said, making us all turn to him. "Why did Dr. Burgis let me into the drug study if he only wanted crazy people?" Ryan asked me.

I looked at him, surprised by his question. I studied his face and was surprised by what I saw. He was serious! He honestly didn't know. I reached out and touched the side of his face and spoke gently to him. "Ryan. My husband. You are crazy."

He blinked a couple of times, I could tell by his face he was thinking hard about what I said.

"No, he's not," his mother said firmly.

I looked at her. Surprised again. She didn't know either. I guess it was pretty bad news until you got used to it. I didn't know. Being crazy was normal for me and it wasn't anything I could change. I spoke gently to her also, trying to tell them as compassionately as I could.

"The doctor was a bad man, Mrs. Bryant, but he was also a very smart man. He let Ryan into the study because he was crazy." She looked unconvinced. I went with the easy to understand facts. "Ninty-five percent of all mental illness is hereditary. If someone else in your family has it you can have it too. It's easy to see where I get mine from."

"Shut up," Mother mumbled, her head still down on the table.

I looked back at Ryan. "I love her, so please don't think I'm being mean, but Rain is the absolute craziest person I've ever met. And you're her brother. Are there any other crazy people in your family?" I asked. Ryan nodded but didn't say who or how many.

My mother raised her head. "If he's crazy, Sky, how on earth can he take care of you? He won't even be able to take care of himself." She didn't say it angry or ugly, she just said it like she actually wanted an answer. That was fine. I had a good answer to give.

"Ryan is crazy, but he's not the same kind of crazy as me. That's why this will work."

"What kind of crazy is he?" she asked.

I looked back at Ryan. He still had his blank face on but his eyes were moving around. He was thinking everything through.

"Not my kind of crazy, Mom," I said again. I didn't want to tell if I didn't have to.

Ryan's father didn't believe me. He was shaking his head no. "Sky. You're just confused, honey. Ryan's not mentally ill in any way. Dr. Burgis must have included Ryan in the drug study just to make sure he'd get our Rain. To give us two reasons to keep coming back to take those pills." He looked at the little pile of pills in front of Ryan with anger. "Ryan's not crazy." He looked up to his son who was staring blankly off into space and added, "He's not himself right now, but he's been through a lot in the past few days. We all have."

My mother still had her head up, listening. She sighed and said, "They're not going to believe it till he tries to kill himself." Her voice was flat, emotionless.

"What!" Ryan's mother shouted, shocked.

"That's so mean!" I yelled at her.

"It's the truth, Sky. I didn't believe you were totally nuts till you jumped out that window when you were seven and almost killed yourself." She laid her head back down on the table ending her part in the angry discussion.

But that was weird. I wondered if it was one of those strange "mother's intuition" moments. She'd had them before, so it could be. How did she know though? Maybe it was a lucky guess? She was scary that way sometimes.

I didn't want to tell, but if it was the only way to help Ryan then I guess I had to. I looked at Ryan and reached out and turned his face to me. He eyes focused on mine and he gave me a whispered, "Yes, my Sky."

"I need to tell them about this morning, Ryan." His eyes tightened up. He was embarrassed. "Don't be ashamed of it, Ryan, you couldn't help it. And they're your family; they need to know so they'll understand. I'm not ashamed of how God made me. I am crazy, he made me this way. And God made you just as you are, for me. Crazy and all. And I love you just the way you are. You're mine. May I tell them about this morning, Ryan?"

He closed his eyes and nodded his head. I looked back to his anxious parents who were leaning forward against the table, dreading and waiting to hear what I would say.

"Mr. Bryant, Mrs. Bryant, if I hadn't of yelled at Ryan and made him stop hurting himself he would have killed himself this morning. He started hitting his head against the wall in the shower; blood was all over the place. But it's okay. I took care of him. I got him to stop. I held him while he cried. I'm his wife. That's my job now."

I looked back to Ryan. His eyes were open again, a blank dazed look on his face. I knew he was still going through it all in his head. My poor crazy husband. He needed me.

"Ryan. Don't worry. I love you. And I'll be here to take care of you when you're crazy like this morning. And you will take care of me when I'm crazy. We need each other. We crazy people have to stick together."

That made him look at me. He studied my face for a moment before he smiled at me. "Yes. We do." He leaned over and kissed me, then reached out and picked up his glass of water, gathered the pills in his hand and took them all at once. If nothing else proved he was crazy that sure did! I would have choked for sure!

Ryan's father prayed for the food and a bunch of other things. He prayed for a couple of minutes. It was nice. He prayed for me and for Ryan. He prayed for my parents and he prayed for Rain, Mary, and Bethany. He even prayed for Believer and Sky Dragon. It was nice. I had never heard someone pray like that before.

He finished and we all started in on the food and everything seemed so much better. We avoided talking about touchy subjects like "Dr. Burgis," "the Pills," or "Craziness." Ryan was smiling and talking now; his old Ryan smile was back and his mom and dad seemed happy too. My father also seemed happy but Mother still had her head down on the table. I could tell she was still listening to us.

"I can't believe my daughter is married. I still feel like she is a little girl. Time has gone by so swiftly."

Ryan's mother spoke to my father, "Just imagine how we feel, Mr. Han. Both of our children got married yesterday." She took a bite of her steak and chewed as she looked over my shoulder where Believer and Sky Dragon stood silently behind me. She seemed to frown before continuing her conversation with Father. "My Rain married Believer. You *do* understand that Believer is your daughter's 'son'?" she asked.

"Yes. I know now," father said.

"Wow! You do!?" I said. I couldn't hide my surprise.

My father nodded, "Sky Dragon was kind enough to explain it to me, Sky. I'm sorry about yesterday. I did not understand."

"Good," Ryan's mom said firmly. "I'm glad you're not going to argue about it. It's hard enough to understand without trying to make it make sense. Your daughter has two grown sons."

"Yes," my father agreed.

"So, we agree then—my daughter is married to your *grandson* Believer, and my son Ryan is married to your daughter Sky."

"Yes. I agree."

"Wow. Your mom is good," I told Ryan.

Ryan was smiling with his old smile back on his face. "Your dad doesn't seem too bad either. As long as he doesn't beat me up in front of everyone again, I think I like him."

"He wouldn't beat up his own son-in-law," Mrs. Bryant said. "Our family is tied to yours pretty tightly now, Mr. Han."

"Oh God. I think I may faint," my mother groaned. Her head was still lying on the table but now she covered her ears like she couldn't stand to hear anymore. We all ignored her and kept eating. Talking away.

Then Ryan's mother looked back to Believer and spoke to him, "Believer, you're part of this family, why are you way back there? There's room at the table for both of you."

"Yes," said my father firmly. "Sky Dragon. Believer. Come."

"Yes, Grandfather," Sky Dragon said happily. Ready and pleased to obey my father and join us at the table.

Believer took a moment. He walked up slowly and eyed my father for a second with his bright red eyes blazing, thoughtfully, before speaking. "Hello, Grandfather." His deep voice rumbled.

"Hello, my son," my father answered back. He didn't seem disturbed at all by Believer's hesitant greeting and ominous stare. He seemed happy; his eyes sparkled as he looked at his two grandsons with obvious pride. It did make sense though, what self-respecting Chinese man wouldn't want a Dragon and a Cloud Prince for sons?

"Well, Father. You wanted me to have sons. Some piece of you that would live on after you died and after I died. Would one son who is a Sky Dragon and one son who is the Prince of Clouds make you happy, Father? Ryan and I will still make some the old-fashioned way, but they are your grandsons. Pieces of your soul."

Father's grin was infectious. I think it was the biggest smile that I had ever seen on his face. "My grandsons!" he said with feeling. "Sky Dragon and Believer 'Prince of Clouds'! Yes, my daughter. You have made your father very happy!" Dad looked like he was about to bust. We all laughed.

Ryan added, "And we're working hard on getting some the old-fashioned way too."

We all laughed. Mother groaned. Occasionally she would color our happy conversation with a groan or a muttered cuss word. We didn't mind. Ryan was happy. Father was happy. Ryan's parents were happy. Believer and Sky Dragon were both very happy. I was like my father, I had never been happier. My face hurt my smile was so big. And then there was my mother—she was—well—dealing with it.

Emma and Mary

✦

Mother May I

"WHAT THE HELL is that?" Emma said as she knelt down to pick up Mary's comb. A long roll of what almost looked like play dough was stuck up under the fancy marble vanity. Underneath where no one could see it.

"Whaaff arr you taffing abouf?" Mary said while still brushing her teeth, head down over one of the sinks.

Emma crawled under and looked at it. There was some dust under the marble vanity but none on the weird thing. It looked new. Fresh. She reached up and pulled at the weird play dough roll and was surprised to feel something metal and hard underneath. She pulled harder and started to work at it with her nails and with a little effort the eight inch long roll, like a hotdog, came off. Emma examined it closer, scratching at the surface until she got down to the shiny metal and something that looked like an antenna. She stood up and showed it to Mary who was flossing now.

"Look at this thing." Emma stuck her strange "discovery" right in Mary's face. Mary's eyebrows went up in surprise and she paused in her dental hygiene, took her floss out, and smiled at Emma sweetly.

"You are straaange Emms. That someone would save all their used up gum, for like, a billion years, in one long super disgusting 'gummy wad' and hide it under the sink is really freaking gross. But that you would find it, and then actually touch it—" Mary did the grossed out cootie dance for a second then stopped suddenly and asked. "You didn't taste it did you?"

"NO!" Emma shouted, giving Mary her squinty eye glare. "This is serious, Mary, stop dorkin' around and look at this thing with me." She showed Mary where she'd rubbed some of the sticky play dough material aside to reveal shiny metal underneath and another spot that looked like an antenna running down the side of the thing.

"Holy shit! That's even grosser!" Mary backed away like Emma was holding a snake in her hand, her face frozen in disgusted horror.

"What the hell?" Emma said, surprised at Mary's reaction.

Mary pointed a finger at the thing and shouted like a broken record. "Eeew! Eeew! Eeew! Eeew! Eeew!"

"What the hell's wrong with you!?" Emma shouted.

"It's a vibrator!" Mary shouted back. "That's got to be some freaky remote control vibrator thingie someone before us stashed in here! And you're touching it with your hands! Eeew! Eeew! Eeew!" Mary continued her broken record "Eeew!" cry as she did a new version of her cootie, gross out dance that involved some hip thrusting action.

Emma watched the whole production stone faced. "Freakin-A Mary, stop acting like a five year old for just a minute! This is serious!" She held it up and waved it at Mary as she spoke, "Don't you know they're listening to every word you say right now!"

Mary froze as she watched Emma bring the thing up to her mouth and speak to it. "All right, you assholes!" Emma spoke to the thing. "I hope you had fun listening to us, you little shits. I bet you hid these thing all over the house."

Mary, getting a little concerned about Emma's sanity, asked, "Emma, why are you talking to the ucky vibrator?"

Emma threw the "thing" onto the floor and stomped on it. "They've been listening to everything we said!" Emma said angrily.

"Who's been listening to us!?" Mary shouted, still totally confused. "The vibrator people!?"

"It's not a vibrator, you dork, it's a bug! A listening device! Those military assholes have been in here. I bet they bugged the whole house so they could listen to us." Emma bent down and picked it up. It was a little flatter now.

Mary looked at the thing in Emma's hand. Then she let her magic out and felt around her and felt the thing. Emma was right. It was a bug. She closed her eyes and stepped closer to Emma and put her hands on top of Emma's. "You're right Emms. Let's go tell our Father."

Emma looked at Mary. Surprised. Mary's eyes were still closed. She looked lost in her magic as she ran her hands over Emma's and the bug. Last night before she went to bed Mary had tricked her into saying that Cornelius and Cathryn were her mom and dad but then everyone had just gone to sleep. This morning, Emma was thinking she would start her work as a servant here at the house, but instead Mary had kept her with her all morning, doing nothing, sleeping half the day away. Emma was confused. She didn't know if Mary was just playing around with her or what. Mary was a little crazy so she might just be playing. But whatever game Mary was playing at, she was right, the King did need to know about the bug.

"Let's go show him," Emma said.

It took a while to get the King. They got distracted by all the bugs. After Emma found the bathroom bug Mary found one in the bedroom, hidden in a vent. Then as soon as they opened their door Mary found two right outside in the hallway. And that was when Emma took charge. She made a servant bring her a note pad and a pen and started the systematic and very organized pest removal program, going from room to room with Mary "feeling" for bugs. They commandeered a few servants, taking them away from their housekeeping chores and putting them to work collecting and extracting the little digital pests from their various hiding places.

Emma's discovery was accidental and lucky, but Mary was walking death to the digital infestation. She found everything, no matter where it was hidden or how clever its camouflage as she pushed her magic through the floors, walls, into the roof, and every piece of furniture as she walked along. One servant held a basket that the others were dumping the bugs in and the basket was getting heavy. Some were super tiny. Some big and fancy. One that they found slipped into the top of a palm tree even had a miniature satellite dish attached to it and a telescopic camera that could pan left and right and zoom in and out.

When they finished the upstairs they took their little search party outside and searched the courtyard between the other buildings and then went to the Guest Hall. They were expecting to find it crowded with newcomers but it was empty. A servant told them that all the newcomers had been ordered to attend a gathering in the Cathedral Hall where Princess Bethany was going to sacrifice a goat. After the sacrifice the newcomers were going to give their oaths to the King and Queen and be given places of service. Emma and Mary took advantage of the Guest Hall being empty and searched it from top to bottom for bugs.

Emma put a check mark in her notebook beside "the garage" with a satisfied grunt. "That's it for the garage, Mary. Only the garden, the area out front, and the downstairs of Amen Hall to go. Are they through with their big get together yet?" Emma asked as she eyed her note pad. She'd kept track of every bug, where they'd found it and what kind it was. Emma had even made a list of which "newcomers" had bugs or anything like a bug in their personal belongings. They found some very interesting items in their private stuff. Some people were in seriously deep shit, but Emma was in the zone. The "hunt" fit her suspicious nature perfectly and her squinty eyed glare roved over long-time servants, newcomers, and each room with equal suspicion. Even the long-time, trusted servants were watching Emma with worry as she and Mary searched through the senior servant rooms and rifled through their personal belongings like they owned the place while Emma scratched notes in her little pad.

"Yeah, let's go Emms. Bethany's finished," Mary answered. "She's doing some other magic right now, I got no clue what, but she's done with the really nasty stuff." Everyone felt the magic crawl through the house when Bethany sacrificed the goat. It was powerful, and for a minute Mary had to stop the bug hunt while the massive wave of dark magic rolled through. They could all feel that Bethany's powers were getting stronger. And darker.

"Good, if they're done in there, let's go," Emma said. "Let's show King Cornelius before we go any farther."

Philip, one of the servants helping with the hunt, dropped a final camera bug into the basket as Emma watched, marking down what kind it was and where it was found.

"We're done, Manuel. Let's go see the King," Emma said to the servant who carried the big basket of collected spy gadgets for them.

"Yes, Princess Emma," he answered.

"I told you, stop calling me that," Emma griped, giving him the evil eye that he ignored. All of the servants had insisted on calling her Princess all morning and Mary kept referring to King Cornelius as "our father" no matter how much Emma complained. Emma had almost given up griping but this one last protest seemed appropriate.

She was nervous. They were about to see the King and Queen and Emma didn't know what would happen when she did. For all she knew they would tell her to report to the kitchens or go home, back to her old life and her real parents. She was still freaked out by the idea of having new parents just because they decided you were theirs. Emma didn't know what to think. She liked them. They seemed great. And if she stayed here she would be close to Jane—and Mary. Which would be nice. But she didn't have any magic like the other Princesses and she wasn't pretty or special or even a witch. She was just Emma. So why would they want her to be their daughter? Why would they make her a princess? It didn't make any sense.

"Let's go see Dad," Mary said and started down the hall still with her eyes closed. Emma growled and followed.

They entered the Cathedral Hall where King Cornelius was holding court. Cathryn and Cornelius both sat in high-backed chairs on a raised platform, about three feet high. A crowd of almost three hundred men, women, and even a good number of children sat on folded chairs in front of them. They were apparently coming forward one by one or by families and presenting themselves to the King and Queen. Byron stood to the side and directed the proceedings while other servants buzzed about, taking care of the crowd and their pedestal seated sovereigns.

"...of our own free will we present ourselves as your humble servants. Please, allow us to serve you. We want to stay. We want to make this our home," finished a man in his late forties with a receding hairline but a strong muscular build. He knelt on the ground before the King and Queen, head bowed now. Beside him, a somewhat plump woman with blonde hair and a full round face knelt with her head also bowed. Behind them were three children, the oldest about fourteen and the youngest about ten with the other somewhere in between. All blond boys. All kneeling.

Emma and Mary stopped at the edge of the room, waiting for the King to finish with whatever he was doing before entering and causing a scene with all their bugs. Mary even opened her eyes finally so she could "see" and "feel" what was happening.

"I accept your oath and that of your family, Nathan Sykes and I—"

"Wait!" Emma yelled as she remembered writing down *that* name on her notepad and her mouth went off all by itself before her brain could get it to shut up. She had one of those weird out of body moments, where she thought about grabbing the word out of the air and shoving it back inside her mouth or hiding it somewhere in the room but out of sight. Under a chair cushion, behind a painting. Anywhere! Somewhere other than out there! Her voice echoed loudly all around the hall.

Three hundred plus heads turned to the side entry where Emma and Mary stood. Once the echo finally died it was quiet for about ten full seconds before Cathryn spoke. "Yes, Emma. You have something to say, my child?"

Emma swallowed the lump in her throat. She didn't know what to make of that, but she tried not to think, just act. She marched forward with her notepad and ignored the hundreds of eyes on her. The kneeling family were so red faced they seemed like they might catch on fire. Whether from embarrassment, fear, or anger, Emma didn't know or care. The Sykes family were spies.

Emma was about to open her mouth to say "Queen Cathryn" but stopped herself before the words got out this time. Emma swallowed, took a deep breath, and said it. "Mother. May I ask him a question?" She closed her eyes, waiting for them to tell her she was crazy or to yell and send her home, or off to the kitchens to scrub pots and pans for the rest of her life, but that's not what happened.

"Yes. Of course, Emma," Cathryn replied.

Emma opened her eyes. Cathryn and Cornelius were both smiling at her and so was Mary who had walked up beside her and slipped her hand into hers without her even noticing. Emma's heart was in her throat and she felt lightheaded, but she had work to do. She walked forward, still holding Mary's hand and stood before the Sykes family.

"Mr. Sykes. Will you be a trustworthy servant? Will my—my mother and father be able to trust you?"

"Of course!" He puffed up, like even being asked was an insult he should never have had to endure. His plump little wife eyed Emma sideways as well.

Emma referred to her clipboard and called out, "Manuel. Bring item number fifty one, fifty two, and fifty three, please."

There was a murmur from the crowd. "Silence!" Byron the steward hissed. He gave the waiting crowd a passing sweep of his angry glare and they went quiet immediately.

After just a few minutes Manuel jogged out with three items in hand. One looked like an old book. Another was a pen. And the last item was a clip on tie. Manuel held them in his hands.

"Bring them here. Let Mr. Sykes see them," Emma ordered.

Manuel brought the items over and held them up in front of Mr. Sykes. The pen and tie lying on top of the old book.

"Are these yours?" asked Emma. She opened the hollowed out book and held it up, showing the PDA and a variety of bugs and listening equipment hidden inside which she dumped out onto the tile floor at his feet.

Mr. Sykes looked surprised, but he stayed in character. "Those aren't my things." He shook his head. "I don't know what you're trying to prove but I've done nothing wrong! I'm an honorable man. I came here to serve. But if this is how I'll be treated then we'll take our leave of this place now. We don't—"

"SILENCE!" Cornelius bellowed. He was red faced and angry, standing in front of his chair.

The noise of his angry shout died quickly. Too quickly. And it was silent. It seemed like the whole house went quiet with a hush in the air that you could almost feel. Even the King and Queen looked around in surprise at the odd effect for a moment before looking back to Emma.

"Please. Continue, my child," Cornelius said calmly as Lucius and five other male servants gathered together around the unfortunate family. Mr. Sykes was still stubbornly defiant. Returning stare for stare, but his wife had eyes only for the tile on the floor. The children huddled closer to their mother, away from their father.

Emma turned back to Mr. Sykes. "Are these your things, Mr. Sykes?" she asked again.

"No," he replied, keeping up his "lie to the grave" gambit.

"Mary, touch him. See if he lies, or if he is an 'honorable man' like he says he is," Emma said without any real satisfaction now that it was just about over. She felt bad for the family. Not for Mr. Sykes, but the kids were frightened and trying not to cry.

Mr. Sykes cringed as Mary moved forward and touched him. She barked out a laugh as soon as she put her hand on his wrist. Mary held him for only a few seconds before letting go. She said nothing but moved away with a smile on her face and went back to Emma and held her hand again.

"Lucius. Take him," Cornelius said.

And Lucius did. Stepping forward and taking Mr. Sykes in hand and hauling him before Cathryn and Cornelius who were both standing now, staring down at the man. The mother and her children were herded to the side by other servants.

"Emma, is there anything you need to add before I deal with Mr. Sykes?" Cornelius asked.

Emma looked at Mary and gave her a bump with her shoulder. "Mary, you touched him, what's up with this guy?"

"Oh." Mary snapped to. She'd been out of it, somewhere else in her mind entirely, daydreaming away right there in the middle of everything, but she snapped back to the here and now with her natural default, big smile. "Oh yeah!" she said brightly, "He's recording everything right now father. His belt is bugged, and so are the shoes of his youngest child Dalton. His wife is actually the one who started this. He didn't really want to come here but she pestered him into it. Her sister works for a magazine." Mary shook her head sadly and added, "I do feel sorry for the kids though. He's going to divorce her for this. This was the last straw. He's sick of her shit."

Cornelius spoke, "Leave them with nothing but the clothes on their back. But search the clothes carefully, with this family—who knows?" Cornelius grunted and he and Cathryn sat back down in their chairs as he finished. "Burn all their possessions and cast them out of Amen Hale. So mote it be."

"So mote it be," echoed voices all around the hall. From the Queen to the servants, even most of the newcomers.

Once the Sykes family was removed from the room, Emma spoke up again, "Father, there are others. Others I need to talk to."

For the next thirty minutes Emma interrogated newcomers who had brought things with them they knew were forbidden before they passed the gates. Some, like the Sykes family, had devices on their person which Mary found. There were nineteen who were cast out. One older man in his fifties who had a recording device and a small digital camera hidden in his stuff was forgiven and allowed to stay, mostly due to Mary's request for clemency on his behalf.

When the Queen asked her why he should be showed mercy, Mary answered, "He fits here, Mother. And he has a kind heart. And he's sorry."

The Queen accepted him, but only if he agreed to become a bond slave of Amen Hale. He chose to be a slave over being cast out, forced to live his life in the outside world. A world where magic only happened in the movies, vampires were myths, clouds were things in the sky not people walking down the hallway, and goat bites were stitched or stapled but not healed.

And that was how Calvin Leonard Pyle became the first bond slave of Amen Hale. Cathryn even let him have his pocket recorder back. It was a device designed for recording personal thoughts, not private conversations. And she told him to keep his brand new leather bound journal. She said that it would now be a Book of Shadows for all Amen Hale. A book of remembrance to be kept in the Cathedral Hall for all to see. So far, his journal had three days recorded, starting Tuesday night when Pyle saw the video on the internet of Black Rain lighting the Murderer's Candle. Mr. Pyle wrote down everything in his journal. He also recorded his personal feelings. How he felt about what he had seen, and his thoughts about what it all meant and where it might lead.

"You are part of the castle now, Mr. Pyle. Like the soil in the garden or one of the bricks in the walls of Amen Hall herself. You are part of this place. What is left of your life will be lived here, and your story will be told here, and it will end here. As my daughter has said, you fit. So mote it be."

"So mote it be," others in the room echoed the Queen's words.

Once Mary and Emma finished with the people who had cameras and recording devices in their rooms, the King and Queen started working with the newcomers again, accepting their oaths of service. The oath was to serve faithfully for five years and a day, at the end of which they would have an opportunity to leave or stay *if* the King and Queen let them renew their vows.

The only other option available was to wholly give yourself over, not as a servant, but as property. Slaves. Like Mr. Pyle. Wholly owned until the day you died or were killed. Cornelius explained the two oaths when they first started and told the newcomers that no slave would ever be cast out of Amen Hale. He left unsaid whether that meant that a poor slave would be kept "no matter what" or that he would be killed.

Mary helped, touching each person before they made their vows of service. They were accepted or rejected solely based on what she felt. It seemed a far better way to go about the whole process and it sped everything up, but it did cut down the number of people accepted. Of the nearly three hundred newcomers who wanted to give their oaths, they ended up keeping only a hundred and seventy four; all the others Mary rejected and sent away. Cathryn and Cornelius gave the "Mary approved" newcomers places of service within the kingdom. Some they placed with Lucius as guards, some as kitchen help, some as gardeners and a dozen other things that needed to be done around the Hall. A few they just gave to Byron for him to fit in where help was needed. They continued, without a break until the last person was "touched" a little after one in the afternoon.

As soon as she finished "touching" people, Mary curled up at Cathryn's feet, lying down right on the pedestal where their chairs had been set up, like she was tired. She of course had taken Emma with her, holding her hand and dragging her along. Emma sat on the platform with Mary's head resting in her lap as she watched and listened carefully to everything, making notes in her notepad to refer back to later. She was determined to make herself useful somehow.

And that was when Rain walked in, holding hands with Bethany, who was all clean and beautiful now. Rain's hair and dress moved and danced like it usually did, moved by some invisible wind that blew only on her and ignored the rest of the world. The feeling of power coming off her was beyond awesome. The atmosphere, the feel, even the lighting of the whole room seemed to change as soon as she walked in.

A few of the newcomers silently went to their knees, sliding out of their folding chairs and kneeling right in front of their seats. There was a rush of whispered voices as the newcomers and servants spoke to one another. The King and Queen stopped what they were doing, watching silently as the two girls entered.

Rain and Bethany ignored everything and everyone else in the room but took one look at Mary and Emma curled up at Cathryn's feet then went straight to Cornelius. They climbed up on the pedestal and curled up at his feet without saying a single word to anyone. Emma didn't know if they were actually tired or if it was some part of their being witches that made them want to make things match, like a mirror image, and even things out. Or maybe they really were tired, like Mary, from doing magic all morning.

Emma saw the looks of wonder and awe on all the faces as they looked at the four "Princesses" and the King and Queen of Amen Hale and felt odd and out of place. She still didn't understand how or why she was in the middle of all this magic and wonder when she was just plain old Emma.

In between taking notes, she stroked Mary's hair. She knew it helped Mary to be touched, so as often as she could she ran her hand over the long, snow white hair with its one stubborn green stripe up front that always fell across Mary's eyes. Emma listened closely, took notes and stroked Mary's hair. It was all she could do.

While everyone was working away with the newcomers, the cooks had been busy, working franticly to make one very dry "bloodless" goat into something that was actually edible. They'd prepared five different dishes hoping that at least one or two of the attempts would be found acceptable if not entirely pleasing. The King and Queen and their four daughters went to one of the private dining rooms where a meal had been prepared for them and their guest of honor, "Mike" the goat.

Emma Hale

Loved

EMMA WATCHED THE jittery server and gave him the full force of her squinty eyed stare as he placed a couple of the unwanted ribs onto her plate. She glared, but she didn't yell at the poor man. He still looked troubled by whatever Mary had done to him when she had touched him. All it had looked like was a simple touch on the back of his hand, but for Mary that was all it took sometimes. Whatever vibes this guy had given off were too much for her to handle and Mary looked white and shaken.

Bethany, Rain, Cathryn, and Cornelius stopped their happy conversation as Emma slid her chair back, stepped over to Mary and wrapped her arms around her where she sat in her chair. Mary immediately buried her face into Emma's chest but didn't say a word.

"What's wrong with Mary?" asked Rain.

"What happened?" Bethany asked. "What's going on?"

"Are you okay, Mary?" asked Cathryn. She started to rise out of her own chair.

"It's okay. I think she just scared herself," Emma answered for Mary who was pressed up against her with her arms wrapped around Emma's middle, not looking at the others.

Cathryn hesitated between sitting back down and getting up and going to Mary.

"She just needs a few minutes and she'll be fine, Mom. I'll take care of her." Emma held Mary protectively and stroked her hair.

Cathryn sat back down and the conversation at the table resumed as Emma did what she needed to do to "fix" Mary.

Rain and Bethany shared a WTF look together. The two were not all that surprised to find out that they had a new sister today, but they were totally freaked to find that the new sister was Jane's grouchy friend Emma. At Rain's wedding yesterday when all the other guests were gathering all around and fawning over them, carefully being polite, Emma had been downright stand-offish, moody, snappish, and utterly unimpressed by all their "witchiness" and "power."

She was still moody and full of dark, squinty eyed glares and even a sharp comment or two, but none of that mattered. Anyone could see that she loved Mary fiercely already. And it was obvious that Cathryn and Cornelius were completely taken with Emma as well. Rain and Bethany took all this in as they sat there listening to their new mother and father and watching as their new sister looked after Mary.

"Wait till you see the wall Cornelius!" Cathryn's eyes were aglow with the wonder of what she'd seen. She acted as if the wall were the greatest wonder of the world, wrapped around Amen Hale like a gilded picture frame for their new magical Kingdom. "The surface is so flawless it reflects the field of flowers around the border of the property like a giant mirror and creates the most amazing visual effect. It looks as if the land no longer ends but goes on and on and on, filled with nothing but flowers. Remember not to bring any of your jewelry, watches," she paused to sip her wine, her face concentrating, "and don't forget your pen when you go to see it. Leave it on your table. You may need to switch to an old-fashioned pencil for a while."

"She got me a wonderful new pen as last year's surprise anniversary present," Cornelius chuckled as he explained Cathryn's concern for his pen to his new batch of daughters as Cathryn sipped her wine and laughed with them. And then they had a good laugh as Rain told them about Cathryn's clothing malfunction this morning, and she even told them about the man whose glasses had fallen to dust.

Bethany told everyone about Cathryn bursting into her room, thinking she'd killed her maid and getting scared to death when the "dead" maid grabbed her arm. And they had almost split their sides laughing when a much-recovered Mary told about Emma this morning and the first hot-dog shaped "bug" she'd discovered under the bathroom vanity that looked like a vibrator. Cathryn had laughed so hard she cried and cried! And then she yelled at Mary for making her ruin a second pair of panties in one day, a new personal record! Mary told their new mother that it wasn't her fault if she couldn't hold her pee.

It had been wonderful, like a real family, everyone laughing and telling stories and enjoying each other's company. It was almost magical. Even grouchy Emma had laughed and smiled right along with her sisters.

Soon Cathryn and Cornelius got back to more serious talk as Rain told them about the changes and additions that she (with Trisha's help) had made to Amen Hale. The wall, the curse around the wall, and the new building off to the side of the garage for holding the traveling archways. Old cracked and worn sidewalks had been transformed into beautiful gleaming white stone paths trimmed with flowers, plants, and trees.

Rain had changed the wall down by the river to make it run along the shore-line like a bulkhead, but she made the wall thicker and added stairs from the ground leading up to the top of the wall where she created an amazing covered walkway so people could still look out across the expanse of the river and enjoy the view while remaining safely behind the walls and spells of Amen Hale. The long dock and the two boat houses she'd transformed into water and done away with altogether. She had doubled the size of the Guest Hall and created a large underground storage area beside the garage that their twenty seven foot box truck could easily drive down into and then unload food, materials, and supplies.

She removed the magical quiet that she'd placed over the smaller walled garden and instead placed the magical bubble of quiet over all the land of Amen Hale from wall to wall, keeping the sound of jets and military equipment from the outside in the outside world and away from Amen Hale. Rain explained to Cathryn and Cornelius how she'd altered the spell of quiet so that it also blocked all radio, cell, and TV signals as well. Cornelius grumbled that he wouldn't be able to see the news anymore, and Cathryn shushed him and reminded him that at least they wouldn't have to worry about people spying on their private conversations with all their fancy spy gadgets.

The style and look of all the new buildings matched the existing Plantation style of Amen Hall except the large imposing structure down close to the river which was totally alien. Rain called it *The Hallow*. It was a large three-quarter circle structure, open to the sky in the center and built like a Roman style theater but with a modern design and feel. Its construction appeared to be black granite stones. Within was seating for two thousand people arranged in twenty-one ascending rows of seats. It was an ideal place for the King and Queen to hold court and meet with everyone in the Kingdom at once so they would no longer have to jury rig the Cathedral Hall as a meeting hall.

The Hallow was amazing, but Rain said it wasn't the big things that were the most impressive parts of what she had done today as she flew around with Trisha, she assured them; it was the little things. Everywhere, inside the new buildings and out all across the grounds, little miracles were waiting to capture the eye and cause you to stand still and stare in stupefied wonder. Magical gardens, fountains, unbelievable statues, crystal, granite, and floral archways dotted the property everywhere. Shaded rose canopies followed the paths in places and perfectly placed vines were arranged like art, placed in ways that would have been impossible to grow in any natural way.

It was a garden, but there was no attempt made to dumb down the fantastic elements and make it feel more mundane, like a modern world "victory garden." The gardens and grounds and buildings were alien, strange, but they were also painfully beautiful, wondrously crafted. From what Rain described, the wall she'd made first thing this morning was surely nothing but a frame to hold the real work of art.

"I can't wait to see it all," Cornelius said excited. "You've been busy today, my child."

Rain nodded. "I had help. Trisha has an amazing imagination, and it helped so much to pull the ideas right out of her head. All I had to do was fly around and watch as it all happened. But I still need to finish the traveling gateways. They're formed, but I didn't know where you wanted them to open. I know we need to connect to somewhere soon so Lucius can bring in some food."

Cathryn nodded. "Just open one gateway now, Rain. Remember, we're meeting the government this afternoon and I'll want you to be there. And so will Lucius."

"Where would you like me to make the gate to? Some place in America? Paris? China?"

Cathryn and Cornelius discussed it for a while and decided that a place not in the U.S. would be best. Some place that no one expected them to be.

"Paris sounds nice," said Cathryn. She reached over to take Cornelius by the hand. "We've always had a wonderful time there. And Byron speaks French, so he can make sure things go smoothly."

"Paris then," Rain said. "I'll do it as soon as we're done with lunch."

"We'll need money, Rain," Cathryn said.

"Gold, silver, or precious stones? I could try to make paper money, but it has serial numbers so I'm not sure how that would work." Rain crinkled her brow as she considered the problem.

Cornelius shook his head no. "Don't worry about paper money. Just make some gems and a few gold bars, Rain. Not big ones," he cautioned. "Just some small ones that Byron will be able to trade without attracting too much attention. It could be a dangerous trip."

"I should go with you guys," said Bethany. "If it's dangerous maybe I'll get to kill someone."

Cathryn shook her head no this time. "Bethany, you'll stay here. And let's hope we don't have to kill anyone."

"Yes, ma'am," she pouted. Bethany had finally managed to eat and hold down her food. Her pale color had improved some already. She'd been able to eat everything that had at least some of Mike the goat in it. And she was also able to drink some grape juice and the one glass of red wine that Cathryn let her have, but the fancy pastries and desserts, the vegetables and fruits she didn't touch.

Bethany actually said that her favorite was the plain, rare strips of meat that Chef Andre had browned lightly and others he'd intentionally burnt, covering the charred and rare strips with different flavors of exotic sea salts from different parts of the world. Each salt created a different flavor mixing with the differing textures of the char and rare meat.

They'd all enjoyed the chef's "goat lunch" creations. Even Emma had eaten some of Mike though she complained about the gamey taste as she reached for her second rib and asked Bethany to off a lamb or step up to a bull next time to which Bethany gladly agreed, her little eyes drifting off to visions of the delightful bloodbath that would create.

"Did the FBI say anything else during your visit this morning?" asked Cornelius.

Cathryn said, "No. We didn't talk much on what they wished to discuss during the visit. Mostly Rain just needed to deliver her three W messages."

"W Messages?" Cornelius inquired.

"The warning about the Wall. The warning that the Way to enter Amen Hale would be through the gateways and she also spoke to them about the Witch."

"The Witch?" he asked.

"Yes, Kendal," Cathryn said reluctantly.

"Hey, did you guys find out where Kendal is? Is she okay? Is she at home at her trailer?" Bethany asked suddenly. Hearing Kendal's name spoken aloud had made her remember again that they were supposed to be worried sick over where she was and that she was missing.

Cathryn answered, "The FBI is going to find her for us, Bethany. We talked with them this morning. They will either have her with them when they come at four or they will tell us where she is."

Bethany looked to Rain, who was looking down at the table, her face blank as she examined a fancy dessert in front of her, avoiding the rest of the eyes at the table. "But that sucks! She's been missing for almost two days now. We don't need them to find Kendal!" Bethany shouted, upset. She kept her hurt and angry eyes on Rain for another minute then stared at Cathryn who returned only a sympathetic look but said nothing further.

Bethany's mouth set in a firm angry line. This had gone on long enough and she intended to find Kendal right now. "Let's just use magic to find her. Rain can find her." She leaned into the table toward Rain . "What's the holdup. Just do your thing and find out where Kendal is. What's the deal?" Her eyebrows were drawn down in an angry line, but Rain wouldn't look up. "What are you waiting for!?" Bethany shouted at her, and Rain jumped in her chair.

"Leave her alone, Bethany!" Emma shouted, her own eyebrows set in a matching glower as Bethany turned her angry gaze on her. Beside Emma, Mary watched wide eyed and miserable, but she didn't join in the argument one way or the other.

"Why!?" Bethany shouted back at Emma. "Why should we wait? I want Kendal back right now. Why should we wait for the stupid FBI to find her?" she demanded. "Rain should just do it now!" She looked at Rain who was looking more upset and troubled by the second, still fidgeting nervously and looking down into her plate.

Emma stood up and shouted back at Bethany, "She doesn't want to do it because she knows it's going to be bad news, Bethany! Very bad news! She wants to wait a few more hours before she has to deal with it! So just let her have her few more hours before she has to go off and do horrible things she doesn't want to do!"

Bethany froze. "Bad news?" Bethany said. She looked around the table at all the faces one by one. Cathryn, Cornelius, Mary, and Emma. Rain wouldn't even look up from her plate. Bethany's bottom lip started to quiver.

Emma's heart snapped like a dry twig—and that was that. She got up, walked around the table to Bethany, and hugged her. If it worked for Mary, Emma figured it would work for other witches too. And surprisingly enough Bethany clung to her like there was no tomorrow and cried. Emma held her and comforted her and loved on her.

No one said a word. They all watched Emma. She wasn't a witch. She didn't have any powers. But she was taking care of Bethany. Just like she had taken care of Mary. Just like she was looking out for Rain and trying to take care of her too. They looked at her and they loved her. Emma Hale was home.

Phillepe and Michael

Just Another Day at the Office

T HE DOOR OPENED at Or et Pirre Precieuse Echanger de Paris. A very tall older gentleman in a gray suit exited the establishment, carrying a large suitcase in one hand and escorting a woman dressed all in black with the other. She was covered from head to toe, a black scarf covering her head, shades her eyes, and her ankle-length black coat covered everything else. It was obvious the woman was young. Very young and very rich. That was who this particular store catered to. The "Gold and Gem Exchange of Paris" also had other patrons who lingered outside, ready and willing to take advantage of a business opportunity when it presented itself.

Phillepe and Michael had received a call from their contact inside the Echanger and knew about the cash in the suitcase. They followed the pair as they crossed the crowded square and were absolutely delighted to see them turn off into the little used, narrow passage between the shops that led down to the main boulevard. It almost seemed like they wanted to avoid the public eye. How convenient. So did Michael and Phillepe.

They were only a dozen paces behind as the girl and the old man entered the narrow brick cobbled passage. They dashed forward. Phillepe swung his gun like a club. The old man was too tall to hit in the head, but he brought the weapon down right between his shoulder blades and he crumpled to the ground with a grunt. The girl turned just in time to be punched dead in the face by Michael with all his running force behind the blow; she flew back against the wall then tumbled down the stair a short distance before rolling to a stop, slumped against a curve in the downward sloping passage.

Phillipe quickly bent down and grabbed the suitcase that the old man had dropped and both thieves turned and ran back to the top of the alley, but they crashed into absolutely nothing! A barrier like an invisible wall prevented their flight! It went from wall to wall at the end of the alley, sealing off the entire passageway.

"Merde! What the hell is this!?" Michael ran his hands over the invisible barrier then hit it with the butt of his gun as hard as he could twice. Phillepe slid his hands along the edges, feeling for some way past the invisible wall. People were looking at them from out in the courtyard as they pressed their hands flat against nothing and beat on the invisible wall like two violently deranged mimes; they were attracting unwanted attention.

Both men turned and charged back down the alley to make good their escape in that direction. Phillepe kicked the old man as he passed by and sent him crashing back to the ground. The girl was leaning up against the brick wall, her face a bloody mess as she watched them come toward her with only one eye open. One solid black eye. She watched the gun point at her. Unafraid.

Michael pulled the trigger on the weapon as he ran by without even giving the girl a look.

Bang! The shot rang out.

Michael was angry, things weren't going well. The two men picked up speed at the end of the narrow passageway that descended steeply as it reached street level but they crashed headlong into another invisible wall with the force of a couple of bugs striking a windshield. This time they'd both done themselves damage—lots of damage.

Phillepe groaned, his head felt like it was split wide open, dried blood was on his face and his neck was so stiff he could barely move it. He could feel that his hands and feet were tied. That was bad. That meant that whoever had him tied up wasn't the police, which was very bad. He heard voices and opened his eyes a crack. He was in a warehouse. He could see that Michael was still unconscious, or dead, lying beside him. He was also tied, hand and foot, which meant that he was probably still alive.

About thirty feet away a dozen men were quickly loading two trucks. The young girl from this morning stood talking with a tall, powerfully built man wearing a black trench coat. The way he stood and his spiky black hair reminded Phillepe of a soldier. He was probably ex-military.

"What time is it back home?" the girl asked in English.

The man answered, "It's almost half past three. Time to head back. We'll return tonight and work through the evening. He turned and looked right at Phillepe and asked, "Mistress, do you want me to kill them now?"

"That would be too kind, Lucius, and I'm in no mood to be kind. Load them with the rest of the groceries." Her voice was cold as ice and sounded oddly flat. Frightening.

The soldier bowed his head. "Yes, Mistress."

Phillepe's vision was quite blurry at a distance. He couldn't see her face or see well enough to know she now wore only a black dress and not a coat. He felt the strange, otherworldly feel in the air, as if he'd stumbled into someone's nightmare. He discounted it easily. The feeling seemed quite normal under the circumstances.

The soldier ordered some of the men to load the prisoners. Two men came over and grabbed Michael. He groaned as they lifted and carried him toward one of the waiting trucks. Two others grabbed Phillepe. He looked about as they carried him, trying to see and remember anything that might be helpful if he ever got away from these people.

He noticed the tall, old man from this morning walking over to the girl. Phillepe felt a small bloom of hope ignite within him. The old man looked unharmed. None the worse for the beating he'd endured or the fall on the stairs. And if the girl was here and talking, she must not have been too badly hurt either even though Phillepe had seen the damage Michael had inflicted with his punch. Even if the bullet had missed her, the girl had definitely been injured, and he knew the soldier wanted them dead, but perhaps there was still hope for mercy. If they were both basically whole perhaps he could talk his way out of being killed.

Optimistic thoughts swam like little "hope" fish through Phillepe's throbbing head as they hefted him into the back of the truck. Six men climbed in with them and settled into seated positions in the rear. They didn't bother with closing the back, leaving the roll down door at the rear of the truck open. Phillepe figured that they couldn't be planning on going very far or very fast. Which was good. At least they planned on staying in Paris. And perhaps his friends would find him and

Michael soon. Perhaps there was still a chance to get out of whatever he'd gotten himself into. If the old man and the girl were not too badly hurt, perhaps they would show mercy. Perhaps. Perhaps.

"What do you think they'll do to them?" one of the men in the back of the truck asked another.

"God only knows. But I know what I'd like to do to them," another man answered back. His voice filled with rage.

Phillepe's hopes dimmed. He opened his eyes so he could see who was talking and found the man staring right at him.

"This one's awake."

"Good. The Princess wants them alive," answered another man, older than the rest. "Jackson, tend to their injuries."

A young man, Jackson presumably, came over and rolled the still unconscious Michael onto his back and started his work. Jackson's face was a grim mask of outraged disgust. "That these *bastards* would hurt our Princess, that their filthy hands even touched her! Why should they be allowed to breathe another breath of our air? It makes me want to barf!" Jackson complained bitterly as he went about his rough ministrations.

The truck started and lurched into motion. The older man spoke again, "All we could do is kill them Jackson. Can you imagine what Princess Bethany will do once she sees her sister?"

"Is that why she hasn't healed herself? To show them what they did?" asked Jackson as he crawled over to Phillepe and rolled him over.

"I'm not sure. It's not my place to question why the Princess does what she does."

Jackson worked on Phillepe's face and his head, roughly putting a bandage over his split open flesh.

"Who is the woman in black?" Phillepe asked, but he spoke in his native French.

Jackson looked at him with contempt. "Speak English or shut up."

American. *They must be Americans*, Phillepe thought. Only an American would be offended that you didn't speak their language when they were in another country. No other people were so arrogant.

"Who is the woman in black?" he asked in English.

The older man stepped over and looked down into Phillepe's face. "You didn't even know who she was. All you knew was that she was a woman that had a suitcase filled with money." He shook his head as he looked down at Phillepe. "A woman you killed. For money."

"But I didn't kill her!" Phillepe winced. His head throbbed; raising his voice had been a mistake.

"Yes. You did kill her," answered the older man with certainty.

He winced but forced the words out. "No. No! I saw the girl before you put me in this truck. She is alive!" He had seen the girl and the old man! They were both alive!

"Don't call her a 'girl,' you filthy dog. Tape his blasphemous mouth shut, Jackson."

"Yes sir," Jackson answered.

Phillepe shouted over and over that the girl was alive until they taped his mouth shut. All of his shouting woke Michael and they taped his mouth shut too. The truck stopped. Both men were lifted out of the truck and hauled out of an underground garage, across a green lawn, and into a large white house then laid on the cold tile floor in a large room with a high cathedral style ceiling.

Phillepe was surprised that the room was packed with hundreds of people. On a pedestal in the front of the room sat an older man and woman in high-backed chairs, looking down on everyone like a King and Queen. Stretched out on the pedestal where the "King and Queen" sat were three teenage girls gathered at their feet. Two had odd tattoos in the middle of their foreheads.

Four chairs sat on either side of the pedestal. On the right side, the first two chairs were empty, but the next two were occupied by a young man and a beautiful young woman who wore fiery crowns on their heads. Phillepe blinked and strained his eyes to try to see better, but it didn't change what he saw. It looked like two crowns, fiery burning crowns, resting right on their heads!

Phillepe looked to the other side of the throne. In the first chair sat a beautiful Oriental girl with blond hair. Beside her sat a young man with sandy blond hair cut short in a spiked style. Sitting in the next chair was a huge manlike monster. His body looked like a collection of angry, billowing clouds, somehow holding themselves together in one place instead of spreading out across the room. The clouds inside the huge body were constantly on the move, crashing about, and a throbbing light came from the creature's chest that almost looked like a heartbeat. His head held the basics of a face, a long, lipless slit of a line for a mouth and two glowing red dots for eyes that hung suspended in the midst of the rolling clouds that made up its head.

In the next chair was another monster, a dragon man! It had the basic form of a man and even wore clothes, but had a long neck and the head of a dragon or lizard. This creature had the same glowing red eyes as the cloud giant in the chair beside it. Phillepe's head was reeling, where on earth was he and who were these people!? What were they!?

There was a loud uproar from the crowd, angry or shocked voices called out, "Oh my!" and "NO!" and "O Princess!" and "What happened!? Who did this!?" Dozens of outraged voices. Angry, shocked voices. Frightened voices.

The man and the woman sitting in the throne-like chairs and the girls on the platform stood. They all looked beyond murderous. And then it felt like thunder itself was unleashed as a roar bellowed from the cloud man so loud the room shook! The monster burst up from his chair and flew across the room to where the young lady from this morning stood. Phillepe hadn't even noticed that she'd entered the hall or that she was the cause of the hue and cry of outrage.

The giant stopped just short of embracing the girl, his raging red eyes studying the damage. She stood close to where he lay on the ground and Phillepe could see her clearly now. His heart sank like a stone dropped down a bottomless well. Her face was a bloody ruin. Nose broken, pushed to one side, one eye was completely swollen shut, but that wasn't the shocking part. The top left side of her head, starting at the hairline and going up from there *was missing*. Blown away by a bullet. A hunk of skull the size of a hand was gone and the brain beneath was mashed and mangled and easily visible through the gaping hole.

Phillepe felt all hope of mercy die a horrible death as he stared at the results of his and Michael's morning labors. He laid his head flat on the cold, marble floor and closed his eyes. Off to the side he heard a woman get sick. Vomiting. Again, his handiwork. Phillepe tried to stop listening or hearing anything and squeezed his eyes shut tighter.

He started framing some type of prayer to ask God for forgiveness, but his prayer kept coming unraveled as he thought about all that God would have to forgive should he even be so inclined to do such a thing. Dozens of brutal strong arm robberies. His part in at least three other murders. A hundred other mean and hurtful things he'd done to people that deserved better. He tried a few more times to pray but then gave up. Phillepe tried not to listen as he waited for the end.

Hillary and the Happy Idiots

The Key

HILLARY PACED BACK and forth with her cell phone pressed to her ear. She and her staff huddled together in an impatient knot of frustrated activity a dozen steps away from the red line that soldiers had painted on the ground. Everyone respected the red line. If, in an absentminded second, an agent stepped across the line, his cell phone, car keys, gun, and the zipper on his fly would pay the price for his lack of focus and instantly turn to sand. The most disgusting inconvenience by far was getting a mouth full of white gritty sand if you were unfortunate enough to have a lot of old style silver fillings or crowns.

A few of Hillary's older staff members opted to remain behind once they realized that their expensive metal dental implants were in jeopardy. Some of the agents and soldiers with old injuries requiring metal plates or metal pins had been withdrawn and reassigned to safer areas. "Crossing the Line" as they were calling it, had to be prepared for and the delegation led by Ms. Clinton *had* prepared for it. All jewelry, watches, and rings had been removed, dress slacks with draw string ties or elastic waistbands had been acquired, plastic buttons on pants, old style #2 pencils had replaced fancy ink pens, and notepads with plastic comb binding purchased at a truck stop up the road had replaced fancy personal computers, phones, and PDA devices.

Everything on their side of the line was solid, normal, and predictable, but pass the red line and you stood in a place where magic ruled—where a mentally disturbed seventeen-year-old girl who thought she was a witch was making all the rules. The mood of the soldiers and agents had changed. The incredulous stares, the derisive banter and mocking laughter were gone now, and the anger from the many soldiers who wanted to storm the house and take everyone inside into custody and kill any who dared to resist was gone. Forgotten and replaced with new sentiments. Fascination. Wonder. Awe. Fear. Excitement. Confusion. Even envy.

It was evident on most of the faces when they first saw the wall and stared at its impossible perfection and beauty, but the wall was inert and therefore somewhat easier to dismiss than the curse on metal which extended a hundred feet from the wall all the way around Amen Hale. The curse was very much alive and easily experienced personally. Spare change and scrap metal was getting scarce. Soldiers and agents couldn't resist seeing the impossible for themselves and kept reaching across the line with empty cans of soda or a handful of coins so they could watch as the man crafted metal changed to white sand before their eyes.

The advent of the wall and the challenge of trying to find a way to open the gateway had everyone in an uproar. What was planned as an official State meeting to take place at 4 pm had been transformed into a crazed "witch" test with the U.S. government scrambling around wildly as they tried to find someone who could open the magical gateway.

Hillary and her group watched and waited with growing impatience while the experts made repeated attempts. So far they'd failed miserably. It was ten past four, they were already late. The much anticipated and planned for meeting with the self-proclaimed "King and Queen" of the upstart nation of Amen Hale might not happen today if they didn't find a way to open the gateway soon.

Over twenty different psychics, FBI brains, and profilers had taken their turn and stood before the strange mirror table beside the gateway arch. The same thing happened every time. The person would stand before the silver mirror and speak to the reflection of themselves they saw in the mirror. The reflection itself didn't speak back but words would appear in the mirror that they could read and respond to and thereby carry out a dialogue with the reflection of themselves.

The conversations were always similar. Those who made the attempt said that talking to the mirror was like meeting someone friendly and even concerned about them individually, but the topics of discussion often veered off in odd directions, concerning common events or deep seated personal problems. Often the reflection in the silver mirror knew surprising personal facts, sometimes embarrassing or troubling facts. The experts and psychiatrists who spoke to the mirror thought there was a highly intuitive and intelligent force or personality inside the mirror itself that basically just wanted everyone it met to have a nice day and be good to themselves. They'd taken to calling the mirror Dr. Phil.

If the individual talking to the mirror tried to direct the course of conversation or demanded that the gateway be opened, the reflection would vanish. If they let the reflection talk and lead the conversation where it wanted, the encounter could last a while. One lasted almost ten minutes and seemed promising but it eventually ended with failure like all the rest.

There were a variety of different reasons the reflections gave for not opening the gateway. A couple of times it said that it didn't feel it was worth the price and it wouldn't open the gate. Sometimes the reflection told the person wanting to open the gate that they couldn't handle paying the price or that if they did pay it they might lose their mind entirely. A few people were told by their reflections that they simply didn't belong in Amen Hale under any circumstances and not to go there even if someone else opened the gate. Others were told that it just wasn't something for them to get involved in. It was infuriating.

These failed experts and psychics huddled together nearby, shaking their heads as they eyed the group of misfits that Agent White had assembled. This morning after the Black Witch and her adoptive mother paid their little visit on the gate and created the wall and the gateway arch, Agent White made some plans of his own. He sent some of his men to the nearby mental hospital of Pembrooke in Lake City Florida to collect a couple of their more interesting patients. He had five potentials, three of whom thought they were witches, one that swore she had some magic powers of her own, and one girl who was violently suicidal. They all wanted to go to Amen Hale and live there forever, not just open a gate.

Agent White also collected about a dozen of the more colorful specimens that were waiting in the line beyond the military checkpoint, wanting to get into Amen Hale to live here and make it home. White had done all of this over the fierce objections of his superiors, but now that the FBI's best and brightest had come up dry he could almost taste vindication on his tongue. It tasted good.

White sauntered over with the help of his cane wearing a relaxed smile as he approached General Prichet whose tight, angry, pinched up face and stiff as a board posture seemed his opposite in every respect. "General Sir, are you willing to at least let my people try? I think it's safe to assume that your experts have failed."

"Wipe that shit eating grin off your face, White," Pritchet complained. He hated the fact that White had acted on his own, against orders, and brought in civilians that they couldn't keep quiet, control, or coerce. Pritchet was a practical man, a soldier, who liked things crisply ironed, polished, and in their place. He hated this whole crazy situation, but he was tired of being on the receiving end of the irritated gaze of the Madame Secretary who he noticed was looking his way right that moment and looking far less than pleased.

"Go ahead, White, let your happy idiots have a go at it. I'll make sure I use your name when I talk to the Secretary so you get the credit you deserve."

Agent White smiled as he surveyed his group of "Happy Idiots," as General Pritchet liked to call them. White turned to one of his men who stood nearby. "Dumont, start with our potentials from Pembrooke. Let the young ones go first," White ordered.

The group of witches and oddballs sat together on the grass by the shoulder of the road about thirty yards away from the red line, within sight of the black glass archway and the mirror table. They were surrounded by guards and a few handlers from Pembrooke for the five patients that came from the institution. The group waiting in the grass already knew that the government was hoping to use them like a key in a door so they could get inside and speak to the witches, but they didn't care. Every one of these people wanted to live inside Amen Hale with the witches and never come back. Whether the witches wanted them to live there or not they were all about to find out.

The agents brought forward a young "mental patient" from Pembrooke and led her to the mirror. She wore some ratty jeans and an old T-shirt she'd written all over with an ink pen. She also had some demon tattoos, black nails, and some piercings. She certainly looked the part. She seemed to make some headway at first but failed a short time later and turned and walked away from the mirror without making a fuss. The agents escorted the girl away and brought a new one from Pembrooke to the Mirror.

"I told you to wipe that shit eating grin off your face, White. This whole thing is just a damn waste of time," General Pritchet griped.

Agent White's grin broadened. "I got a fifty that says my 'happy idiots' get done what your 'brilliant idiots' could not." White chuckled as the General stomped away. It was gratifying because he knew Pritchet was a betting man, but he didn't want to take his bet. The General could taste something too. White bet it tasted like crow.

They lead Izzy to the strange mirror table. Its base looked like a black glass vanity with a shallow bowl, almost like a sink but without a drain. The mirror was amazing, made out of solid silver, but there didn't seem to be anything else to it, other than what you might see in the reflection. The agent who brought her over walked away, leaving her alone before the mirror. The mirror only spoke if the person standing before it was alone.

Izzy waited and looked into the depths of the silver mirror. She saw words form in the glass above the reflection of her face.

Hello.

She read the word and smiled. "Hi," she answered back. The "Hello" faded away and more words appeared above her reflection.

Are you having a good day?

"No. My life sucks," Izzy said simply. Honestly.

Life sucks sometimes. You've got to deal with it.

"No. I don't think I will. Not anymore."

Why not?

"I'm just sick of trying."

So what are you saying, Izzy? The words hovered above her reflection in the mirror.

"How did you know my name? I haven't told you my name."

I know all about you, Izzy. I know everything about you.

Izzy thought about that for a minute—then accepted it. Why would it lie? She didn't matter enough to be lied to. "Then you know what it's like in there."

I know.

Izzy glanced to the guards and the staff from Pembrooke. This was the first time in a year and a half that she'd been away from that horrible place. And even then it had just been to go to the hospital. She'd been a patient at Pembrooke for four years now. "I can't stay there. And they won't let me out. They'll never let me out. Not now. Ever."

I know, Izzy.

"I've got to go somewhere. I can't stay there. I've got to get away!" she pleaded.

You could write on the mirror and ask for help and the mirror would show it to someone for you. Or you could tell. Talk to one of the soldiers. Someone not from Pembrooke. Maybe we can get moved to another facility. We could still have a good life, even if we are locked up. At a new place things would be better, even on the inside.

"I don't want a life on the inside."

I know, but I wish you'd reconsider.

"Screw this, you gonna help me or not?" she said angrily. She thought about just walking away from the stupid thing.

Don't go! I'll help you, Izzy.

Izzy looked at the words. She doubted it. "Then help me," she dared.

A knife appeared in the glass, floating in the air beside her reflection. Izzy turned her head and looked where it should be if it were real, but there was no floating knife. She turned back to the silver mirror and the knife was still there but only in the mirror. Words appeared above her reflection again.

Take the knife, Izzy. And if you're really going to do it, then do it right. Cut deep, and bleed out. Cut your wrist and let the blood go into the basin. I'd rather have you end it here, with me, than tonight in some ugly cell with that scrap of ditch glass you hid in your shoe.

Izzy wiggled her toes experimentally. The piece of green glass was still there. Words appeared in the mirror again.

Do it here. Do it now. This is a better place. Reach in and take the knife.

Izzy's throat was dry as she reached toward the silver mirror. She wasn't even surprised when her hand passed through the plane of its silvery surface. It was cold in the mirror; she felt as if she were reaching into a bucket of cold lake water. Her hand closed around the wooden handle of the knife and she drew it out of the surface of the silver mirror and into her own world. She studied it for a second. Felt the wooden texture on the grainy handle. She looked back into the mirror. Her reflection looked back at her. She didn't notice that her reflection no longer mimicked her reactions perfectly. And she didn't notice the storm of excited activity from the watching agents. The knife was in her hand and the world was a simple place. A place she understood. Words appeared again.

Are you sure you want to do this, Izzy? Her reflection's mouth moved now, though the words still appeared and disappeared above her head as she talked. *You can still stop. You don't have to do this, you know. You might find some new friends at a different facility. I'm sure I could get us to one of the other places, like the one in Gainseville you heard about.*

The mirror was trying to talk her out of it. Her face in the mirror was worried and concerned. Izzy almost laughed. The knife wasn't the kind of help she expected but she'd definitely take it. It was safer. This was much safer. For all she knew, even if they let her into Amen Hale they would just turn around and throw her back out again. Or maybe it would be worse inside Amen Hale than it was at Pembrooke and they'd just lock her up in there too. No. She had all the help she needed. She lifted her good hand and kissed the tips of her fingers and pressed them to her reflection in the mirror. Izzy looked at her face, she smiled at herself. Her reflection looked sad, but she smiled with her.

"Thanks—for the help, I mean. The knife is great. Bye," she told herself awkwardly. She wasn't in the habit of thanking anyone for anything. She stepped up to the basin but paused for a moment to study her wrist. She'd done this before. There were lots of scars. She hadn't had a knife or something sharp enough to cut her wrist deeply or properly for almost two years now. The mirror was right; she needed to do it right this time.

She brought the knife down and sliced hard, cutting deep into her wrist. The knife was so incredibly sharp she cut halfway through her wrist before the bone itself stopped her from going farther.

"Aaaee!" She gasped in pain and whimpered and dropped the knife into the basin. She saw the government agents that had escorted her to the mirror begin to rush forward, but she shouted at them. "Stay back! I'm doing what it wanted me to do!" They slowed for a minute but started forward again once they got a good look at her wrist. Blood was gushing out.

CRACK! BOOM! Thunder tore from the sky so loud it threw people to the ground. Soldiers, agents, and members of the diplomatic team for the Secretary ran about in a panic not knowing quite what to do while in the distance alarms were going off everywhere. Car alarms and house alarms set off by the amazing clap of thunder. People and even hard as nails soldiers cried out in fear as if the world itself had been damaged.

Izzy hung on to the basin of the mirror table for dear life. She knew if she fell she wouldn't have the strength to get back up. She watched as the agents in their suits picked themselves up off the ground and backed away from her, wide eyed and terrified. They even restrained the handlers from Pembrooke, keeping them from hauling her away. The men from Pembrooke yelled loudly and argued with the agents.

Izzy ignored them; they didn't matter anymore. She turned back to the mirror. She still held her hand in the basin that was quickly filling with her life's blood. She felt weak and dizzy but also happy. She enjoyed a calm satisfaction, knowing she'd done it right this time. She looked back up at the mirror and saw her own reflection.

Izzy. Please don't worry. The words appeared again over her image.

"You're back. Good." Izzy smiled, her words slurred.

Yes. I'm here.

"Who are you?" Izzy asked.

I'm you.

Izzy studied the words. Her vision and thoughts were fuzzy, but she still knew that was odd. "You can't be me. I'm me," Izzy said.

Her reflection smiled at her. A small smile. A knowing smile. *I'm you too, Izzy. I'm a part of your soul. I'm a friend made just for you. I care about you, Izzy, and I can't let you go back to Pembrooke and I won't let you die all alone. You belong inside Amen Hale. You need them.*

Izzy slouched over the mirror table. It was all she could do to hold herself upright, but she tried to stay steady. She didn't want the Pembrooke handlers to come and take her away. The shallow basin was filled to overflowing. Her blood had begun to spill from the sides of the mirror table. "But I'm dying," Izzy said. "I'm not going to Amen Hale."

No. You're not dying, Izzy. I am.

The blood vanished from the basin. The blood that had overflowed all over the top and stained the ground at her feet vanished as well, and Izzy felt warmth and strength flow back into her body. She looked at her wrist and ran her hand over the place where the deep cut had been; there wasn't even a scar. She looked back into the mirror and was shocked to see her reflection. She was pale and she looked so weak, but Izzy herself felt fine again.

The only person who really knows you is you. And the only person that loves you more than anyone else is you. And the only person who really knows if you need to be in Amen Hale—is you, Izzy. And the only way to open the gate is for a part of your own soul to be willing to die to let you in. I'll die for us, so you won't have to. When you think of me, please don't be sad. I did this for both of us. Her reflection's pale face became angry. Determined. *You were right,* she swore, *it would be better to die than to live that way another minute. You were right, Izzy. It did suck. It more than sucked. Live a good life for both of us and remember always that I love you.*

The reflection in the mirror raised a hand to the glass on the other side of the mirror almost like a wave goodbye. Izzy could see that her reflection's wrist was cut, just like hers had been. Sliced with a knife. It was as if she'd cut her reflection's wrist and not her own. She looked down, searching for the knife somewhere, in the basin, about the table, she looked on the grass but it wasn't there either. It had vanished along with the blood. She looked back to the mirror. Her reflection looked even worse. There were more words.

The portal will only work if you go through first. Goodbye, Izzy, I love you. Then the face in the mirror faded.

"No! Come back! Come back!" she shouted. "Don't die! Come back."

Beside her the gateway opened. There were shouts of surprised victory from the soldiers but those men who'd been close enough to have seen some of what happened were silent as they watched the girl yell at the mirror.

"No. Don't go! If you really love me don't go!"

Agent Dumont had been keeping a safe distance while the girl worked with the mirror, but now he came forward and stepped up to the gateway bursting with satisfaction. He was the agent that White had sent to Pembrooke, and he was the one who'd insisted on this particular girl coming, even though she was a "lifer" and the staff had fought like hell to prevent her from going, which only made him more determined to have her. He laughed as he approached the open gateway, but his laugh tuned into a startled swear as the scene through the opened gateway vanished at his approach like a door slamming in his face.

"Shit! What happened!?" he shouted. "It was open! The damn thing was open!"

"What the hell, Dumont!? What'd you do!?" White's warbly, angry voice shouted from far away.

Dumont looked toward the sound and saw the old man puffing and waddling across the street at a less than blistering speed. He hurried toward the girl who was still shouting at the mirror.

"Bring her over here!" he ordered the agents struggling to hold onto the violently distraught girl who had started to hit the silver mirror with her fist. They drug her toward the archway. As soon as she was in front of the gateway it opened again, showing the outward view from the twin Arch on the opposite side of the wall.

"What happened, Dumont?" White puffed out as he pulled up to an exhausted stop and leaned on a young agent standing beside him to keep himself from falling over.

"I think the girl has to go through first, sir," Dumont guessed.

"Well whatever you do, don't let go of her! Hold her right here till we can get everyone in place. We don't want the damn thing to close again," White ordered then reached for his phone.

"Ohh, sir." The young agent he was using as a cane shook his head sadly. "You forgot to remove your phone before you crossed the line. Your cell's shot now, sir."

White looked at it for a second, went red in the face, and threw the phone to the ground where it shattered. He looked at the young healthy agent he was using as a leaning post. He let go and stood straight on his own two feet. "Run and alert the delegation to assemble quickly! Tell them that we are ready to proceed," he ordered.

In just under five minutes, the group of diplomats, agents, the Secretary of State and her personal staff were in position, organized in a tightly packed group behind the girl who had opened the gate. Two agents held the girl, each holding an arm. She'd already worn herself out fighting them and hung limply in their grasp. They held her out in front of them, quite literally like a key in a door as they approached the Gateway.

Agent White, now the official band leader of the diplomatic parade, limped along behind the girl and the two agents. The delegation of thirty-three passed through the arch and into the Kingdom of Amen Hale. As soon as their party cleared the gate, the image of the other side faded away and the structure became nothing more than a simple black glasslike arch again.

There was no one waiting to greet them on the other side of the wall, so they kept moving down the drive and kept the same basic formation as they marched toward the mansion. They kept the limp girl dangling in front them as they marched en mass down the cobbled brick path as if she were a passport or credentials they might have to present should they be stopped and questioned along the way. They noticed but didn't acknowledge the incredible changes to the landscape. This was serious business and each aid and agent was trying his or her best to bring their "A" game and execute to the best of their abilities without the aid of the ear buds, phones, guns, PDAs, cameras, and gadgets that they'd all come to rely upon.

As fantastic as it was to see first hand, no one in the group was surprised at the changes in the landscape. They'd been briefed on Black Rain's remodeling of Amen Hale as she flew around with her mother and later with Agent Trisha, creating gardens, buildings, walls, and statues at will, shaping them out of nothing but thin air and thought. They'd watched satellite and spy plane footage in their tents, but seeing such wonders on a TV screen was different from walking down a cobbled drive enveloped by an expansive field of too perfect grass, bordered by two ribbons of too colorful flowers, all of it cocooned in an envelope of technology free too perfect quiet. More than one person in the party had the mental picture a Technicolor journey down a yellow brick road pop into their heads, or the past memories of a walk through a Disney theme park, where everything was staged and overly perfect, and bright. There it was fantasy and harmless make believe, but here, the Haunted Mansion was all too real, Sleeping Beauty was a dead vampire buried in the garden, and Snow White was a Black Witch.

The Secretary of State's first official visit to Amen Hale was a poorly guarded secret. Spies were everywhere. Bags stuffed with cash were all the rage as every country with the means was pushing for a place at the table with Amen Hale. They were using every trick in the book to gather the golden crumbs of knowledge that the United States was desperate to hoard back for itself. Though it was based entirely on secondhand statements and rumor, the rest of the world knew of Amen Hale's intentions to remain independent, sovereign, and free from American rule and law. The President was insisting that Amen Hale was an internal affair, but the other countries were soundly rejecting his political speak. The world wanted access to Amen Hale, but at this moment the Americans were the ones on their front steps.

As the group approached the mansion, Byron the House Steward stepped out of the front door and greeted the delegation formally, then surprised everyone when he told them to wait.

"Wait for what?" Agent White asked Byron, confused.

"Till it pleases the King and Queen of Amen Hale to allow you into their presence."

And so they waited.

Black Rain

Buried in the Garden

BELIEVER LOOKED AT me and cried. Tears welled up from the clouds around his red eyes falling to the floor like fat drops of rain, his slit of a mouth parted, the edges turned down. My soul would have cried out, my heart would have broken, and my own tears would have joined his—but my soul was only half here and my heart had stopped beating two hours ago and no tears would ever roll down my face again. I had died. Again.

Instead of crumbling into his arms I stood there, still as stone. As still as the dead body my will propped up like a puppet and my soul used like a window into the world as the rest of me floated in the darkness of oblivion.

"What have you done?" Believer asked me. There was anger in his voice, and I couldn't blame him for it. Believer never forgot what I told him. He kept every single word I said and pondered over them and on me and what made me tick, always watching me with his red eyes. He knew that death could not surprise me, I could feel it coming. My husband knew that I had allowed this to happen, and he was not happy. I hadn't told anyone that I was in danger, and he knew I'd done it on purpose. Last time I had at least told him I was about to die. This time I hadn't. I hadn't told a soul.

"I'm sorry, my love. Please forgive me. But I am what I am."

He walked around me, circling slowly, looking at the damage done to my body, the body he'd held and loved with all his heart just last night. Broken and bloody. Cold and lifeless. I could feel the trembling rage, anguish and hurt that shook the room like silent thunder, coming from my husband.

"Tell me why. Why you would allow this harm to come upon yourself and upon me? Why would you let them kill you, my lady? They have not just killed you, they have killed me. You are my flesh for I have none of my own. You have killed me with yourself. Why did you allow this?" His burning eyes looked down at my dead lifeless face and my one black, dead, pasty eye.

He deserved his answer and I wanted to feel again with a human body. To look into his face and feel my heart race and my skin flush with the shame of what I'd done or to have my heart soar to places I never dreamed existed for someone like me inside his arms and body. To look at him and feel *nothing* was a pain I would not endure for another minute!

"I'll tell you everything!" My voice was raspy and wooden but still filled with need. "But not as I am now, speaking through the shell of a dead body. I'm coming back, my love! I'm coming home to you! Stand back."

I released my hold on the girl who was Black Rain, and the body dropped to the floor stiffly. Voices shouted and cried out. My family—Cornelius, Cathryn, my Sisters, Sky and Ryan, the people of Amen Hale who looked on and watched it all and shared this horror with us. I heard it all. I heard their cries. I heard Byron weeping like a baby. They could not see the shadow of my soul that floated in the air above the still form of the girl I had been. Dead now. Killed in an alley by common thieves. Just like any normal girl.

I whispered to Lucius, my words spoken into his mind and he obeyed me. He stepped out into the middle of the floor and called away my sisters and brother who'd run from their seats and now crowded around my body with Byron and some others. Believer was already standing back, waiting for me to return, but my human family was being difficult.

When they refused to move away, ignoring his gentle urging, Lucius yelled at them. "Let me obey her will! My Mistress has spoken! Everyone move away from the body! Return to your places!"

They gave him surprised looks but obeyed without questioning him. The look on his face was enough to convince everyone that he was telling the truth. They clung to each other, weeping as they backed away from the body and watched as Lucius stepped over to my corpse then called for someone to bring him a knife.

One of the servants stepped forward and handed him a long shiny knife and backed away. Lucius took my right hand and laid it flat against the hard marble floor and started cutting at the wrist. It took a couple of minutes as he sawed through the bone. Though I had no eyes, I could see him. He wept while he worked, his blackened hand holding my wrist fast to the marble floor as he worked at the grisly task.

A murmur from the crowd rose but my family watched wordlessly. Lucius rose to his feet, walked about ten steps away from the girl I had been, knelt to the ground and gently placed the severed hand on the floor then backed away. Every eye focused on the severed hand resting on the white marble floor, and so did I.

I poured my will into fashioning myself a new body using the cells that were already there as the building blocks. It was my DNA and I wanted to come back with the same body so I used my severed hand to build a new me.

The hand twitched.

Everyone jumped. The room watched in fixated horror as a new body formed from out of the stump of my wrist, growing first into an arm then ballooning and adding a torso, then sprouting a head and legs in just over two minutes. My soul slipped inside the familiar shell of my new made flesh and I felt all the sensations that came with having a human form rush at me at once, smells, sounds, air pressure, and cold! The marble floor was pretty damn cold on my bare naked ass!

I released some of my power through my flesh and floated off the frigid floor and up into the air. My body was still in its entirely natural state, but there were certain changes that I had to make to feel at home in my own skin. Changes that made me into the "me" that I now was and wanted to be. My hair changed from a kinky dishwater brown/blonde to a straight, glossy blue/black that fanned out around me like a black halo as it waved about in the currents of power coming from my body, making me look like I floated in water instead of air. My mark appeared on my forehead, my nails went from the colorless flesh tone pink to long shiny black that looked like claws on the end of my hands, and my eyes changed color, the complete globe of my entire eye turning a mirror-like midnight black. I knew this made my eyes appear insect-like, but I didn't feel like "me" without my black eyes. It was who I was.

I spoke and willed my words to carry through all of Amen Hale. "As above, so below. As within, so without. Black is my color and my name is Black Rain! Let the Black Witch now rise again!"

Just like the last two times I had returned from the dead I willed thunder to herald my arrival to the world of my birth.

CRACK! BOOM! Thunder ripped the sky shaking the Hall and all Amen Hale and all who drew breath with bone rattling force. Screams, shouts, and momentary panic quickly subsided as the thunder faded away and rumbled off into the distance. People began to calm as they realized that the end of all things had not come. The house was still standing. And they all still lived. Including me.

"So mote it be," I said. There weren't many, but a few people echoed my words. My mother and father and some of the crowd saying, "So mote it be." I was sure more people would have joined in, but it was just too soon, most of them were too shocked to form words.

I turned in a circle as I floated in the air and looked at these people who were now a part of Amen Hale. Many of them had fallen to their knees. Wide eyes and blank expressionless faces stared back at me, not showing fear or joy or anything. I wondered for a brief instant what this strange expression was I saw on so many faces—until finally it clicked and I understood. It was awe.

I was still completely naked as I floated in the air and I felt no shame as these eyes looked upon me, but it was time to take on the dress that was part of my existence now. I willed my black dress to leave the body of the dead girl on the floor and to form on my flesh. Of course it was now free of the blood and other more disgusting bits of myself that had seeped out of my head and onto the dress, but that left the old, dead me, lying naked on the floor. Yes naked. I wasn't a bra and underwear girl these days.

I looked at my old self, dead and naked, there on the floor and was far more concerned for the dead me's modesty than I was for my own. Perhaps it was because the only consideration that could be given her now was that which was given her by those who still lived. Like me.

"Lucius," I called and he stepped forward. "Please, cover me." I looked toward my old self, and he quickly walked over, taking his black trench coat off and draping it over the still form. "Thank you Lucius. You know that she loved you. She loved us all. Take care of her now. Take her to the garden and find a peaceful spot to bury her. Do not mark her grave. All that she was now lives *in me*."

He looked at me and studied my face for a moment before saying, "Yes, my Mistress."

"I'll go with him. She was my sister." Ryan's voice was thick with barely contained emotions. He looked pale and shaken and even a little unsteady on his feet as he rose out of his chair beside Sky and walked down to Lucius. Sky Dragon stood wordlessly and joined them. I was his sister too and he wanted to help bury me.

I felt the tears slip from my black eyes and trail down my cheeks. I watched them. Everyone in the hall watched as together they gently tucked the jacket around the body then lifted her up and carried her out, leaving behind nothing but the blood on the floor to show what had happened.

With a thought, I cleaned the blood off the floor. People murmured and pointed as the dark stains slowly vanished as if the floor itself had sucked it up. I didn't want it lying there as a reminder of what had happened, and it would have been unseemly to bring someone in with a mop right now, so I just took care of it myself.

"My child," Cornelius called. His voice was somewhat uncertain, like he didn't know how much old "me" was inside this new "me." It almost sounded like he didn't know if I was still his child or not. So I told him.

"Yes, my Father."

He smiled, relieved, and so did Cathryn and most of the rest of the people in the room. "I believe it is time you answered your husband's question. We are overjoyed to have you back, but why did you allow yourself to be killed?" he asked me directly.

I shot a guilty look over to Believer and his glowing red eyes then quickly dropped my gaze to the floor. I floated down to the ground; my hair fell and hung still as I pulled my power back into myself and pulled everything else into myself too. My shoulders hunched, I drew my arms in, and I kept my eyes on the floor as I tried to explain my colossal screw up.

"I'm sorry, Father." I dared a glance at Believer's hurt eyes again then quickly looked back to the ground. I didn't know if I looked as guilty and as horrible as I felt, but I did feel horrible. Horrible that I had put my family through all of this. "I'm sorry, my love. I'm sorry, everyone."

The crowd of faces that lined the walls—the servants, staff, and people of our new little world that I didn't know—they looked ready to forgive and oozed sympathy but those that loved me most still looked hurt and upset and demanding. Believer, my sisters, and Cathryn especially, who finally had some color returning to her face, were far from sympathetic.

"I didn't mean to cause such a mess. I was trying to protect us. To protect Amen Hale."

"How did this protect us, Rain?" Emma asked as she slid off the platform and stomped toward me. She was angry and wrung out emotionally. Her face a mess of shed tears. "You let a couple of stupid thugs blow your brains out! What's the deal!? How did that keep us safe!?"

Bethany slipped off the platform and stepped forward and wrapped her arms around Emma's middle and added in her own hurt, angry, little voice. "Yeah! You scared the hell out of us! What gives!?"

Mary joined them and stepped up to Emma and slipped her arms around the other side of her, turning Emma into a "witch sandwich." Her voice mimicked an angry Ricky Ricardo Spanish accent from the Lucile Ball Show. "You gat some splainin' to do, Lucy."

"I know! I'm sorry! I know!" I shouted, vexed by guilt.

"Girls," Cathryn said, standing to her feet. "Let her tell us *why* she did what she did." She looked down at me, "Go ahead, we're listening. And this *better be good.*"

I swallowed. Damn! My new mother sounded just like—well—*like a mom!* A pissed off mom! Shit! I wondered briefly what she'd do to me if my answer didn't suffice. Would she ground me!? I was a married woman and the Black Witch but I didn't feel like either of those things. I felt like a foolish little girl as I stood before them shuffling my feet. I didn't know what she'd do but I didn't really want to find out. So I explained why I did what I did. Stupid or not, I did what I felt I had to do. I'd probably do the same again.

"As soon as I opened the gateway to Paris I knew I would die there. I felt death whisper to me like a cold wind on my face. It told me my time was short, Mother, but it did not tell me who or what or why. I didn't know the details; I only knew that my life would end in the next hour. I was careful to touch all the others who went through the portal with me to see if anyone else would die, and I knew that I was the only one. And if I was the only one then I thought for sure that the attack would have been from some country or government or some group of religious nuts that wanted to kill, not just me, but all Amen Hale. I thought it may be a sniper on a roof or a bomb or some poison slipped into a drink or some other fancy spy way of killing me. I thought someone would kill me because of who I was, a Child of Hale." I looked hard at my mother and father and then at my Sisters who were listening closely.

"What if one of you were out, walking around in Paris, and someone shot you in the head? I knew that someone was out there and I wanted them to kill me. Me!" I growled. "Not you! I wanted to make sure they never had a chance to kill my Sisters." I looked to my new parents. "Or my Mother and Father." I looked away to the rest of the crowd who was hanging on my every word. "Or any of my family. I thought for sure it would be a government or a group or some super secret cult of crazies that would kill me. Someone that I could then rend and destroy and make an example out of so horrifying no other living soul would ever dare raise its hand against a Child of Hale!" I finished with a little heat of my own but then I dropped my eyes back to the floor. It was easy to hear the shame and regret in my voice as I finished.

"But that's not who killed me. They didn't even know who I was. I died for something stupid, not something grand, like protecting my family. I died just like any normal person would die. I was killed by a couple of thieves who wanted my money."

"It's not stupid and it's not a wasted life!" Sky shouted. She surprised everyone as she flew out of her chair across the hall and landed beside me then wrapped her arms around me. She faced my mother and my sisters with a determined set to her jaw. My outspoken advocate continued to fire back, doing far better than I had.

"She did the best she could! And think of the good she has done. Who knows how many people those bad men have murdered, and how many more they would have killed if she hadn't of stopped them. They are bad, bad men and she stopped them! That is not stupid. And yesterday she died for all of us when she got blown up in that limo. We would be dead. All of us, even the vampires and Sky Dragon and Believer would have died if Rain hadn't of died for us. And she's only died once today so she's doing great!"

"Doing great?" Mary asked, confused. "Huuh?" Her face asked the question.

"She died twice yesterday." Sky paused in thought then turned to me. "Was it twice or three times?" she asked me.

"Completely dead or just soul death?" I asked.

"Completely dead."

"Just twice yesterday," I admitted, confused by the strange direction of the conversation as Sky turned back to my mother with a big grin. Cathryn and Cornelius both appeared to be as confused by Sky as I was; their eyebrows were drawn up as they listened, polite smiles in place.

"See! She died twice yesterday and she's only died once today. She's doing great! Maybe she'll get through the whole day tomorrow without dying once. But whatever happens, I won't judge her for dying to save the ones she loves. I would do it too, but I can only do it once. She can do it for us more than once. I think that's why she loves us all so much."

I looked over to Believer and into his bright red eyes and I just couldn't wait any longer. "Believer, I need you," I said, and he came over, opened his arms wide, and wrapped Sky and me in his embrace at the same time.

I just relaxed in his powerful arms, safe and back where I belonged. Beside me I watched as Sky reached up and turned Believer's head away from staring down at me and toward her. She gave him a level look.

"She's still going to love you. Even if she dies. She doesn't forget her old life, even if she is a brand new, Rain. She'll probably just love you more each time because the whole world will be new to her each time. Like seeing a beautiful sunset for the first time or seeing you smile for the first time. Each time she comes back, she will love you, but it will be new again."

"Each time she comes back?" The clouds around Believer's eyes darkened at the grim thought.

Sky's eyes narrowed also as she looked up at his huge cloudy face. "Believer. She's the Black Witch. She was a mess when you found her and she's going to stay a mess!" Her voice was firm. "Do you think you can fix her? You can't. You'll just have to love her messy. Okay?"

That confused him. Hell, that confused me! Believer's face went through a couple of emotions as I watched but finally he settled on "thoughtful" as he looked down at me and his Sky and nodded.

"The delegation from the United States, my King," Byron's voice called out. "They have finally opened the Gateway and are on the drive, approaching the house."

"We'll need a few minutes, Byron," Cornelius answered.

"Yes, your Majesty." Byron stepped off to delay the entrance of the Secretary of State.

Sky looked from Believer to me. Then over to where my Sisters were climbing back onto the platform at the feet of Cathryn and Cornelius. "Rain. Go to your place," Sky told me.

I clung to Believer's arm like a stubborn child. "I don't wanna."

She gave me a hard look. She wasn't giving in. "Go to your place. He will be here for you when you're done. We still have to see the government people and we all need you, Rain. I don't do government people; you know I can't handle that kind of stuff. So go to your place!" She ordered, then pointed to the platform and gave me a shove with her other hand.

It didn't help. I wasn't able to go anywhere; Believer's arm still held me tight.

"Believer. Let her go and go to your seat right now." Sky didn't yell but Believer obeyed immediately.

He released me and stepped away. His red eyes stayed fixed on me as he half walked, half floated across the room and settled back into his chair. I kept my eyes on Believer's eyes as Sky herded me over to the platform where my Sisters' waiting hands grabbed me and drug me up with them and then buried me in their hugs.

Cornelius spoke, "Before we admit our government guests, what do we do with the men who killed my daughter?" His voice was cold but businesslike. He wanted it decided so we could move on to other things. It would cause lots of questions having two hog-tied Frenchmen flopping around on the floor when we invited in the Feds.

"Rain," Cornelius asked, "What would you have us to do with them?"

"One of them is for Bethany's birthday; she's turning fourteen tomorrow."

Bethany's face lit up. "Oh yeah! I completely forgot about my own birthday. Wow! I can't believe you remembered!"

"Of course I did, honey," I said as I hugged her and looked up to Cornelius. "Father, may we have a feast day tomorrow for Bethany? We can have a sacrifice at noon and a feast that night."

"That sounds like a wonderful idea," Cornelius said, smiling broadly. "I didn't know it was your birthday tomorrow, Bethany." He put on an affronted air. "You haven't left me very much time to find you a proper present, my child." He turned back to me, going serious again. "Which one is for Bethany?" he asked.

"She may have the one in the green shirt; he's the one that punched me in the face, then shot me in the head. He's the one who murdered her own sister in cold blood and I'm sure his blood and soul and sins will taste the sweetest to her."

"Thank you, Rain." Bethany's voice was filled with longing as she stared at the man in the green shirt lying still on the floor. He was awake and listening to all we were saying, his eyes wide with terror, not defiance.

"How the hell am I gonna be able to top that!" Mary complained. "What am I going to do for her, run out and find a serial killer for her to eat?" She crossed her arms over her chest. "That's just not fair!" she pouted.

"Mary, you've already got me beat," I said sweetly. "All I did was get her a tasty snack. You found her a Sister." I pointed to Bethany who had already crawled back into Emma's arms.

"Oh yeah," Mary said, face thoughtful for a moment, then apparently deciding I was right, she brightened right up. Emma played along and gave Bethany a squeeze and she giggled. Mary shouted at me triumphantly, "Ha! In your face, lady! I kicked your ass! My gift rocks!"

Bethany and Emma laughed while Mary bobbed her head and gave me the "talk to the hand" gesture. Others in the hall laughed too, caught up in the light-hearted silly nonsense of it, though I was sure that most of those listening and laughing didn't understand half of what we said; they just laughed because we did and they needed to laugh the same as we did.

"That's enough playing around, girls!" Cathryn scolded. "We need to let our government guests in and we don't have time for games or riddles. Rain, what do you want to do with the other man?"

"I'll take him to the crypt tonight, Mother. The Queen of the Damned and her Dark Prince will rise tonight and they will be hungry."

"Then it's decided," Cathryn said.

Cornelius stood up and looked out at the tightly packed crowd standing all around the hall, meeting their eyes squarely. "Though I knew a day might come that would bring a human sacrifice to Amen Hale I am surprised that it has come so soon. We surely did not want this. But here we are." Cornelius paused and looked at Cathryn who nodded her consent.

"Let them reap what they have sown, my Lord," she said as she looked at the men who had hurt her child.

Cornelius nodded, turned, and addressed the hall again. "These men have killed my daughter!" he shouted loudly, face dark with righteous anger. "You saw with your own eyes what they did to my child, your Princess. They are nothing to us but food now. Do not waste a sympathetic thought on them. If you have sympathy to spare, or grief to bestow, lend it to the families that these men have left weeping. They are murderers of innocents. We do not know how many others they have killed, but we do know that it is finished. One man will be given to the vampires, the other we will sacrifice at noon tomorrow. It will be a human sacrifice. And we will have a celebration tomorrow evening for Princess Bethany. His flesh will be made available to any who wish to taste it. I myself have never tasted human flesh before. It should be a memorable event." His eyes challenged the silent crowd for a moment, as if daring anyone to voice a word of dessent before declaring loudly, "So mote it be!"

"So mote it be!" the hall echoed back loudly. It was clear that their King expected a reply, and they'd given it.

Cornelius released the people of Hale, allowing them their freedom for a few moments before admitting our government visitors. I watched as those helping ready the room rushed about preparing tables and chairs for the delegation while the cook staff and servers rolled out tables and stands for the appetizers and refreshments they planned to serve. But most of the people were free to simply relax for a few precious minutes or run to the bathrooms which were in high demand.

All around the room people talked in groups. Some looking grave, or serious, but many others laughed and chatted away. The hall was filled with the life and hum of hundreds of different voices. Even the sound of children playing was welcome. This crowd did not bother me. They were not strangers. They were ours. Children of Amen Hale. I actually liked the busy activity and energy of it all, it made me feel more alive and part of the living world again, which was exactly what I needed after walking around as a corpse for two hours.

Musicians tuned up noisily in a corner and Cathryn and Cornelius busied themselves issuing orders and supervising the preparations. We girls made ourselves comfortable on the platform at their feet and let the chaos go on around us.

The condemned men were removed, hauled away like bags of garbage—very, very important bags of wiggling garbage. Human trash whose highest and best use would soon be realized. Food. I watched as a servant walking along beside them reached out and smacked one of the men on the ass, almost like a football player would do to one of his teammates, but this wasn't a friendly gesture. A wicked grin was spread on the man's face as he laughed and joked with some of the other men of Amen Hale standing nearby. I realized with a little jolt of shock that they were looking forward to tomorrow's feast. They were looking forward to the sacrifice. And maybe the flesh too. Human flesh.

"Isn't it a strange world we live in, Emms?" I said as I watched the doomed men disappear out the back doors.

Emma had Bethany leaning up against her chest and was stroking her hair as she looked out at the room. "Strange." She said the word but didn't say any more, like her brain was in neutral and just that one word had reached her while her fingers pulled their way through the long black/red strands of Bethany's hair.

I scooted over and joined her, running my own hands through Bethany's beautiful mane as I spoke to Emma. Bethany seemed to have nodded off, relaxed and happy and finally full from her lunch with "Mike," and at peace now that I was back. I looked down at Bethany. She looked like a little sleeping angel resting in Emma's arms.

"Tomorrow our sweet little sister here is going to kill that evil man and we're going to eat him—and I'm okay with it. Actually, Emma, I think I'm more than okay with it."

Emma blinked and focused on me. "Okay with it is fine; that guy blew your brains out, and I hope Bethany makes the dirt bag pay for it." Her face fell a little. "But *more* than okay sounds creepy. How much more than okay?"

My own brow furled as I did some honest introspection. I almost didn't say, I didn't want to scare Emma, but she was my sister. I had to be honest with her. Who else could I be honest with if not one of my sisters?

"Emma, I'm scared, I think I'm becoming a monster. I'm looking forward to it. All of it. The bloody sacrifice. The death. Eating his flesh. I'm looking forward to all of it," I said honestly. I was worried about myself. Would I become less and less human each time I died? How many more times would I have to die before I changed into a monster that I wouldn't recognize as "me" anymore?

I watched as Emma shook her head no. She looked unconcerned. "You're not becoming a monster, Rain. Your husband is a monster. You're becoming a witch."

That stumped me. I was still stuck thinking that through when Emma asked a question of her own. "Will you take me with you tonight, Rain?" Her eyes begged.

I didn't have to ask what she meant, I knew. She wanted to go with me tonight when I carried the man to the crypt for Dan and Jane to eat when they rose. "Of course, Emma," I said and watched as she wiped at her eyes. I realized that Emma was always trying to take care of us. Bethany and Mary and even me. Even when she yelled at me earlier, it was just because she cared about me and didn't want me to hurt myself. And she still wanted to take care of Jane too.

"Mary, take Bethany from Emma for me."

Mary did as I asked without asking why, sliding the sleeping angel out of Emma's arms and onto her own lap. I scooted over and pulled Emma toward myself. She went stiff and pulled back for a second as she looked into my midnight eyes, but then she relaxed and scooted toward me all on her own, leaning back against me. I slowly slipped my arms around her, and she let me hold her. I didn't blame her. She wasn't the only sister still learning to trust her sisters. She tilted her head and looked up at me and I looked down at her. I watched her eyes as she studied my face.

"Why did you make your eyes turn black?" Emma asked. "They were normal when you made your new body."

"It feels right for me to have black eyes," I told her.

"I saw you naked." Emma blushed for me, just remembering. "My God, Rain. The whole damn Kingdom saw you naked! All the way naked!" she whispered, scandalized, but then her eyes squinted up and cut to the crowd as if she were seeking out those evil men who may have enjoyed the view too much.

I laughed. Her face tilted back up to me with a questioning look, still so serious even in the face of my easy, relaxed smile. "Emma, I really don't mind if everyone saw me naked. I think that's another witch thing. Being naked. My husband doesn't like it when other people see me, but I don't care if they do. Sometimes I actually enjoy being naked now. It's feels nice."

"Did you know that your lips are real blue, like they would be if you were cold. You're not cold, are you? From dying?" she made a pained face.

"No Emma, I'm not cold. They're just kinda blue like that, I'm not really sure why."

"It's okay. They look nice like that. They're—different. And you can call me Emms if you want." She reached up hesitantly and touched my lips. It was such a delicate, gentle touch, her long fingers tracing my lips while she studied them. "Is all the hugging you guys do a witch thing, or did you hug like this before you became witches?" Her hand reached higher and she touched my forehead, my coven mark.

"I was a hollow shell of a girl before I became a witch. I usually didn't care enough to hug anyone back then. So for me at least, yes. It is a witch thing," I answered her question as honestly as I could. "Mary was a hugger before she became a witch, but now she has to touch people. It's part of her power. And Bethany doesn't have to be a hugger, she's an angel, everyone wants to hug her and she is kind enough to let us."

She was quiet for a while after that. I did nothing while she lay against me, lost, deep in thought. When she looked back up at me, it was there in her eyes, the set of her jaw, her face reflecting the decision she'd already made. Somehow I knew what she was about to say before the whispered words passed her lips.

"I want to be a witch."

"Girls, it's almost time for our visitors to come in," Cathryn called to us. "I'm not sure how this will work with all you girls at our feet like this. Are you sure you wouldn't prefer to have seats of your own? Are you going to stay up here on the platform from now on, all stretched out like this?"

"This is our place, Mom," I heard Mary telling her.

"Are you sure, Mary?"

They kept up their discussion about the seating arrangements but Emma's eyes were still on mine.

"Are you sure about this, Emma? It costs something to be what we are."

"Tell me," she asked. She looked serious. Too serious. Already decided.

Emma didn't strike me as the kind of person who changed her mind once she made it, and even though I truly wanted her to be with us, I didn't want her doing this without knowing what it would cost her. Sooner or later. I placed a hand on the side of her face and called a memory out of my own mind that I wanted her to see and sent it into her mind.

Emma's eyes rolled up into the back of her head and her eyelids closed half way; her eyes moved around and her head made small little twitch-like movements as she watched my memory through my eyes. I held her and waited. I wondered what she would say when she knew.

Emma

Sorry Mom

I FOUND MYSELF in some strange house, standing with Bethany, Mary, and Mrs. Bryant, but I wasn't in control of my own body, and somehow I wasn't overly freaked out about it. Even though I wasn't in control, it felt as if I were doing and saying what I was suppose to be doing and saying. Before I could think much on what was happening or how I got here a door in front of us opened and a policeman stepped into the house. He quickly shut the door behind him, but not before we caught a glimpse of the massive crowd outside and were hit with the riot of noise and flashing camera lights that squeezed through in that one brief moment. The cop froze there at the door, clearly surprised, as he looked right at me. After eyeballing me up and down his gaze shifted to Bethany and Mary.

His expression soured. He got angry, rude, and even nasty with his comments. I watched as Mary lost it and spouted some strange line of cryptic rhyme gibberish as she danced around. Suddenly, the policeman was thrown backwards and held up against the wall! He was pinned there by Mary's powers until Rain's mother, yelled at her and got her to stop doing whatever it was she'd been doing.

I saw Mary's confusion as she stood there, dazed. And then the confusion became fear, fear at being so totally out of control. Together we led her over to the couch in the living room and sat her down. By now I had guessed that I was in Rain's house, her trailer. And I'd also guessed that I was seeing a memory and seeing it through Rain's eyes. As if I were Rain.

"Are you feeling okay, honey?" Rain's mother asked Mary.

Mary looked flushed and confused as Mrs. Bryant chased at the continual tears running from her eyes with a tissue. "Sorry, Mom," Mary said quietly. Apologizing for whatever it was that she'd done. I noticed that she was calling Rain's mother "Mom."

"It's okay, Mary. You didn't mean to do it," Rain's mother said, and she looked at all three of us for an appraising few second. "Ryan's been telling me about the problems you girls are having—now that you're witches. And about you girls having 'accidents'." She looked right at Mary when she said this and Mary nodded. "From what I've seen and from what Ryan has told me, you girls don't handle 'strangers' or 'rudeness' very well at all and it just set's you off."

She turned her eyes onto Bethany. "And you, young lady," she lifted Bethany's chin to stare straight into her face, "need to be careful when you talk about 'blood.' You get way too excited about it." Bethany's eyes went wide and she nodded her head. Not denying it.

Rain's mother gave all of us a sad look then let out a deep sigh. "Wasn't it easier when you girls were just normal girls? If you were normal girls you wouldn't have to worry about having accidents and hurting people." She looked right at Mary and said, "Isn't there any way you can give this up and stop being witches and just be girls again? Wouldn't it be better to quit this now, before someone gets hurt? No more magic, no more accidents, and no more crazy people wanting to burn you?" She looked over at the front door and the two police waiting with Ryan and a man I recognized as Rain's father. "And no more police," she added firmly.

She gave all of us another pleading stare. "Can't you girls go back to being 'Rain,' and 'Mary,' and 'Bethany'? It would be better. You could still be sisters and Bethany, you could still stay here, honey." Rain's mother reached over and took Mary's hand. "Twice just this morning you've lost control, Mary. What are you going to do when it happens and you can't stop yourself even though you want to!? What are you or Rain or Bethany going to do when someone's not around to keep you from doing something horrible? With idiots like that madman with his bullhorn screaming Burn the Witch it's only a matter of time before something horrible happens. This is no good for any of you girls. Just let it go, and be girls again." She pleaded, then stopped and stared at Mary and Bethany, and at me too, hoping we would say something.

As I thought about what I might say if I were really and truly there in person and not in memory I heard Mary's soft reply beside me. "Sorry, Mom. I'm scared, and I don't want to hurt anybody." Mary bowed her head, almost like she was ashamed of herself. "But I like it—I don't want to go back. I like being special—" Mary looked right into my eyes, Rain's eyes, but it was as if she were talking to me and not Rain as she said, "I'd rather burn as a witch than live as a normal girl." Mary bowed her head and closed her eyes.

Mrs. Bryant looked surprised and disappointed. She thought she'd been getting through to Mary.

"Sorry, Mom," Bethany said next.

"Sorry, Mom," I finished. Rain's mouth was moving, Rain's voice saying the words, with me inside her, looking out of her eyes.

"Sorry, Mom." though the words didn't come out of Rain's mouth a second time, I still said them for myself as her—our—mother stared into my eyes.

Black Rain

How to be a Witch

EMMA BLINKED A few times as the memory ended. I watched her. She said nothing for a few minutes and I could tell she was thinking through what she'd seen. When she spoke her voice was grim, but there wasn't a shred of doubt.

"When I do it. What do I have to do?" She said "when" not "if."

My throat was dry and I had to swallow. I was happy. And I was sad. This would cost her but it was her choice. I told her what she needed to do, but kept it simple. I didn't bother her with the Wiccan Rede and I did not worry over a coven cloth or her waiting a year. I told her what I felt was needed to become what Mary, Bethany, and I were. I told her that, and nothing more.

"You need to choose your new 'witch name.' It can be Emma Hale if you choose it to be. Or it can be whatever feels right to you, but it will be your new name forever. Your birth name will mean less than nothing to you once you take your new name. You may feel led to claim a color or a title as your own. Do and say what feels right to you in the moment, Emma. Trust your feelings and let the witch inside you lead you. A witch is a creature of passion and not always reason and it will be frightening to truly let go. But this is what we are, Emma."

The noise in the room was lessening and I leaned even closer, whispering quietly, "You'll have to stand before others and declare yourself."

"How?" Emma asked.

"You must stand and name yourself and say your new name. Then name your color or any title you claim as your own. Then you must declare yourself a witch three times, saying, "I'm a witch, I'm a witch, I'm a witch.""

"Is that it?" Emma asked.

I shook my head, it was a small movement but what she could already see in my eyes made it seem like a shout. "You'll also need to bring some type of an offering; it doesn't have to be money or something expensive, but it does have to be something personal. Something that means a lot to you."

"What did you bring, Rain?" Emma asked.

"I brought a piece of paper that told a secret. The very darkest secret of my heart. And then I told everyone."

A look of utter terror crossed Emma's face for a moment before she quickly banished it and locked it away, back inside her heart, down deep inside. I worried for a second about what horrible terror she hid within her soul, but then I cast the worry away like it never existed. It didn't matter what it was. I loved her. I wanted her with us, but she needed to let it go.

"Emma. They must know," I whispered and watched as her eyes took on that crazed, fearful look again. "If you want to, we can do it tonight, when we're alone, but do it when it feels right, Emms. And do it for yourself."

Emma nodded, looking resolute but troubled.

People were finally settled in the room so we both sat up and scooted over to Cornelius's feet. The little platform that the servants had hastily erected wasn't designed to have four teenage girls lounging on it as well. It was too uncomfortable, too narrow, and it was somewhat wiggly on the front right corner, but I didn't want to move. Mary was right, somehow: this was our place. The others all had thrones but there would never be thrones for the daughters of Hale. Sitting here at Cornelius's feet didn't feel humbling or odd in any way; it felt right to me.

I made some quick adjustments to the platform to get it up to code. With a thought, I made the platform a taller, wider and more comfortable. The thin padding on which we lay became full and comfortably plush and some additional raised and shaped forms pushed up from the wood beneath the padding, wrapping around the two high chairs to give us girls something to lean on and to give the flat expanse some shape and edges.

I heard the buzz of the crowd. Excited whispers rose from those who noticed the change. Beside us, Mary was leaning back against Cathryn's feet holding a sleeping angel in her arms. I wrapped one arm around Cornelius's leg and kept the other arm around Emma to make us match. I released just a little bit of my power, and Emma smiled as the length of my blue/black hair she held lightly in the ring of her fingers began to dance about, waving gently back and forth as power flowed from my body and down through my hair. People rushed to their places and gathered to watch and witness what was about to happen while others stood ready to serve in some way during the meeting. The room quieted.

The back doors that led to the garden opened and Sky Dragon, Lucius, and Ryan came back in, silent and grim faced as they took their seats. I noticed the glances they shot in my direction as I lay here on the platform with my Sisters. Sky Dragon looked worried about me, Lucius looked heart sore but focused, and Ryan looked angry. They had just buried me out there and here I sat like nothing had happened. Ryan probably felt like I should have been out there with them, mourning myself, sorrowing for the "me" that died instead of being in here, living my life. I tried not to notice their faces and put my mind to other things as Byron led in a parade of government suits, FBI agents, and one very familiar face. Hillary Clinton. The Secretary of State.

Izzy

Pissed

IZZY WAS UP and walking on her own two feet again, but it wasn't much different from being carried. One of the agents kept a tight grasp on her at all times. The guy who held her now had huge meaty paws, one of which he had wrapped bruisingly tight around her forearm as they entered the house. Izzy didn't care. She was pissed.

She wasn't pissed about *not* being dead. She was used to that. She'd come close lots of times, real close twice, and she'd really done it right this time. The knife had been so incredibly sharp, the blade falling from her hands so quickly. The edges of her vision had dimmed and the welcome numbness had spread through her body just like before. Each of her heartbeats had thudded loudly in her ears, the thudding slowly changing to a roaring like when your ear is pressed up to a seashell.

But then it all stopped. Her wrist was healed in an instant and all the blood vanished out of the basin and went back inside her body. Instead of killing herself like she wanted, Izzy ended up killing her reflection. A reflection friend that had been nice to her and knew all about her, even the secret things. She was the first person Izzy had met in years who actually helped her when she asked for help. Her reflection had given her a knife and said that she loved her and that she was her friend.

Plain and simple, Izzy was pissed. Izzy was pissed because her friend in the mirror died. And she was also pissed because she was still nothing but a prisoner, even after her friend had died to get her into Amen Hale. It was like she died for nothing. The hand clamped tightly on her arm pulled her along with the group as they passed through the house.

She was in Amen Hale but she knew they wouldn't let her stay here. The staff at Pembrooke had made the FBI promise to return her, no matter what happened. Izzy heard the agents agree to do just that. But before they sent her back to that hellhole they would march her back to the arch when they got ready to leave. Like a key. Over and over. Back and forth. In and out, until they were done with her, and then they'd send her back.

Izzy thought about the mirror table there at the archway. She wondered what she would see if she looked in now. Her mirror self was dead. If she looked in the silver mirror would she see just her normal reflection now or was that gone too? Killed. Murdered along with her mirror self. The Izzy in the mirror said that the only way to open the gate and let Izzy in was for her to die. But whose stupid rule was that!? Izzy didn't want her reflection to die! She didn't deserve to die! Sure, she'd wanted to die herself but not her reflection. Her reflection friend had been nice.

Izzy felt blindsided. This was a pain she hadn't been prepared for. Like finding a new, hidden part of herself that she actually liked, only to have it taken away, murdered right before her eyes. Izzy thought about it—the gate and the whole damn stupid situation and came to one solid conclusion. THIS SUCKED! Who the hell does this to people anyway!? Whose stupid ass rules were they following!? That Black Witch that made the stupid gate. So the Black Witch had murdered her mirror self. That bitch! That sorry, mu-tha-fucking bitch! And it had all been for nothing! They wouldn't let her go. These thoughts rolled around in Izzy's head as they entered a huge room and stood before the King, Queen, Princesses, Lords, and Ladies of Amen Hale.

There was some boring formal introductions as the King and Queen greeted the Secretary of State and the Secretary of State greeted the King and Queen. Blah. Blah, blah. Blah, blah. They had Izzy hidden at the very back of the pack. She could hardly see a thing except the heads and backs of big FBI guys who stood all around her blocking her view, but then the King started to introduce the others in the room, names that didn't matter until he got to one name that Izzy recognized.

"And this is my daughter, Black Rain."

"YOU BITCH! YOU GOD DAMNED MURDERING BITCH!" Izzy screamed like bloody murder before a big sweaty hand clamped over her mouth and shut her up. She fought with the man holding her, but he was too strong and he quickly wrapped her up tight. She could hear the angry murmurs and voices from the crowd of people that lined the walls and the worried whispers from the group of agents and government flunkies in their suits that surrounded her in a tight nervous knot standing before the King and Queen.

She heard Hillary's voice as she complained to the King and Queen about the Gateway and what it had made Izzy do to herself in order to open it. Then she told them that this was no way to treat guests that they had invited to come and meet with them. She almost sounded like she was glad Izzy had called the Black Witch a bitch. Izzy's mouth curled in a smile under the sweaty hand clamped over her mouth.

"Release the girl. I will speak with her now." It was a female voice that sounded very much like she expected to be obeyed. That *not* obeying wasn't even an option.

The guy holding Izzy had turned around facing away from the platform as soon as she started screaming so she couldn't see what was happening, but now he turned back around. Izzy could see that a girl in a black dress had climbed off the raised platform she had glimpsed when they first walked in. After a quick whispered discussion the guy holding her finally lifted his hand from her mouth and then let her go completely.

Izzy rubbed her numb, aching arms as she walked forward. She knew she'd have bruises tomorrow. Bruises that looked like men's hands. Izzy walked past the government agents and Hillary in her snappy business suit and toward the girl in her black dress standing in front of the King and Queen. She just stood there and watched her coming with her strange eyes. They were solid black. And her hair was moving around like it was alive. So was her black dress. Izzy felt the creepy vibe coming off her as well, but she focused on what this Black Witch bitch had done to her and pushed that to the front of her mind. She killed her friend.

"So. You're the Black Witch?" Izzy said as she stopped just a few feet away from her. The girl nodded. "You murdered my friend, you bitch," Izzy said with an acid smile.

The girl didn't get upset about being call "bitch" but did ask a question. "Was she a nice girl?"

Izzy was so surprised by the question she started to answer, "Yes. She was nice, and she listened to me—and she—" Izzy clamped her mouth shut; she'd forgotten herself for a moment. She'd almost forgotten that she was supposed to be pissed! "She was nice!" She spat out her words. "And you killed her. You murdered her! You!"

"Yes. I am a murderer. It's what I do," the witch admitted without any shame at all. "But what I don't understand is why you even care if the girl in the mirror died. I mean, you *just* met her. Why so upset? Did you care about her?" She smiled a little and leaned in, "Did you love her already? So soon?"

"What's it to you!? Bitch! What? Would it make you happier if you knew that you killed someone that I loved? Would that DO IT for ya!? If you killed someone I cared about!? You're one sick bitch!"

And then the Black Witch stepped closer and "sniffed" at her. Izzy's eyebrows shot up and she backed up a step. "Stop sniffing at me like some kinda dog, you bitch!"

The witch sneered, her eyes narrowing as she looked at Izzy and her expression changed to one of contempt or even disgust. "And you call me a murderer. You stink of death. You don't want to live. Do you?"

Izzy didn't answer. She looked down at the floor so the witch girl couldn't see how surprised she was. She moved her toes in her shoe, the glass was still there. Hidden. She could still end it tonight. She would end it tonight.

"I've smelled this stink before. You smell like Rain Marie. You want to die. You want to kill yourself."

"So what if I do!?" Izzy yelled at the witch. "It's my life! Mine! I'll end it if I want to! When I want to!"

The Black Witch nodded with what looked like grudging acceptance and sniffed again. She shook her head sadly. "You'll still do it tonight."

"Shut the hell-up!" Izzy shouted. She shot a quick, worried glance at the Feds who were listening closely. She didn't want this witch to rat about the piece of glass hidden in her shoe. Somehow, some witchy way, this girl knew and if she ran her mouth they'd take her perfect piece of glass for sure!

"Don't worry about me, girl. It's all you. Like you said. Your business. I won't tell them a thing. But don't worry, I can smell death on you, they won't be able to stop it even if they tried to. And they certainly will try, but only you can stop it now. But you won't. You're settled on your course." The witch paused and tilted her head to the side as she considered what to do.

Hillary stepped closer over the objections of her aids. "What is she talking about?" Hillary addressed the King and Queen. "I don't understand what your daughter is trying to say, but understand right now that this girl is in our care, she is not to be harmed in any way."

Queen Cathryn answered, "I assure you, my daughter doesn't want to hurt this girl. I think she's trying to find some way to help her."

"Help her!?" Hillary's voice was incredulous and angry, though still controlled. "This girl has doctors and professionals who can help her; she doesn't need your daughter's kind of help. The poor girl should have never been brought here in the first place and what she went through at that gateway certainly made her condition worse. We can watch her and make sure that she doesn't hurt herself. And make sure she gets the care she needs. We will take care of the girl."

"Take care of me!?" Izzy yelled. "Don't you get it! I don't want your help, lady. Just leave me the hell alone! I don't want to go back to that place!"

"Who is this girl?" Cathryn asked. "Where on earth did you find her? Is she insane?"

The girl was obviously suicidal and they had mentioned "doctors" and "professionals." Hillary's angry gaze fell on Agent White who was looking rather unwell at the moment, like he'd eaten something that disagreed with him.

He cleared his throat with a cough then answered the Queen's question. "She is from a nearby mental health facility. She is somewhat suicidal, and we were loath to use the girl, but everyone else failed to be able to open the gateway. I assure you, we tried a good number of others before we allowed this poor girl to make the attempt." His voice was defensive but respectful.

Cathryn was familiar with most of the mental health facilities in the state of Florida. The local Wiccan and Pagan community often came to her for help with family or friends that became unbalanced mentally, and she'd had the unfortunate task of sending a few of these troubled souls off to a number of those facilities. She also had the challenge of trying to get others out. It was easy to get people in but nearly impossible to get anyone out.

"Which facility is she from, Agent White?"

"Pembrooke."

Cathryn and Cornelius shared a disgusted look between them. The absolute worst of the worst. The most stringent, restrictive, and difficult facility in the State of Florida. Pembrooke was a certifiable nightmare.

All of the cursing and yelling had woken Bethany and she was still trying to catch up with what was going on. "Is Pembrooke a bad place?" asked Bethany in her sweet little voice.

"Yes, honey. It is a very difficult place to live," answered the Queen.

"Is that why she wants to die, Mom?" asked Bethany as she stared right at Izzy. The honest question voiced so clearly seemed to slice through the air like a knife and Izzy cringed as if the words had cut her.

"I think they sent her there because she tried to kill herself, honey. But yes, being there will probably make her want to die even more."

"That's so sad," said Bethany.

Rain spoke then. "Mother, please help me. What should I do? " she asked, her voice sincere as she looked at Izzy.

Cathryn looked doubtful as she studied the girl. Izzy didn't look up; she kept her eyes on the floor. "Is there any real hope for the girl?" Cathryn asked.

"Not a snowball's chance in hell. Not as she is. She can't live alone; someone will have to watch her always. Be with her always. Care for her always. Even if she lives through today, death will whisper to her tomorrow."

The Queen nodded then spoke to Izzy herself. "Child. Are you determined to kill yourself or do you want help finding a way to live? I am offering you help. My help. The next word out of your mouth will be the most important word you have ever spoken in your life. You will say the word 'please' or you may choose any other word your heart desires. Now speak, and decide your fate. So mote it be."

"So mote it be," almost four hundred voices echoed the Queen's words, spoken by all those who lined the walls and served around the room. Once the echo faded away the room went silent.

"Please." The whispered word was heard by all in the silent hall.

The tile floor right beside the Black Witch darkened and then surged upward; a mass of amorphous gray material rose into the air and quickly shaped and formed itself into a beautiful silver mirror. It was oval, six feet tall and four feet wide. The mirror hung about six inches off the ground, suspended in air. People oohed and aaahed and a buzz of quiet conversation rose in the hall as everyone watched the Black Witch working her magic.

The Agents, wound tight as a spring ready to pop, moved everyone in their group back as far as they could go without mixing into the crowd along the walls. Hillary watched and tried to make sense of what she was seeing with her eyes. Izzy, on the other hand, wasn't impressed at how the mirror was made or at the witch who made it; she was worried about the mirror itself. What would she would find if she looked inside? Would her friend be there, or would her reflection be gone? Dead forever.

"Look into the mirror," the Witch told her, almost as if she could her thoughts. "Let's see if your nice friend is ready to live again, not just in your heart, but out here where you can see her and speak to her again."

"She can live again?" Izzy asked.

The witch smiled. "Souls can't die. Your friend was a piece of your soul and souls are eternal. When she died, she went back to the one who made her. She went back to you. Back to your soul. She's inside you right now; I'm sure you can feel her inside you."

Izzy placed a hand over her heart. She had felt something happen, deep down inside herself when her "mirror self" died. Even now, that very moment, Izzy felt something. Something down inside herself. It felt like she wasn't completely alone within her own body. She hadn't given it much thought, but she hadn't truly felt alone since she'd walked away from the mirror.

"Look into the mirror and your friend will live again, here, in this world." The witch stepped away from the mirror to give Izzy some room.

She came hesitantly, one slow step at a time until she stood in front of it and looked inside. At first there was nothing there, but then her reflection took shape in the shining metallic surface and words took shape in the mirror over the head of her smiling other self.

Hello again Izzy.

"Hi," Izzy said, somewhat shyly. "I'm glad you're back." She felt odd talking to someone who had died for her only a short while ago.

So am I. I didn't think I'd be coming back to this life again, but I'm glad I did. You need me.

"I know," Izzy said with feeling as her eyes started to tear up. She ordered them to stop. She refused to cry.

You've already gotten us into another mess now, haven't you?

"Yes," Izzy said. She shrugged. "Sorry. But at least you're back."

True. Her reflection self conceded the point, then smiled, *And thanks. I missed you.*

Izzy blinked, doing her best to fight her tears back. "You did?"

Yes, I did.

The Black Witch slipped up beside Izzy and looked into the mirror with her. "Hi there!" said the witch in a happy voice with a great big smile.

Izzy watched as her reflection stopped mimicking her actions and moved independently, all on its own as it looked at the witch.

So, you're the Black Witch. Izzy's reflection looked surprised and curious as she looked at the witch.

"Yes, but just call me Rain, I'm no one special. I'm just a friend. Like you." The witch smiled. "Would you like to come to live in our world for a while? You need to talk some sense into yourself before she ends up killing you both. Or if she's absolutely dead set on doing herself in, I'd love to have you stay here with us. You know, you don't have to die when she does, although I know you'll want to. I wanted to." The Black Witch looked caught in some private painful memory for a brief moment before she continued, but without her smile. "There's really no sense in both of you dying tonight."

The Izzy in the mirror looked surprised and confused beyond words. She looked from the witch to "herself," who stood beside the witch looking confused beyond words as well. The girl in the mirror recovered first, her words appearing in the mirror. *Okay, I guess. If there's some way you can get me out there where Izzy is. That would be good. She needs me.*

"Good," said the witch to the girl in the mirror. She looked back to the girl outside the glass. "What's your name anyway?"

"Izzy."

"Well, Izzy, you need to give your friend a name."

"What?" Izzy asked. "A name?"

"Yes, she needs a name. She's a real person, just like you, and she needs a name. The girl who made me did not name me and I was forced to name myself. But that was cruel. Your friend deserves a name. A name given to her by the one who gave her life because it will mean more to her if it comes from you. Your friend loves you."

Izzy took a step back. She gave this strange girl a hard look, with her crazy black eyes, weird forehead tattoo, and living hair flipping all about her shoulders. She stood there, enduring the scrutiny wordlessly, smiling again.

"How the hell do you know about all this stuff?"

"Name your friend, Izzy." The smiling witch ignored her question.

Izzy turned back to the mirror, to her mirror self. The Izzy in the mirror was no longer even trying to copy her movements but was watching her, looking into Izzy's face. She looked expectant, excited even, as she waited to hear what name she would be given.

"Do you have a name that you would like?" Izzy asked the "her" in the mirror.

The girl in the mirror shook her head. Words appeared over her head. *This is weird, but she's right. It seems so strange that she knows so much about me, but she's right. It would mean so much more to me if you named me. A name you want me to have. Whatever you pick, Izzy, I promise, I'll love it too."* Her mirror self smiled and watched as Izzy thought hard on what to name her.

"Lizzy. I name you Lizzy."

"Excellent!" said the Black Witch. "I *like it!* You'll be like twins. Like sisters."

The witch stepped back from the mirror and threw her arms wide and chanted her words in a sing-song rhyme.

"Mirror image with a soul.
Your second life just minutes old.
You are needed by the one
From whose soul your soul has come.
From the land beyond the glass,
To our world you now shall pass.
Not in shapeless spirit form,
But with a body you'll be born.
As above and so below,
Flesh and blood and life bestow.
Open now and set her free,
Izzy's friend, so mote it be."

A straight line of light split the surface of the silver mirror from top to bottom and light poured out as the mirror opened in the middle like two doors swinging out. Blinding white light flooded the room and people shielded their eyes and looked away as a girl stepped out of the mirror. As soon as she was out, the mirror shut, sealing the blinding white light away and then the whole mirror faded away, dissolving back into the ground and disappearing entirely leaving nothing behind but the marble floor.

A new girl stood with the Black Witch and Izzy. She looked *exactly* like Izzy. Same face, same hair, same clothes, same shoes. But very different facial expressions. Izzy looked like she was about to faint dead away, but Lizzy had an enormous, ear to ear, smile on her face as she looked around the room, taking in the sights like she'd never seen any of them before. She breathed in a huge deep breath of air and then she laughed.

"This is so wonderful!" Lizzy looked at the Black Witch, who wore a small happy smile. "Thank you for my life," she told her.

Rain shook her head. "Don't thank me. Izzy is the one who made you. I helped her, but Izzy is the one who gave you life. You're a piece of her soul. She even cussed out the Black Witch because I killed her friend, a friend that she loved. That would be you."

Lizzy looked at Izzy. "Thank you for making me and giving me life. Thank you. It's wonderful to be alive," Lizzy said with a big smile, but Izzy looked troubled and confused.

"No Lizzy, it's not wonderful for me. How can you even say that, you know what it's like for me. It will just be worse now. They won't let me stay here. They'll make me go back to Pembrooke. I won't even have you with me in my heart now that you're out here." Izzy couldn't take it anymore; her strength vanished, her desire to fight died.

She sat on the floor right there and curled into a ball, crying quietly. She covered her face with her hands so no one could see or hear. Lizzy ran over and stood over Izzy protectively and looked back to Rain, then to the Feds, then the King and Queen.

"You're not going to make her go back there, are you!? They rape the girls at Pembrooke! They are monsters!" Lizzy shouted as she stood over Izzy, not sure what to do or how best to protect her.

"NO!" Izzy yelled from where she lay on the floor, then fell to mumbling, "You can't tell, you can't tell, you can't tell, you can't tell—" saying it over and over as the others in the room stared at the twins.

Cornelius and Cathryn both stood up. "Lizzy," Cornelius called her name and she turned and faced him.

"Are you the King of Amen Hale?" Lizzy guessed.

"Yes. I am."

"Then help us! PLEASE!" Lizzy pleaded with all her heart. "Izzy can't go back to Pembrooke. She just can't!"

"Lizzy! Be at peace, child!" Cornelius shouted and made a calming gesture and Lizzy settled enough for him to speak. "You and Izzy are both welcome to stay here and live here and make Amen Hale your home. But you understand that Izzy is a very sick girl and she will need your help. Will you be willing to take care of her and watch over her and keep her safe while you live here with us?"

Lizzy seemed confused by the question. "That's all I want to do! I want to take care of her. I love her. She made me. With some help from Rain," she granted with a glance in her direction before looking back at the King. "I never want to leave Izzy, and I'll be glad to keep her safe. I know she's hurt and messed up and she hates her life right now, but it's not her fault. I promise I'll help her. I'll be glad to help her!"

Cornelius nodded. "Can you recall all that Izzy has been through at Pembrooke?"

At her feet Izzy's mumbling got louder, "You can't tell! You can't tell! You can't tell!"

Rain bent down and tried to comfort her, whispering kind words to the troubled girl as Lizzy spoke to the King. "Yes. I remember everything. I remember all her life that we shared. I know all of it."

Cornelius nodded. "Then you will need to sit with Agent White and tell him what has transpired at Pembrooke that has made Izzy so upset, and any other place where Izzy has been mistreated in the past. I want names, places, and the details, even if they are painful memories. This may be difficult for you, my child, but it needs to be done only this one time. I have spent some time with Agent White and found him to be a capable and seasoned man of honest character. He may ask some questions as you speak, don't fear to answer. These men will not take you or Izzy away. Amen Hale is now your home."

"What about Izzy?" Lizzy looked down at her with worry. "She shouldn't hear any of what I'm about to say. It would be bad for her. Very bad."

"Believer," Cornelius called.

"Yes, my father," he answered in his deep rumbling voice as he stood in his chair to his towering height of almost eight feet tall. It seemed that Believer claimed Cornelius as his "father" since he was married to one of the girls he claimed as his daughter.

Cornelius looked surprised, but he smiled. "Believer, my son. Would you and Rain please carry Izzy to the Reading Room where she can rest on a couch? Keep her safe, but remember that she is very resourceful, she may yet try to harm herself."

"WAIT!" shouted Lizzy. She reached down and snatched off one of Izzy's shoes without so much as a "may I." Everyone watched as she dug around inside the shoe and came out with a wicked looking piece of green glass. Then she bent down to her own shoe and took out another identical piece of green glass, a mirror image of the first piece. "That's what she was going to use to kill us with tonight," said Lizzy as she held the pieces out in her hand, displaying the evidence to the room.

"Not anymore," said Rain. And the two pieces of green glass vanished.

Believer moved forward in his odd, half walk half floating gait then reached down and gathered Izzy up into his powerful cloud-like arms.

"Be careful with her please!" said Lizzy as she looked at Believer with worry.

Believer's massive head turned toward her, his eyes glowed brightly but with compassion not menace. His slit of a mouth turned up in a soft smile as he spoke to Lizzy in a deep, resonant rumble. "Do not worry for Izzy. I promise that my wife and I will keep her safe till you come for her."

The three of them left the Hall together.

"Dr. Burgis," called Cathryn, "please go check on the health of the child and have the servants bring anything that you require for the girl."

"Gladly, your Highness," the Doctor answered and stepped away from the side of the room where he'd been standing with Jane's parents, Mr. and Mrs. Miller.

The government agents broke into hushed conversation as they watched Burgis walk from the room. They wanted the doctor badly. They wanted him, his research, and his pills.

"Agent White, would you and one assistant please go to the garden parlor with Lizzy and take her deposition? What value you choose to place on her words and what you do with this information is entirely your business."

"I would be glad to assist in taking the girl's deposition, King Cornelius," White answered. He turned back to one of the men behind him. "Watkins, come with me, please."

Cornelius looked over at Hillary. "Call it what you will, Madam Secretary. Political asylum has an official sound to it. Sanctuary adds a certain human touch. But if you must paint me the villain, then call it child abduction. But whatever you choose to call it, Izzy will be staying here in Amen Hale. This is now her home. Her friend and sister Lizzy will be taking care of her for the rest of her life, however long that is."

Agent White hobbled out to the front of the room with his partner. "Come this way, Lizzy. I assure you, I'm here to help."

Lizzy didn't move; she stood frozen in place. Her head whipped to Cornelius then back to the two FBI men.

"She's only a few minutes old," Sky spoke from her seat. "She's new, and she's scared of the men. They're cops. She was being brave when Izzy was out here, but now she's scared. The things that happened to Izzy are a part of her too." Sky's brow was creased with worry as she looked at this new "friend" named Lizzy.

"I'll go with her," Dana said and stood. David, of course, stood with her.

"Thank you, Dana, David," Cathryn said, unable to hide her surprise. "I'm sure Lizzy will feel much better having you go with her."

Everyone watched as David and Dana stepped forward. The couple with the burning crowns had passed as almost a minor oddity while they remained seated and silent, but now that they were out in front, hundreds of eyes watched them in wonder. Beautiful crowns of blue, red, and yellow flames circled their heads but did not burn them, their hair, or their clothes.

Lizzy was staring at the burning crowns as Dana and David walked up to her. She didn't know what to make of them either but Dana's attitude toward the "cops" seemed to reassure her.

"Don't feel bad, Lizzy. I don't trust cops either," Dana said and she gave Agent White and his partner the totally evil eye until they turned and shuffled off to the garden parlor on their own.

"Why do you not like the cops?" Lizzy asked her.

"In my first life, the cops killed me, and David had to raise me from the dead. So I have serious cop issues now. I can't freakin' stand um." Dana took Lizzy by the arm and kept talking to her as they walked from the Hall following behind White and his partner. "So now I'm on life number two, just like you."

David followed a short distance behind the two girls.

"I'm on life number two, too." Lizzy said with a little laugh. "What was your first life like, Dana?"

"I was an evil, sadistic, cold hearted bitch in my first life. Wasn't I, David?"

"True," David answered. "But I still loved you. You were my bitch."

Dana was laughing as their small group left the Hall.

Cathryn and Cornelius

Matters of State

"MADAM SECRETARY," CORNELIUS addressed her directly, "Now that the girl is being cared for properly, perhaps you and your people would care to enjoy the hospitality of Amen Hale and rest for a few moments before we get started discussing matters of State."

"Yes. An excellent suggestion, King Cornelius," Hillary replied.

And that was what they did. After the brief respite with drinks and hors *d'oeuvres* and fifteen minutes of polite conversation they started the meeting. Hillary began with what she hoped would be received as excellent news and set the tone for the rest of their evening. In a long flowery drawn out way, she informed Cathryn and Cornelius that the United States intended to allow Amen Hale to exist and that the President had granted it autonomy as its own independent nation located within the borders of the U.S., provided they could give a number of guarantees in return. The men with her produced an official looking document and placed it on the table.

Queen Cathryn spoke, "How very kind of them, Cornelius. They intend to 'allow' us to exist and generously see fit to 'grant' us autonomy and graciously the U.S. government deigns to 'give' us our independence."

Cathryn looked at Cornelius who wore a huge smile on his face and they both burst out laughing. Others all over the hall also laughed, the sound echoing off the high ceiling and filling the house. Hillary and those with her, however, did not laugh. Not a chuckle. Not even a smile.

King Cornelius raised his hand and the room quieted. When he spoke his full, rich voice was friendly but firm. "The United States of America intends to bestow these unspeakable riches upon us *IF* we 'give' certain guarantees. You realize, Madam Secretary, you are trying to give us what we already possess in full measure and then make us pay for it with promises. We owe no man or country anything. If I were a politician I would make broad sweeping promises of a hundred different kinds concerning our conduct. But I'm not a politician, I'm a King. It will not take ten pages of parchment to hold my words nor will it take a team of lawyers to interpret my meaning. When I speak for Amen Hale, I speak the truth. And if you want to hear me speak the truth then hear this now."

Cornelius leaned forward in his chair and the air itself seemed oddly tuned to the tension in the room. "We have no desire to interfere with the affairs of nations, Madam Secretary, though I know you wish it were otherwise. Nor do we plan on redressing the plights of the world. We will not be feeding the hungry, clothing the teeming masses, or curing cancer with magic pills, nor will we be gifting the rich and powerful of this world with immortality, and we will not be raising loved ones from the dead unless we feel obliged to do so. How my children use their power is our business and ours alone, but have no fear, we have a very finite sense of the world. We do not wish to damage it in any way."

"You can cure cancer?" someone spoke up from the group behind Hillary.

Heads turned among the visiting delegation as they searched about among their own number to find who had spoken out of turn, but the man made it easy, taking a step forward. He was indistinguishable from the others in his suit and tie, except for his face, which was filled with emotion, not the blank business-like stares the others wore like a part of their uniform.

"If you can cure cancer, why not give this gift to the world? How could you possibly keep that knowledge to yourselves? You can help so many people. My daughter has cancer. She's dying."

Other agents stepped up to grab this rogue member of their party, but Hillary waved them off, waiting to see how such a heartfelt plea for help would be treated. It was a damn good question.

"Do you believe in God, Agent Shellhouse?" asked one of the young witches who lounged at Cathryn's feet. Her long hair was snow white with one bright green stripe up front that set off the color of her bright, green eyes.

Agent Shellhouse seemed surprised that the girl knew his name and surprised by the religious nature of her retort. "Yes" was his short, crisp, one word reply.

"Then pray and accept His will," Mary said without emotion. The cold rebuttal was chilling.

Shellhouse reeled for a moment then fired back angrily, "Do you believe in God!?"

"No. Say it right. Use my name. Like I did yours. Mine's Mary Fae," Mary supplied helpfully in short little sentence bites. "Go ahead now. Ask again." Mary gave him a smile and an encouraging little wave with her hand as she waited for him to chew up his sentence and spit his words back out.

The man took a moment but managed to restructure his question as requested. "Do you believe in God, Mary Fae?"

"Yes" was Mary's short, one word, crisp reply. The exact match of Shellhouse's answer. Mary smiled and clapped her hands like she'd completed a puzzle of some kind and so did the other two tattoo marked girls on the platform, applauding her.

It was such odd behavior that it was obvious, even to their visiting guests that this wasn't an attempt at cruelty but was some odd behavioral quark. Hillary and her group took this as further evidence of mental instability among these girls who saw themselves as witches. Government psychiatrists, profilers, and analysts had already been studying their peculiar behavior and marking the way in which the girls liked things to even out and balance.

"You believe in God?" Hillary interrupted, hopelessly unbalancing the word equation that Mary had just gotten balanced.

Mary looked unhappy as she turned her bright green eyes onto Hillary. "Yes. I've touched too many people now, too many lives. I've felt too many souls who believe in God to not believe in him myself. Rain is one of the absolute worst to touch and I touch her all the freakin' time. She's even spoken to people who have gone to heaven. And she's gone to her own hell three times now too." Mary seemed to ponder that for a second before moving on. "I am the Green Witch, and my power is life. I can feel and even see the cords of life that bind all things back to the one who made all things. So yes, Mrs. Clinton, I believe in God." Mary's eyes seemed to glow as she gazed in their direction, looking out at them. Her gaze shifting about moving around the room, apparently seeing things invisible to everyone but herself.

"Can't you see that *YOU!* are the answer to my prayers!?" Shellhouse shouted suddenly, still trying to make his case and get his daughter the help she so desperately needed. "I'm asking you! I'm begging you! Please, please help my Bree! She won't live through another month of chemo." He took another step forward, and the other agents finally restrained him and pulled him back toward their group.

On the platform Mary closed her eyes and put her hand out in front of her and a ghostly white rope became visible descending down from the high ceiling ending right inside the chest of the agent who's arms were now held by two other agents, one on each side.

"Do you see it?" Mary asked no one and everyone with her eyes closed.

"Yes," the man breathed out. "But what on earth is it!?" He was looking down at his chest with an expression of horror.

"It is the way home," Mary said. "Your daughter has one too, but I've already shown you too much." She lowered her hand and the ghostlike filament vanished from sight but not from memory. "Trust him or don't, curse him or bless him, forsake God or follow him, it's your choice, but leave me the hell out of it. It has nothing to do with me anymore. I believe in God—and I fear Him."

That said, Mary turned away and quickly crawled across the platform on her hands and knees toward Emma who reached out to hold her but as soon as Emma touched her Mary jumped as if shocked.

"Emma!" Mary shouted, her face filled with surprise and fear.

"Bring me a blanket!" Emma ordered, and a servant dashed off to fetch one.

"Is she all right, Emma?" Cathryn asked as she came over to check on Mary.

"She will be," Emma answered as she hugged a shivering Mary.

A servant ran up to the platform and handed the blanket up to the Queen who draped it around the two girls as Emma soothed Mary.

"It's okay. It's my choice," she heard Emma whispering to Mary.

"Remove him from the Hall," King Cornelius ordered. Once the problem agent had been taken out, he continued. "That is a perfect example of why we will be isolationists. You tell me, Madam Secretary, where would it end if it ever truly began?" Cornelius shook his head as he looked toward the doorway through which the distraught man had just exited. "Everyone has a sick loved one that they want healed. A wife or a child they want raised from the dead. No one wants to die. Everyone wants power and magic of their own. And whether you believe in God or not, my daughters do," Cornelius affirmed again. "Rain especially. And she has some very firm beliefs concerning the use of power. But that is our business and we will keep our own counsel concerning these matters. Some knowledge is forbidden and I feel we tread on dangerous ground with this line of discourse and therefore we will speak of other things. Like money."

"One of your areas of true expertise, Mr. Hale," said one of the agents toward the back of the group that Cornelius recognized instantly as Thaddius Stockwell.

The video of Black Rain broke on the web and went viral on Tuesday and that was the catalyst that started the police investigation and IRS activity as they probed into all of Cornelius's business dealings looking for anything suspicious. Federal Agents arrived at 6 am Wednesday morning and searched Amen Hall. They seized computers and records and took photos of valuables, antiques, and jewelry which they planned to confiscate when they returned with a court order while Stockwell did his damndest to terrorize and coerce cooperation out of Cornelius. It had been a three-hour meeting which would have been more aptly described as an interrogation. It ended with Stockwell telling Cornelius that the IRS had frozen all of his assets, over twenty million dollars in a number of banks and offshore accounts. Stockwell had grinned as he told him that they planned to indict him on charges of money laundering and tax evasion if he even lived long enough for that to happen. Stockwell's grin was ear to ear as he contemplated out loud and at lenght how Cornelius's Russian clients would thank him for his keen accounting services. Cathryn had wept and wept during that meeting when a gloating Stockwell told her Amen Hale would be sold at auction or turned into a state run tourist trap. Cornelius smiled now as he looked down at Stockwell.

"Agent Stockwell! What a surprise. What a difference a day can make, wouldn't you agree?" Cornelius gave Stockwell a feral grin. "By the way, it seems you were right about the Russians. They did kill me!" Cornelius laughed, but no one else did.

Dark looks were directed at Stockwell by many in the hall, and curious, even suspicious, scrutiny came his way from the other agents who stood around him. The girls on the platform smiled as they enjoyed the sound of their father's laughter. Bethany rose from where she sat at his feet and crawled right up into his lap, pulling her legs up and making herself comfortable right there in the chair with him. Cornelius didn't seem to mind at all and he draped one arm around the child he claimed as his youngest daughter.

"I'm afraid I'm not following this," said Hillary. She didn't like playing catch up and that was what she was doing now. "Would you or Agent Stockwell please explain what you're talking about?"

Cornelius obliged happily, "Your man Stockwell here was kind enough to call some of my Russian clients yesterday and let them know that my records had been seized. I'm sure he would say that he hoped to apply pressure on me to get me to cooperate with his investigation. He laughed in my face and tried to guess who would be the best to call as he thumbed through my rolodex."

Cornelius gave Hillary a wink and a grin. "Since he was complicit in my murder and I have already paid the ultimate price for the crimes of which I am accused,

I shall confess to all." Cornelius chuckled as he looked over at the ashen face of Agent Stockwell as he confessed his crimes with a smile.

"Yes, Stockwell, I was engaged in creative accounting practices to protect my wealthy clients from paying a collective net tax burden of 68%, not counting the inheritance tax. Next to my ancestor, Nathan Hale, I consider myself a true pacifist. He would have raised a militia and started a revolution. In his day he was labeled a patriot. But today he would have been labeled a 'homegrown terrorist.' But me. Money laundering." Cornelius shrugged as best as he could with Bethany in his arms, still wearing a happy grin. "I was fighting the good fight, just in a more peaceful way. However, in one way it seems I have surpassed my most worthy namesake." The happy grin vanished. "It would seem that I have more than one life to give to my country. And this, Agent Stockwell, *is* my country. Amen Hale is mine, and you sir, are not welcome in it."

Cornelius watched as Stockwell excused himself and walked toward the doors. Two grim faced servants escorted him out of the Hall.

"Now where was I?" said Cornelius.

"Money," supplied Hillary.

"Oh yes. Thank you. A topic easily covered." Cornelius smiled. "We simply have no need for it. We can make almost everything we need. We seek nothing from the outside world for ourselves. Our population is currently four hundred and seventy-three souls, or seventy five now that we have Izzy and Lizzy. We intend to expand to a thousand or fifteen hundred at most, but no more, I think. We have absolutely no plans to engage in high finance or the affairs of the powerful. Other than food and some of the most basic items of life, we do not need money. We will not damage the world's economy. If you choose to forbid us access to American soil then we will simply go to other nations with our needs for trade and travel and leisure. We want to live in peace and quietly take care of our own, like Izzy and Lizzy, but with that said, I do believe it's time we discuss the dirty business of yesterday afternoon." Cornelius's brows cut into a deep V as he eyed Hillary and her delegation. "Who destroyed the military convoy and the limo carrying Black Rain yesterday afternoon?"

"That's a more difficult question than you might think," Hillary replied. "It was an odd group of current and ex-military from a number of different countries. Even the soldiers involved in the attack didn't know who was in charge. There were French, Italian, Chinese, and even some German soldiers in the group. The men we've questioned all say that they were acting without the permission of their governments. When we ask why they did it, they all say the same thing: that the threat posed by Black Rain and the others from the drug study was too great to allow them to live. All the men appear to be deeply religious. We're looking into how big a part that played in this."

"How is it playing out in the news?" Cornelius asked. "Believe it or not, I haven't had a chance to watch the news since I rose from the dead, so I have no idea of how the world or America has responded to the attack."

Hillary let the comment about his so-called "resurrection" pass without challenge and just answered his question. "The European governments are claiming ignorance and are making a public show of surprise at the actions of their own soldiers. U.S. forces are on a war footing we haven't seen since the Cuban Missile Crisis, and some in Congress have started calling for all troops oversees to be recalled immediately to bolster our numbers at home. There is serious talk of abandoning our bases in Germany, South Korea, Iraq, and a dozen other countries altogether. The rumor mill in the press suggests that these nations who were involved in the attack were afraid of the tactical advantage the U.S. would gain with Black Rain here in America. And now these same nations that tried to kill her are contacting us and insisting on having the right to 'kiss her' instead." Hillay sneered, coloring the words and the intentions of these countries as ugly and two faced. "They want their ambassadors to have access to Amen Hale. They see Rain as a wishing well and are demanding the right to cast in their coin."

Hillary kept her face all business, but inwardly her heart did happy cartwheels as she watched the grim faces in front of her process her play on words. Rain was still out of the room so she felt at liberty to talk freely about her. Black Rain's presence changed the atmosphere in the entire Hall—the lighting, the air, the way sound carried, and more. Hillary was overjoyed to have the girl elsewhere while she spoke with the King and Queen and tried to make some type of progress in dealing with these people. The meeting had been a complete bust on many points, but they were still gaining valuable intel and priceless insights into this incredibly bizarre situation. Just seeing how the power structure was arranged was fascinating. It truly was like stepping into the pages of a child's fantasy novel.

But Hillary knew that the reality of what was happening here was a lot uglier than the pretty picture that Cornelius and his wife were trying to project. The noble and fatherly king and his motherly queen didn't exist. They were make-believe. Cornelius was simply a lying and manipulative con man. A desperate criminal who was about to lose everything and go to jail. An incredibly lucky con man who had this set of uniquely fragile and mentally unstable teens fall into his lap. And now he and his wife had control of most of these children that were a part of the drug study as well as the others who'd developed powers of their own. If these people would actually *stay dead*, Hillary would suggest that Cornelius and Cathryn be removed, permanently, for the good of the teens and the security of the country. But these people had a nasty habit of rising from the dead, and if they tried and failed things might go badly. Very badly.

Hillary continued with her attempts at negotiation. "Over 233 American soldiers and thirteen civilians died when these people tried to assassinate Black Rain. Now these same nations that attacked us insist on meeting with you, Nation to Nation. Whether you wish to be an isolationist or not, or even pacifists, your existence has just cost a hell of a lot of American lives. Young Americans that have given all they had to keep you safe. And if these nations get more aggressive, it very well could mean war. What then, King Cornelius? Will you stay behind your wall and watch the country Nathan Hale died for burn or will you help us? Your daughter is the one who got us into this mess in the first place."

Cornelius considered what she said, but another interruption from one of the girls turned the whole discourse into a screeching train wreck.

"Bullshit," Emma said simply. "It's bullshit. Someone knew what was going on or they wouldn't have tried this. There's no damn way those countries would have allowed those soldiers to come here unless someone up the ladder in our own government gave them the okay. Hell, I'm just seventeen but I've got the sense to know grade A bullshit when I smell it. Am I wrong on this or what?" Emma glanced around at those on the platform, seeking support for her bovine feces hypothesis.

Cathryn certainly seemed to be taking her seriously. She looked intrigued as she sat forward in her chair. "Emma. I have yet to see you be wrong in anything you name, but let me ask you a question if I may. And don't laugh, this is a serious question, but it will sound silly. But don't laugh. Mary that means you too."

Mary was still half wrapped up in the blanket she shared with Emma, and Cathryn gave her a hard look and waited until Mary nodded before she asked her question. "Emma, did you just think or guess that it was all bullshit, or did you 'feel' it?" she asked. "How did you know?"

Mary didn't laugh but she did slap a hand over her mouth to keep back the giggles that wanted out. Emma was stone faced as she thought about the question. Something made her speak—she had felt something—she couldn't describe what or how or why but it was something.

"I felt it."

Hillary was frustrated beyond reason. How many times would this meeting degenerate into nonsense!? "Are you trying to say that we attacked our own people or that someone in our government allowed this to happen? Don't take offense here, but you think that I'm lying to you because Miss Tate here 'felt' bullshit in the air? Am I following this or did I miss something somewhere?"

Some of the Feds and those with Hillary actually laughed at that witty repartee, but Hillary could see that she wasn't winning any points on the other side of the table and she quickly moved for a subject change. Fortunately she had a couple of perfect ways to get the job done quickly.

"King Cornelius, I assure you that I had no prior knowledge of this attack, but while we are on the topic of being honest, how do we know we can believe anything you say? You just confessed to being a career criminal. You're a professional liar, so how does the U.S. government trust you to keep your word since you're unwilling to commit your words to a written form? And what are we to do about the parents of the children that you've abducted? Mary Hillman's parents are keen to have their daughter back home and the parents of Emma Tate spoke to me just this morning. I assured them that I would ask you myself to return their daughter to them. They want Emma to come home. Miss Tate's not even a witch like the others and her parents are very vocal in their desire to have her back home."

"Tell my folks not to sweat it," Mary said. "Bethany and I are gonna go hang out at Rain's house for movies and pizza tonight; we'll be there at eight. Could you tell my folks to meet me there?" She waited for an answer but got blank face back from Hillary. "Well, you gonna talk to my folks for me or not?" Mary asked again, annoyed.

"I've got it!" one of Hillary's aids answered. "Eight pm tonight at the Bryants'. They'll be there." He had a pad and pencil, scribbling away.

"Thanks, Harold," Mary answered. Of course, she knew his name. He looked up from his pad and she gave him smile and a wink.

Hillary ignored the interruption and focused on the one girl who wasn't a witch. "Miss Tate, you can come with me when I leave. You're not a part of this. You can walk out of here right beside me if you want and be back with your parents. This is not a safe place. You should go home where you belong."

"No one is making me stay here, except me." Emma sounded sure of herself as she spoke. "If you think I don't know how crazy this is then you're wrong. I do. And it is crazy," she admitted. "But I want it. I choose it. This family. This life. This fate." Emma turned away from her and stared at Mary who was wrapped in the blanket with her.

"Is there anything that you would like us to tell your parents?" Hillary asked sadly. "Any message for them?"

"Yes," Emma said. She closed her eyes and took one deep breath, then grabbed Mary's hand. Together they crawled forward and slipped off the end of the platform. The two girls walked hand in hand to the center of the open space between the two groups and stood facing Hillary.

"Tell my parents this for me." Emma turned and faced Mary, who was crying quietly as she looked at Emma, but Emma smiled at her and spoke loudly for all to hear. "Tell them that I found something in the fire that I cannot live without. So let me burn with her. My name is Emma Hale. White is my color. I'm a witch. I'm a witch. I'm a witch." Emma kept her eyes on Mary as she spoke to Hillary. "Could you tell my mother one more thing for me please?"

"Yes. Of course," Hillary answered. "What is it that you want to tell your mother?"

"Tell her I'm gay," Emma said, and then she leaned forward and kissed Mary. And Mary kissed her back. The wild rush of adrenaline shooting through Emma's body mingled with the tingling sensation on her forehead and the wonderful feel of Mary's silky soft lips sliding against her own. It was a riot of passion and feeling that went beyond explanation. Emma didn't need to look in a mirror to see the mark on her forehead. She knew what it looked like. She knew what she was. And now, so did everyone else.

Kendal Flame

A Star Falls

THE HALL WAS quiet as the two girls walked back to the platform hand in hand; they kissed again quickly before climbing up onto the platform where Cathryn, Cornelius, and Bethany were standing, waiting for them. Cathryn and Cornelius said nothing about the girls kissing and acted like there was nothing odd or in any way deviant in their affection toward each other.

They gathered around Emma, hugging her and looking at her new coven mark. A sickle moon surrounded by four stars was there on her forehead shining brightly. All the girls' tattoos were brighter than ever now that four of them were together in the same place. The four stars were the witch colors of the four witches. Black Rain was the black star, Mary was the green, Bethany was the red star on the left, and Kendal's star had been a red one on the top right, but that star had changed color—now it was white. Kendal's red star was gone, Emma's white stood now stood in its place.

"Kendal," said Bethany sadly. "She's really gone. They need to tell us about Kendal, Mom."

Cathryn nodded and held Bethany and together, like a family, the group turned and looked back at the waiting group of Federal agents and those who accompanied the Secretary of State. They all looked a little shell shocked and none too pleased after hearing Emma's little speech and seeing the two girls who said they were sisters acting very "unsisterly." Hillary and the others looked disgusted and suspicious, as if they were waiting for the next shoe to drop any moment, watching for the servants to start handing out cups with poisoned Kool-Aid.

Cornelius spoke. "Madam Secretary. It's time we heard the news of our missing witch. What has happened to Kendal Flame?"

Hillary had hoped that this would have waited until later, much later, but she turned to Agent Shaw and waved him forward. Shaw had a yellow envelope in his hands and he approached the platform and handed it to Emma who then handed it to Cornelius. Everyone watched as Cornelius walked over to his chair, sat down, then slipped the 8x12 glossy photos out of the envelope and held them in his lap. He looked at each one for a minute before picking up another photo from the stack. There were fifteen photos to go through and the room waited in silence and watched while their grim faced King put down one photo and picked up another. When he was done he put all the photos back inside the envelope and sealed it up.

"Emma, please hand this back to Agent Shaw."

Emma did as she was asked wordlessly, then went back to Mary who was shivering again. Cathryn picked the blanket up from the platform and wrapped it around the two girls.

"Be brief. Tell us what happened," Cornelius said to Shaw.

"She was abducted at a gas station five miles from here late Tuesday night. They drove her to a secluded wooded area on the north side of town where they murdered her." Agent Shaw seemed like he would like to stop there but then added the additional grisly details. "She was abused. Crucified upside down and then burned alive. We have agents working the case right now. Evidence at the scene suggests religious extremists were the ones responsible."

Cornelius and Cathryn quietly discussed Kendal with the girls. They asked if she had anyone whom she cared about that should be cared for now. Her mother, a niece she always sent a birthday card to every year, and Steve, her boyfriend of four years, were the only people that the girls knew of that Kendal cared about. Cornelius had Byron bring some cash, a hundred thousand dollars, which was given to Agent Shaw. Cornelius asked him to see to the funeral expenses and any travel expenses incurred by the family and to divide the rest up among the niece, her mother, and Steve.

Cathryn came off the platform and took about ten minutes to tell those in Amen Hall about who Kendal Flame had been, how she had lived, whom she had loved. Mary stepped forward and added some herself, telling a couple of short stories about Kendal that made everyone either laugh or cry. Bethany spoke also. Her sweet little voice broke over and over as she told how Kendal had given her a place to hide from the men who tried to hurt her and how she finally took her away from her horrible mother who wanted to put her out on the street as a whore so she could get more drug money. Rain wasn't there, but Mary told how Kendal had taken in Rain and what a mess she had been when they first found her, wandering the streets of their trailer park like a zombie, wearing nothing but black.

Then Cathryn told all those in the Hall again exactly how Kendal had died. It was a solemn room. No one had come expecting to be present at a funeral, but now they had seen Rain die before their eyes and rise again. They had watched Lizzy be born again and walk from the mirror and now, here they were, at yet another funeral. Everyone in the room had been thorough a wild emotional marathon, a wearing roller coaster of highs and lows. Cathryn was brief and ended with a few final words of thanks to Kendal for the love and life she had shared with them and then told the group of agents that they had thirty final minutes to speak their peace.

Hillary spent her thirty minutes trying to secure a number of promises or commitments which she did not receive. The only reassurance Cornelius gave was that they had absolutely no plans to meet with any foreign governments, nation to nation. Emma described Amen Hale's foreign affairs policy as "Don't call us, we'll call you." A frustrated and worn out Hillary actually smiled and told Emma that she liked it.

Cornelius thanked them for coming and called for Lizzy and Izzy to be brought back into the Hall. Cornelius then told his government guests that Rain had been murdered earlier that day while she was traveling abroad in the world and that she had risen again from the dead. Hillary and her party took that news without flinching. Like it was just another day at the office in "crazy town USA" but Hillary did ask where Rain had been when she was attacked.

"Abroad," Cornelius reiterated and went on speaking. He told them that the man responsible for the crime had been captured and would be sacrificed tomorrow at noon.

"Sacrificed?" asked Hillary.

"Yes. A human sacrifice," answered Cornelius.

Hillary was beyond caring about one idiot that pissed these people off, but Cornelius noticed the worried whispers from the others in her group. "We are a sovereign country. Our ways are not your ways." Here he paused to look over to

Mary and Emma briefly before continuing. "As you have your fun tomorrow and watch us with your spy planes and satellites I wouldn't want you to think we were sacrificing an innocent man. He is a criminal and a murderer. And I have no doubt you were already curious as to who we buried out in the garden earlier this evening. It was the body of my daughter, Black Rain. And let me remind you that the borders of Amen Hale are not to be breached, should some inquisitive person in your government want to send someone over the wall with a shovel."

Cornelius looked back to where Lucius stood and nodded. Lucius came forward carrying a huge wicker basket of spyware, bugs, and listening devices which he dumped out in front of the Feds. They glanced briefly at the electronic spyware garbage but mostly their eyes drank in the sight of Lucius himself. The man they all used to know as Major Tom Benistin.

His tanned, leathery skin was smooth and pale now and his somewhat balding, blond hair was gone, replaced by a full head of short spiky black hair. He was about twenty pounds lighter now and his sky blue eyes had changed to black. He looked twenty years younger, lean and powerful. His face, intense. There didn't appear to be a shred of doubt in the man; his body and posture was one of someone who knew his place and was standing in it. Many of them also noticed that one of his hands was now as black as night. Lucius was an impressive persona as he stood there and eyed the visiting group of his ex-associates while they returned his scrutiny and studied him like some exotic creature—no longer human—something else now—and no one was quite sure exactly what.

"If men enter Amen Hale again, uninvited, I assure you, Madam Secretary, there will quite literally be hell to pay," Cornelius cautioned. He smiled and ended the meeting on that high and encouraging note. Agent White and Lizzy entered the Hall with David and Dana. David, Dana, White, and his man Watkins all looked sick to their stomach and so did Lizzy as her red eyes quickly scanned the room for Izzy.

"Where's Izzy?" she asked.

"She's coming now, Lizzy," Cathryn told her.

Believer entered the Hall a moment later, walking in alone and Lizzy hurried over to him.

"Where's Izzy? You were supposed to keep her safe! You promised!" she accused. Looking behind him, around him. "Where is she!?" Lizzy shouted.

Believer put his hands up in a calming gesture. "She's right here, Lizzy." Believer touched a cloudy hand to his chest. "My Love asked me to hold her and Izzy within my body so she could rest and recover. They are coming out right now."

Believer lowered himself to his knees in front of Izzy. Everyone watched as a hand pushed its way out of Believer's chest, then an arm, legs, and then Rain and Lizzy both emerged from the billowing rolling clouds that made up Believer's body.

They both wore odd expressions on their face and were soaking wet as they stepped out of his body. Together, they both looked up and exhaled at the same time and a cloud of steam came out of their mouths. They laughed together playfully as they watched the hot vapor curl up and away.

"You were right, that was cool," a happy Izzy told Rain.

"It would work a lot better if it were colder in here," Rain commented as she watched the last wisps of vapor vanish away.

"Are you okay!?" Lizzy shouted as she looked her other self up and down.

Izzy was smiling. She looked calm and in her right mind as she answered, "Yeah. I'm better now." Izzy looked back over to Believer who was still on his knees and was watching them with his red eyes that looked like burning coals floating in the midst of rolling crashing clouds. "Thanks, Believer. That was—nice." She sounded very sincere.

Believer smiled at Izzy, his slit of a mouth running from one side of his head to the other. "You are most welcome, Izzy. And welcome to Amen Hale. I'm glad Rain and I could help you," he answered in a deep, rumbling voice.

"What did he do to you?" asked Lizzy as she looked at Rain and Izzy who were both soaking wet.

Izzy sighed happily, "Well. First, he just held me for a while, and then he hugged me."

"He hugged you, while you were inside of him?" Lizzy asked, her face scrunched into a confused question.

Izzy nodded, eyes wide. "Oh yeah. It was amazing. Like floating inside a cloud, I never touched the ground. And then they let me rest for a while, and—I think I fell asleep for a while." She looked over at Rain who nodded helpfully. "Rain was inside him with me, and that was nice. I felt so safe in there." She looked back to Believer. Rain was now wrapped in his arms and they both were looking at her with warm smiling faces.

"I missed you," Lizzy said shyly. She sounded jealous of Believer and all of Izzy's attention that he was getting. She noticed that Izzy was missing a shoe. "Oh crap, your shoe, I bet your feet are cold!" She dashed off to the side of the platform where the shoe had flown when she pitched it after taking the glass out of it. Lizzy ran back over and sat down in front of Izzy, grabbed her wet foot and started working it back into the shoe as Izzy struggled to keep her balance.

"Take the sock off! It's all wet and squishy!" Izzy complained as she tried to keep from falling on her butt.

Rain dried herself and Izzy with a thought so she wouldn't have to squeak every time she took a step while Agent White and his assistant rejoined their party and David and Dana resumed their seats.

"Agent White, I trust that you have what you need," Cornelius asked him.

White nodded. "Yes, King Cornelius. I believe I do. It was a very—informative session." White left unsaid what was plain to read on his face. He had some work to do. At Pembrooke and perhaps a few other places as well. After a few final farewells, Lucius and Sky Dragon led the government delegation out of the hall and toward the gateway out at the wall.

And so ended the first official state visit between the Kingdom of Amen Hale and the United States of America.

Black Rain

Nothing Is Scarier Than Love

BELIEVER AND I slipped to the side of the room out of everyone's way as Cornelius and Cathryn spoke for a few minutes and then released the people of Hale from where they stood their weary vigil all about the Hall. Instantly the room flooded with noise and activity. I was glad I was out of the way because it got crazy fast and the platform got rushed by a tidal wave of excited people. The crowd gathered around Mary and Bethany and Emma like they were rock stars, everyone wanting to meet them for the first time and talk to them for themselves. Others surrounded Sky and Ryan and David and Dana, although they gave the burning crowns some cautious space. Even Sky Dragon seemed swamped with hangers on and I laughed and pointed to him.

"Believer! Look at your brother!" I heard his deep rumbling laugh join my own. We could barely see Sky Dragon through the press of people, asking him questions and wanting to speak with him or even just touch him and see what he was made out of. I wondered for a minute why I wasn't being rushed like everyone else until I noticed that I was, but my crowd was very different.

People were forming a ring around our little alcove hiding place, up against the wall. They were making a half circle about twenty feet back from us, dropping to their knees, and looking at us worshipfully. Looking at me actually. There were more than two dozen men and women, and more were coming, walking over and kneeling down quietly and joining the others already on their knees. They didn't say anything to us and they kept their distance, being respectful of our personal space in our little out of the way niche, but at the same time they wanted to be near me.

"Look at Izzy and Lizzy, my love." Believer pointed to them. He was so tall he was looking out over the heads of those gathering around us. Believer noticed me on my toes trying to see and lifted me up into his arms.

A group of people had gathered around Izzy and Lizzy, welcoming them to Amen Hale. They were smiling and laughing with them and Izzy was laughing and smiling too. It was good to see her happy. Lizzy was happy too, and she was right beside Izzy. Right where she wanted to be and needed to be. It was a much happier ending than mine had been with Rain Marie, the girl who had made me. And it was a better ending than the one Izzy had planned for herself tonight, bleeding to death, all alone in a little padded room. This was better. Even if she lost her mind and still killed herself tonight, at least she wouldn't die alone. Alone sucked.

One of the servants called out for everyone to please go to the dining hall. "Dinner is now served!" His voice rang out but very few people moved toward the exits. The kitchen staff had been working away, preparing to feed the four hundred and seventy-five hungry souls that now called Amen Hale home but everyone seemed content to ignore dinner altogether and crowd around the royalty of Amen Hale. A few words of encouragement from Cathryn got people going in the right direction and the room finally started to clear as people headed toward the Grand Dining Hall that I had formed this morning.

I watched as a few of the kneeling people around us rose reluctantly to their feet and headed off to dinner but others stayed where they were. I wondered what I should do as I watched one man who looked like he was praying. He rocked back and forth on his knees as he looked right at me, his lips moving soundlessly.

Should I tell all of them to stop? Should I forbid them from doing—what exactly *were* they doing anyway? Were they worshiping me? Were they praying to me? It was all wrong. It was all sin. But then—I had prayed to "me" too. I didn't know what to do.

Believer was looking at my face, studying me as I looked at the crowd and he could tell that I was uncomfortable. Undecided. Confused. So he took care of me. "Rise. Go to dinner now, my friends." Believer's voice rumbled kindly to the last dozen or so still on their knees and they finally rose and walked away leaving us to ourselves.

Soon the only ones left in the Hall were the servants who were working and cleaning or those who were the royalty of Amen Hale. A King, a Queen, some Lords and Ladies and a big bunch of Princesses. Believer and I were still hiding out in our spot beside the wall. He held me in his arms as I watched the room with him. I was enjoying being still and apart from everyone, just watching the others. They were my family. All of them.

I watched as they stood together, talking and laughing and playing. As I watched, some white puffy clouds appeared over Ryan and Sky's head that quickly shaped into two cloudy crowns that glowed and sparkled like blue diamonds next to David and Dana's burning crowns. Everyone laughed for a bit, then Sky let their crowns fade away and they all started talking of other things.

We stayed apart. Believer held me, and we enjoyed the stillness as we watched them for a while, until Sky Dragon broke away from the group and ran over to our quiet little niche. The ridges over his reptilian eyes were pulled together, making him look angry or worried.

"Brother, a group of them want to go over to Rain's parents' house tonight for dinner and to spend some time watching movies. Lucius has two dozen men he's sending with us but I would feel better if you came too. It's not safe out there."

"No one will leave Amen Hale till I have seen them first!" I commanded, my voice filled with a power that lashed through the Hall and snapped every head my way. Sky Dragon's eye ridges shot up as I continued in a voice that I hardly recognized as my own. Filled with power and more.

"You will bring those who wish to go before me! If they smell like death is waiting for them, I will know it! I will smell it—and I will be very, very pissed off." My skin felt warm as my temper flared and my power began to spill free. The thought of danger to my family had my heart to racing, and I ground my teeth as dark thoughts formed unbidden in my mind. I still didn't even know what had happened to Kendal, but I knew she was dead. Kendal was gone but I would not let that happen to the rest of my family!

I WOULD NOT!

My hair blew about my shoulders like I stood in a gale and the light around me seemed to change color too, becoming more amber, a more somber tone of white, like my mood had darkened the light itself and shaded it with my rage. The air itself around me felt alive with my power and I began to glow.

People screamed. All over the room servants and even my own family cried out, plates fell to the ground—and people fell to the ground—some falling to their knees or just turning away, shielding their eyes to keep from looking at me as my power raged through the Hall. I felt Believer's arms wrap around me and hold me to his chest and try to cool me and my raging temper and I heard him groan.

Only the horrifying thought that I was hurting him helped me get myself under control again. My rage broke and I pulled in with all my will and brought my power back within myself. "Believer," I said quietly. All I could see were his arms. Rolling clouds. His body and arms were wrapped around me, cooling me, but now the only thought in my head was terrified worry that I may have hurt him somehow with my power.

"Believer! Are you okay!?" I shouted.

"Yes, my love. I'm all right." He said the words, but he sounded subdued. Believer didn't lie but something sounded off.

"Let me see you," I said.

"Rest a while first, you're still upset, my love, I can feel your heart. It's still racing." His voice sounded a little more like himself, and that sounded exactly like what he would say, so I calmed down.

"I'm not angry anymore. I'm just scared now," I told him.

"Believer." I couldn't see him but I heard Sky Dragon's voice. "How is she?"

"She's resting, my brother, but she'll be fine. Do as she asked and gather those who wish to go."

"All right. Will you be staying with her now or will you be coming with us?"

"Please, go with them," I whispered to him.

Believer growled his complaint and his body rumbled like the soft roll of distant thunder that gently vibrated my body and bones like the purring of a galactic-sized cat, but Sky Dragon had heard me tell him to go and he answered me himself, sounding relieved as he ignored his grumpy brother.

"Thanks, Sis. I'll go bring the others to you so you can smell them."

I rested for a few minutes and listened to the noises around me and spoke with Believer. He still didn't let me see anything and carefully kept me covered in clouds and I wondered why, but he described what was happening. It was soothing, listening to his deep voice as he painted the picture that he would not let me see.

The hall had been mostly empty, only a dozen people had fainted but they had all revived and were up and on their feet again and seemed none the worse for the experience. A few plates and dishes had been broken and one man had hurt his arm when he fell into some glass on the floor. Believer said that Dr. Burgis was already attending to the man, stitching the cut. When I said that I could heal him Believer laughed and said no. He said that the doctor looked very happy to be of use and that it looked like a very small cut anyway. He told me that Sky Dragon had already explained to my family what had upset me and why I lost my temper. He said that no one was upset or angry at me. Everyone was fine.

"Those going to your parents' house are ready to see you, my love. I'm going to release you, but I want to tell you quickly about a few other changes. It's nothing bad or harmful in any way, but you should know now so it does not surprise you."

"What changes?" I asked, worried.

"You are glowing, my love. As am I."

"How bad?"

Believer laughed. "You'll see. A few of the servants who were standing close to us have had their hair change color a little. Some white streaks in their hair, and they also are glowing, but not like you. Or me."

I could hear my family talking in hushed tones; it sounded like all of them, close by, listening. "Okay, let me out, let me see them and make sure they'll be okay before they go."

Believer took his arms away from my eyes and stepped back and I could finally see the room. It was still standing, and servants were moving about like before, doing their work. In front of me stood my family; they looked okay except for the way in which they looked at me. Wide eyed and staring, but some of them looked away from my gaze. Dana looked at the floor and Bethany looked over me, like she was staring at the ceiling and she looked ill. Some of the others squinted as they looked at me like I was hurting their eyes. I raised my hand and looked at it.

"Yep. I'm glowing," I said, stating the obvious. It wasn't ridiculously bright but there was an obvious glow coming out of me. Somehow my skin seemed too thin or translucent now and some of my power shone right through. I missed my old thick skin that kept all of me hidden inside and out of sight.

"How do you feel, Rain?" Cathryn asked. She squinted as she looked me in the face.

"Fine, Mom. Sorry I lost it. I didn't hurt anyone, did I?"

"Oh. We're all fine, dear," Cathryn said adding a tight smile to her tight eyes.

"Bullshit," Emma said, her flat voice stating the truth when no one else would.

Everyone except Emma laughed like that was the funniest thing they'd ever heard, including Cathryn, and some of the tension seemed to vanish as Emma doled out her squinty-eyed glare at all the laughing faces like she was daring anyone to say she was wrong. I wondered if I'd missed something. It didn't seem that funny.

Cornelius spoke once everyone had a good laugh at Emma's expense. "Of course our Emma is correct. As she always is it seems." He gave her an affectionate smile and she nodded, content with that word of praise from her new father as Cornelius continued. "Perhaps 'fine' is a bit too strong a statement. To put it simply, my child, we are all amazed, and—still recovering from seeing your power."

Cornelius glanced away briefly from my eyes before continuing. "Feeling you unleash your—anger or power or glory or whatever that was—I can't think how to describe it. It was quite an experience." He squared his shoulders and forced himself to stare into my face for a moment. "It was godlike, my child."

"Hey! No blasphemy till I'm out of ear shot please," Ryan complained.

"Oh! Oh my word!" Cornelius turned red as he looked back at my brother and his frowning face. "My apologies, Ryan. Quite thoughtless of me—sorry."

"Godlike?" Ryan said and raised an eyebrow at Cornelius and then looked down at Sky. She just shrugged and cuddled up next to him. She didn't look concerned one way or the other.

"I should have worded it another way, Ryan. I meant no offen—"

"Yeah, yeah, yeah," Mary cut in, "come on God lady, sniff us, we're late already." She pushed to the front. "My folks are meeting me at your parents' house and I'm in for a hell of a lot of yelling tonight so sniff us already, so you don't go all 'END of the World!' on us again." Mary mimicked my voice exactly and even used her own magic to make her words echo around the Hall, scaring the hell out of the servants. Again.

She stepped forward, put one arm high in the air and pointed to her arm pit with her other hand, waiting to be sniffed as she gave me a wicked grin. I laughed along with the others, gave her pit a good sniff and then did the thumbs up.

"No death. Just some good old nasty Mary funk. Next!" I called out. The assembly line for the sniff test went quickly and thankfully no one else made me sniff their pit.

"Blessed Be," I said out loud happily when I was done checking the last person. No one was facing death on this trip.

Lucius and some of his new security detail arrived but waited at the doors for the group to exit. I was surprised to see that they all had guns. Lucius could come and go through the gateways as he wanted now, so who knew what else he may have been buying in Paris. Guns and clothes for sure. All of his men had identical black leather jackets, pants, boots, and fancy belts holding all their guns. Just looking at them made me worry. I'd be glad when everyone got back to Amen Hale. Back to what was now our home.

I wished them well and told them to tell my mom and dad that I loved them. Believer, Mary, Bethany, Ryan, Sky, Sky Dragon, and her mother and father who planned to call their driver from the Bryants' and head home from there. My glowing husband followed the group as they headed toward the kitchen area and the magic door that would take them to my bedroom in my parents' house.

My skin was glowing some but Believer's was worse. It was as if he'd absorbed the light down into his center and now his gray rolling stormy clouds were lined in silver light as if there was a tiny sun hiding inside his body, trying to shine through the clouds. He lit up the hall as he walked along with the group. He had always looked amazing with his rolling billowing clouds constantly crashing about, but now he looked awesome! And even more beautiful than before.

He waved at me before disappearing through the doorway that led into the kitchens with the others but only a second passed and the doors flew open as Mary came charging back into the Hall. Mary ran straight up to Emma, threw her arms around her, and KISSED HER! Right on the lips! And Mary wasn't playing around either; she did it like she meant it! And Emma looked like she was more than happy with it! She kissed her right back! Mary pulled away, put a hand over her mouth, giggled, then dashed off without saying a word, disappearing back through the doors to go with the others.

I knew my eyes had to be as big around as saucers, but no one else seemed freaked out in the least. Not Cathryn or Cornelius or even David or Dana—or even Emma! Everyone just started talking again, like everything was as normal as normal could be. Same ol', same ol'.

Same ol', same ol', my ass! White rabbit with a wrist watch! What—THE—hell—was—THAT!? What the freakin' hell was goin' on!? Did I really just see what I just saw? What was next!? I could almost see the group of acrobatic midgets as they burst through the doors and started their cartwheels and flips, swallowing swords and spitting fire. And here came the marching band and girls in tights waving their parade flags around with "WTF!" spelled out in bright red letters on white fields. And then the one-eyed one—

"Rain honey? Rain!" Cathryn said. "Are you okay?"

I blinked and look at her. She was looking at me along with the others like I'd missed something. They all eyed me with concern. I wondered how long I had been gone.

"Sorry. I'm sorry, I was just daydreaming again, Mom. I'm okay."

"Rain. You don't have to apologize for it." She came forward and gave me a hug and kissed me on my glowing forehead and felt my brow with the palm of her hand. I noticed the tightness at the corners of Cathryn's eyes as she looked in my face and check me out. I hoped this damned radioactive glow wore off soon so everyone could look at me again without needing shades. "You're still a little warm, Rain. Try to stay calm. Come to dinner with us where I can keep an eye on you."

"No, I can't." I reached up and took her hand off my forehead. "I need to take that man to the Crypt right now, before it gets any later. Jane and Dan will wake up tonight and I don't want to be in there when they do."

Cathryn nodded, then called some servants whom she told to bring the man I needed, bound and gagged for me. They rushed off to do her bidding. "You should take some servants with you to keep you safe and to carry the man for you."

I laughed. It was a strange laugh, unlike myself. Whispers of power danced around me for an instant, somehow caught up in the sound of my laughter.

My new mother looked a little unsettled, but she tried again. "You shouldn't go alone."

"I'm not. Emma's going with me, Mom."

She looked at Emma with surprise. "You are?" Emma nodded.

"Leave your daughter to her business, Cathryn," Cornelius told her. "Let's go eat before our household leaves us nothing but bones on a plate and few empty bottles of wine for our dinner."

"Oh hell no. Let's go, David," Dana said and started to pull David toward the Dining Hall.

"You're that hungry?" David asked.

"Hell no! But you only let me drink two glasses of wine earlier today," she complained. "After all this shit, I need to get wasted, David. I'm sorry." She looked over at him and was surprised to see that David held a lit cigarette in his hand. He handed it to her wordlessly. "I thought you wanted me to quit."

"We've got time, love. We've got time," David told her as he held the door open for her and they walked out.

"They're such a beautiful couple," Cathryn said wistfully as she watched them go out.

"I agree. Let's get going." Cornelius slipped his arm through Cathryn's and started guiding her toward the doors very much like Dana had done with David but with much more grace. He definitely wanted some solid food for dinner, not just wine.

"Be careful, Rain. Keep her safe, Emma!" Cathryn called to us as Cornelius pulled her along and out the doors.

The Cathedral Hall was empty, except for the two us standing in the middle of the room and a few scattered servants, cleaning.

"What on earth was that, Emma?" I asked her. "With you and Mary?" I added when it seemed she didn't know what I was getting at.

"Oh. I forgot," Emma said. "You weren't in the room. You don't even know about the mark." Emma was looking right at me and I finally focused in on her forehead and my eyes went wide.

I couldn't believe I hadn't noticed it before; it was right there, big as day, staring right at me from her forehead. I noticed that Kendal's red star was gone, replaced by a white star. "Emma, you—" I began.

"Yes," Emma said, cutting me off. "I did."

"And you did it in—"

"In front of God and everyone," Emma finished my words again.

"But, what did you bring as—?"

"An offering?" Emma finished my sentence yet again, and a slow wicked smiled stole onto her face. I realized that the little witch was having fun, watching me freak out in tiny little bites. "I had my offering with me." Her smiled deepened and she stepped closer to me. "I brought the same thing you did, my Sister. The very darkest secret of my heart."

I gave her back one of her own squinty-eyed glares she liked to dole out as I thought it through. "You like girls!" I somewhat guessed and sort of accused.

"Yes," Emma said without a hint of shame.

"You like Mary." I squinted my eyes further, adding up the pieces. Assembling the clues.

"And?" She looked at me. That stumped me for a bit, but then the light came on and it made perfect sense.

"And you like Jane!" I said triumphantly.

"And—I like you," Emma said as she looked at me with an intense, smoldering gaze that made me realize with a scary little thrill that *I*—was on the *menu!* And Emma was HUNGRY!

I swallowed and blinked. My brain slipped into neutral for a moment and the gears ground and slipped as I tried to think of what to say. I stuttered out, "But—umm. Aaah. You know, I'm married, Emma," I said uncertainly. This would definitely go to the top of my list of weird things. Or almost the top, I amended, as I considered how weird my life was these days.

"I'll talk to Believer," Emma said. She didn't sound discouraged in the least by my matrimonial status. She raised a hand to her chin and bit her index finger as she eyed me up and down and thought through the "married" dilemma. "Perhaps if I ask real nicely Believer will share you with me, if I promise to love you with all my heart too. But that's hardly a bargain because I already do." She tilted her head to the side as another thought occurred to her. "Or maybe I could just join you two."

"JOIN US!" I squeaked/shouted, shocked out of my mind. TOP OF THE LIST! TOP OF THE *DAMNED* LIST!

Emma laughed as she watched me freak out. "Yeah," she said with a big smile.

"You're serious!" I accused, my bottom jaw hanging open as I stared at her with my black eyes.

"Yes, Rain." Emma shrugged. "Unless you just don't like girls in that way. Period. Ever. End of story. I'm okay with that if that's what it is. I love you and I always will. We're Sisters." She eyed me with something that was definitely NOT a sisterly look as she added, "But if I can have you, I want you, Rain. You're beautiful."

I could tell that she meant it. My heart was pounding and I could feel my power rising and starting to get away from me so I closed my eyes and took deep breaths, trying to calm down a bit. I didn't want to have another melt down.

"Please. I need a minute," I said between deep calming breaths. In and out. In and out. In and out.

Emma was silent. I kept my eyes closed as I continued to talk. "I really didn't see this coming."

"That's the funny thing," I heard her voice say. "Mary did. From the first second she touched me, she knew, and she still wanted me. Mary saw everything I kept hidden from everyone else, down inside my heart, and she still loved me just the way I am. She wanted *me*. She wanted Emma."

I didn't have to see the smile on her face to know it was there. I could hear it in her voice. She was smiling as she thought about Mary. Emma really loved Mary. And not just as a sister. Emma LOVED Mary. It sounded nice. Not dirty. Not wrong. But if they were a couple, then—"Won't Mary get upset? You guys are together, right?"

"Mary already knows how I feel about you."

"I don't know," I said honestly. "I really don't know if I like girls that way. Let me think about this some, Emms."

"Kiss me. It's the quickest way to see if you like girls."

Yeah, right! I thought. I opened my black eyes and looked at her and raised one suspicious eyebrow.

"Don't be stupid!" Emma grumped, giving me a self-righteous frown. "I'm not trying to cop a feel or trick you into getting drunk and going into a dark closet with me or asking you to play strip poker or spin the bottle! I'm not some silly boy with their stupid little games. I know it sounds weird but it's the quickest way to see if you like girls. Just kiss me, Rain. And you'll know. You'll either like it," she made a face, shrugging with one half of her mouth, "or you won't."

Damn! She made it sound so *reasonable*. "How do you know this is the best way?" I asked, trying to be reasonable too.

"I kissed a girl once. When I was twelve. We were practicing," she squirmed for a moment then added, "for kissing boys." She looked embarrassed at this remembered situation, but she shook it off and boldly asked me again. "Kiss me. If you don't like it, I promise I won't ask again. *I can't lie*," she whispered.

Oh God! My eyes darted left and right. Servants were still around and some of them were even listening to us as they worked. One woman's eyes were as big as saucers as she pushed her wide broom over a spot that already looked swept.

"Right out here, in front of God and everyone," I whispered, instantly terrified.

And just like that Emma looked so serious. Serious and pissed. I really couldn't blame her for being pissed. I knew I was being a wimp.

"Yes! Out here in front of God and everyone!" she snapped. "I don't care who sees me. I already told everyone anyway. The servants know what I am. My old mom and dad know what I am. My new mom and dad know." She threw her arms up in the air as she finished her tantrum with a shouted "Gay! Gay! Gay! So mote it be! Isn't that what we witches say!?"

Emma stepped closer and got right up in my face and looked me dead in the eyes. "You were right, Rain!" she growled. "You told me what it would take to become a witch. And it's exactly like you said it would be. I had to let go of everything I kept bottled up and let my passion take control, *and I did.* I let go of everything, and now it feels like I've been turned inside out." She closed her eyes just like I'd done earlier to try to keep calm. She took a few deep calming breaths of her own but kept talking with her eyes closed, just as I had. "The crazy thing is—I like it. This feels right. I can feel it. I feel it all around me."

I felt something around me as well. Something new. There was a faint hint of a new exotic smell in the air. I stared at Emma. It was her magic. Of course she had magic. Just like Mary and Bethany, it was starting for Emma now. She had power of her own. I wondered what my new Sister's power would be.

She was so close to me as she stood there with her eyes closed that my eyes had no place to go except her chest or her face. So I looked up at her face. Emma was tall, scarecrow thin, and her cheek bones stood out making her eyes the focus of her face. Her eyes were closed but I knew they were an unassuming chocolate brown that looked very plain until she used them on you. Her complexion was nice, but she still had a few blemishes on her cheeks and the beginnings of a break out across her shiny brow. With a thought, I banished them forever and made her skin spotless perfection. I modified her pale flesh. I gave her a light golden completion, like a perfect summer tan.

"I felt that. What did you just do to me?" Emma asked. She didn't sound worried at all, and she didn't open her eyes.

"I made your skin perfect and I gave you a tan. You won't have zits anymore. Just keep your eyes closed and hold still. I'm still working on you."

She nodded but said nothing and kept her eyes closed. Emma's eyes were the focus of her face but her eyelashes were barely there, and her brown eyebrows were thin too. I made her eyelashes become full, long, and dark and made her eyebrows dark but once I was done I wasn't happy with it and I started over and reshaped them again. I worked on her eyebrows and lashes for a while, playing with them and fine tuning until I was more than satisfied. Emma was all about eyes, so they had to be perfect. I added some shading, almost like makeup, to make them stand out.

She had brown eyes. *Should I change them?* I wondered. I didn't ask; I just did it. Her eyes were still closed but that didn't bother me. I changed her iris color hidden behind her lids from brown to what would be a shining, copper gold. An unusual color, but I didn't want to use a common color for her; I needed something different, something unique.

I made her nails long and changed them to the same metallic coppery gold to match her new amazing eyes. There was something wild about Emma now, and it made me want to make the body match the girl. Wild. I moved to her hair. I didn't know what color to go with so I kept it brown, but I changed the color to a deep golden brown and changed the texture, making it silky soft, full, and luxurious. I didn't make her hair straight like the rest of us girls; I gave it some wave and body and made it grow long, almost down to her butt.

Emma didn't open her eyes, but she did lift her hands to her hair, feeling the length. She frowned. "I don't want long hair, Rain. Make it short. I've always wanted it short."

"How short?" I asked, surprised.

"Short."

"Really?"

"Yes." She said it. She meant it. I changed it.

I shortened it a little at a time, trying to find a "look" that looked like Emma to me. I made it very short and spiked, like a boy's hair and I styled it. For color I went with black. I cringed, waiting for her to scream as her hands went to her head and felt the length, but she didn't yell. She smiled as she felt what I'd done.

I noticed her teeth needed work. I placed a hand on each side of her face and opened her mouth with my thumbs. She still kept her eyes closed as I did this and even tilted her head down to me. I'm sure she was hoping for that kiss, but I was all business, looking at her teeth. Since I was remodeling I might as well be thorough.

I was tall for a girl at 5'7", but Emma was positively crane-like, standing six inches taller than me. I couldn't see what I needed to without a bucket to stand on. "You're too damn tall, lady, get on your knees for me," I ordered.

She did as I asked and dropped to her knees and I looked into her mouth. Her top teeth were so-so/okay but her bottoms were a mess. With a thought, I fixed Emma's teeth, making them absolutely perfect, pearl white and straight. I gently closed her mouth, making her bite down.

"I fixed your teeth, Emms, but I'm no dentist, so tell me how that feels. I've never done teeth before."

She opened and closed her mouth a time or two, testing my work. She still had her eyes closed but a hint of a smile touched the corners of her mouth. "Thanks. I know my bottom teeth were gross. But I've got a gap between my teeth now. Here, I'll bite down and you can feel it from the side."

"How?" I asked.

"Just put your finger in my mouth, right on the side so you can feel the gap." She clamped her teeth together and tilted her head to the side she wanted me to feel. This was getting weird.

"This is kinda awkward, Emma, me sticking my finger in your mouth right after you asked me to kiss you."

"Ain't it though?" Emma said, still with her eyes closed. Her mouth was set with a happy, wicked smile.

I couldn't help it. I smiled too. "You fucking witch," I said, but she could tell I was trying hard not to laugh.

"You've already started, you dork! Now fix me!" She laughed and tilted her head to the side for me to feel her teeth.

"All right, all right," I grumbled. I willed the long black fingernail on my index finger to vanish down to the quick and did as she asked. I slipped my finger into her mouth, running it down between the smooth slippery teeth and her warm cheek. I felt the gap where her teeth didn't meet up, top to bottom, with my finger and then Emma leaned her head the other way and I felt the other side. I thought about being able to see through her skin and flesh, like an x-ray, and my vision altered. I watched with my new sight as I did the work I wanted.

"How's that?" I asked when I was done.

"Wonderful," Emma said.

I was still looking at bones and teeth, past her skin as Emma did a few experimental bites. I saw that everything matched up perfectly and let my eyes return to normal vision, surprised to find myself looking right down into her mouth now that she was on her knees. I could see her new perfect teeth. I closed her open mouth with my hands, tilted her head to the side and put my finger in her mouth again, running it across her smooth, perfect teeth. There wasn't a gap any longer— but I already knew that.

Emma tilted her head the other way. I felt the other side. I remembered when Emma had touched my lips earlier, running her fingers delicately over my lips. She said they were blue. She said they were different. I pulled my finger out of her mouth and did as she'd done to me earlier. I traced her lips with my wet finger, barely touching as I went around her thin lips and I felt Emma shiver under my hands. She swallowed like her throat was dry. My own mouth went dry as I watched what my touch was doing to her.

What the hell was I doing! I snatched my hand away like I'd touched something hot.

"Lips!" I blurted out. "Do you want me to do your lips, Emma?" I said in a rush, not because I wanted to do her lips, but because I had to say something! Anything! Before things got out of hand! And I didn't want her thinking I was touching her lips because of something sexual! Shit! Was I?! I could feel something—like my passionate witchy side was trying to rise up within me and get me acting in the moment and doing what "felt" right. Just because it felt right.

But I didn't know if this was right for me! Emma had Mary now, and I had Believer. But knowing how she felt about me was making it hard. Knowing that she wanted me. And knowing that Emma loved me was—was—was damn confusing! And I was married dammit!

And then there was an odd feel in the air. All around us.

"My lips? Really? You can do my lips too?" Emma said, drawing my confused attention back down to her face. She was touching her own lips now, showing her dazzling smile and she looked up at me with her new gold eyes.

My bottom jaw fell open. My God! HER EYES! They were so beautiful! I stared into them—speechless. Dumbstruck and confused. *How!?* I wondered. I couldn't have done this. I knew I was no Picasso or Michelangelo, but the eyes staring back at me said that I was all that and more.

The copper gold eyes I was lost in went wide as Emma watched my reaction, and then her face collapsed into stricken, panic. "What the hell!?" She sounded alarmed. "It's either really, really good, or freakin', barf bag nasty bad! So which is it!?" she demanded.

When I didn't respond right away she tried again but with an edge of desperation in her voice. "Some help here! Do I need to walk around with a bag over my head now or what?" Emma frowned and glared at me with her new eyes as she waited for my answer.

"Please. No bag," my quiet voice replied.

Emma arched one lovely eyebrow and grunted.

"It's good," I whispered.

She watched me, studying me intently, like my face was a mirror that she could see her own face in. "So—you like it?" she asked, still studying my face.

I nodded. "Do you want a mirror, Emma?" I asked, still staring, still trying to figure out how I'd done what I'd done. Even if you paid me a quadrillion bucks I couldn't tell you how I'd done it.

Emma smiled a bit as she watched my face. "No, Rain. I don't need a mirror. I need lips. My lips are too damn thin and they don't have any color. Can you make them black for me?"

I frowned. She frowned as she looked at my frown. "What's wrong?" she asked.

"Emma. You've just become a witch. You really need to be careful. The changes we make now may be the way you are forever," I warned her.

"You mean like Mary's hair." She reached up and touched her new hair and took a moment to admire her new golden nails. Emma smiled as she ran her hands through her hair, feeling the new short cut and the way it spiked at the top.

"Can you even imagine Mary without that green stripe being in her hair?" I told her. "I can't. She wouldn't be Mary without it. It's part of what she is now. Like my black eyes. I'm not 'me' without them."

"I'm not afraid to change." Emma was dead serious as she spoke. "As long as I'm still Emma on the inside, I'll be fine with changing the outside. Now make my lips black." She said it without a shred of doubt in her voice. "And I want an ass," she added and gave me such a sad smile. "I've always wanted a nice ass."

Honestly, how could I refuse a request like that? First, I willed her lips to fill out, giving them just a little more plump and curve, and then I changed them to a shiny, glistening black that looked wet and sinfully delicious.

Next I brought my will to bear on her body. I had Emma stand up so I could see all of her. I wondered for a moment about the best way to add "ass" to someone as tall and skinny as Emma. She was all skin and bones. I finally decided to start by making her whole body more athletic, so I did it that way. Her body toned with added muscle like a professional athlete and I willed just a little additional padding on her rear.

"Turn around," I told her. She did.

I looked at her, but the dress she was wearing hung on her like a sack and hid everything underneath. If she expected me to work on her ass, well, dammit, I needed to see her ass! I willed all her clothes to be gone. And just like that, she was completely naked before me. Emma didn't say a word, but her spine stiffened and her hands reflexively shot to the areas that needed coverage.

"So. How does it feel to be naked, Emma?"

She let out a strained, nervous laugh. "It's kinda weird."

Then she noticed that every servant in the hall had stopped doing whatever tasks they were about. They all stood, staring at her. Men, boys, girls, women. About a dozen people. Emma's head whipped left and right as she eyed each of them in turn until they either looked away, up at the ceiling, down at the floor, or busied themselves, going back to their work.

The moment she had that handled, six men pushed through the doors at the far end of the hall, carrying a man who was bound and gagged. We were standing right in the middle of the room and the newcomers (being men) stopped and stared at Emma, eyes wide, as they gaped at her naked body. She let out a little squeak! She faced them, keeping her naked rear pointed away and tried to cover her front as much as possible with her hands.

"Awkward, ain't it?" I smirked.

She squeezed her eyes shut tight and tried to relax, but I could tell that I'd finally gotten to her. Her cheeks went red with embarrassment and she was shivering, but I wasn't ready to give her clothes yet. I was still working on her ass.

And looking at it. The work I'd already done was obvious; she was muscular now, but not grotesque at all. I was being very, very careful, taking away in some places and adding a bit more definition in others to balance her body out. I walked around her, shaping her flesh in ways I never had before, but I couldn't see everything I wanted to see; Emma's hands were in the way hiding some of the best spots.

"Stand straight! And move your hands!" I ordered roughly.

"You fucking witch!" she growled with all the dark venom she could summon, but she did exactly as I asked, standing straight and tall, arching her back, and even throwing her arms wide so I could see everything that there was to see. Her squinty eyed glare had been transformed into a thing of power and shocking beauty. She stared daggers at me with those eyes as she ground her perfect white teeth framed by her amazing black lips.

I circled her, admiring her beauty, occasionally reaching out and tracing my long black nails across the plane of her perfect back or down one of her arms that she held outstretched, feeling the muscles and tone of her flesh. Across her chest and her new firm breasts and down, I traced the grooves of her well-defined stomach.

Emma was beautiful. And she was our Emma. I looked up to her angry, burning eyes again and saw that they no longer burned with embarrassment or anger. Those flames had been smothered by a different kind of fire that burned hotter. She wanted me, right now. I stepped up to her and ran my hands up the sides of her body, starting low with my hands on her bare ass and rising slowly, over her hips and up her sides, around her shoulders, up her bare neck until I buried my fingers in her short spiky hair. I brought her face down to mine at the same moment I felt her arms wrap around me and pull me against her naked flesh.

"Please, let it be beautiful," I whispered my prayer to myself just an inch from her lips.

"So mote it be," she breathed and kissed me.

Bull Dandridge

Desecration

DELTA ONE HAD crept over the garden wall shortly after full dark and disabled the two sentries who kept watch at the rear of the garden. The boys in their white lab coats had armed them with a custom-made concoction, thanks to the scrapings they'd gathered the previous night, and it took only fifteen minutes for the powerful acid to burn through the wall and into the crypt.

The intruders quietly slipped through the ragged hole then down a steep stairwell until they reached a lighted hallway at the bottom of the stair. The hall was illuminated by glowing crystals set into the ceiling. Each of the tiny glowing points of light above were reflected in the perfectly smooth red glass floor below like shining stars floating in a sea of blood. The walls were smooth and bare of any markings and were made out of the same nearly impervious white material as the outside of the Crypt.

The soldiers moved forward silently, searching rooms, finding them all empty until they came to the last room at the end of the hall. Inside they saw them, lying on a bed in the center of the room. A seventeen-year-old girl and a seventeen-year-old boy. Dead. At least in the way that mattered and made them human. Innocent victims of the doctor and his drugs as far as they were concerned. Instead of the Derm pill, a drug designed to clear up acne, they'd been given dangerous mind-altering drugs that made their own wild imagination come to life and turn them into real vampires.

The scene in the room was too personal to have any flavor of the erotic, even though they were both nude. It looked as if they had made love and then died in each other's arms. When the team first entered, the men were hesitant to touch the couple, but now they moved in and grabbed limbs roughly, as if by being extra harsh and businesslike they could drown out the wrongness of the whole horrible situation. Human hands, hearts, and minds were not meant for this type of work. Machines or wild animals or mindless beasts were better suited for the defilement of the dead.

"What the hell are you waiting for? Pull um apart!" Bull ordered and two of his men reached toward the bed and the two naked figures that lay upon it, wrapped in each other's arms.

"Damn! They're heavy!" Stitch complained as he pulled on the girl's white arm.

"Come over here and feel this, Bull. This isn't like any skin I've ever felt before."

"Screw that!" Bull snapped. "We got no time! None! Just get it done. If we stopped to check out each whacked out piece of shit in this hell hole we'd be here till hell frozes over. I want that female bagged and over that wall in five minutes or its your ass."

"Hold her arm, Stitch, and brace yourself. I got an idea." Tiger got into position, his arms wrapped around the male as he put a huge booted foot right in the naked chest of the female. He pushed with his foot and pulled with his arms. The huge black soldier grunted and strained, veins standing out in his arms and neck as he tried to separate the male from the female that he clung to with a death hold like steel. Stitch hung half off the side of the bed with both of his arms wrapped around one of the girl's arms and his feet braced against the side of the bed as he tried to hold on.

"WHOA!" Stitch yelled as the girl came loose and her dead naked body flew off the bed and crashed into him like a ton of bricks, knocking him to the ground and pinning him to the floor. The dead girl's legs and arms were all around him, her cold dead face rested against his, and her eyes stared into his.

A couple of the men in the room laughed as Stitch lost it and freaked, kicking and twisting around like a man possessed to get the dead girl off and get clear. Bull walked over and grabbed the girl's body and heaved her up off the panicked soldier and clear of the floor letting Stitch scramble away until his back slammed up against the wall of the cavelike room.

"Bag," Bull said, his voice all business.

Red held open the black canvas bag while Bull lowered the girl's body down into the waiting darkness. Her skin was soft and to the touch felt like human skin, but her body was solid and heavy, like a rock. To look at her you'd guess the girl weighed 90 to 100 pounds at the most but she felt more like 180 or more. Her eyes were open and staring sightlessly, like any other set of dead lifeless eyes Bull had seen, and he'd seen his share over the years, but these were different in one very important way. They weren't decomposing like a normal corpse's would after almost three days of being dead. And the smell was all wrong. No smell of death hung in the air, but there was a sweet floral smell instead. Like a bunch of roses were in the room, only there were no plants or roses anywhere.

Stay dead dammit! Stay dead just a little while longer! Bull thought to himself as he reached down and gathered the long black hair that hung outside the bag in his big fist and shoved it down into the sack on top of the girl's white face, hiding her from view before he cinched up the bag.

By the time he was done Stitch had worked through his issues, recovered his cool, and was ready to go. Bull didn't say anything to him, he just let Stitch and Carter take the black canvas bag and get going, up the steep steps and back to the hole they'd burnt into the side of the crypt.

"Bull, I'm ready over here, but I gotta ask. We still doin' it this way?" Tiger held a huge axe in his hands made out of a hardened plastic that was unaffected by the curse around the wall.

Nothing the team had with them tonight had metal except the two guns they'd taken off the guards from Amen Hale they had knocked out on their way in. All of their gear was dense plastic, cloth, or wood. And they were missing three members of their team who had metal plates or dental reconstruction that would have been damaged by the curse if they had tried to go over the wall. Those men waited for them in a helicopter on the other side of the wall just past the range of the curse.

Bull gave Tiger a look. The big black man never went soft, even when asked to do horrible things. This was a first for him and he looked troubled as he flexed his hands on the wooden handle of the big plastic axe. The rest of the team stopped and stood still, waiting to hear what Bull would say. Bull didn't have a problem sharing some of what he knew. Some of it he could tell. The obvious parts. So he spilled it.

"The suits are worried that these two are contagious. They said that these two could make others, and if this got out, vampires could spread like a plague. And on top of that, they're worried about how the male will control all the witches with his mind once he rises. He could make them do whatever he wants. And they think that when these two start walking around again they're going to be out of control and crazy for blood. God only knows what kind of mess it will be. They don't want to take that kind of chance."

Bull gave each of the four men still in the room a quick look, meeting their eyes. "We can't have 'real' vampires out there. If it was my call I'm not sure I wouldn't do the same thing. But it's not my call, or yours. If this all goes to hell, then it goes to hell. This is the job. Let's get it done."

"What about the female? Why are they keeping her alive, Bull?" asked Tiger.

Bull's eyebrows shot up. This was a bit much. It almost sounded like he was going to have a problem here and his eyes got tight, but Tiger didn't back down.

"Bull. If they want them dead I'm totally good with that. I'm with you, it's not my call, killing them makes sense." His hand flexed on the handle of the big axe. "But they don't want them both dead. They want to keep the woman alive. And if the lab coats get their hand on her—" Tiger shrugged. They all knew that the guys in the lab coats never changed, they had no souls when it came to their shit. It's just the way things were.

"So what are you saying, Tiger?" The fact that this was the only time in six years Tiger had shown even a split second of hesitation gave Bull cause to keep listening.

Tiger looked up to the top of the high stairs where Stitch and Carter had probably just cleared the Crypt, headed for the wall and the waiting helicopter on the other side with the body of the female vampire. He looked back to Bull. "I say we kill um both, Bull. You know what they'll do if they get that girl. We don't want vampires running around out there. And I think it would be a lot more merciful for the girl to never wake up than to wake up and find out what happened. This is dirty. This is bad."

Tiger looked at the naked male, stretched out on the bed; his dead staring eyes seemed lifeless but still somehow accused the men who had taken his love. His arms were still bent and frozen into shape, missing the body they had held only minutes ago. The feel in the room was spooky, like any moment the wretched cup would be full to overflowing, the desecration too vast to go unanswered and the dead themselves would rise to speak their peace.

The creepy vibe filled the room and the men from Delta One shifted their feet nervously as their leader rubbed his chin, considering what to do. None of the others said a word. Bull knew that meant they all sided with Tiger on this. Busting into this Crypt to rip these two kids away from each other, right when they thought they were about to rise again and live forever like some kind of fairy tale was a damned cruel thing. Any idiot could tell from the way they died that these two kids loved each other.

But fairy tales belonged in books, not buried in a garden on the banks of the St. Johns River. Life wasn't a fairy tale. Life was ugly and full of shit problems that someone had to face and fix. And today that someone was him. If the blackest and foulest of deeds truly needed to be done, then they damn well needed to be done. But none of that explained why they wanted the girl alive. Tiger was right.

"I hear you, Tiger," Bull finally said. "I'll consider it. But either way, this one's dead. Now get busy."

The big man nodded, stepped up to the bed, and swung the axe.

The Bryants

Witch Etiquette 101

M R. AND MRS. Bryant had planned on having a peaceful evening
with Bethany, with the three of them curled up on the couch watching
movies together, but the evening had somehow ballooned into a crowd
of almost twenty unhappy people packed into their double wide trailer. Mary started it when she decided to come with Bethany, and then she invited her family to
come and soon others had begged their way into the living room as well, other
parents also hoping to see their missing children here tonight.

No one was sure exactly how many of the others were coming with Mary and
Bethany. Mr. Bryant couldn't find the heart to turn away the parents of those with
children involved so the "pleasant" evening was a thing of the past. An oppressive

haze of tension and frustration filled the room like cigarette smoke in a crowded bar as parents paced the floor and complained to one another about the whole ugly, impossible situation.

And to make it worse, the girls were late. They were supposed to arrive at eight and it was almost nine. The Bryants explained to their guests that Bethany, Mary, and the others were going to travel to the trailer that night by using the magic door leading into Rain's bedroom. Everyone had taken a tour of the house and saw Rain's bedroom with its "magic door" painted flat black.

The door was still covered with Bethany's blood and showed the abuse it had suffered at the hands of the police who kicked it in on Wednesday. The lock was broken and the wood around the door frame was splintered, but it still worked for what the girls were using it as. A magic door.

At first, it seemed that everyone accepted the magical transportation as possible, but the girls were late now and people were getting impatient. Mary's father and the others started to whisper mockingly that the "magic door" was broken—but all doubts were gone and the room went silent as soldiers dressed in black marched into the room, pouring out of the empty bedroom. Just like magic.

"Who are you people?" Mr. Bryant demanded boldly, blocking their way forward.

The man in front answered him politely. "Sir, we are the Royal Guard of Amen Hale. We will be outside this home while the Princesses and the Lords and Ladies of Hale are visiting here." That said they walked around Mr. Bryant and out the front door of the trailer.

Everyone pressed against the walls and made room as more than twenty heavily armed men trooped by, their marching feet making a rumbling sound on the floor as they made their way outside. The last of the soldiers stopped in the middle of the room; his was a face Mrs. Bryant recognized.

"Lucius, where on earth are the girls?" she demanded.

"They will be coming through soon, Mrs. Bryant. I wanted to make sure it was safe before they arrived." Lucius studied the people in the room, obviously looking for threats.

Everyone there studied him right back. Lucius had no weapons or guns visible like the other soldiers in black but somehow that just made him appear even more dangerous. More than one set of eyes lingered on his curiously blacked hand or wondered at his pale complexion.

"Is Princess Mary's family present?" Lucius asked the room.

"Mary Hillman's her name! And she's *OUR* daughter!" came the harsh reply from a tall man leaning against the bar in the kitchen. He was wearing jeans and a flannel shirt; he had a long mustache and his long hair was worked into a ponytail that ran down his back. He looked like a construction worker with his sun darkened face and muscular build. He gave Lucius a murderous glare as he walked into the living room and stood beside a blonde woman who had to be Mary's mother.

She was holding the hands of two frightened girls, ten and maybe twelve years old; both had blonde hair and green eyes like their parents. They looked exactly like little "Marys" except for their hair. Mary's hair was white now with one colorful green stripe up front, but Mary's family were all golden blondes.

Lucius gave the angry man a friendly smile meant to reassure and settle him down. "Yes sir, I can see that she is." He gave the Hillmans a friendly nod. "Mary is the one who asked that you be here tonight and she's looking forward to seeing her mother and father again. And I'm sure she'll be delighted to see her little sisters as well." Lucius gave them an easy smile.

The Hillmans all exchanged surprised glances. They'd been told all kinds of horrible things, a hundred different stories each one worse than the one before and now they simply didn't know what to believe. Emma's parents had scared them to death with their version of events. They swore up and down that their daughter had been flat out stolen! Abducted! Kidnapped! They'd seen Bethany's mother on the TV saying that her daughter had actually been stolen from her by Mrs. Bryant herself and then sold to the Hales for money in exchange for sex.

While they didn't believe that for a second they were still very pissed at Mrs. Bryant for almost the same reason. Mrs. Hillman was home yesterday afternoon when Mrs. Bryant showed up and begged her to let Mary come with her. She'd been with a policeman at the time (and she'd been so upset). Both of them were saying that Bethany had hurt herself and run off to hide at the Hale house and they needed Mary to show them where to go, so she let Mary go with them. But then Mary didn't come back home.

The Hillman family was quite upset with the Bryants. The crazy stories about magic and witches they'd heard while they waited for Mary to show up sounded like nonsense. The Hillmans preferred the more understandable version, that an eccentric wealthy couple named Cathryn and Cornelius Hale were claiming Mary as their own daughter along with a few others. Mary's mother and father came here expecting a fight over Mary still being theirs, but now it seemed like they weren't going to get one after all.

Mr. Hillman scratched his head looking a bit confused as he asked, much more calmly. "So, Mary asked for us to be here herself?"

"Yes, she did. But for your own safety and the safety of all those in the room I must ask that you please refrain from calling her 'Mary Hillman'."

"Why?" demanded Mrs. Hillman, her anger and suspicion flaring. "Mary Hillman is our daughter's name! She's OUR daughter! Ours! You hear me, you freak!?" She spat out her insult.

Lucius raised his hands, palms open in a pacifying gesture which drew every eye in the room like a magnet straight to his blackened hand like he was about to cast some type of magic spell. Lucius noticed everyone looking at the hand, grimaced, and quickly put his hands back down by his sides again and made another attempt at getting the room ready for the royal visit. Mary had warned him that it was going to be difficult and she'd been right.

"Please, for the safety of everyone in the house, call your daughter Mary, Mary Fae, or call her my child, daughter, or any other pet name you prefer. Call her anything you like, but please, do not call her 'Mary Hillman'."

"But why?" asked Mr. Hillman. "I don't see what the problem is. That's her name."

Lucius answered him but addressed the whole room as he spoke. "It may be hard for you to believe it or accept it, but your daughter is extremely dangerous now, Mr. Hillman. She is far more dangerous than those soldiers who just passed through this room with their guns. Your child is a witch now. Not the pretend kind, but a real witch. With real magic. And her magic can and does get away from her if she's not careful or if others around her are not very careful in how they conduct themselves. Certain things, or stress can make her lose control of her power, and if that happens there can be accidents."

Lucius paused and ran his gaze across the quiet room before letting it end on Mary's parents again. "Mrs. Bryant can tell you more of what it will be like to have a witch as a daughter, but it's not my place to explain such things. It's my place to keep them safe. You must not call the witches by their birth names."

"He's right," Mrs. Bryant said, drawing everyone's attention. "My Rain almost killed herself the last time I insisted on calling her Rain Marie Bryant. I'll never do it again." She looked away from the angry accusing eyes of the Hillman family and didn't give any additional advice.

"Is Mary changing her name like Rain did?" asked one of the Hillman girls as she looked up at her mother.

"No dear. Not our Mary. Mary's not like Rain. She doesn't wear black all the time and she doesn't forget her own name. Or her family," Mrs. Hillman answered her daughter and then set her challenging gaze upon Lucius.

Lucius could see that the gentle approach had failed so he tried a rougher approach. "CALL HER WHAT YOU WILL!" he shouted loudly, surprising everyone in the room. "But if Princess Mary loses her temper and has an accident and ends up killing one of the other guests here tonight because you insist on calling her 'Mary Hillman' then let the guilt and the responsibility for that choice rest squarely on your head! You have been warned! My job, and the job of the twenty men outside this trailer, is to protect Mary and Bethany. But if they hurt you, they may become so upset that they end up hurting themselves as well. So by protecting you, I am also protecting Princess Mary and Princess Bethany. Now I beg you, for the sake and safety of your daughter, and for all of those in this house, that you heed my warnings."

A dropped pin could have been heard in the silent room. The reality of danger, like static electricity, filled the room. Eyes darted to the dark hallway that the girls would be walking out of any minute.

Lucius continued what he'd started, but more tactfully, as the room was still reeling from his bluntly delivered shock treatment. "Princess Mary and Princess Bethany are dangerous. Caution is needed, but not fear. If you observe a few simple rules of conduct the evening should be pleasant, and safe, for all of us."

Like a flight attendant explaining to a group of terrified first time fliers how to use their seat cushions as floatation devices, ears pricked up and people leaned in to hear his instructions on what *not* to do so they didn't end up dead. Or worse. Their imagination filling in the gaps and dreaming up all manner of possible horrors.

"First, don't surprise them. If you have some shocking news to tell them, do it, but do it calmly and tactfully. While you speak with them don't let your own emotions get away from you, and please, *don't yell at them*. Do you all understand me?" Lucius paused as around the room heads nodded.

Mr. and Mrs. Bryant didn't need the speech, but they both nodded their heads along with the others in the room as Lucius doled out his instructions to the party crashers. They approved of the crash course in witch etiquette that Lucius was administering before the girls arrived and any opportunity for prevention was lost. Better to prevent an accident from happening than to do damage control after one of the girls hurt someone or hurt themselves.

"Again, do not call them by their birth names. Use their fist name or any name for that matter, but not their first and last name together. Don't act surprised or offended if they do something involving magic. No screaming or running from the room. Just relax, take a deep breath, and go with it. Try to stay calm and respectful. The witches may act peculiar so be prepared for odd behavior. Mary must have space, do not crowd her or touch her."

Lucius paused here again to make sure he was understood. "Again, do not touch Princess Mary. Let Mary come to you and touch you first. If she touches you, don't be surprised if she has some type of reaction. It may seem almost like she loses herself for a moment if she touches you but this is normal for Mary. Just give her a minute or two and she'll recover. If she seems dazed for longer than a couple of minutes or deeply troubled, back away, and have Mrs. Bryant attend to Mary at once."

"My God, is it that bad for her?" asked Mary's mother, her face begging to be reassured and told no.

Lucius carefully kept his face blank; facial expression of any kind may have been interpreted as mocking or cruel. "Yes. It is that bad." He gave his short answer then eyed the room as he finished "Witch Etiquette 101."

"One last piece of advice before they arrive. Don't be rude to them. Especially when speaking to or in the presence of Princess Bethany. Do not insult the King and Queen of Amen Hale in her presence. To do so would be unfortunate and dangerous for all of us."

Lucius left the details unsaid but the point had been made, the room was alive with caution now. He added a few final words of caution concerning Sky, Ryan, Believer, and Sky Dragon. He tried to prepare them for their first glimpse of the cloud men. He explained that they could talk and laugh and be offended just like anyone else. He also said that Believer would probably go outside the trailer to stand guard because he was too tall to stand inside the trailer without bending himself almost in two.

"Could you introduce me to the rest of your guests now, Mrs. Bryant?" Lucius asked as he surveyed the room and the people he didn't recognize.

Mrs. Bryant did the introductions, first introducing Lucius to the room as the "Captain of the Guard of Amen Hale" and then she went around the room. Mike and Hanna Hillman, Mary's mother and father, and her two sisters, Kaylee and April.

Careful to use his "human hand" Lucius greeted each person warmly with a hand shake and a smile as Mrs. Bryant introduced them. The simple, normal gesture of a warm handshake improved the dark mood in the room immensely as he worked from person to person, even taking the time to shake hands with the Hillmans' daughters. Mary's grandparents were there. David's father, Mr. Hodges, was there hoping to see his son arrive with the others. Mrs. Bryant introduced Emma's mother and father, both tall and rail thin dressed in dark colored business attire looking grim and worn. It had been a long endless day and night for both of them.

"Will Emma be coming here with them?" asked Emma's mother as Lucius shook her hand.

"I'm sorry. Princess Emma chose to remain behind."

They looked so disappointed as Mrs. Bryant continued the introductions. Rain's grandmother was there as well as Jane's uncle Billy who asked if Jane and Dan were coming and was hugely disappointed with the answer he received as well.

Mrs. Bryant hesitated for a moment on the last person who had been tucked away in a corner the entire time, but the girl stood and introduced herself to Lucius before she had a chance to do it for her.

"Hello, Daddy," said a voice Lucius didn't expect to ever hear again.

"Anna Lee?" His face showed how shocked he was at seeing his own daughter in this room. She was sixteen, her short brown hair was cut in a bob, and she had on a blue sweater and a pair of faded old jeans.

She looked at him for a moment before coming closer. She stopped about five feet away, like that was as close as she could stand to get. Her manner was business-like as she addressed her shocked father. "They said that you were dead. Mother said you were dead. The people on the news said that you were dead. General Yates stopped by the house, he said that you were dead too. Are you still my dad?" She paused for a moment before she added the sting. "Or not?"

Lucius closed his mouth, smiled just a bit and nodded his head, like she'd told a good joke at his expense. One that he deserved. "Yes. And no."

"What the hell does that mean?" Anna Lee asked, steady as a rock as she looked at him. At his face. His eyes. His hair. And the rest.

"Yes. Because *I am* still your father. And no. Because I'm not the father you remember me to be." Lucius reached down to his belt and grabbed a radio. Everyone heard as he spoke into it. "We're just about ready in here. Is the area outside secure?"

"The area is secure, Captain. The soldiers that were already here are being very cooperative," came the reply on the other side.

Lucius turned back to his daughter and his eyebrows shot up. "What on earth have you done to your hair?" he asked her.

Now it was her turn to look surprised. "My hair? What'd you mean?" She looked totally befuddled by the question.

Lucius laughed, a great big laugh which was followed by a big smile that came easily to his face. His daughter stared at him like he'd just grown a third eye or two extra heads, her mouth hanging open just like Lucius's had when she surprised him.

"Anna, what did your mother say? God, it had to be mouth full." He shook his head and chuckled as he waited for an answer. "Come on now, you're going to have to tell me about it. Your mother would never allow you to cut your hair. Is this recent? When did you get up the nerve to do it?" Lucius took a step toward the frozen girl that was his daughter.

Her eyes stayed on his like he was a pod person from another planet that had eaten her father and replaced him somehow. Lucius reached out and touched her hair, and sighed as he eyed just how short it was.

"You know, I'll miss the long hair too. But," he nodded, "I guess you were due for a change. Just like me."

Anna Lee blinked and still seemed to be trying to understand how this smiling happy man who seemed so at ease and comfortable in his own weird pale skin could possibly be the man she knew as little more than a parental robot. Someone who rarely, if ever, noticed anything trivial like hair and never actually spoke to her about something other than the three necessities in life: grades, long term goals, or schedules—and most important of all, how to stay on schedule.

"I'll be busy for a few minutes, Anna, but get me a plate and some pizza and we'll sit together once I'm free. You still need to tell me all the details on the hair story. All right?" Lucius stepped up to her and gave her a hug.

It took a second, but the girl hugged him back just briefly before he stepped away with a final word, "Regular coke, no more diet coke for me, Anna Lee, and just plain cheese pizza if they have any left. All right?"

"Okay?" she managed to mumble out as she stared after him.

The others in the room had watched the whole odd little scene and were as wide eyed as the girl as Lucius disappeared down the hallway headed toward the magic door.

"Here you go, honey," said Mrs. Bryant to Anna Lee as she pressed a plate with a slice of cheese pizza on it into her hands; she also handed her a can of regular Coke.

Anna looked at the pizza and then studied the can of Coke in her hand. "But Dad always drank diet Coke. That guy can't be my dad," she said as she looked at the can.

"Honey, you have short hair now. You changed. Your dad drinks regular Coke now. He changed."

The girl looked up into Mrs. Bryant's face. "But he used to be a horrible asshole. Now he's almost—nice." She said it like the word tasted bad in her mouth.

"What's so bad about that?" asked Mrs. Bryant kindly.

Anna Lee looked frightened as she explained, "I'll tell you what's wrong with that, I know how to deal with 'asshole dad.' I'm used to him. But not this guy." She held up the can of regular Coke and gave it a vicious angry shake like it represented the "nice" dad. Anna's eyes went to the front door like she was thinking about bolting.

"Just give him a chance," Mrs. Bryant urged. "You came all this way, Anna. Just eat some pizza with your father and tell him all about your hair and see if you like this nice dad that you have now." She noticed tears pooling in Anna's eyes. "What's wrong?"

"I wonder where asshole dad is." Anna wiped at her eyes. "He was an asshole but I knew that he loved me. Even though he was an asshole. Where do you think he is?" It was rhetorical and she didn't really expect an answer, but Mrs. Bryant gave her one anyway.

The words came out smoothly, like she had already asked herself the same question. "Your asshole dad that loved you is probably in the same place as my angry rebellious daughter named Rain Marie Bryant. My Rain Marie loved me too.

Even though she disobeyed me and broke all my rules and lied to me. I loved her too." Mrs. Bryant wiped at her own tears now but gave Anna a smile. "My Rain Marie is now called Black Rain. I love Black Rain, and she is my daughter, but things are different now. Just like it will be for you. Your father is now Lucius. And things will be different."

Anna let herself be guided to an out of the way chair to wait for her father. Mrs. Bryant left her there and went off to talk to other people. Anna wished she had a great story to tell him about her hair, about the God awful fit her mother threw—but she had just cut her hair that morning and her mother hadn't even seen it yet. Anna didn't even have a good story to tell. So she sat there and waited for her new dad to come and spend some time with her as she held his plate of cold cheese pizza and his can of shook up regular Coke.

Hidden Agendas

---◆---

Pillars of Power

THERE WERE ALWAYS conspiracy theories flying around D.C. A certain paranoid portion of the populous loved nothing more than to mull over the latest far-fetched tales of corruption, cover ups, and the secret agendas of those in power. Many obsessed souls and others simply out to make a buck spent their days and nights blogging on the internet and writing junked up novels about secret societies bent on influencing the wheels of government. Very few people in the mainstream ever took them seriously, and yet the rumors were always there. Stories. Questions. Mysteries. It was like hearing a rustling noise in a dark, quiet room. You knew it was probably roaches, but no one ever seemed to know how to turn on the light, or possibly no one cared enough to turn on the light, or just maybe—no one was *allowed* to turn on the light. So the roaches remained an easily dismissed noise in the dark.

But no more. The crises room was in full swing, the light was on, and roaches of the two-legged variety were running for cover. Eight senators, nineteen members of the House, and more than a dozen others from the Federal Reserve had offered to resign and testify, but before they did they wanted assurances that they would not be criminally prosecuted for their part in the attack. They wanted to retain their generous pensions. They wanted to keep their fantastic government (taxpayer) provided health plan and security.

David Brenner repeated the same sentence for the fifth time—the legalese, complex semantics and sheer number of words had shortened each time until Brenner was reduced to speaking in plain English. The President and his group leaned together, whispering quietly.

Brenner and the Justice Department's legal team was saddled with the onerous task of defending those government officials implicated in the rocket attack. There was a full-blown, forceful investigation underway into the attack that killed Stan Reese, Director of the FBI, along with two hundred and seventy other soldiers and government agents and a number of civilians. It was nine pm, Thursday evening.

The President himself had called this special session and most of the people in the room hadn't slept in the past twenty-four hours. Dozens of smartly dressed soldiers in their finest dress uniforms stood ramrod straight, lining the wood-paneled walls of the circular room. And they were all armed.

The members of the Justice Department objected loudly the moment they entered the room and saw the armed soldiers. They loudly cited the specific House rules that this action violated. They called it an act of madness. The work of a President wild with his own power. They called it an outright abandonment of the rule of law and a dozen other legal and even street talk slams.

From a seated position at the table the President replied to the red-faced men in a calm sure voice stating that so long as the continuity of government itself was in danger, the soldiers would remain. That statement alone seemed to bring into question what other rules would no longer be honored, what other laws could not be counted upon to shield and coddle their creators. It raised the stakes of the meeting right through the magnificent domed ceiling high overhead.

The room itself was clearly divided. Brenner and two others from the Justice Department sat with five private attorneys and their staff at one end of the long table. On the other side sat the President and his staff. Both groups huddled at opposite sides of the massive conference table whispering, plotting, and scheming.

All of D.C., The White House, Capital Hill, Congress, the entire city itself had an uneasy, wild, unsettled feel. The past twenty-four hours had been absolute madness as the President tried to keep up with the incredible events taking shape down in Florida with the Black Witch and Amen Hale. On top of that was the international pressure from the world powers as they vied to ingratiate themselves to the Black Witch or applied pressure in the opposite direction, insisting that she and the other teens be destroyed immediately. And everyone wanted to find out more about the drugs used to create these teens with such fantastic and frightening powers.

But even in the midst of all that was happening, the attention of the Capitol was focused on what was happening in this room as the power players of D.C. had their influence, reputations, and quite possibly their lives sucked into an unstoppable black hole. Two words were being whispered by reporters, clerks, congressmen, and janitors alike—High Treason.

As everyone now knew, there was a modern but no less secretive version of the Masonic Order alive and well in D.C., and its members had supplied intel and other assistance to the foreign forces behind yesterday's attack. All the oaths of secrecy that they'd sworn were now worth less than used toilet paper as desperate senators and representatives attempted to roll on one another like panicked teenagers, trying to beat one another to an immunity deal.

There were some very pissed off people in this group as well because they believed that they'd been lied to. For any normal thinking person it would have been no big surprise that a secret society would lie to its own members, but the self-important arrogant, power-hungry members sure didn't see it that way. They acted surprised, hurt, and outraged at what had happened. None of them were willing to talk without immunity to prosecution, but they had confided in the legal counsel provided them by the Justice Department, who then related their version of events (off the record).

The leadership of this group that called itself "The Order" had come to the conclusion that Black Rain and the other teens from the drug study were far too dangerous to be allowed to live, but they also knew that the United States government would never have the intestinal fortitude to do what they felt needed to be done. The word had gone out that this secret society would help any group or country that wanted to make an attempt on the life of the Black Witch and the others. Those with positions of power provided information on the location, status, and abilities of the kids in the drug study and even provided tactical information to the teams that launched the rockets used in the attack. These senators and representatives swore (off the record) that they anticipated a car bomb or having the teens killed by sniper fire, but they all vehemently denied ever being told about plans for a massive rocket attack right in the midst of a U.S. military convoy as it rolled through a major U.S. city.

Mitch Hunt asked, "Do you have the list of names and all the other documents here with you?"

"Yes," answered Brenner. "If there's an immunity deal, we are prepared to hand over everything right now. We'll also provide details on the organization itself, international contacts, and well-documented and detailed records of their activities over the past twenty years to help make this worth the price."

Heads leaned together and whispering started again at the Presidential side of the table, but after only a few minutes the President stood and the whole room went quiet.

"All right. Give us the damn documents. We'll sign the papers."

"You'll sign the documents yourself? As they stand?" asked Brenner, his voice unable to hide his doubt and surprise and as soon as the initial shock passed—suspicion. He waited for the other shoe to drop and it did.

"As long as one or more of the names on your list don't kill the deal for everyone, I'll sign it. If a few names need to come off the list, then do it. You've already talked to them, you know who to let hang to make sure the whole thing doesn't turn to shit for everyone. This has to be sold to them—" the President pointed away from the table, indicating anyone and everyone outside the room, "not just me. People are panicked enough without dragging this nightmare out for weeks and months. The American people will be confused enough and a lot of them will believe that the White House itself is part of The Order, no matter what we do or say to convince them we're not. America can't afford this shit right now, not with what we have happening in Florida and with the rest of the world breathing down our necks. We need this settled fast, and nothing is faster than everyone on that list resigning tonight and giving a video-taped confession for the American people to see."

His voice got harder and meaner as he added, "That part is non-negotiable! No taped confession, no damned immunity! And no double talk. No bullshit political speak. No one saves face when they give their testimony, I want it short and ugly. You're all bastards that betrayed me and the trust of the American people. There is no justification for what you did." He glared down the length of the table. He may not have trusted the men he now faced with sensitive political secrets but he'd certainly trusted every last one regardless of political leaning to not be outright traitors.

It took Brenner a moment to quiet the angry whispers of the private lawyers on his side of the table. "You'll guarantee immunity from prosecution, provided we offer up the biggest bastards," Brenner clarified before the shouting started.

The lawyers representing those "biggest bastards" shot to their feet, vehemently rejecting this development. Everything broke down into bedlam for a few minutes until two of the private lawyers were removed by soldiers, who first confiscated their cell phones before leading them from the room.

As the door shut the President filled the uneasy silence, speaking calmly. "There are bigger concerns gripping our country than jumping through hoops to make sure we destroy every last son of a bitch who had a hand in this." The President paused to take a drink from his white mug bearing the presidential seal. No one spoke and he didn't rush. He sipped, then carefully set the mug down before continuing in a conversational tone. "Give me the ones at the very top who deserve to burn and I'll cut the rest loose. Of course I think it's a shit deal, David. If it were up to me, I'd have all of them lined up on the Green and shot for treason on live TV. My approval ratings would go through the roof, but it doesn't work that way in the real world. That's what got us to this point in the first place. If you meet my terms, we have a deal. I have other problems to deal with that are more important than high treason."

"Mr. President," Brenner said, "I'll need a few moments to amend the list of names. As you accurately stated, a few of the names on this list would ruin the deal, and as general counsel for the entire group, I believe it is in the best interest of the vast majority of my clients that I let the biggest bastards hang. May I have thirty minutes, Sir?"

The room quickly broke into activity as the details were discussed.

Mary Fae

Finding Someone Special

G ASPS. THAT ODD sound that a quick intake of breath makes when it comes unbidden. A few quietly muttered curse words. The sound of movement, feet shuffling, the wood floor of the trailer groaning and complaining. People moved toward the other side of the living room or retreated behind the other side of the open kitchen bar, while others just pressed themselves against the walls of the trailer to get some space between themselves and what had just entered the room.

Believer, The Prince of Clouds.

"O my Lord, Believer! What happened to you!? Are you all right!?" Mrs. Bryant shouted in alarm as he took a few more hunched over steps into the living room.

The seven-foot high ceilings within the trailer were forcing him to bend at the waist and lead with his head and his red burning eyes. Beautiful rays of gold and yellow light slipped past the clouds here and there, shining onto walls and faces that stared in open-mouthed wonder at the radiant giant in their midst. It was like a piece of the sun had hidden itself somewhere within Believer's body.

The clouds within him continued to roll and crash about perpetually, but this newly added element of light transformed him. His whole body was like a constantly changing fantastical sunset, a living canvas of brilliant sky that rearranged and transformed minute by minute. Darker clouds in one place became edged with silver light while others caught fire with a hundred different hues of gold, red, and burnt orange that painted his body while at the same moment rays of light slipped out between gaps in his clouds, the beams like a celestial gift, lighting those who sat in darkness with no light of their own. Believer had been fascinating and puzzling to look at before, but now he was something else altogether.

A rumble of subdued laughter rose up from the midst of his body before he spoke. "Hello, Mother. Don't be concerned. I am unharmed. I believe this will only be temporary, it's already dimmed some," his deep rumbling voice answered her as she stepped closer to him, looking at him with concern.

Mr. and Mrs. Bryant were the only ones in the room who stepped closer. Their visitors were in a state of shock as the warm comfortable blanket called "reality" was snatched away, exposing their minds to this raw new knowledge—that fantasy was indeed fact, that the impossible was actually quite possible, and that the laws of the universe and physics were in truth—baloney.

Am I really seeing what I think I'm seeing? was written on faces all around the room. They all knew he was coming, but seeing was altogether different from hearing. Wide staring eyes drank in the sight of Believer, The Prince of Clouds.

"But why on earth are you glowing?" asked Mr. Bryant.

A sweet little voice answered from somewhere behind the clouds, "Because Rain freaked out, Mom! She almost fried us all to a crisp with her power and Believer had to grab her and hold her till she calmed down!"

Bethany squeezed out of the hallway, past Believer and into the living room. She was barefoot, wearing nothing but her red and grey witch dress and a great big smile. "Hey!" she said happily and ran over to Mr. Bryant's open and waiting arms.

"Believer. Is Rain all right?" asked Mrs. Bryant as she looked up at him. She didn't have far to look since he was bent over.

"Yes, Mother. She's well. Rain just lost her temper for a moment, and I helped her to calm down. We are fine."

Mrs. Bryant would have asked a hundred more questions, but the others were entering the room, stepping around Believer. Sky Dragon, Lucius, Sky, Ryan, and Sky's mother and father stepped into the room. Sky's mother already had a condescending sneer on her face as she eyed the trailer. Mr. and Mrs. Bryant busied themselves with the task of playing host, making introductions and attempting to make this evening's gathering as enjoyable and as safe as humanly possible.

The mood in the room became much more relaxed and a whole lot less crowded as soon as Believer and Sky Dragon excused themselves and stepped outside to keep watch over the trailer and its important occupants. Somewhat relaxed conversations filled the room while the newcomers enjoyed cold pizza and sodas. Most of the guests were gathered around Sky, Ryan, or the Hans plying them with questions and avoiding Bethany altogether.

Lucius's warnings about the witches were still fresh on everyone's mind, but after a couple of minutes Mrs. Hillman couldn't take it any more and strode over to Bethany with a determined look on her face. Bethany had been over at the Hillmans' house dozens of times and she'd fed and fussed and mothered the girl as much and maybe more than anyone in the trailer park other than Kendal, so witch or no witch she was going to talk to her about Mary because Mary still hadn't entered the room.

"Bethany, where the hell is Mary? She's supposed to be here," Mary's mom demanded, her voice testy but carefully not yelling.

Her husband loomed over her shoulder, standing right behind her, but he kept quiet. Mr. Hillman didn't know Bethany as well as his wife did so he was letting Hanna do her "thing" and be a mom. Mike usually just read the paper or watched TV while his house full of girls just absorbed the additional little female body without his notice or opinion.

Bethany answered with a shy smile. "She was nervous, Mrs. H., she had to go pee."

"Because she knew we'd be here and she thought we'd yell at her, hum?" Mary's mom guessed with just a hint of sympathy and a fair measure of "mom" angst. "We're not going to yell. We're beyond wanting to yell at her."

A little crease formed on Bethany's brow at that, then she shook her head no. "It wasn't you, Mrs. H. When Lucius told us that Emma's parents were here, that's when Mary got all nervous and jumpy and said she needed to pee."

"Emma?" Mrs. Hillman turned and looked over to the tall, gaunt looking couple that stood on the far side of the room speaking with Mr. Han. "Why would she be more afraid of Emma's parents than her own?" Mrs. Hillman grumped.

Bethany gave a happy shrug. She didn't know. "She'll be here in a few seconds, Mrs. H. Honest. She really wants to see you guys. And I've missed you too."

Bethany's innocent little angel face stared up at Hanna and she looked exactly like the same little girl she remembered. Just a little girl, not some horribly dangerous and frightening witch! She ended her cautious reservations and gave Bethany a good firm hug then started to mother her just like she did whenever the poor girl would appear at her table for breakfast or lunch or even dinner with Mary. A few mornings she had come into her living room to find the girl sleeping on her couch or in Mary's room curled up on the floor. Of course, Hanna knew that there must have been a good reason for it, so she never questioned it. And never complained.

"My Lord, child. What have you gotten yourself into? Why'd you run off like that? Are you all right? Rain's mother and that police man said you cut yourself up. Have they been making you stay? Can you girls come and go as you please? Do you have a safe place to sleep? Did anyone touch you?" (That last was a question she always asked Bethany that didn't get asked to most children)

Mrs. Hillman stopped in mid sentence as a very familiar tattoo appeared on Bethany's previously naked forehead. A crescent moon surrounded by four stars. One red star, one green star, one black star, and one white star. "Bethany, that horrible nasty tattoo you girls got on Monday night just appeared on your forehead; that means Mary's here now, doesn't it?" Hanna hadn't believed Mary when she tried to explain why her new ugly tattoo just vanished when the police car carrying Rain and her brother Ryan pulled away from their trailer Wednesday morning. She believed now.

Bethany nodded and Mrs. Hillman followed her gaze. She leaned around her and looked toward the hallway. They both spotted Mary at the same time. Her shock white head of hair was peeking out into the room. Impossibly bright colors like "shock white" and "neon green" made peeking around corners in a sneaky fashion impossible for Mary, but she still tried. Almost everyone in the room saw her at the same time.

"Eeep!" Mary let out a startled noise and vanished back down the hall. Bethany giggled. Mary's mom started toward the hall.

"I'll go get her, Hanna," Mrs. Bryant called. "Just give me a second to calm her down and bring her out."

Mrs. Bryant headed after Mary, but Hanna Hillman was faster; she rushed over and thrust her arm across the entrance to the hallway blocking the way. Hanna Hillman yelled right in Mrs. Bryant's surprised face. "You just stay out here dammit! Don't you think you've helped us out enough already!? Mary's my daughter! You hear me?"

Lucius came rushing over as did Mike Hillman along with Mary's two little sisters who squeezed past all the other adults and stood beside their mother while Mike and Hanna gave Lucius and Mrs. Bryant a looked that screamed "Parental

Outrage!" Mrs. Bryant and Lucius both withered under their combined glares and quickly backed away.

"Come on, Mike. Girls, wait right here." Hanna's two younger daughters both nodded. And with that said, Mike and Hanna Hillman went after their oldest daughter.

Rain's black and bloody room was empty. There was only the bathroom and one other door in the short hall. The door had a Marlins poster and some other baseball paraphernalia on it.

"Must be their boy's room," Mike said as he reached for the handle. The door was unlocked and he opened it. Mary was sitting on the bed, head down, rocking back and forth with her eyes closed.

"Hi, Mom. Hi, Dad," she said without looking up, as if she could see them standing there even with her eyes closed.

"Can we come in, Mary?" her mom asked from the open door.

"Yes. But don't yell. And please be careful." Mary kept rocking. Back and forth. Eyes closed.

"Are you okay, Sunshine?" her father asked, his voice filled with emotion. He was almost in tears as he looked at his oldest daughter and what she'd become in just a little more than the day she'd spent away from them. Mary looked like an emotional basket case. Eyes squeezed shut, rocking back and forth.

"I can feel you getting upset. Please, Dad. Don't. I'm okay. Don't be sad." Her voice was on the edge of tears too, from hearing her father's voice and feeling the emotions in the room.

"What's happened, Mary? What's wrong, honey?" Mary's mother asked. Then she recalled what Bethany told her. "Are you afraid of Emma's parents for some reason?"

Mary stopped rocking, her body stiffening.

"Why are you scared of them people? They seem all right," asked her father. "Is there something bad about them? Do they want to hurt you or something? I spoke with them for a while tonight. They're as mad as hell about their daughter being stolen away but you didn't have anything to do with that. They don't have any reason to be upset with you darlin'. And I won't let them near you. And you got that guy Lucius out there. He can just ask them to leave if you want."

"No, Daddy," Mary said. "That would be wrong. I just, I don't want to touch them. EVER," Mary said with feeling. She shivered like the thought alone had chilled her to the bone.

"What on earth about them has gotten you so spooked, girl? And what's all this that guy Lucius spouted about you not being able to touch people? He said that you might lose control of yourself or have a seizure if you touched someone. What on earth is happening, Mary? You didn't have any trouble touching us yesterday before you left with Mrs. Bryant. You were a witch then just like now so why can't you touch people now? What's wrong, Mary?"

"Wow. Was that just yesterday?" Mary shook her head in disbelief. "I swear, yesterday feels like a thousand years ago." She took a deep breath, rolled her shoulders and sat a little straighter on the bed before continuing. "My power as a witch is growing, Mom. Yesterday, when I was at the house I couldn't even talk to the trees or hear the whisper of the world or speak to the animals or see the auras or the cords that bind all things."

Mary finally opened her eyes and looked at her mother and father with her normal vision; at the same time, laid on top of everything she saw was a dazzling array of colors. Auras. Not just coming from her parents but also other objects in the room. Her gaze was pulled to the desk by the wall. An old Bible and a notebook beside it glowed yellow and gold in her vision. A memory flashed through her head, the notebook was Ryan's journal. She'd touched him, so she knew what was written in it already. It made her smile.

Her attention was pulled to a guitar hanging on the wall that glowed brightly. On the floor, a wadded up shirt. Dirty laundry glowed in a hamper also, other little objects in the room begged for her attention.

"Mary, are you all right?" her mother's concerned voice asked as she took another step into the room.

"What?" Mary blinked. Realized she'd flaked out for a minute. "Oh. Geeeze. I got all trippy looking at the auras in the room. Sorry. I get distracted real easy when I use my human eyes to see. I see so much more than anyone else. It's hard to stay focused on just the stuff everyone else sees," she explained.

"So, you're seeing things now. Hallucinating?" her father guessed incorrectly.

Mary laughed. A happy clean laugh. "Mom. Dad. We might as well get this over with. Let me touch you," Mary said.

"Are you ready for us to touch you, Mary?" asked her mom.

"Well. I'm gonna have to touch you sooner or later. I hope neither one of you is a serial killer or did something really sinister like steal the recipe for the secret sauce or something because I'll damn sure know if you did. When I touch you, I'll know everything. I can't even stop it if I wanted to, it just happens when I touch people now."

Her father looked concerned, but her mom looked embarrassed and she gave them both a reassuring smile.

"I promise to *try* not to freak out when I see your private stuff. I love you guys. But I'm not going to go through my life not touching you. So come here and let's do this. And then I'll know all there is to know and it won't matter anymore. And don't worry about me knowing all the sex stuff. I've touched every soul in Amen Hale. And I touched a bunch of others who wanted in that we ended up kicking out. Over five hundred people. Believe me when I say this, I have seen EVERY-THING."

Now her parents looked even more worried. "So. Just by touching us, you'll know what we've done—through our whole lives?" her father asked, sounding doubtful. One eyebrow was cocked up in a curious expression that Mary had never seen on his face before. It made her smile. Something new, every minute, and life just kept going.

"Yep!" she said happily. "It's like living out a whole new life each time I touch someone because I'll know it and them so well, it's like I've actually lived it myself. I keep all of the lives that I've lived deep down inside me so I don't lose the Mary that is really me to all the rest. At first it was really hard to keep me 'me,' but now I have things under control. They're all inside me, and I can call on pieces of those memories if I want. But *only* if I want. I really do like being ignorant. Because my Mary is a seventeen-year-old girl who likes to have fun. And she's a total airhead sometimes. And flakey. And she likes to play and cuddle. And she's a witch. Which makes her crazy. And makes her me." Mary tilted her head to the side, a little smile on her face as she spoke about herself in the third person.

Mike and Hanna Hillman exchanged a troubled glance and walked over to the bed. They each sat on one side of their daughter but were careful not to touch her yet.

"Mary. Why are you scared of touching Emma's parents? What is it about them that you don't want to know?" asked her mother.

Mary looked at her in surprise. "Snap, Mom! You were actually listening to me. That's a good question."

Her mother gave her a frustrated look. "Of course I was, kitten. I may not understand all this witch shit, but if you're gonna be one, then I gotta understand you at least. So if I understand how this works, if you touch someone, right away you know what they've done their whole life. Now why would that be bad to do with Mr. and Mrs. Tate out there?"

Mary looked at first her mother and then her father. "Okay. I'll tell you. But keep an open mind. This is going to sound weird, but just go with it. And also, you guys should know that I can't lie anymore." She reached up and tapped her forehead tattoo with a finger. "It's a witch thing. Thought you should know. So if I say something, you can believe it. No lies. Never for me. So mote it be."

"And you really remember the lives of all those people you've touched?" her father asked. He wanted to believe what Mary was saying, but he was still doubtful.

"I speak twenty-three different languages now, Dad. I am a vascular surgeon. I've lived the tax time life of an accountant. I am a cook. I'm a lawyer. A worthless drunken bum. A school teacher. A soldier. A whore. A preacher. A stay at home mom. A construction worker. I've lived in most every city in America. I've been poor. I've been rich. I remember being in war. I remember being evil and hurting other people. I've raped and I have been raped. I've lied, I've cheated, I've stolen, I've run from the law. I've spent years in prison and been raped in there too. I've lived in the Amazon, eating bugs and worms just to say alive." Mary laughed, a big grin on her face.

"One life I collected was so amazing it's hard to even believe it's real. It was about 10 pm. The auto pilot was fixed on the tiller and I was down in the hull asleep. My sailboat was sailing in open ocean about nineteen miles out, off the coast of Florida east of Miami, when I ran right into the side of an aircraft carrier! They were doing some stupid military maneuvers or war games and were running silent, with all of their lights off, so the men on deck didn't see me or notice my tiny mast lamp. I guess the guy on the radar watching out for little shit in the sea like my tiny boat was asleep, getting a doughnut, or taking a leak or something, but my boat, Jasper's Pride was crushed. Those bastards just kept going, like nothing happened and let me sink out there. Water started pouring in. All I had time to grab was one flipper, a sleeping bag, my mask, and a snorkel. I did have a little pocket knife in my pocket but that was it. The boat was gone and I was floating out there in the ocean at night."

Mary's parents were drawn in; they were both leaning close as their daughter told them a story of a life she had lived and yet never lived, but she spoke about it with the feeling and passion of someone who had experienced it, lived it, tasted the salt water, and felt the thrill of this life and death experience.

She continued, gesturing here and there, her voice animated as she told her tale. "I used the knife to cut a hole in the end of the sleeping bag and crawled in and stuck one leg out of the bag and put my one flipper on that foot. The bag was wet but not sodden, it was made of some waterproof material that helped keep me afloat and helped keep me warm as I started to swim."

"Swim!" her father blurted out. "Where the hell did you swim to, them bastards left you out in the middle of the damn ocean?" He asked with real concern, totally forgetting that Mary had never set foot on a boat. He was captivated by the story. He squirmed on the bed beside her with nervous energy that had no outlet. His whole being wanted to jump in himself and help his little girl swim her ass out of there. Or get a boat and go save her himself. Call the Coast Guard! Something!

"It was lucky for me that it was one of those magically clear nights without a cloud in the sky. The kind you can only find out in the ocean, in open water. Believe it or not, from almost twenty miles out, I could see on the horizon line the glow of Miami off in the distance. That place gives off so much light pollution it's like a freaking beacon. I stayed calm and steady and used my one flipper to start swimming toward the light. I just kept at it, kicking and kicking. When I got tired I switched legs. When I got really tired I'd rest and float a while. A few times I felt something come up and taste the sleeping bag. It tore some of the fabric out one time and didn't like the flavor."

"Oh my sweet lord, what was it?" her mother asked.

"Sharks, Mom," Mary answered with a wicked smile. "Big sharks. They left after playing with me for a while and I kept swimming. I swam all night and part of the next day and finally came ashore right on Miami beach at about 1 in the afternoon. I was lucky the current was in my favor, and that the sharks didn't bite the meaty part of the sleeping bag, and that I had my mask and snorkel. I walked up that sandy beach, past all the freaked out tourists, right up to some stupid tiki hut stand and ordered a beer. That was the best tasting beer I have ever tasted in any of my lives. It tasted like liquid life as I drank it. It was so cool, *so refreshing*— and for so many miles I'd been thinking about that beer and promising myself, over and over, that if I kept kicking, and swimming that it would taste better than any beer ever drank by anyone who ever lived on the face of the earth. Damn if I wasn't right."

They sat on the bed in a strange state of reverent silence. Magic was in the air, touching Mike and Hanna Hillman. The tangy smell of the sea filled the room. The exhausted feel of life, fought for and won. Victory of spirit. Mary's father swallowed like his throat was dry and his eyes went wide as he looked at his daughter who smiled at him. He could almost taste the cold beer, wetting his parched mouth and sliding down his throat—*and damn if it didn't taste good*!

"What about Emma's parents, Mary? Why don't you want them to touch you?" her mom asked, breaking the spell.

Mary sighed and the feel of the room vanished away, everything drained back to normal. "I've got the flavor of them from touching Emma, and I do NOT want to touch them. I don't want them in me. They're not bad people. They're good parents in the traditional sense. They provide for her, take care of her physically. But they're cold. Mechanical. Distant. Living in their home is like living in a public place filled with polite and helpful strangers. There's no intimacy. No hugging. No touching. Even their fights are robotic and without sparks that fly in a home where love is. They care for her, but not in the way she needed. Emma was dying for love that they could have given her but they didn't. Or couldn't. She even tried to tell them. Twice. Which is amazing, because Emma doesn't do second chances. They sent her to counseling like she was the one with the problem."

Mary sighed. "It's not really their fault though. I think it's just how they were made. It's their flavor."

"Flavor?" Her father made the word a question.

"Each life has a flavor. A taste. Everyone thinks a little differently, remembers differently, hopes and fears and hates differently, and they all love differently. For some people, it's like they're just barely alive. Their life is so dim, and they have no passion at all. Their whole life is soft and quiet, and all they have is muted shades of what could be bright, vibrant colors. It's so sad. Most people are in the middle, a mix of things. But there are a few who are very special, though to look at them you'd probably never know it. Great thinkers. Amazing artists. An amazing ability to focus. One man had such a kind heart that it almost made me want to not be 'me' and switch out. And another had such a vivid imagination that she could close her eyes and envision whole worlds that were so real it was like magic. But of all the people I've touched—no one is like Emma."

Mary's voice softened. Her smile became more private, more personal. "Emma came to Amen Hale last night with Jane and Dan. She wanted to be there when the vampires were put in their grave. The second I touched her, I had to have her. Emma is one of those special people, but she makes all of them look like shadows next to her. Flickering candles compared to a raging fire. Emma loves. The second I touched her I fell in love with her. I saw how she loved Jane. Her friend that turned into a vampire. I saw how much Emma loved her. The only word I could think to describe it is—FIERCE!" Mary growled out the word, then closed her eyes and licked her dry lips before she continued.

"I wanted her to love me like that. It was so beautiful. I had to have her. And I knew just what she wanted, what she needed, so I gave it to her. I held her and loved her with all of my heart and held nothing back because Emma does not hold back. Emma loves. So I had to do the same." Mary stopped talking and stared off into space, lost in her memories.

"Mary. Are you saying that you and—this girl—are a couple?" her father asked carefully.

"Yes."

"But you like boys, Mary," her mother said.

"But I love Emma," Mary answered.

Without saying another word, Mary reached out with both hands and touched her mother and father and added them to her collection.

Bull Dandridge

Housewarming Party

T HE AXE BIT through the last portion of tough flesh and Dan's leg came off just above the knee. It had taken ten powerful strokes with their hardened plastic axe to sever the limb. There was blood, but not in buckets; only a small amount spilled out of each severed limb, but it was all adding up. The white sheets looked like a butcher's table top.

"This ain't working fast enough!" Bull stepped up to the bed. "That bed keeps absorbing the force of the blows. He'll take forever to finish like this."

He grabbed the torso. It still had one leg and one arm attached. The severed and ruined head and the other arm and leg lay in pieces on the bed that the couple had used for their wedding night. Bull drug the body off the bed and onto the hard, glasslike red floor.

Tiger started swinging again. He grunted. "Thak!" The axe struck. Grunt. "Thak!" Grunt. "Thak!"

Huge big swings, muscles corded and pulled as the big man brought the plastic alloy blade down on the arm with all his strength. Grunt. "Thak!" The arm came off at the forearm.

"Much better! Now the other leg," Bull ordered.

"How many pieces this guy need ta be in, Bull. He's dead." Red's strong Jersey accent colored his words.

"Fine. You make the call, Red. But remember. These people have a bad habit of coming back from the dead. After what we did to him and his girl, you feel comfortable leaving him like this or do you want more pieces?"

Bull watched as Red thought that through seriously.

Grunt. "Thak!" The sound of the axe started again. Red and Bull watched as Tiger pulled it free and raised the bloody axe overhead again; his bald head was beaded with sweat as he tensed for another swing.

"More pieces would be nice, Sir."

Grunt. "Thak!"

"Yeah. Thought you might make that call. Take that axe from Tiger, he's slowing down."

"Tiger. Switch out," Bull called.

"Let me free it." Tiger's big booted foot pressed against the torso as he tried to break the blade free from where it was buried. The body on the floor made a strange gurgling sound, like air coming out of a punctured tire.

The four men in the room froze. Everything started moving at the same time. The severed arms and legs on the bed, the one arm on the floor, the one leg on the torso, all kicking and flexing and grabbing and writhing like the worst cliché scene out of a zombie movie. Only this wasn't a movie. This was real. A variety of curses and swears echoed in the cavelike room.

"Oh no you don't!" Tiger grabbed an arm that was trying to crawl over to the body and threw it across the room where it landed with a crash.

"This thing's trying to pull itself back together, Bull!" Tiger called, readying the axe for another swing.

"We'll use the acid we used on the wall. Let's melt this bastard!" Bull shouted.

The partially severed leg sealed itself back to its stump on the torso like the whole body was liquid and pliable. It started to kick out blindly, wildly, spinning around in a thrashing circle, making Tiger jump out of the way. The other severed hand crawled like a terrifying spider across the floor toward the body but was grabbed by a member of the team named Keno, while Bull ran to the bed and threw a sheet over the mangled head that was reforming rapidly. White light poured out of the one undamaged eye. Bull was careful not to look into the light as he covered the head and began to wrap it up, being mindful of the furiously biting mouth.

"Muther fucker!" Keno shouted as the hand clamped down on his forearm.

The sounds of crunching bone and screaming filled the room.

Jane

A Waking Nightmare

I FELT MOVEMENT. Somehow I knew I was in the air. Moving in the air. Where was I? Where was Dan? Where were his arms? They had been around me when I died. Where was Dan?

My eyes opened. Darkness. Cloth. A few inches away from my eyes. What was happening?

Dan's voice cried out in the muddle of my waking mind so loudly it shook my body.

"JANE! Wake up! JANE!"

"Dan?"

"JANE! Soldiers have taken you out of the crypt! I'm still in the crypt. They're trying to kill me right now and they're going to try to kill you! YOU HAVE TO FIGHT, JANE! Wake up and start fighting, start fighting, Jane!*"*

"We have movement. She's awake!" a man shouted nearby.

Soldiers. Soldiers were trying to kill Dan. Right now. And they were taking me away form him.

RAGE. It filled me like liquid fire. We were supposed to be safe! We were in the crypt where it was supposed to be safe! NO! My arms and legs pushed and strained to move but they were held to my sides. I was wrapped around with cords of some kind. Strong cords. With all the strength I had I kicked and pushed and pulled and writhed. The tape that they had wrapped around my mouth tore and I roared!

"Back up! The tape's torn. Her mouth is free!" A soldier. Nearby. '

"Dan! FIGHT THEM! DAN!"

The cords around my body held me. I struggled and roared and writhed, but the cords held. I felt almost mummified. I looked down and could see in the darkness what looked like thick metal wires wrapped around my entire body. It looked like a steel wire cocoon.

"They have me tied up, Dan! Metal wires! I can't break free!" I shouted in my mind frantically. I waited for an answer.

"Check the wires! Are they breaking? Be ready to put her down if it looks like she's about to break free!"

"The wires are holding, Sir."

"She's stopped struggling!"

"DAN!" I called again frantically into the night of my mind. No! NO! Dan said they were fighting with him! What if they hurt him! What if they were hurting him right now? What if they had killed him?

I went still. Cold.

"Dan," I spoke aloud. I waited. "Dan." I waited. "Dan."

"She's calling for the other one, over and over. She must not be able to hear him anymore, either that or he's not answering."

"He must be dead then," said another voice. "We aren't out of their range yet."

They kept talking but I stopped hearing the words.

Dead. My Dan. My Dan. Dead.

My Dan is dead. I finally put the words together in my head. They still didn't make sense. How could Dan be dead? We were going to live forever. Love forever. This isn't how our story ends. He was going to hold me forever and love me forever and it was going to be beautiful and wonderful for all eternity. We were in a safe place. Dan couldn't be dead. He was my life. My mate. He was made for me. Only me. The darkness and echo of my own thoughts was the only noise within my mind. I was alone.

"No."

I thought I would be angry. Filled with seething endless wrath. Outrage. But it wasn't there. The only thing I could feel was emptiness. Not even coldness. No cry for vengeance. Just emptiness. I was empty except for my memories of him. Dan had filled my soul with life and joy and fun and a reason to live. But now. Nothing. Dan would want me to fight. To live. But I didn't want to live another second, let alone forever. Not without him. Not without my Dan. What was the point?

"Dan." I spoke once more and then started shutting myself down like someone turning off the lights in a house a room at a time. I stopped breathing. I stopped moving. I stopped hearing the noises of the soldiers talking around me and the whirling noise of the helicopter. I stopped everything. Without Dan I had nothing. I was nothing. Empty. I was emptiness. Only my mind was still there. I knew I could end that too when I was ready. I could just cease to be and let it all end. I wasn't really alive anymore anyway. I was already dead, only my will and the magic it made kept me alive and I had no will to live without him. Without my will I knew that the magic would die and all that was left of what I had become would disappear into nothingness. Emptiness.

I let go of everything except my mind.

I drifted in a motionless sea of quiet night. Without feeling. Without sight. Without sound. Without smell. Empty. Just me and the emptiness. All alone except for my memories of Dan that rushed to fill in the open empty expanse of my mind like flood waters washing across a desert. But memories, no matter how wonderful and beautiful were just memories. I was still alone.

Rain had been wrong about keeping us safe, but she was right about one thing. Death sucked when you were alone. It really sucked.

I waited in the emptiness while my mind flooded with the leftovers of my life. Alone.

Black Rain

Hell Comes Calling

EMMA REACHED OUT and touched the liquid-like surface of the silver mirror I formed on the wall of the Cathedral Hall. She pushed a single long-nailed finger into the surface and beyond then pulled her hand back quickly and smiled, fascinated, as ripples echoed across the silver surface where she'd disturbed the quiet of its reflection.

Emma wasn't naked anymore, I'd made her clothes to wear. But as with her hair, she had her own ideas about what she would wear in her new life as a witch. She'd insisted on wearing pants, but I had chosen what kind. They were white, made from a material that looked like very expensive leather that I molded to her body like a second skin. It was a fit only magic could create and she looked positively indecent in it, but with her new body, she'd look indecent in anything she wore.

The short-sleeved red and white top that I made for her looked almost normal until she turned around and revealed that it was completely backless with only one thin strap at the neck to hold it in place. The material simply hung down the front. Any sudden movement or long stretch would reveal her perfect breasts to the world.

Emma didn't complain about my totally "hoish" choice of attire I made for her. She asked if I liked it and smiled when, embarrassed at myself, I confessed that I did. I made her a pair of red calf-high boots that added another inch and a half to her six foot one inch frame. I finished off her ensemble with a belt made out of brilliant red rubies the size of dominos with a circular black onyx clasp.

Her tattoo glowed as bright as her beautiful smile as she played with the mirror that I made to take us into the vampires' crypt. Emma's otherworldly beauty was breathtaking. Not of this world. I knew I should be worried about what this much change would do to her, but it was hard to worry because I liked the changes as much as she seemed to. She was beautiful. And she was happy.

"Can we go through now?" she asked me.

"You'll need to wait here till I make sure it's safe, Emma. I have to make sure they're not already awake. I won't risk you getting eaten if they're awake and too hungry to think straight. I'll be okay if they kill me on accident, but I won't risk losing you."

Emma's face darkened, her stunning copper gold eyes squinted at me, and her black lips pressed into a tight line.

"I can't risk it," I said. I looked at her and even the thought of her in pain made my heart squeeze tightly inside my chest.

Emma watched me, her eyes focused on the hand that I had pressed to my chest then she studied my face for a moment more before nodding grudgingly. "All right. But don't be gone long."

"Would you like us to carry him for you, Princess Rain?" asked one of the servants holding the Frenchman we were about to carry into the vampires' crypt as a waking meal for Jane and Dan. Breakfast. This would be the only "breakfast" that they would ever have (as they would never sleep again), so I was glad we could make it special with this little surprise.

I studied our prisoner and almost laughed. *Who went ape with the tape?* I wondered. His mouth and jaw were mummified, hidden under a mound of silver duct-tape. His arms were bound behind his back and his feet were bound about at the ankles so that he couldn't walk or stand without assistance.

Six servants had escorted him into the Cathedral Hall and two of those men now held him erect, each holding an arm. The Frenchman's eyes were alert and observant. He seemed calm. As if he were a willing participant in what was happening. Maybe he just didn't care.

I noticed that these men, our guards, were having a hard time not looking at Emma. Of course they'd already seen all of her earlier and what she wore now wasn't much better than being naked. Too bad for them she didn't like boys.

I grabbed the Frenchman with my mind, like an invisible hand fashioned from my will alone. "Let him go," I said.

The two servants glanced at each other then obeyed me. They opened their hands and stepped away. The man did not fall onto the floor like they expected but remained erect, held in place by an invisible force that did my bidding. He hung, suspended in the air an inch off the ground. All eyes watched as he floated toward me. His eyes flitted about as he realized he was levitating but his calm held.

I came closer and looked into his face, studying this man who had robbed me and helped kill me for money. His muted grey eyes were interesting but not stunning. He looked to be in his early thirties and had that sense of being a simple and hard man. Practical.

"Do you speak English?" I asked the man.

"He does, Princess Rain," one of the servants answered for the doomed man.

The duct taped prisoner nodded in confirmation, bobbing his head up and down in a quick jerk. I didn't remove the tape. I didn't want him to speak, only to listen to my words and understand me. His next spoken words out loud would be voiced to someone I could not speak to myself and that was his only worth now. That, and the warm living blood that pulsed through his veins. He was food. And maybe a phone. I felt no sympathy or empathy for the man. His death did not seem cold or cruel to me. It just was.

"You understand that you're about to die?" I asked him.

His eyes closed and he nodded again.

"Are you in any pain at all? Does your head hurt?" The bloody cut on his forehead looked nasty and painful.

His eyes opened. He looked surprised. He studied my solid black eyes curiously. He nodded slowly this time.

I willed his body to heal and the cut on his head sealed itself, his split lip healed, and even the crook in his nose that must have happened years ago straightened. His eyes stared at me in suspicious thankfulness.

"I've done this kindness for you. In exchange can you do something for me?" I asked him.

He looked confused, but he nodded and raised both shoulders at the same time. "Sure, but I'm about to die, so what can I do?" was spoken by his body language and easily understood. His spoken words were not needed, but they were what I wanted.

"When you see God in just a few minutes, and the brightness and power of his glory drive you to your knees and make you cry out that He is Lord. Please sir. As you worship him before you are judged by him, I would ask that you remember me in your heart at that moment, that some small part of what I am may worship him too."

That was not what he expected. His surprised eyes looked into my solid black gaze and I watched the mysterious light of revelation dawn within this hard murderous man. It was the sight of eyes that believed. Truly, 100% believed. Perhaps it was the imminent fact of his death or maybe it was the common way I had spoken to him, like God was a real person and not a phantom idea without shape or form. Who knew what had done it, but that magic switch had been thrown inside his head and I almost wished it hadn't been. He'd been so calm and even accepting before, but now he writhed like a man possessed.

"Well shit," I muttered crossly.

But the doomed man wasn't the only one that I'd weirded out by my unusual request. The six servants who stood nearby were looking at me and the writhing Frenchman with wide frightened eyes.

"What the hell!?" Emma shouted as the man struggled wildly against his bonds, his eyes bulging and frantic. A red spot had bloomed in his right eye as he strained against his bonds with every ounce of strength he had. "What the hell's wrong with him?" Emma asked again.

"Yes. Exactly," I answered lightly, but Emma and the six servants standing nearby stared back at me with blank questioning faces. My sad attempt at being witty with such a horrible subject had died the grisly death the effort deserved. I made a second attempt with all the gravity the topic should have received the first time.

"A second ago this man didn't believe God was real, Emma. Now—he does," I explained.

"So this guy freaked out because he believes God is real now?" Emma asked, still not able to understand his wild reaction.

"He doesn't want to burn, Emma. He's afraid of the judgment of God. He's afraid of hell."

"Hell," Emma said. Not really a question.

All eyes watched as I nodded gravely. "He'll be there in less than an hour. Maybe sooner."

Fear, dread, terror—it spread like a contagious airborne virus, first blazing to life in the eyes of the doomed man, then spilling over into the servants in their worried glances at the frantic Frenchman. They watched his desperate writhing with renewed interest, as if they could see the licking flames of hell even now, rising up through the mosaic tile floor and making the man squirm even more.

And I saw the spark of it grow in Emma's copper gold eyes as understanding came, bringing with it—FEAR. The fear of God. I watched Emma's face as fear burned brightly for a moment but then faded like a red hot ember spat out of the fire, glowing brightly for a moment before going grey and cold. The fear was replaced by a small smile that slipped onto her lovely face as she gazed at me. I wondered why and what she could possibly be thinking inside her unusual mind, but I didn't want to speak and ask about "hell" or "God" or anything that would scare her and spoil the smile, so I said something else instead.

"You're beautiful," I said, without thinking how odd a thing this was to say to a girl.

Emma blinked in surprise as did the men standing nearby; they'd all heard me say it—and they'd seen us kiss just a few moments ago. Instantly, I felt like a complete and total idiot! I looked down at my feet to hide my red face, flushed with the evidence of my embarrassment right there for all to see!

SHIT! That sounded so, so—boyfriend/girlfriendish! Now you've done it, Rain! *But I didn't mean to egg her on!* I answered myself. It was an accident. It just slipped out. *Yeah! But it sounded so weird!* But she is beautiful. *Yes! But you didn't have to say it in front of six men!* So what if I—

"Crack!" The odd noise ended the argument going on inside my head and made me look up. I was relieved to see that everyone's attention was captured by the same sound; they were all looking at the thrashing man suspended in air who was now emitting a disgusting, gurgling sound.

One of the servants came over and inspected him. He ran a hand over our prisoner's duct taped face. "Blessed Be!" he exclaimed. "He was trying to scream so hard that he broke his own jaw! I think he's drowning in his own blood!" The men standing around all looked horrified by this grim revelation.

At least he's getting in some good practice before he starts screaming for all eternity, I thought to myself, careful to keep that thought safely in the shadows of my own mind. Who knew what they would do if I uttered that aloud?

The man had stopped screaming and seemed to be whimpering now, and every couple of seconds we could see his throat move, his Adam's apple bobbing up and down as he was forced to swallow his own blood or drown. I didn't want him eating the vampires' breakfast, which was weird, because "he" *was* the vampires' breakfast. I made a mental note to add this situation to my list of weird things.

With a thought I fixed his jaw and stopped his bleeding, and right away he started screaming again. I sighed. Oh well. *Practice makes perfect,* I thought as I turned back to Emma.

"I'll be right back for you, Beautiful, just let me make sure it's safe to visit first."

I quickly pushed the doomed man through the mirror and almost fled through the shimmering wall myself to escape the watching eyes of the servants who had heard that last bit.

Emma's hungry eyes watched as I vanished into the mirror. One kiss, no matter how long and passionate and wonderful would not be enough for her. She hadn't humiliated me by asking me if I'd liked it. After our kiss, I was the one who felt awkward, embarrassed, and shy, even though she was the one standing there completely naked in the middle of the huge room with the servants looking on. I seemed to lose the capacity for speech as I stood there until Emma spoke first.

She had promised me that she would not try to kiss me again until she had spoken to Believer. Then she smiled at me, called me a dork, and asked if I could "please" make her some clothes.

I walked along the tunnel-like cave lost in my happy thoughts, the floating Frenchman following, pulled along by an invisible tether, hovering a few inches above the ground like a red balloon tied to the wrist of a wandering child at a fair.

"Hehehe." A little laugh escaped as a wicked thought occurred to me. She'd promised not to kiss me. I hadn't promised not to kiss her. Hmmm.

A hand came out of the darkness and grabbed me, snatching me off my feet! I felt a blade as it was pressed to my throat.

"Don't move or say a word! Not one word!" said a gruff male voice at my ear, his hot breath right in my face. I could feel the prickle of his stubbled face scrape roughly on the flesh of my cheek and I felt terror build in my chest at the feel of unwelcome male hands holding me roughly! I was terrified.

I nodded before I thought to do anything else or that I didn't need to worry about what this man did to me. My trembling fear was the natural reaction of a woman when she's attacked by a man, horrible fear and panic. That same idiocy all of us females complain so bitterly about when we see it displayed in a scary movie, where the girl freezes or freaks out or just stands there and screams until she gets stabbed or eaten by the monster instead of running away. This reaction seemed hard wired into me. I wasn't human, or mortal; I could crush the earth like an empty beer can with only a thought—but I was still a girl, and my first reaction was that of a terrified girl.

He must have felt my fear and the trembling of my body because he eased his crushing grip on me and lowered me down to the ground. "Just relax. We're not here to hurt you. We'll be gone in a just a few minutes, so just stay still. There's nothing to worry about." He still had his knife pressed to my throat.

A second soldier, face blacked out, emerged from the darkness; the whites of his eyes were bright and wide as he looked at me and my forehead. "SHIT!" he swore quietly. His attention was still focused on my forehead.

"Yeah. Shit," said the man holding me calmly. He sounded confident, in control.

"Which one is she, Blue?" asked the new soldier, younger and smaller than the one who held me.

"Black Witch," said the man holding me, who I guessed was named "Blue."

"Holy shit. Has she tried to do anything?"

"No. But come here and check out this guy behind me. He's all tied up and floating in the air."

The soldier slipped out of my sight. I finally recovered from my initial shock and was able to think again. A big hand was covering my mouth so I couldn't ask any questions, so I thought about what I had already heard. The soldier had said that they weren't here for me—and if they weren't here for me—then that must mean—

My blood ran cold. Goosebumps sprang up on my arms. They were after Jane and Dan. They were here to kill Jane and Dan. What would I do if they had killed Jane? What would I do? What would I do? What would I do? I began to shake.

"Easy, girl! Don't do nothing stupid!" The point of the knife bit into the flesh of my throat.

I willed my flesh to heal and then for my skin to become impenetrable. I drew in a deep breath and closed my eyes, but the man holding me lost it and tried to stab me. I didn't know exactly what moved him to action, but he pushed as hard as he could, trying to drive the knife into my throat.

"Drop her! Drop her!" the man shouted as he stabbed. He kept trying the knife on my throat and back with no success for another few seconds, then he dropped the knife and wrapped both of his arms around my head.

I willed my bones to stay unbroken and my limbs to stay in place a moment before he tried to twist my neck off my shoulders. And then a second man was there, lashing out, trying to stab me with his own knife. I had ultimate power, but it was all held inside a girl's body that weighed a hundred and twenty pounds, and the two huge men smothered me, ripping away my clothing as they tore and slashed at me in a mad blur of limbs.

I'd had enough. I willed fire to spew from my mouth, and it poured out like a flame thrower, as if I were a human dragon. First one man then the other disappeared in a wash of orange and red flames, and I collapsed to the floor as the hands holding me turned to ash or burning stumps. I closed my mouth, ending the spewing inferno as I lay on the floor of the cave.

I was covered in blood, ash, and gore and my dress was mostly burnt or ripped off; only a few tattered smoking shreds remained. I coughed and tried to hold my breath as I picked myself up off the floor and willed the fire and smoke to go away. At my feet were the charred remains of two soldiers. Parts of them were gone, burnt to ash, but other bits were still recognizable for what they had been only a minute ago. Men.

Behind me I heard movement. I turned, unhurried, to see the Frenchman struggling to free himself with one of the knives that had been dropped on the ground. The surging power within me was held, a constant thing. Controlled. No longer threatening to burn my flesh to cinders. My hair moved about me in a easy breeze of power as I turned to go, leaving the Frenchman to his efforts. Unimportant.

I needed to check on Jane and Dan. I walked down the hall and toward the bedchamber. I saw movement up ahead. Soldiers in the doorway. Shots rang out. "Pop! Pop! Pop! Pop!" On and on little flashes of light danced and bullets shredded more of my dress from my body, and the force of their blows drove me backwards. Soon everything went silent again.

I didn't want to kill these men until I had spoken with them. I willed the air in the room to become thick, wrapping around the men and holding their bodies still but still allowing them to breath. I moved forward. Two men stood motionless at the entrance of Jane and Dan's bedchamber.

Their eyes followed me but they did not move or speak. One soldier held a knife gripped in his hand, his hard face set in a determined scowl with his teeth gritted together; the other was a younger man, Mexican, holding a tube-like object that looked like a gun or weapon. I passed them by and entered the room where just this morning I had seen Dan and Jane, safe in each other's arms.

I looked at the empty bed. At the bloody white sheets.

The empty bed. The bloody sheets.

My eyes searched the room. Standing to one side of the room were two men, frozen, each wearing gas masks and holding one side of a body-sized black canvas bag. Smoke was rising out of the open bag. With a thought I slashed the bag from top to bottom and the contents gushed out onto the floor like the insides of some sea creature's stomach, spilling its horrors onto the deck, revealing the unfortunate souls that it had eaten.

I could recognize bits, floating in the brown sea of steaming liquid that covered the floor. Before it reached my bare feet I willed the brown liquid to vanish along with the toxic fumes that had started to make my throat raw as I tried to breath. On the floor, I recognized a finger. A kneecap. Part of a leg. A piece of torso. Another piece. An unrecognizable scrap there. There was so little left.

I slowly went to my knees on the floor. Where were my tears? I felt numb. Somehow I wasn't even surprised. I had been too happy. Just moments before my world was perfect and beautiful, even wonderful, but it had been a lie. It was all my fault for forgetting what I was. As within, So without. I was like a pile of shit wrapped up in a beautiful box with a black bow. I'd even fooled myself. I thought I was giving the ones who loved me something beautiful when I gave myself to them, but I was wrong. Sooner or later the lid came off—and what I was would take its toll on those who put their trust in me. I was a murderer.

"Death is all around me. Love and death and murder," I said out loud.

Jane and Dan had trusted me to keep them safe and I had let them be murdered in their beds. I had promised to keep them safe. Somehow I had lied. A witch wasn't supposed to lie. But it seemed that a Black Witch could.

I loved Jane. I loved Dan. I had done what I was born to do, kill that which I loved the most.

I had killed Rain Marie. I had killed Brendon. And now I had killed Jane and Dan.

EMMA! What would Emma do when she found out!?

"Oh! Oh God! Nooo!" My whole body went warm and then cold, then warm and cold again. I felt light headed and dizzy and swayed on my knees, seeing dots in my vision. Emma would kill me and I would let her. I would beg her to do it. Over and over!

Or worse. Emma would kill herself. I heard it like an echo: "I kill that which I love the most."

I began to shake uncontrollably. I took a shuddering breath into my shaking body. I smelt. I smelt—roses. Just the weakest of smells. A faint trace of that sweet fragrance still hung in the air.

My eyes opened and I focused on the floor beside me. The finger was moving. Then I noticed that all around me, where I knelt, all the little pieces and bits of flesh scattered on the floor were trying to move, struggling toward me like I were a loadstone that drew in death like a magnet did metal. Instead of shrieking and running from the room like a sane person I closed my eyes and pulled in my senses, focused them, and felt the death around me.

Dan! I felt him! Here in the room! His were the pieces and parts, but Jane was not here; she was truly already gone. But Dan was still here, although I could feel him slipping away even now. Going—the smell was growing fainter each second.

"NO!" I yelled.

I didn't open my eyes, but I willed the finger and the other pieces of his flesh to come together and form his body anew. I poured my rage and power into my will as I felt him fading away.

I opened my eyes. Standing before me was Dan. Remade, nude, perfect, whole, and complete.

Dan looked at me for a moment, then scanned the room. Apparently satisfied that I was safe, he smiled, then toppled over onto the floor. The smell of roses surged powerfully then fled the room. I felt it like a rushing wind as it sucked the last bit of what Dan was out with it—and then he was gone.

No Jane. No Dan. "They're gone."

If I had only been here an hour earlier I could have saved them both. Or even a minute earlier, I could have saved Dan. I had saved him, but he didn't want to live without his Jane. He'd let himself go. They were both dead.

I was still on my knees. I felt detached from all reality. My living fantasy was a living nightmare. I was an unnatural abomination. A murdering horror. As within, so without. A shred of a soul that was created for the sole purpose of killing those that I loved whether I wanted to or not. Who would be my next victim I wondered? Believer, my father, Ryan, or just some innocent without a name that I would kill just because.

I was damned. I had died and God had cast me out, into a hell made just for me, my own oblivion. But I had stubbornly returned where I was no longer welcome. Surely my punishments would be endless. Since I insisted on living here where I did not belong God would devise a hell for me here on earth so intricate and painful that it will make brimstone, wormwood, and hellfire into cool water and a warm comfortable coat by comparison. This moment must be only the beginning of sorrows, the beginning of His wrath, but I had to admit, as an odd smile bent up one trembling corner of my mouth—it was a damn fine beginning.

Black Rain

A Fate Worse than Death

I MUST HAVE fallen asleep or passed out, but I woke as I felt a wet rag on my face, wiping at the grime and filth. Cooling me. I opened my eyes expecting to see one of our servants, but it was my murderer. His face was sooty, and a red blistered burn was on one side of his head and his hair looked singed on that side. He had a shred of damp cloth in his hands.

His eyes watched mine as he wiped my face again. Gently. I noticed that he was missing a shirt sleeve. Must be what he's using to wipe my face, I thought. I didn't care why he was still here or why he hadn't run away. Unimportant.

"Princess. Please. Please drink." His words were clear but still colored with a French accent like you hear in the movies. He held a black plastic canteen up to my lips.

I swallowed, but the water stung my sore throat as it went down and I turned my head away and started coughing, which also hurt. Cold water spilled down my neck and back, making me shiver as I raised a hand and massaged my sore throat. The fire, and then the fumes from the acid must have hurt my lungs and throat. My exterior was impervious, but it seemed I hadn't made my insides quite so untouchable.

"Merde!" my French murder swore quietly. "Forgive me, Princess. I did not mean to wet you so—"

"It's okay." My voice came out thick and low.

"Please take another drink, Princ—"

"Shhh," I urged.

He shut up but held the canteen ready. I couldn't feel my legs at all. They tingled like they'd fallen asleep. It seemed strange to still have human conditions like thirst, circulation problems, numbness, and pain when I held this much power within my body. But it felt right to be weak and be strong at the same time. For some reason human weakness made me feel connected to this dream of a life far more than limitless power did. So mote it be.

I raised both of my arms out to my sides. "Help me up."

My murderer carefully put his arms under mine and lifted me onto my feet.

The three soldiers in the room were watching me. The two men who had been holding the canvas bag, and another man that I hadn't noticed before, who leaned up against a wall, his bleeding arm wrapped up and cradled in his lap. The two men outside the door couldn't turn their heads to see me. I looked over to Dan's nude body, lying on the floor, pale and perfect. And dead.

I took one deep breath. My legs tingled, pins and needles. I wanted to stand on my own, but couldn't. I did not want to use magic to make it happen. What to do? I needed a chair. But then I looked at the room. There was no chair in the room and the place was a shambles. The bed looked destroyed, the bloody sheets torn and all over the floor. Camo and black colored military gear—bags, plastic bottles, jackets with plastic zippers, and such were scattered all over. An array of bloody bandages littered the area around the wounded man against the wall.

My eyes fell on a large axe, lying on the floor near the bed. *They used an axe on them*, I thought. These men came here, broke into their grave, drug them out of their wedding bed, and chopped them into little pieces and melted them with acid.

Evil. The word hummed in my head.

Murderers. Echoed soon after.

They were just teenagers. They were in love. These men had to know that what they were doing was wrong. Evil. It made my stomach turn to look at the axe and think of the little pieces that had burst from the bag of acid, but I refused to look away until I felt it coming.

I pitched forward and vomited. My murderer struggled to keep me upright with his arms around my middle while at the same time trying not to touch me indecently. I went again. Again. And once more, then dangled, panting and exhausted, limp as a rag in his arms. He pulled the damp cloth from where he had tucked it into his belt and wiped my face clean without saying a word.

I struggled to stand. It took a minute, but I finally stood on my own power and waved off his arms. I took a deep breath and filled my lungs with the sickly, sour smell of my own vomit.

I looked about me. I looked at the men who had murdered my friends and an odd thought occurred to me. I was a murderer too. And my Frenchman was a murderer. And these men were all murderers. Wow! It was a regular "Murderers' Convention" down here and I hadn't even known. I must have missed the memo. Perhaps my invitation got lost in the mail. I'd have brought chips and dip or at least dressed better.

Somehow a laugh burst from my mouth stinging my sore throat. The sound was hoarse and rough and sounded insane in my own ears, but I didn't care. "It's like AA," I said to them. "We're all murderers. We're all addicts." I had to stop to cough, which was annoying.

I willed my body, throat, and lungs to heal and filled myself with strength, not just "power," and I released some of my power through my flesh. Instantly I became light as a feather on my feet. My hair that was lying still and lifeless now rose and waved about behind me. I stood straighter and spoke cheerfully now to my fellow murderers, letting my imagination go wild and not even trying to reign it in.

"I apologize, guys. I didn't know that we were having a meeting tonight. I can't believe Dan and Jane left the place such a mess. Just give me a minute and I'll clean up for them."

I thought about the bed and all the loose items in the room (except the axe) coming together in the middle of the room and everything broke apart into a billion little particles like sand and drifted on air toward the center of our now bare room. An oval table with seven comfy chairs formed where the bed had been. The room seemed larger now without the bed and table that had been on the side of the room. I walked to the head of the table.

"All right, come on everyone and take your seats. We're ready for our group therapy now. It's time to share," I said encouragingly, my voice upbeat. The eyes of the soldiers looked frantic and worried as did the Frenchman.

"You guys are new, but don't be shy. There's no better way to work through your problems than to share them with others who have the same problem, so let's all take our seats and we'll get started."

I willed the air holding the men secure to wrap them like a second skin from their shoulders down to their toes and leave their heads and mouths free. I walked the men toward the table like robots and had them sit in the chairs. Even the Oriental man who had been slumped against the wall rose with a shout of pain, walked over, and took a seat at the table. I stayed at the head of the table. The smiling hostess.

"Everyone stay calm and do as she says," said the oldest one.

"You must be the man in charge of this fine group of murdering bastards," I said with a bright happy smile for him. "I'd say I'm glad to meet you, but," I gave him a thoughtful nod of my head, "you did just butcher two people that I love more than my own soul, so I'm not really very happy to see you. I know that's not a good way to start group but we all need to be honest with our feelings."

"Shit, she's fucking nuts, Bull!" said the skinny man with the wild eyes.

"Listen! The lady wants to talk. Talking is *good*," the older man urged.

Even I could hear the unsaid communication. If she's talking to us, we're not dead, and maybe, just maybe, if we talk long enough the cavalry will come or we can find a way out!

My attention was drawn to the Frenchman. He stood beside the only empty chair looking very uncomfortable. "Did you wish for me to sit also, Princess?" he asked.

"Are you a murderer?" I asked him.

"Oui," he said without hesitation, then sat in the chair.

I smiled. "I'll start, and then we'll go around the room. Okay?" I cleared my throat that did not need clearing just to set the mood. "Here is the way we will do this. First, say your name, then say what you are, then tell the group about at least one person you murdered and how you did it. I'll start. My name is Black Rain and I'm a filthy murderer. I murdered my own child. I had an abortion." I looked to the man beside me. He was a huge black man with a shiny bald head.

"They call me Tiger," he said in a deep rich voice. "But my real name is Malcom Tiege. I'm a murderer. I killed a woman in Iraq by accident when I was trying to shoot the guy beside her. I didn't mean to do it, but I killed her." Weak, not what I wanted, but I let it go and looked to the next seat which was the Oriental man with the hurt arm.

"My name is Keyno," he said, his voice filled with so much pain it was hard to make out the words. "I'm—I'm a murderer. I've killed women and children taking out a target with laser-guided bombs. I was painting the target for the bombs to drop." Very weak.

And the next man, Spider, was the same. A bomb blast with collateral damage. They were playing my game but not the way I wanted to play. My smile was gone now. The leader of the group was even worse; he said that he'd ordered men into action even though he thought the orders were shit and had gotten men killed.

My Frenchman went next, his was much better. "My name is Phillepe. I am a filthy murderer. A thief and a bastard. I helped kill you, Princess, and two others before you."

I looked at the last man, the big angry man who had been by the door. He didn't look like he was going to play the game like the rest. I could tell he was going to be different.

"My name is Red. I'm a soldier. I follow orders," he said in his deep, gravely voice and eyed me with a look that would intimidate almost anyone alive. His body didn't move but I could see the cords in his neck flexing against my hold on him. He ground his teeth together making a squeaking grinding sound. He looked like he wanted to kill me with his bare hands. The others all started shouting.

"Red! Play along dammit! That's an order!"

"You're gonna get us killed!"

"Don't piss her off, Red!"

"Easy man!"

I willed the air holding the other men to shut their mouths and keep them quiet so Red and I could finish our pleasant conversation. It was quiet but the silent communication continued, with the other four men giving Red desperate eye contact, begging or ordering him to give in, go along, and get with the program.

"Red," I said. He turned back to me, visibly calmer. It seemed he was going to try to play nice. It was a wasted attempt because there was no nice in me, but my voice was calm and I even wore a smile as I spoke to him. "So what happened in this room? It was just orders. None of it stained your soul. You didn't do anything wrong. You committed murder but it's not your bad. You're white as snow on this?"

The corners of his eyes tightened, like he could smell a trap built out of words. He answered calmly, cautiously, carefully now, like he could feel the danger drawing closer and the only weapon he had to hand was his voice.

"We knew it was a horrible thing to do, but we had our orders. Just like in the Bible, sometimes King David asked his men to do horrible things that were evil, but his men obeyed him anyway. They were soldiers just like us. They obeyed their king. Just like us."

I was shocked! I laughed out loud! "You MUST BE shitting me!" I barked out, and laughed some more, a wide amazed smile hanging on my face as I spoke. "You're gonna go all Bible on me after you just butchered two kids in their beds with an axe? There's no way you can walk away from what you did in this room and not feel darkness weigh down your soul." I gave him my best "you're full of shit" look.

I saw the first faint evidence that a conscious dwelled somewhere within the man. He looked embarrassed by the attempt himself, a small twitch worried his check for a moment and his eyes darted to the side of the room where Dan's naked body lay crumpled on the floor before he hardened his face and returned his newly focused gaze back to me and made another attempt to justify his sin.

"I didn't say I wouldn't have nightmares about it. This was some horrible scary shit! But it wasn't our call. We're soldiers following orders. And these were horrible orders that we didn't like, but we did what we had to do, what we were ordered to do. We're sorry for your friends, but someone was worried that they'd go crazy once they rose from the grave and start killing people, or maybe even make more vampires, and then it would spread like a plague. Vampires all over the place, killing people. That was why they did this. It was their call. Again. Their call! NOT OUR CALL!" he said emphatically, like "not our call" was chiseled somewhere in granite on a wall, and therefore nothing could be laid at his feet. He was untouchable. His character, above reproach. His actions, too noble to be questioned, all because it was "NOT HIS CALL."

I was done with him and his bullshit excuses. "Red, I believe you. And since you were the only man in the room that said he was not a murder, I'll even let you go. You really shouldn't be in our Murder's Anonymous meeting anyway. You're too good for us. So get the hell out." I released the man from the grip of air holding him in his chair.

He flexed his arms for a moment, shot a quick glance to the man named "Bull" then pushed back his chair and stood up and started to walk away.

"Red," I called to him before he reached the doorway. I willed air to hold him there and keep him silent while I turned him around so I could see him.

He didn't look surprised that I'd stopped him. He looked like he expected it. He was ready to die, confident he could handle it, almost eager to face it. He was a soldier. He'd faced death over and over. Like a lover he'd been courting for years, and now she was finally ready to take him into her arms. Death and Love were all around me; I saw it in many places others did not. He thought her kind and loving. I smiled at the idea of arrogance in general. My own and others.

"I have some new 'orders' for you. Before you go," I spoke in rhyme, letting the words fall from my lips, not even knowing what I'd say from word to word,

"As above and so below, a secret mission I bestow.
Take the axe up from the floor, take it home and through your door.
Greet your loved ones with a kiss, then cut them up in little bits.
Use your skills and hunt them down, sneak and move without a sound.

All your family, every one. Brothers! Sisters! Mothers! Sons!
When you've butchered all your kin, lay the axe to all your friends.
Kill and chop and swing your axe. Follow orders! Don't be lax.
Avoid capture if you can, plot and think, scheme and plan.
Perhaps when you are finally done, when you stand before God's Son.
When He shouts, 'WHAT! HAVE! YOU! DONE!'
'Not my fault!' you will say. 'Not my call!' Not on that day.
'I had orders!' you may protest. 'I had to obey!' you may contest.
'You did have orders!' God will say. 'My golden rule you disobeyed!'"

I floated out of my chair and hung in the air before them like a half naked, burned, and bloody vision of divine judgment. The rags and shreds of my black dress waved about and my hair billowed around me like I floated in water not air. Power made my voice echo and vibrate in the room as I spoke, but I did not shout the words.

"Do unto others, as you would have them do unto you. So mote it be."

Red had gone pale as a ghost. I released my hold on him and he staggered, putting a hand out against the wall to keep from falling to the floor. I released the air from the mouths of the other men in the room. They were all white as ghosts as well. No one talked, though they could if they chose to. They were speechless. They seemed to shrink down into their chairs, avoiding my gaze as they watched Red.

He staggered forward. It seemed as if he were fighting against himself as he placed one big booted foot in front of the other in halting steps. But each step came quicker than the one before and soon he stood over the axe.

"Please, I'm sorry for what I did. Please don't do this!" Red whimpered. He started to cry as his big hands wrapped around the handle of the axe. He struggled, trembling, fighting against the force that possessed him.

"Pardone!" said my Frenchman murderer. He rose from the table unsteadily, a hand across his stomach looking pale and sick. "Forgive me, Princess, one moment, I—I will be sick." He came out of his chair and ran from the room in a flash. Odd. I'd just lost my cookies right here in the room. I let him go. "Unimportant" was the word that came to mind and felt right. Familiar.

The whimpering, crying, and pitiful begging coming from Red as he lifted the axe into the air and watching the French murder lose composure worked like a key in a hidden door. The four hard as steel men at the table were reduced to absolute "mush." No resistance remained. No fight. Just a white blinding roar of terror showed on each face and the knowledge that there were *indeed* worse fates than death. And "death" was exactly what Red was wanting.

"SOMEONE KILL MEEE!" The big man bellowed so loudly it hurt my ears, like sheer volume alone could force the action he wanted into being. Once he ran out of steam he drug in another ragged breath and started again. He strained to look at me as he begged for death. "Just kill me! I deserve it, lady, witch, please, just kill me! I should have never come in here! You warned us not to mess with your family, so I deserve it! I deserve it, so kill me, but don't make me kill my family. Me! Just me! Kill me!"

I heard Phillepe vomit somewhere in the distance, the gagging and retching sound mixing and blending beautifully with the ragged breathing and begging of this man before me. I did not turn my head away from the wretched sight of him. I watched and held my arms out like his suffering was the sun and I was a flower sucking in the rays of his heartache and torment like nourishment for my fiendish darkened soul. He saw no pity in my black eyes, only death.

He turned his efforts to the men held motionless at the table. "Please kill me! Kill me, Bull! You've got to let someone know! Kill me! Put me down! Have someone put me down! Keno, kill me! Spider! Tiger! Blue! Squirrel! Where are you! Kill me!"

I wanted him quiet so I gagged him with air again, shutting his mouth and ending his yelling.

"Suck it up soldier!" I growled as I floated in the air over the middle of the table and looked down at him with angry eyes. "How the hell will you complete your mission if someone kills you? And if you keep yelling you'll get yourself captured or killed. Now stop being such a spineless shit. Any man who's brave enough to enter a vampires' lair and butcher them in their bed has what it takes. Now take your axe! Go. Follow orders. Bits and pieces, Red. Bits and pieces. And don't feel bad about it. Remember. *It's not your call.*" I hissed out those last words.

He was hardly recognizable as the same hard as iron soldier that had stared me down only minutes earlier. His face was red and mottled, green and yellow snot running from his nose and mashed along his cheek. He was wet from tears and sweat and he wore an odd expression. Something new. Beyond terror. Beyond horror. He stared forward but looked beyond what was in the room, like he could see the sights and carnage that awaited—bits and pieces. Mothers. Sons. Daughters. Children.

I felt the beginnings of a chill up my own spine, but then my gaze fell on the axe and anger, warm and comforting, seeped though my whole body driving out the chill. I was content with what he faced as due penance for me and mine, but I doubted that God would be so easily impressed. Eternity in hell was a long damn time to burn.

Without another word Red turned and walked out of the room.

I floated delicately down into my own chair and sighed. "Well. I think Red has made a real breakthrough, don't you?" I said with a happy smile.

They stared at me like I was the devil herself in the flesh. I let my smile die and moved forward with our first meeting of MA (Murderer's Anonymous). So far it had been very satisfying. Now I wanted to see if I could make our meeting informative as well. "If you lie. You get the same. *Or worse*. Now who feels like sharing?"

I had no end of ready takers. They argued among themselves to see who would tell me the next morsel. I learned some amazing things, but one revelation took my breath away, gave me hope, and made me weep at the same time. Jane was alive. They hadn't killed her. They'd just stolen her away.

But her Dan was dead. I knew she would not live without him. I didn't think I had any tears left. I was wrong.

Emma Hale

Counting The Cost

E MMA NOTICED THE surprised stares directed at her by the young
male servants nearby and was instantly outraged, thinking their looks were
because Rain had called her "Beautiful" before she vanished through the
mirror. She gave the closest servant her squinty eyed gaze and demanded to know
what his problem was, intending to ruthlessly crush any homophobic issues these
men may harbor.

Dale, the unfortunate servant she'd focused on, quickly explained to his very
angry Princess that her coven mark had vanished, which caught their attention and
made them stare. Emma quickly rushed over to the mirror and stared in surprise
at her naked forehead as Dale explained that it was normal for the mark to come

and go. He told her that the same thing happened to the others when they were all alone. Her coven mark would vanish until there was at least one other witch nearby.

Emma nodded, totally embarrassed that she'd thought the worst of these men standing with her. Emma put a hand to her chest. Her heart was still racing like she'd been running sprints and all she'd done was lose her temper for a few seconds. And it happened so quickly! She closed her eyes trying get her heart rate down and get herself back under control. She loathed the idea that other people knew more about what she was now than she did herself. She was a witch, but she had absolutely no idea what that meant.

Emma wanted an owner's manual! She wanted something that she could read through and get herself up to speed on what *unexpected* thing to expect next. After a few minutes she opened her eyes and contented herself with pacing back and forth in front of the mirror like an exotic caged animal while she waited for Rain to get back so she could yell at her for not warning her about the mark, but the longer she waited the more she worried.

She tried not to overreact. Rain had said that she needed to make sure it was safe first, and she had to take care of the guy and get "breakfast" all served up and ready. She didn't want to cry "Wolf!" and cause an alarm just because Rain was taking her time—but something felt wrong. This was too long. Rain said she'd be right back.

More pacing. More worrying. More closing her eyes, trying to stay calm.

"How long has it been, Dale?" Emma asked for the fifth time. She had her eyes closed again.

"More than twenty minutes now, Princess."

Emma opened her eyes. That was too long. "I felt it! I knew it!" Emma turned to the waiting and very worried faces of Dale and the other five servants standing with him. "Run and get the King and Queen and let them know that something's wrong! Rain's in trouble! Tell them what's happening."

Without a word Dale took off, as fast as his feet would carry him out of the Cathedral Hall and toward the Dining Hall where most of the inhabitants of Amen Hale were still enjoying the evening meal. Emma looked at one of the other men. "Get some men and go check the garden, make sure nothing's happened to the Crypt."

"Yes, Princess." Two of the others took off at a run.

"Get Lucius and the others on the phone and have them get their asses back here NOW!" Emma ordered the remaining servants.

The men looked stricken. A young well-muscled black man answered. "Princess. Phones don't work in Amen Hale anymore. We can't call them and they can't call us. You'll have to go and get them yourself or we'll have to wait until they return."

"Go and get them myself?" she asked.

"Through the magic door in the kitchen. They used it to travel to Princess Rain's home."

Emma took that in and nodded. She remembered the door and knew right where it was from when she'd traveled here with Rain for her wedding. "Come with me," she ordered the last three men, then took off at a fast walk, heading toward the kitchen and the magic doorway without the first clue as to what she'd do when she got there. She'd never done magic before, but people she loved were in trouble, and she was damn well going to try to do something! If she didn't get the stupid magic door to work, then they'd find her there, clawing her way through the wood with her shiny new fingernails when they finally came back home!

Three grim-faced servants followed in her wake as she marched into the kitchen. They pushed through the busy kitchen, earning startled looks from cooks, servers, and scullery maids who gawked as they passed. They went down the dark hall in the back of the kitchen and stopped before the storage room door.

Emma grabbed the handle and froze before she twisted it. With effort, she forced herself to release the knob and take two deliberate steps back. Emma studied the door. She looked at the hastily traced outline of four hands that had been pressed to the door above the writing and then tried to read the message on the door.

She growled in frustration as she tried again and again to read the elusive words, which must have been written in some magical way that make whatever was written there turn to gibberish for anyone who didn't have permission to read it. But she should be able to read it!

Frustrated and angry, she ignored the writing and looked at the traced hand prints instead. Four prints, four witches, which meant that one of the prints had to belong to Kendal, the witch who had been murdered by psychos. She lifted one hand to her forehead and touched where her mark should have been, but it had vanished, gone, until one of her sisters returned. Maybe that was why she couldn't read the words?

In the hall behind her the servants she'd brought waited, watching her every move as she tried to puzzle out what to do next. She also heard other worried voices coming from the kitchen heading her way. She tried to ignore them as she focused again on the magical message written on the door.

"A hand placed here will open the way, at any time, on any day." She couldn't read the line but she knew what it said from when she'd first came through the door. Back then she'd been able to read it, but that was 'before'. Which made no sense! Whatever! Reasoning that "the hands" were the key to working the door she approached it from that angle alone. The smallest one had to be Bethany but the others were practically the same size; it would be impossible to tell which was hers (or which one had been Kendal's). She hoped Kendal's mark was now hers, like a birthright because she'd taken her spot in the Coven. Maybe that was why it wasn't working she worried.

She ignored the sounds of the growing crowd behind her, whispering, watching her fumbling attempt to open the door. But embarrassment wasn't part of her character when it came to someone she loved being in danger. Emma would do whatever she had to do for someone she loved, but she simply had no clue as to which of the hands *she* belonged to or if the door would even work for her at all since she wasn't Kendal.

"You can do it, Emma." Emma recognized Cathryn's voice and turned to find her "new mother" standing with the others in the crowded hallway behind her.

Cathryn paled, astounded by Emma's new appearance. She cataloged the changes one piece at a time: face, hair, body, the glittering ruby belt wrapping her slender waist. But as her eyes drank in the sight, Cathryn kept talking; like most women, she was able to manage two things at once without hurting herself. "All of your sisters can open this door, Emma. You have the power to do it also. The magic is in you; I can feel it even now. You have to trust yourself and find your own unique way to let your magic come out."

Emma frowned. Without saying a word she turned back to the door, studying the hand prints and the writing again.

"Sometimes closing your eyes helps; try that," Cathryn suggested. "Stop looking at the words and the marks, close your eyes and try to feel which is the right one."

Emma's head snapped back to Cathryn, surprise on her face. "I've been doing that a lot already."

"Doing what?"

"Closing my eyes. I've been closing my eyes at really odd times." Emma stepped away from the door, her brow furrowed as her thoughts turned inward, self searching, as she examined that realization closer.

It's just like what Rain and Mary and Bethany do when they get upset or use magic. I'm becoming one of them. I really am becoming the White Witch. She reasoned this out for herself, not upset by the idea of becoming a witch so much as she was concerned that she'd started closing her eyes without even being aware that she was doing it, or even *why* she was doing it. The change seemed spontaneous. Manifesting with no warning at all. To Emma, it felt like having a nervous habit—like stuttering, nail biting, or nose picking—appear in a flash and then blend itself seamlessly into your life as if it had always been there. TA-DA! A new "tick" or disgusting habit, right there, like magic.

Emma wasn't concerned by the changes she'd made to her body, but the changes to what made her "Emma" absolutely terrified her. She immediately began an intensive self-inventory of who she was. She wondered what other changes were steeling up on her without her even being aware enough to acknowledge the change, or the loss, and check it off her mental list as another part of the price she'd agreed to pay. She needed to add it up! Emma wanted to sum it all up, look over the bloody pile with her squinty eyed gaze, give a grim nod and say—"Yep. It ain't pretty, but there it is. And, yeah, I'm good with it."

THAT! was how it was supposed to work. THAT! was what she'd planned on. But THAT! was not what was happening! It was one thing to lose yourself a piece at a time, but it was something totally different to not even know what it was that you'd lost! She tried to focus her mind on her goals, her plans, her extensive list of internal "issues!" that she constantly dealt with, but for some reason her thoughts were wild, unpredictable, and as well disciplined as wind driven leaves.

Think about EMMA! Think about ME! She pushed herself harder. It was part of her nature. Emma needed to be organized and add things up, and this was a price she'd never counted on having to pay! Never even dreamed she'd have to pay! Emma wasn't aware of the growling sounds she made or that she backed up and flattened herself against the wall there in the hall, arms held out in front of herself, thrashing about to keep others at bay.

Her eyes were open but she was lost within herself, not seeing or hearing what was happening around her. With a chill certainty she knew that this couldn't be fixed, somehow she knew that things would never add up again for her the way they had before. Never again. She'd forever be unstable, volatile, unbalanced, unpredictable—even to herself, changeable.

I've lost my mind. I've gone insane. Emma laughed because she did not cry, but her body needed some emotional release right then so she laughed instead of crying. After a few moments she stopped and congratulated herself on at least figuring out this much. She knew that she'd gone mad. And she knew that the price to become a witch was higher than she'd ever dreamed. She thought about the loss of her mind, the thing she valued most, and she laughed and spoke to herself, she didn't even realize that she said the words out loud where others could hear.

"I didn't want this! I'm not good with this. Not good." Emma stubbornly pressed forward with her attempt at introspection. She was making some horrible discoveries, but she was learning about herself, which was what she wanted, so she pressed on. She tried to think about what other "non Emmaish" things she'd done since becoming a witch just hours ago, and the shameless way she'd chased after Rain and finally kissed her flashed in her mind like an amazingly powerful memory, complete with color-sound-texture and lots of emotion.

She felt the flush of that moment on her skin again. A prickly heat and a nervous excitement started to overwhelm her body and she forced herself to *STOP!* Don't *think about RAIN! Think about ME!* She ruthlessly drove her thoughts away from the memory and back to the path she wanted her thoughts to follow. *Am I still Emma? What else has changed!? What else is gone!? GONE! GONE! GONE!*

She raised a shaking hand to her face and finally focused her eyes on what was in front of her. She stared at the hand and confusion gripped her. She wiggled the fingers. It was the hand of a stranger, or had her hand been severed and replaced by some alien appendage while she slept? She turned it, studying it. The inch long, copper gold nails gleamed like the metal claws of some monstrous machine in the dimly lit hallway.

"Emma, are you all right!" A voice close by.

Emma met the strange woman's eyes. The tattooed, blonde lady was staring at her, concern and worry marring her lovely features. Emma had only a foggy, vague sense of recognition.

"Emma! Thank the Goddess! Can you hear me? Are you all right, child!?" Cathryn's heartsore voice was filled with relief.

Emma leaned in and studied the woman and her upset face. Her—mother's upset face? "Mom?" she wondered.

Was this woman her mother? She didn't look like her mother. Emma felt like she'd been dropped into a blender—everything was all mixed up and swirled around so that she didn't know up from down, her body and her mother's were all mixed up. She watched as the blonde woman's face softened. Emma watched with growing unease as the woman walked forward and hugged her. She stiffened, her spine and body becoming an iron rail.

Why is she touching me! The thought screamed through Emma's head, and she tried to pull away, but the lady kept holding onto her, refusing to let go. Emma struggled wildly. Then froze. Then struggled again, but the woman held onto her tenaciously, refusing to let go. Emma closed her eyes and took a deep breath, trying to relax. She hated being touched by people, but this lady would not let go! Emma was exhausted but she tried to pull away again, trying to claw and scratch, but the blonde woman fought her hands down and clung to her in a death grip and Emma started to panic. She couldn't get away!

I CAN'T GET AWAY! She screamed within herself and without as she fought on. *I can't get away! I can't get away. I can't get away.*

Emma quit struggling, gave up, and slumped in exhausted surrender, still held in the woman's arms. And that was the moment she first felt it. She didn't know exactly what it was at first, but she definitely felt something that she'd never felt before. The woman lifted one of her hands and touched Emma's face and she felt it again. It was right there, on her hand as it gently stroked her cheek and brow.

Whatever this stuff was, it was coming off the hands and arms of this woman. Determined arms that held her tight, refusing to let go.

The tattooed woman spoke, and it was there again, somehow mixed in with the comforting words that Emma heard but did not "hear." Curious, Emma reached to her mouth and felt the words and this strange new substance pass through her fingers, and with a small thrill of comprehension, she understood what it was that she felt.

It was Love.

This woman loves me, she thought. She knew it. She more than "knew it," she felt it!

Emma lost herself all over again in this odd new discovery, fascinated by it, exploring it. She examined this strange new element, this love. It wasn't completely intangible, it had a feel to it, a physical aspect to its character. She ran a hand across the bare flesh of the woman's arm and rubbed her fingertips together. It was a sensation more than a texture she felt between her fingers. It wasn't heat or cold, or a slimy or gritty feel, it was something she didn't have a name for because she'd never felt anything quite like it before.

She didn't worry herself with questions about "why" she could feel "love," but simply accepted it for what it was, an awareness of its presence. She couldn't see it with her eyes in a practical sense, but she still knew it was there. She could touch it and grab it with her hand. It had a quantity and a quality and other unique details. It moved about. Little wisps of it floated in the air around her, left over bits from the woman's words.

She used her cupped hands to gather in a small cloud of it and brought it to her face and inhaled. It did not make her choke or gag, like smoke or water if they got into your lungs, but it did calm her. And it even made her thirsty for more. She put her fingers in her mouth and sucked the alien substance off her fingers and swallowed, tasting it. Consuming it. She didn't taste it with her palate; the stopping and tasting point for this substance seemed to be deep inside herself where she felt it settle within the core of her body and even down into her bones.

Emma ran her hands across the woman's face and gathered a good handful and brought it to her mouth and licked it from the palm of her hand and ate it. Like a twisted dimmer switch, her dim perceptions bloomed into bright crystal clarity. Love was there. Coming off of this lady's skin, hair, and even the words that came out of her mouth in little puffs, curling out into the air. Love. Emma breathed it in, tasted it, she held her hand in front of the woman's mouth as the words came out, surrounded by and filled with love.

She thought she understood the nature, type, and flavor of this woman's "love" now. It was one that she was totally unfamiliar with but had always wanted to know for herself. Emma had dreamed of it so many times, night after night, lying awake in her bed, staring at the ceiling. Dreaming of it. Aching for it. Longing for it with all her heart but never once shedding a tear for what she desired with all her soul to know.

A mother's love for her child.

"Mom?" Emma asked, her tentative voice hopeful and pleading at the same time.

"Yes, Emma. I'm here."

Emma felt the love coming off this woman. It tasted like her mother's love but she looked nothing like her mother. She closed her eyes and stopped looking at the unfamiliar face, at the blonde hair, and the tattoos on her arms and just "felt" the truth instead of using her eyes. Her rigid body softened the rest of the way as she surrendered herself to the truth of what she felt with her eyes closed. Emma felt the love, and she returned it. Emma loved this woman who loved her like her daughter. This mother.

"I love you, Mom." Emma said the words and knew without opening her eyes that her own words were also filled with love.

Slowly and cautiously she wrapped her own arms about this woman who was her mother and waited to hear what she would say next, oblivious of anything else happening in the dark hallway or in the world around her. It was easy to shut out everything else with her eyes squeezed tightly shut. It was better to feel her than to look at her. It was less confusing. There was no doubt at all in this woman or in the love Emma felt rolling off her, and she was steadied by that confidence as she drew it deep within herself and let it warm her. Calm her. Love her.

This mother—her mother—"Mom" rocked her gently, back and forth, as she spoke. "I love you too, Emma. I'm here. I'm here my child."

Emma drew the love into herself, like parched desert ground drinking in water after a drought that had lasted through seventeen long years with her birth parents. They had been detached to the point of neurosis. Cold and distant. Loveless. Quiet. Somber.

"It's okay, Emma. Just rest, dear. Just rest."

She did as her mother asked and rested in her loving arms and stopped worrying about what she'd lost or who she was or what she was or even why she was.

"I'm good," she whispered quietly as she slipped off to a peaceful sleep. "I'm good with this."

Believer

Last Rites

THE STORAGE ROOM door swung open and Believer, the Prince of Clouds looked out into the hall, his red eyes growing bright as he took in the scene. Queen Cathryn sat on the floor, leaning against the wall steps away from the open door holding a girl he did not recognize in her arms who was either sleeping very soundly or was dead. King Cornelius was kneeling beside her looking drawn and grave, and very relieved to see him.

"Believer! Come with me. Rain needs your help!" Cornelius's desperate words were spoken while he rose to his feet, turned, and charged off, down the hall without waiting to see if he was followed.

A human stampede began as male servants who had been lining the walls and crowding the kitchen also turned to follow their King. Believer did as he was bid, following Cornelius effortlessly, somehow passing through the crowded hallway like smoke, appearing on the far side right on Cornelius's heels as he ran toward the garden and the vampires' crypt.

Once Believer moved out of the doorway he'd been blocking with his enormous body, Lucius and Mary charged out just in time to watch as everyone went dashing off after Cornelius.

"Where are the others!?" Cathryn demanded from where she sat in the floor before Lucius could take off running after the rest.

"They're still at the Bryants'. Believer and Mary insisted on returning early. What's happened here?" Lucius's eyes studied the strange creature lying in Cathryn's arms trying to make sense of what he knew must be "Emma" from the mark that appeared on her forehead. Mary stood still as stone, looking down at Emma.

"Go back!" Cathryn ordered Lucius ferociously. "Bring our people home immediately! We have been attacked!"

Lucius paused only a second, looking as if he would die if not given more information, but then he nodded, stepped back into the storage room and pulled the door closed.

Mary was frozen and speechless. Comprehension evaded her as she stared down at Emma, like a small snake trying to swallow a large egg; she wanted to understand what she was seeing but was having a hard time getting her brain to wrap around what was right in front of her.

"Breathe, Mary," Cathryn told her.

Mary sucked in a quick lungful of air once. Again. Her brain started working a little better as her lungs continued the action that had been momentarily crowded out by shock.

"Is she—"

"Emma is sleeping." Cathryn answered both questions she saw in Mary's eyes, then told her more. "Rain changed her body. She was fine. But then she had an episode."

Cathryn was tired, worn out, and roughed up. She had scratches on her neck and hand and blood had soaked through the bandages wrapped around her arm. Her hair and clothes were messy and dirty and she was wet with sweat and old tears, long dried.

"Emma's magic came upon her suddenly, and it was very difficult for her to let go of what she was and to accept what she has become. For a while she lost herself completely, lashing out, yelling, and laughing. I was so scared she would hurt herself. She didn't even know who she was or who I was, not until the very end."

"Her memory came back at the end?" Mary's voice was just a quiet whisper as she asked.

"No. I'm not all that sure that it did. She just knew what I was and that I loved her—and that was enough for her."

Mary took a step closer, but just one. She didn't want to disturb Emma while she slept, and she was scared of what touching her would do to Emma or her right now. But she ached to touch her. She had to know..

"Who attacked us?" she asked instead of asking what she really wanted to ask, which was more questions about Emma.

"Government soldiers we think. We're not really sure. They cut into the vampires' crypt earlier this evening. Of course we didn't know they were in there when Rain went to check on Jane and Dan right after you left to go to the Bryants' house with Bethany and the others. We haven't heard from Rain for almost an hour now. Our people have the crypt surrounded and there are no enemy soldiers inside the walls right now. David has scared everyone away with what he's done, but we were waiting till Believer or Sky Dragon returned before we went inside the crypt to see what's happened down there. The cloud men are the only ones who can't be killed by the vampires, if the vampires are still alive that is," Cathryn added grimly and stopped to swallow and wet her worn throat before continuing.

"If Jane or Dan yet live they may be hurt or too dangerous to be around humans. Cornelius wanted to wait for Believer or Sky Dragon. I'm sure he's already sent Believer inside the crypt by now so we'll know more soon."

Mary sat down on the hall floor, like her legs had given out. "Rain can't die, Mom. That can't happen. It's impossible." Mary said the words but her voice broke as she spoke.

"I hope you're right, Mary. I hope so." Cathryn sighed deeply and closed her eyes and leaned her head back against the wall.

More than two hundred men and even some women and children were gathered around the crypt or marching around the walls, making sure the area was secure. Flashlights and torches now lay in a heap on the ground or had been turned off and tucked away into pockets, no longer needed. About three hundred and fifty yards straight up, fixed in space directly above the crypt hovered a giant ball of yellow burning fire.

It looked exactly like a miniature sun and was visible for miles around in every direction, reminding those who saw it from a distance of a nighttime shuttle launch but one that did not lose its brightness or waver in its consistency or in its position in the sky. There was also no billowing cloud of white and grey smoke obscuring the ground beneath its perch, nor did the burning sphere unleash the roaring thunder of rocket engines the space shuttle emitted when it transformed night into day. The burning sphere was about the size of a two story house and it illuminated the area around the crypt and all Amen Hale from wall to wall as if it were high noon with its yellow tinged light.

Standing grim faced with the others holding vigil outside the crypt were a young man and a young woman wearing burning crowns on their heads. Curses were shouted in the night. Many angry curses. Amen Hale was angry. To the cameras watching from spy planes and satellites orbiting high overhead, the Kingdom resembled an angry ant nest at the eye of a much larger angry ant nest. Beyond the walls, planes flew, trucks and equipment moved, and soldiers surged about while further away panicked citizens living nearby fled and vehicles choked the highways and byways and back ways. It closely resembled the traffic nightmare caused by hurricane evacuations as tens of thousands fled the area and the raging inferno burning in the sky over Amen Hale that many were calling the Fallen Star.

Chaos ruled the night on both sides of the black glass walls. The people of Amen Hale knew that the crypt housing the sleeping vampires had been violated and that their princess, Princess Rain, was inside the crypt when it was attacked. And Black Rain was missing, but that was all they knew. Worried, angry faces of distressed men and women watched, waited, and hoped. Some even prayed as Believer's glowing form vanished inside the jagged dark opening the intruders had made in the back side of the Crypt.

Believer glided down the dark stairs, his own body giving light to see by as he glided down the steep descent, but halfway to the bottom he stopped. A soldier lay face down on the steep stair. A knife protruded from his back. His dead hands still gripped tightly to the handle of a black axe that looked covered in blood and gore.

Believer looked at the knife again, thinking it unlikely that his wife or the vampires would have killed this axe-wielding soldier with such a weapon. He wondered who had? He floated the rest of the way down to the foot of the stair and found another dead man who had received the attention of the axe-wielding soldier, but also may have been the one responsible for the knife in the soldier's back. The man had been decapitated and his body had been cut into little pieces. The clothing did not look like that of a soldier's.

Believer looked closer at the severed head and recognized him as one of the men from France who had attacked Rain earlier that day. Instantly his anger rose and his whole body trembled. A noise like rumbling thunder shook the room as Believer's eyes burned bright with his wrath. The severed head and dead lifeless eyes of the Frenchman stared back at him unimpressed. He was beyond the reach of anything Believer's anger or wrath could do to him thanks to the axe-wielding soldier.

Believer moved on down the hall but did not get far before being stopped, again, because of dead men littering his path. Two more soldiers. Both burned to death. Believer pressed on gliding the last twenty feet. He entered the vampires' bedchamber.

Dan's nude and still body rested on the top of a table that now resided in the center of the room where the bed had once been. Seven chairs surrounded the table but only one was occupied. The room's lone human occupant was an Oriental man, another soldier, who sat stiffly in his chair dragging ragged breaths, in and out.

He turned his head and looked at Believer as he entered the room, but he didn't rise up out of the chair. He looked morbidly pale and bloodless in complexion. Believer stepped closer and could see that his shirt had been ripped open and someone had punched a fist-sized hole into his chest and ripped out his heart. The heart hadn't gone far though; it lay on the table right in front of the man, still beating, still alive. And the soldier was somehow still alive enough to admire the missing organ as it did its thing, beating away, just not inside his body.

The Oriental man seemed to be unable to move anything but his head. He appeared to be held in place by the same magic that caused his unusual "heartless" condition. Believer recalled ripping someone's heart out with her bare hands was one of the threats his wife was fond of using. Although, the last time she'd threatened to eat the heart after she tore it from someone's chest. He was glad she had not eaten this man's heart, but then *she may be saving it for later.*

This thought troubled him, but he was immediately warmed by another thought. *She's alive!* This knowledge helped end the constant thunder-like rumble coming from his cloudy body. He calmed himself enough to think. He tried talking to the man.

"What happened here?" Believer's deep, powerful voice demanded.

"Black Witch killed me." The man's voice was soft, airy, and clipped. He took a gasping breath. "And she cursed me." Another ragged breath. "Can't die until after," another ragged breath, "I answer your questions." Gasping ragged breath. "And give you her message."

"Where is my wife now?" Believer rumbled.

"She didn't tell us." The man took a sucking breath. His air supply seemed to have a four-word maximum capacity before he required another breath of air. "Where she was going—but she did leave—messages—I have to give you—before I can die—and—I want to die." The man's voice was a ragged, whistling whisper, but his words were understandable. The ragged hole in his chest kept stealing his air pressure, and it made little disgusting flapping noises like a punctured tire as the man breathed in and out.

He grimaced, his face twitching and contorting in pain as he struggled to talk and breath. Apparently death had not diminished his ability to feel pain. "Are you—really—her husband?" he asked in his ragged whistling whisper as he looked at Believer's cloudy body, wondering how a flesh and blood girl could be married to a cloud man.

"Yes. I am her husband," Believer said as he pulled back a chair opposite the living dead man and seated himself.

They regarded each other across the table. Dan's nude, lifeless body and the man's bloody twitching organ lay on the table like evidence of the crime, carefully laid out for inspection.

"I have a message—for you.—She told me to—tell her husband—not to worry.—She said to tell you—she didn't die this time—she loves you."

Believer was relieved to hear from his wife, but surprised that she had left a living dead man behind as a message device. Believer had never been "creeped out" and didn't recognize the feeling in the way any human would have, but he did feel unsettled by the situation. It was disconcerting having this ruined man convey such a sentiment, from her to him, with his whistling gasps. He reminded himself what this man was, what he did, and dispelled the uncomfortable feeling as he looked down at this soldier. Perhaps delivering this message served more than just one purpose? Perhaps this was part of his punishment that she meant to inflict. Part of her anger and wrath she wanted this man to endure.

"Did you try to kill her?" Believer asked, his voice rumbling with anger.

"Not at first.—We came for vampires.—She came in before—we could finish them."

Believer looked at Dan's body on the table. The body looked intact but it also looked dead, but he had no idea if that meant that Dan was "dead" dead or just "asleep" dead. Dan's dead body might actually be alive. He looked back to the Oriental man whose slanted eyes were squinted in pain. He looked alive but must be dead. Death just wasn't simple to figure out these days.

The Oriental soldier's tormented gaze kept going back to the animated muscle beating on the table. Blood had soaked the man's clothes and pooled at his feet. He appeared to have no more blood to bleed, but still, he lived. And apparently this man would live until he had answered Believer's questions and delivered Rain's messages.

The man's distress and torment touched something within Believer, some part of him that came from she who made him, his Sky. Some compassionate part of his soul wanted this ended quickly to give relief to this man. Believer tried to push the feeling away. Perhaps this man did not deserve his pity. Perhaps he actually deserved to suffer even more. Perhaps his wife had already been more merciful than she should have been. Although he had to admit to himself, when in a foul mood, mercy was not Rain's dominate character trait. But who knew what this man had done. He turned his burning red gaze onto the man.

"Tell me who you are. Tell me why you came here. Tell me what happened here tonight. And then you can tell me the rest of your message so you can die."

Believer listened as in ragged, wheezing, whistling gasps, the man told him everything. He was part of a group of soldiers that had been ordered to move against the vampires. The man told Believer his name was Keno. He told Believer everything he knew and briefly what happened when Rain arrived before they could finish off Dan with the acid.

Believer asked more questions about the Frenchman and the dead men out in the hall and Keno told him about the horrible curse that Rain had set on one of the other soldiers, a man named Red. Hearing about the curse made even Believer go quiet for a moment as he considered what his love had almost unleashed in her fury. He thought about the man with the axe in the stairwell and was glad that he had died before he could carry out the curse. Believer told Keno about the knife in the back of the man with the axe and studied his surprised reaction to this news.

"This news shocks you greatly. I can see it on your face. Tell me why," Believer asked. He was still totally confused himself as to what could have compelled the Frenchman's actions. Believer wanted Keno's thoughts and theories to add to his own.

"The Frenchman—heard the curse—Red begging—kill him—damn nice of—French guy.—Still—didn't think—he would—do that—for Red." Believer watched as Keno shook his head like he didn't believe his own words. His wind capacity was diminishing the more they spoke and was down to two words before he was forced to refill his leaking lungs with more air.

Believer wanted to let the man go, and he knew Keno wanted to be released so he could die, but he had more to tell. When Believer was first created by his Sky, he believed every word he heard completely, instantly, but he had become a careful student of human expression since realizing how often some humans did not tell the truth or only told a small part of the truth and kept other parts hidden. Believer's curiosity to understand what had happened compelled him to ask another question.

"You do not believe that the Frenchman killed Red because he begged for someone to help him die. You do not think it was done in mercy. Why do you think he did what he did?"

Believer watched him carefully. Keno thought for a moment, putting serious consideration into his answer which made Believer value his reply even more when he finally started to gasp it out. "Think he—did it—for—Black Witch—your wife."

Keno watched Believer, his frown, and knew he didn't understand, so he added. "Didn't want—her to—hate herself—later—I think." Keno looked tired, pained. He shrugged. "Just—a guess." He was held upright by a force he could not resist but still he seemed to sag, his eyes again looking toward the beating heart on the table between them.

Believer wanted to be angry at this man, but he was not angry. He'd been trying to deny the feelings that pushed at him, almost like a physical force. Compassion. Care. Concern at the suffering of another. Empathy. All the best parts of what his creator had made within him. Parts of her soul that were parts of his soul now.

"That's enough, Keno. And I thank you," Believer's deep voice rumbled. "What other message must you tell us before you can die?"

Keno looked up and met Believer's red-eyed gaze and was surprised to find no anger there, in the way the dark clouds gathered around his eyes and mouth. No rage or anger, just compassion. Hope brightened the pallid face of the dead soldier. He appeared to rally, and draw his strength together, reassured by the knowledge that the end was near at hand. "I'm sorry, Believer.—You seem like—a nice guy.— I'm sorry—I came here."

Believer looked at this broken and ruined man and felt compassion for this human touch his soul in a way that he could not deny. In a way he would no longer resist. Fat tears, like drops of summer rain, fell onto the table before him.

"I'm sorry you came here too, Keno. For you, also, seem like a nice guy. And you have paid the price for what you have done, but this is enough. What you did to Jane and Dan is between you and them, but I forgive you your sin against me and my wife. May God your Creator receive you with grace when you return to him. Now what is your final message?"

"Thank you!—Believer," Keno said with as much feeling as he could manage through his ruined lungs. He closed his eyes and took a few moments to pray.

Believer let him have this time. While the man whispered, gasped, and prayed, Believer's brother, Sky Dragon, entered the room silently. He raised one reptilian eye ridge as he watched the praying dead man and then raised the other eye ridge as he noticed the beating heart lying on the table beside Dan's nude dead body. He extended his long neck and inspected the ragged hole in the man's chest, looking at his brother who remained silent. Quietly, so as not to disturb the praying man, Sky Dragon moved a chair back and took a seat at the table and waited.

Keno did not pray long. After a few minutes he opened his eyes. He took a moment of surprise to say hello and then in the next ragged breath goodbye to Sky Dragon. "Here is the last—message, Believer."

Believer nodded his large cloudy head formally, accepting, his slit of a mouth pressed into a tight line so that it was invisible in his features. Mixed conflicting emotions and thoughts churned through his soul.

"She said—to stay here—in Amen Hale—where it's safe—till she returns."

The heart on the table stopped beating and a last rattling breath flapped out of Keno's ruined chest. The force holding him erect vanished and he sagged forward, his head and chest landing with a dull thud on the table, pinning the heart under him, like he had finally reclaimed possession of the errant organ. Keno passed from life to death and from this world into the next, his soul going back to the one who made it. Believer watched him go in respectful silence.

"Brother, are you actually weeping for this man who attacked the vampires and your wife?" Sky Dragon asked, his voice balancing on the knife's edge between teasing and surprise or confusion and censure.

"Yes," Believer answered unashamed. "Do you remember what it was like when you were first born, when the world was brand new and confusing, my brother?" Believer waited until Sky Dragon nodded his dragon-like head before he continued. "When I was only minutes old and feeling small in myself, and much less than a person, someone very wise told me that I was most fortunate to be made from a part of Sky's soul. Because our Sky is good. Her heart is good. Her spirit is good. And her soul is good. And that I was blessed to have her make me. Blessed to have her as part of my soul."

"Who told you this, brother?" Sky Dragon asked. Captivated. He had never heard this before.

"My wife. Your sister. She told me this just before she told me that she was like us, a created friend. Only the one that created her was not good. Rain is good because she chooses to be good, she wants to be good, though there is darkness in her soul. It was made there in the way she was formed and she hates it. Kindness and mercy and compassion are a part of you, my brother; do not fight against it when a part of Sky touches your soul. We do not need to fear what is in our heart from the one who made us like my wife does."

"Forgive me, brother," Sky Dragon said as he looked at his brother's sad face.

"Of course," Believer said quietly. "It is in my nature."

Jane

<hr>

An End of the Beginning

I TRIED NOT to think about Dan, but parts of my mind rampaged inside my head completely beyond my ability to control. I was stuck, like an old scratched record playing the same song over and over or a DVD replaying the same images. I felt broken inside my soul. I was missing a part within me that had become essential to the structure of the whole, and now that part was ripped out; the roof had fallen in. The entire structure was unstable and doomed.

With my improved vampire mind I could think about so many things at once, and that was what I did now, only it was a hundred little parts of the same part combining inside me. The same person. My Dan. One part of my mind kept sorrowing about how I would never stare into his eyes again while another completely separate part of my mind fretted over not hearing his voice inside my head and recalled how his words, spoken into the quiet of my mind at an unexpected moment filled me with such a thrill of joy because I was not alone inside myself.

Another part, the feel of his touch, texture, my hands in his hair as the sandy blond strands slipped one by one through my fingers and another part was remembering in perfect detail the day we met in the doctor's office and his note that he had given to me. I still had the after taste of my McDonald's grilled chicken salad in my mouth and I was hot. The pills had made me break out in a feverish sweat, making my hair damp and stick to my brow, and little beads of sweat formed on my hot skin, cooling me.

I remembered Dan's hand as I held it. His palm was sweaty and so was mine and our warm hands stuck together where we held them, down low between us, beside the rail of the chair where others would not see. It felt wonderful. It felt perfect.

Another part of my mind remembered Dan's body moving with mine as we made love and the complete joy and peace we both shared as we held each other and drifted off into death, safe in each other's arms looking forward to our eternity together. An eternity to love and be loved by my Dan.

And though I tried to stop my mind, I could not stop it. As a vampire I knew that I would never sleep again but somehow I now dreamed a hundred dreams at the same time and was totally unable to make them stop or go away. Like a hundred "Janes" were inside my head, remembering a hundred different wonderful memories of the same person at the same time. All memories of a person I would never see again. I knew the past was all I had and I would never add to what I already held, never a new touch, a new kiss, a new word spoken into my mind when I least expected it. I couldn't go on. Not like this.

"Goodbye, Dan. Goodbye, Mom. Goodbye, Dad. Goodbye, Jane. Goodbye, all my friends. I loved you all," I whispered in my mind, and then I let go of that last small shred of my will that sustained me.

I wanted to cease. To end. To become nothing so I would forget what almost was but would never be. As I let go, no invisible cord snatched me away, nothing pulled me toward God or heaven or down toward hell. Ryan had said I was damned. Dan and I had talked about what our fate would be should something like this happen. In a way, Ryan was partly right and also partly wrong. In the sense that I would never be able to go to heaven and never see God, he had been right. That was impossible for us.

But we also would never see hell. We were removed from any 'afterlife', both reward and punishment. And though our physical bodies had no limit on how long they could live as vampires, if they did die, we would die entirely. Our eternal souls were tied, not to an eternal God, but to our physical bodies, something that had both a beginning and an end. Something that could be destroyed or forsaken. We had given up immortality for mortality.

All that held my soul intact was the magic that came from my will and the magic I drew from the blood of souls that we fed upon. Mortal parasites, feeding on the immortal souls around us.

I let go and drifted down into nothing where I knew the open end of eternity waited for me. As I descended further into emptiness, I felt myself begin to unravel and spread out into the vastness around me; becoming one with its darkness. The anguish of my heart faded more and more as parts of me fell away, merging with the void like cups of water poured out into an endless sea, bits and pieces went into eternity and finally disappeared altogether. I could feel my will to live and exist diminish and I felt my magic fade to the dimmest of things. So small now.

A faint spark held against the vast, endless abyss around me.

Finally it came, an end of pain and knowing.

Not hearing Dan's voice no longer hurt because I could not remember the sound of his voice. I could not recall his touch. I could not remember his eyes. Were they blue? or green? I could not—

Nothing.

No voices, no sounds, no feeling, no memory, no thought, no Jane—

Jane

———◆———

Blood

A TASTE.
A taste of life.

This foreign, *alien* force, echoed out across the endless sea of eternity and down into the bottomless waves beneath which I had vanished. The taste of life reached into the timeless black emptiness that I was one with, joined with its endless night. I did not seek it. I was unaware. It sought me. It called to me across the eternity of nothing in which I rested. It wooed me, drawing me together, pulling me back from one end of forever to the other, like a sponge dropped in water. And finally it touched me.

A touch of life—
And with the touch came a thirst.
And with the thirst came a word—"blood."
And with the word came memories.
Beautiful blue-green eyes, staring down into my soul.

Soldiers and Doctors

CPR

"IT HAS TO work! It should be completely involuntary, like shocking a heart when it stops beating." The man in his white lab coat gritted his teeth in disgust as he ran his hand down the length of the plastic bag, chasing out the last few squishy drops.

Blood, thick and almost black in color fell onto the face of the girl lying on the floor of the helicopter. The blood filled her open mouth to overflowing, covered her open staring eyes and her beautiful milk white face, and hid her completely beneath a cold mask of black liquid gore. The girl's beautiful black hair fanned out around her head and acted like a sponge, conveniently absorbing the overflow and spillage.

"All you're doing now is making a mess, Morgan. The girl's dead," complained Dr. Ethan Penlow, his voice filled with the bitter sound of defeat and disappointment.

"This will work!" Morgan insisted as he threw the empty plastic baggie aside blindly. It landed against the side of the helicopter with a sickening splat, barely missing one of the soldiers. Morgan dashed back to the cooler, pulled out a second baggie and hurried back to the girl.

Juggling the cold slippery baggie while pushing his glasses back up onto his nose, he took the scissors from the front pocket of his ruined and bloody lab coat and sliced the corner of the plastic bag, then upended it, squeezing its contents onto the girl's face as well.

The other two white coated men in the helicopter stood well clear, giving Morgan space to go nuts. They both kept a sharp eye on the baggie he held in his hand, ready to dodge if he pitched the disgusting projectile in their direction. Red bloody bags tended to make a mess of shiny white lab coats.

Her lip twitched.

"Look! Look! She moved! I knew it! I saw it! I knew it! I saw her move!" Morgan shouted triumphantly in a childish "I told you so" manner.

Immediately the two other men crowded around in a flurry of excited activity. Dr. Penlow put on the headphones attached to the monitors, checking for any internal sounds within the girl's body. Breathing. Heartbeat. Blood flow. Digestion. Anything. The other two men checked the other monitors that searched for detectable brain activity or any change in body temperature.

Minutes passed. Listening. Checking and rechecking.

Nothing.

"Dammit," Dr. Penlow growled. He took the headphones off and chucked them on top of the girl's motionless body like it was nothing but a piece of furniture now. He retrieved a handkerchief from the inside pocket of his lab coat and wiped the sweat off his face and then wiped at the blood stain on his new tailored pants from kneeling beside the body.

"Morgan. Are you sure you saw her move? How could you possibly see anything with her face covered like that?"

"I'm telling you, she moved! Her lip twitched! I saw it," Morgan insisted angrily.

Penlow and Caprella shared a quick glance and a mutual shake of the head. "No brain activity, zero temp change, and no internal sounds, Morgan. Absolutely nothing. It's over. You're just seeing what you want to see. You're projecting," Dr. Caprella concluded as he looked over the monitors and machines attached to the girl. "There was no way we could we possibly know that killing the male would kill the female as well. That level of co-dependency isn't what we expected. It's not like anything that's ever been attributed to a vampire before in fiction and it certainly isn't anything like the vampires in the books she was reading when she made her transformation. It makes no sense at all. They can't blame us for this."

He drew his own handkerchief and started to wipe his hands clean as well. "We wanted both of them to study, they were the ones who insisted on killing the male."

Morgan didn't move; he kept his vigil, staring at the bloody face in stubborn denial.

The device attached to the body that monitored sounds beeped twice. Six sets of eyes looked at it. The three doctors and the three soldiers who stood around the doctors.

"Probably just noise from the helicopter," Penlow said. He reached out, unhurried, and picked up the earphones and slipped them onto his head. The others watched. Penlow raised an eyebrow. "We *may* have some sounds coming from the body. Probably noise from the helicopter. But it sounds like—digestion."

His face set into a mask of concentration as he listened cupping his hands over the earphones to try to shield out the noise from the helicopter.

One of the soldiers standing nearby spoke up, "Doctors. Perhaps you should all take a step back if she—"

A cough from the girl shot blood a foot into the air only to have most of it land right back onto her face.

And then quiet. A chill passed over the flesh of the warm blooded and living men inside the cargo bay of the helicopter as if a presence had moved back into the room with them. A red light began to glow from her blood-covered eyes. It was just a dim weak glow shining through the red mask like a flashlight under a red bed sheet but the glow became brighter as they watched.

The three doctors and the three soldiers in the helicopter all took a cautionary step back as if they were unsure if the bindings would hold. The entire length of the girl's body from her chest down to her feet had been wrapped around and around with metal wire leaving only her head exposed. She looked like a human caterpillar in a shiny metal cocoon. Four large cargo straps, designed to hold down heavy equipment and keep it from shifting during flight, fastened her securely to the floor of the helicopter's cargo bay.

They watched in fascinated silence as the open mouth slowly closed. She appeared to swallow. The mouth opened again ever so slowly, like a Venus flytrap waiting for another red liquid fly to land in its toothy maw.

Penlow walked over to the cooler, pulled out another red baggie, and tossed it to Morgan, who, thankfully, caught it.

"Care to continue your very successful treatment, Dr. Morgan?"

Morgan grinned back at Penlow until he looked at the baggie in his hands then made a disgusted face as he reached for his bloody scissors again.

They detected a temperature change after two more baggies. Morgan was being much more careful, pouring in the blood one mouthful at a time and then waiting to repeat the process as the mouth closed and opened again as if by reflex. After another baggie they detected their first sign of brain activity. Nothing typical of a human but a scattering of random indications that something was there. After another mouthful the girl turned her head away and closed her mouth, refusing to take any more blood.

The three doctors discussed this new development while they watched the brain activity continue to increase until the monitor was a meaningless blur of crazed lines.

The girl started to weep. Her face and features were hidden by the bloody gore, but the sound of weeping and the set of her mouth were enough for them to see that the girl wept. Penlow and Caprella remained silent but Morgan could not contain himself; he was too excited to wait another second, let alone a minute.

Dr. William Morgan was a tall, thin man in his early forties with short black hair and a long, clean shaven face. He wore wire frame glasses that balanced atop his thin, sail-like, ridge of a nose in an unsteady rocking perch. His voice was conversationally friendly as he spoke with the weeping girl in his British accent.

"Well, doing better, are we now, love? We were worried we'd lost you for a minute there. You almost died on us, Jane, and we don't want that."

She twitched constantly. Little movements pulling the corners of her mouth tight then releasing, slack, and her eyes shifted constantly under the bloody gore that covered her face. There was no sign that the girl was aware of Penlow's questions and she continued to shake and twitch. When she spoke her voice had an unforgettable, spine chilling quality about it that both fascinated and frightened the hell out of all the men at the same time.

"Let. Me. Die." She continued to shake and her eyes continued roving as she spoke. "No blood. Refuse. Let me die."

It was obvious by the girl's words that she was aware of her surroundings and had the ability to reason and answer questions. It was Morgan who spoke again, too excited to keep his mouth shut.

"Pep up, Jane, we're not going to hurt you and there really is no need to worry. We need to help you adjust to your new—condition—without endangering those around you. Really nothing to worry about at all. Now please tell me, how do you feel? Were you aware while you were in the grave or did it just seem like a period of normal sleep?" His eyes were aglitter with curiosity as question after question poured out.

Penlow and Caprella both cast grieved sideways glances at Dr. Morgan but they remained silent and let their eccentric but brilliant colleague continue his string of questions for the next five minutes nonstop with no response from the girl.

In frustration Morgan got personal to see if he could tease out a reaction and thereby get some usable information or at least observe what her reaction to stress would be. Any reaction would be preferable to what he was getting now, which was nothing. He went for what he was sure was a tender spot as he paced back and forth in front of her.

"You still remember your husband perhaps. What was his name? I'm sure you know his name but it escapes me now for some reason, blast! It's right there—on the tip of my tongue. I knew it. Damn." He scratched his head, still pretending not to know the name while at the same time making it an insult. "Damn. Damn. Damn. Damn. Damn. Oh bother, still, it'll come to me. So tell me now, do you have any memories of your wedding night? We're all physicians, my dear, so don't be shy. You can tell us anything. Were you a virgin?"

"Morgan! What the hell are you doing!? Don't taunt the girl. Not after what she's been through tonight," Dr. Penlow rebuked, but Morgan had already gotten what he wanted, a reaction to his needling.

The girl began to cry again. Morgan nodded to his two companions, muttered a quick insincere apology and grabbed his notebook. He remembered to keep a suitably chastened look on his face while he worked, scribbling away, making notes as he observed the results of his little stress experiment before events moved beyond his ability to recall correctly. He jotted down exactly what he had asked that finally caused the reaction (memories of her husband). He noted the time on his watch (9:45) so he could record how long the girl's distress lasted, then he stuck his pen in his teeth just long enough to turn on his digital pocket recorder, hoping to record any angry retort she may give once the tears ended.

The girl obliged him wonderfully on all counts. After another minute of weeping she sighed and lifted her trembling head slowly from the bloody floor and looked past Morgan directly at Dr. Caprella and addressed her words to him. "Kill me. I don't want to remember what you monsters have ripped from my soul. Finish what you started. Kill me now."

Caprella remained silent. Her every word sent chills up their spines and caused goosebumps to rise on their skin. For Morgan, the sound of her voice acted as a catalyst making his pen pick up speed as he labored to digest this new smorgasbord of tantalizing data.

These men had never experienced the wonder of "magic" or seen the impossible be reduced to the "common" or "ordinary" state of things as it was in Amen Hale. To these three men, just the fact that this girl's every spoken word could send a chill up their spine was like throwing a lit match into a warehouse filled with fireworks. Ideas, theories, and questions shot off in every direction within their minds, all demanding answers and tests and experiments to get those answers! It was explosive.

They studied her. And through the twitching and shaking she also studied them, hearing both what they said and what they did not say. She moved her trembling head and directed her gaze to the final man, Dr. Penlow. Her chilling words were spoken perfectly, unaffected by her roving eyes and trembling features.

"End my life as you did my Dan's and the world will be forever safe from the threat of vampires. I promise, I won't resist the soldiers, just let them kill me, and I will die. I will not stop it and I will not come back. I want to die. Please, just let me go back into the sea of eternal night where I can forget what you have stolen from me. I need to forget."

She rested her head back on the metal floor and closed her eyes and exhaled, becoming still. It looked like she was starting to shut down again and the three doctors shared a moment of quiet unspoken communication between them. Someone had to do something to stop her from letting herself die. If that was what she was doing now.

KEEP HER TALKING! Morgan held up his notepad with the message on it, waving it in front of Penlow. He doubted that the girl would respond to his voice, but someone needed to keep her talking.

Penlow nodded. "Jane. I know we've had a rough start, but I promise, conditions will improve soon."

The girl replied, her voice quiet, but the chilling whisper was impossible *not* to hear even as she became motionless and still. Only the barest hint of air moved in and out of her lungs as her lips spoke her words.

"Did you know that I haven't killed anyone. Not a single person. Ever. I've been very careful. I may be a monster, but I did not want to act like a monster. I did not want to live like a fiend. Slipping into homes, taking innocent lives in the cover of night. Because it is not right to take the life of another. Not right to act like a monster." She paused just long enough to smile. "And so, here we are. Humans, acting like monsters. Monsters, acting like humans. Just. Let. Me. Die."

She breathed out her last breath and went totally still as her mouth clamped shut. Morgan went over to the cooler and took out another packet of blood and prepped it while the others watched the monitors. The girl was fading again, letting herself die. And she'd closed her mouth tight as she said her last word.

"Someone's going to have to open her mouth," said Caprella. "But we're going to have to wait till there's no brain activity to make sure we don't lose a hand. Or worse."

Morgan nodded. "I agree. Once she's flatline and unable to resist we'll pry the mouth open and dose her again."

Three minutes passed while the three men watched the monitors and prepped for the task ahead.

"Status report on N1, Vega." The radio came to life.

"What the hell!" Stitch said as he reached for his radio.

"I thought we were flying dark, Stitch," muttered Carter, one of the other soldiers.

Stitch shrugged. "The General probably just wants to make sure the cargo's still worth hauling. Last time he called it looked like the girl was nothing but a dead stick."

"Vega here, Sir, we're good. Condition of N1 much improved but still touchy. Repeat, condition of N1 moderate. Sir, is Tango clear? Over."

"We've had no contact from the rest of your team. It doesn't look good. Maintain radio silence unless I contact you. Confirm when N1 is delivered. Over."

"Roger," the soldier replied, his voice subdued.

Minutes passed.

"Aaahh!" The girl's still body gasped, she writhed in the wires, and her eyes snapped open. Her vital signs all began to spike! The doctors scrambled around, alarmed and surprised by the whip fast recovery and what could have caused it. They watched, perplexed, as the girl's face transformed; she looked absolutely enraptured as she focused upon the space directly above her head with such an emotional intensity it made the six men in the belly of the aircraft study the ceiling with an ominous waiting expectation. The soldiers tightened their hands on their weapons and watched her and the ceiling, like they half expected something to come right through the whirling blades and metal roof of the aircraft.

After a moment of rapture, she closed her eyes and rested her head back onto the metal deck of the copter, an absolutely blissful smile resting on her lips. Her eyes no longer roved and jerked about spasmodically in their sockets and her wild twitching had ceased; now her face passed through a number of emotions, a luxurious smile one minute to spontaneous laughter to frowning and even weeping once.

It was—unsettling.

"Shouldn't we ask wha—"

"No!" Penlow and Capella shouted at the same time as they scowled at Morgan. Morgan surrendered to the mood in the aircraft and wisely let silence reign.

Another twelve minutes passed in silence as they watched her. The smiling vampire seemed to be in very high spirits now, even bursting into laughter occasionally for no apparent reason.

The radio crackled to life again. "Status report on N1, Vega."

"Vega here, sir. All good. Actually we're too good, sir."

"Explain that, Vega. What do you mean by 'too good?'"

"Sir, if I had to venture a guess, I'd say that N1 appears to be communicating with N2 again. Which doesn't make any sense. N2 is gone. But she's communicating with someone in her head, unless she's gone nuts or maybe it's the witches she's talking to somehow. She's grinning from ear to ear, sir, and I don't like it. Something's happening."

"N2 is still alive, Vega."

The other soldiers shared surprised grumbles as Stitch expressed their mutual confusion. "N2 was down, sir. I saw it. How the hell is he back?"

"N2 refused to 'stay' down. He kept coming back so they had to take him."

"No fucking way!" Stitch spat out; he clicked the button on his handset and spoke into the radio. "Sir, N2 was nothing but soup in a bag when I left; how the hell could it come back?"

"Tango Charlie last contact confirmed that N2 kept pulling back together no matter what they tried, but I'll let them know that the 'soup' has made contact with N1 and is aware. Tango cleared the crypt and the wall just two minutes ago, dragging N2 along with them. They're airborne now and will be heading to the L.Z. with you. When you land, let them know N2 is coming. If they can hold N1, they can hold the other one as well or at least find some way to actually kill the damn thing."

"Sir, did we lose anyone?"

"Only three got out, Vega."

"Down or captured, sir?" Stitch asked. The other three soldiers leaned in but the next words ended hope.

"They are confirmed down, Vega. I'm sorry. I won't contact you again. Stay dark till after the transfer. Over."

"Roger." Then, "Shit," Stitch swore quietly.

The three doctors burst into excited conversation, overjoyed by the news that the male vampire was captured and still alive, but this exuberance was aborted when they noticed the absolutely murderous looks from the three soldiers. The doctors assumed a respectful silence as the soldiers gathered together for a brief whispered conversation about the four fallen members of their ten-man team.

The discussion was brief and business-like, with all of them agreeing in seconds that this mission was the worst fuck-up they'd ever had the misfortune to be a part of. At a final word from Stitch they went back to their positions. The rest of the trip was made in anxious silence with one very happy vampire girl who seemed to be enjoying the trip more than anyone else in the helicopter.

Hillary

Faux Sun

HILLARY CONTINUED SHOUTING at General Thompson who stared back stone faced and inflexible in the face of her rant. "I spoke to the President myself just before we went in and he assured me that there would be *no* further aggressive actions taken against these people! His exact words to me were '*We'll leave them alone for now.*' So what the hell happened just now? Why are the people of Amen Hale gathered around the crypt, General? What happened to the vampires and where did those helicopters go that took off thirty minutes ago?"

Thompson took a step back, restoring some personal space between himself and the furious woman in front of him. He raised his hand and used his thumb to wipe a little spittle off his chin, complements of Mrs. Clinton.

"I spoke to the President. It was a secure line and his orders were clear. The operation carried out earlier this evening was to be kept *need to know* on the basis of the enemy's ability to read minds. No one who went inside was aware of the pending strike. And it's not just your phone that we are blocking; we are jamming all communications to ensure that no information gets out about the strike until later this evening. My orders were clear, and I have followed those orders to the letter, Madam Secretary, as given me by the Commander in Chief of the United States of America. So if you have a problem with it, go spit in his face, not mine."

"And have you spoken to him since they set a new sun in the sky, General?" Hillary asked conversationally.

"I'm still waiting for him to return my call. We're experiencing some communication trouble," the General confessed, finally showing a hint of emotion on his stone face. It was unease.

One of the General's aids entered the room. "Sir. Professor Sweat's team is here."

The General cut his eyes toward Hillary.

"Don't even dream of going there, Thompson. You might be able to keep me from making a phone call because of the President's orders, but if you try to restrict my access further I promise you, I will bury your ass so deep in legal shit you won't even be able to breathe without choking on it."

General Thompson and Hillary Clinton eyed each other for a second longer until the aid, standing in the door way, cleared his throat.

"Bring them in," Thompson ordered.

Hillary gave him an evil smile. "You bastard," she muttered teasingly.

"You bitch," he dared very quietly with his own smile.

Both smiles vanished as the room filled with men in various attire. Some of them wore jeans with colored shirts, one or two wore white lab jackets or business casual attire, but none of them wore a uniform. They were scientists brought in by the government to study and gather data on the constant stream of impossible phenomena happening in and around the teens from the study and the witches of Amen Hale. Eleven men and two women filed into the large, overly impressive room of the home which had been evacuated and subsequently occupied by General Thompson who had set up his HQ in its homey opulence.

Professor Sweat was an energetic man in spite of his ample weight and advanced age. He stepped to the front of the odd assembly of hastily gathered scientists and spoke for the group. "General, you wanted our take on the situation and we are prepared to offer our advice if you're prepared to hear it."

The General nodded.

Sweat nodded in return. "Of this one thing we are all in agreement. Whatever you do, don't harm or shoot or in any way at all disturb the boy who has created the faux sun. If his concentration slips and he loses control of his creation even for a moment it could be disastrous."

"How disastrous?"

Nervous laughs and whispers from the assembled eggheads greeted Thompson's monotone reply.

"If it's truly a fusion-powered event like we believe, and the boy loses control—we're dead."

"How many dead? How big a blast? How large a disaster? And can we stop it?" Thompson tried to cover the bases and squeeze an intelligent answer out that made sense and actually held actionable content.

Sweat answered all four questions, holding up fingers sequentially as he went. One finger, "Every human on earth would die." Two fingers, "Big enough." Three fingers, "Larger than a bread box." He smiled as the fourth finger raised, "Yes. We certainly can stop it."

Hillary stepped forward and challenged Sweat's assumption. "How on earth can we possibly stop something that powerful?"

"Easy," Professor Sweat said confidently. "Someone needs to go over there and *very politely* ask the boy to put his dangerous toy away before he kills seven billion people. I know it's low tech and not very flashy, and it doesn't involve guns or gadgets, but it might just keep us all from dying a horrible death. And now maybe the General can call off the snipers he has ready to shoot the boy with plastic bullets designed to pass over the wall. I would hate to see one trigger happy soldier expose seven billion people to the scorching flames of an imploding star."

"Excuse me," General Thompson said without a word to confirm or deny anything.

Thompson took off and Hillary found herself standing alone in front of the assembled hodgepodge of scientists. "How did you know about the snipers?" she asked Sweat.

He smirked. "Had no clue. It was just a guess, but it was based upon deductive reasoning and the assumption that soldiers are usually idiots with guns."

That earned a smattering of laughter from the group standing behind him, but one older woman in a pea green pant suit cut through the light mood with her concerned voice. "We don't have time for this, Carl! Who's going to go talk to that boy and tell him how dangerous that thing is? The soldiers sure as hell can't do it, they've just pissed in these people's face with whatever idiocy they did earlier tonight. It needs to be someone, *anyone*, not in a uniform."

"I'll go talk to him," piped up a middle-aged man with a raccoon like sun burn from wearing sunglasses while he fried. He was sporting shiny wine-colored shorts and a t-shirt with a Florida Seminoles logo on it.

He boldly stepped forward and grabbed Hillary's hand in an unwanted handshake and pumped it with excessive exuberance as he grinned at her. Three of the man's colleagues, also wearing FSU shirts and matching sunburns, whispered urgently to their friend to "leave the Secretary of State alone!"

"Why you?" Hillary asked as she extracted her hand from his handshake and gave him a glower.

"Why not?" he fired back confidently, both eyebrows raised.

"What the hell are you?"

"Astrophysicist. Dr. Everet Tanner. Pleasure to meet you." He smiled.

She eyed his attire doubtfully and the man looked down at his own shirt, as understanding dawned and he explained. "Oh! The clothes. The FBI grabbed us as we came out of the rally announcing the starting lineup for next season. They brought us straight here. Didn't have a chance to change. We're professors at FSU." The three other men wearing FSU shirts waved at Hillary.

"Fine. You'll do. You look harmless enough. No one on earth would mistake you for a soldier in that get up." Hillary eyed him up and down one more time then snapped, "Let's go."

"What? But how are we going to open the gateway?" the man asked in confusion.

"We don't have time to mess with that damn thing, and I'm not about to open a vein. We're going over the wall."

"Over the wall?" The overly enthusiastic astrophysicist and FSU fan looked far less confident now, but he still followed along in Hillary's wake as she marched from the room with determined strides.

"Don't forget to leave your cell phone and jewelry. It can't go where we're going, Dr. Tanner," she called over her shoulder.

The man's three colleagues stood in a line and hummed the Florida Seminole theme like a dirge and did the Tomahawk "chop" with their hands as their good friend, Dr. Everet Tanner, followed the Secretary of State out the door. On his way to either take one for the team or just possibly save the world.

Jane and Dan

＊

A Time for Blood

I FELT MAGIC—HIS magic! *His* presence!

"Aaahh!" I gasped.

It couldn't be! They had killed him. I heard the truth of it in their voices as they spoke. They'd been absolutely sure he was dead. I'd heard it in Dan's desperate voice the last time he spoke to me in my mind, he even thought he was about to die.

It couldn't be him—But it was him!

My brain tried to reason out what may have happened—how! Somehow he had come back from the dead, just like me, and he had found some way to reach me! Perhaps he no longer had a body and was just a ghost now? My Dan.

"Dan?" I said his name in my mind as I stared up at the ceiling and felt him drawing closer to me.

Very close now. I felt his magic as he passed through the roof of the helicopter. I couldn't see him but I knew he was there, hovering above me, a missing part of my own soul, and my body cried out for the needed reunion!

"Dan!" I called in my head.

He didn't speak back. I didn't hear his voice in my head yet and I wondered why. He was right there, hovering right above me. Was he looking at me right now? At me. His body. His home. His place. Oh! Why did he wait!? Was he in shock? Was he overjoyed? Was he experiencing the same rapture I was? Perhaps he was gathering himself, gathering his strength.

I wondered quickly what it had cost him to come to me like this, like a ghost. I worried for an instant of a second what all of this might mean. What had become of him when they destroyed his body? I dismissed the worry and cast it out like the vile blasphemy it was, rending the thought into a billion bleeding pieces. He was still Dan. I'd take whatever I could get! And whatever he was now, whatever he'd become when he died was here for me now. Dan was here, and I loved him. I felt him drawing closer.

I felt him enter me. His magic, his soul, moved into my soul and dwelt in me completely. As soon as he assumed his proper place within me, I was whole. The broken parts of my mind that were trapped in loops of memory, replaying my past, finally stopped. My entire vampire mind became completely and totally silent for the first time since I awoke from the grave. And then I heard the most beautiful sound I'd ever heard in my whole life

"*I'm right here,*" his voice whispered softly in the new quiet of my mind.

I couldn't reply at first, but he knew I couldn't. I savored just hearing the word. Being whole. He was here.

"*Jane,*" he said it again because he knew I wanted him to. It sounded perfect.

"Dan." I said his name.

"*Are you all right, my love?*"

"I am now that you're here."

"*Jane, you let yourself die. You died.*"

"Yes. But so did you."

"*No, Jane. I didn't die. I refused to die and leave my body. The cold emptiness tried to pull me down, but I refused to go. I stayed there and kept pulling myself back together. It was close, and I almost lost it there at the end, but I held on long enough. Rain came just in time and saved me. She stopped the soldiers and rebuilt my body. As soon as I knew my body was safe, I left it, to come looking for you. I came to save you, but—you already died.*"

"Sorry, my love. And the soldiers didn't kill me. I let myself die. I had to die, Dan; my mind doesn't work without you in it anymore. I couldn't think; I was broken. Dan, I—"

I struggled, trying to think what to say. How could I explain why I did what I did?

"Jane. It's all right. I know how you were broken. I see everything inside you, my love, I know all of it already. I know why you did it. But I'd be lying if I didn't say that you scared me to death. I know what it felt like when you died, Jane. I know everything you felt."

My body shivered with Dan's emotion as it lay shrouded within its steel wire wrappings.

"It was horrible, watching you die, and horrible watching you—let me go. Please, Jane, let's not do that again. Never do that again. Don't let me go again, Jane, never again."

"I'm so glad I'm not alone inside here anymore. But, Dan, where is your body? Are you here and there at the same time? I'm so far away from you. And you almost looked like a ghost when you first got here, what's happened?"

"I left my body completely. I think being able to cast my soul out of my body is part of my new power as a full vampire. My body is back in the crypt with Rain. When we get close enough I'll connect with it again, but right now, everything I am is inside of you."

"Not everything," I pouted. There was a very important part of him that his ghostly self hadn't brought along and I very much wanted that part of him inside of me—as well as his soul.

"Hehehehe. That's my girl." I could almost feel Dan smiling inside me. It felt wonderful. *"Soon, my love. Soon. But first we need to get you free of these wires. And then I want to rend Morgan into lots of tiny pieces. We'll kill the rest quickly, but not Morgan. Him I want to play with."*

Now it was my turn to laugh and I did. I could feel Morgan's body heat as he sat beside me in the helicopter, scribbling in his notepad, unaware that I was laughing about his death. "Maybe I should tell him, Dan. He'd probably find the fact interesting."

"No, love. Don't tell him. Let's keep it a surprise. You know how I like surprises."

I laughed again, but then I thought about what was about to happen. We were going to kill these men. I was going to kill these men. Blood. Death. I didn't feel sorry for them, but it would be the beginning of the killing for us. A beginning that would never end as long as Dan and I lived. We were going to kill these men. And others after these men, I was sure. I wondered what went wrong in the first place. How did it come to this anyway? What happened and how did these men even get into the crypt? We were supposed to be safe. Where was Rain?

"My love, it's not Rain's fault. I'm sure she did the best she could. The soldiers used acid to burn a hole through the wall of the Crypt. Once they got inside, they stole you, then they used an axe to cut me up into pieces. They took the pieces of me and used the same acid they used on the crypt to try and melt me away to nothing. Rain got there in time and stopped them from killing me, Jane, but they hurt her. She looked horrible. If you could have seen her there in the Crypt it would have broke your heart. She looked bad. I should have spoken to her, written a note before I left, but I just took off as soon as my body was safe to come here for you. She probably thinks we're both dead. I'm worried she may hurt herself, Jane."

A cold dark fury settled into me unlike anything I'd ever felt before. I let it spread through me, cold merciless fury that spread out like a living thing from the center of my body, up to my head and down my arms and legs and into my hands and feet. I let the power wash through me until it was finished doing whatever it had done.

"It's time for us to kill, Dan."

"*Yes, my love. It's time for blood.*"

Dr. Morgan

True Colors

THE HELICOPTER TOUCHED down in a weed-ridden field located just behind an old dead gas station a mile from the interstate. As soon as the helicopter began its approach, the four large black semis turned on their lights, illuminating the field. A fancy forklift was already moving forward before the aircraft had even settled on the ground. It approached the side of the helicopter and raised a flat metal scoop to the correct height. The soldiers within slid the girl, still in her metal wrappings, onto the flat metal and strapped her down. Dr. Morgan stepped onto the metal scoop with the body and appeared to be adjusting the straps as the lift backed away with the girl and him still on it.

Then the shooting started. It lasted only a minute. Snipers positioned all around killed everyone with their first volley. Morgan supervised as they loaded the girl into one of the trucks.

"Is she secure, Dr. Morgan? Are we ready to move?" asked one of the men who received them in the back of the truck. He had a German accent, with black, slicked back hair. He wore jeans with a dark leather jacket but was otherwise nondescript and forgettable at a glance. Just a regular looking middle-aged man.

"She's already tried her strength against the cables and they held superbly. I think she's safe enough, Milt. But I'm afraid we can't go just yet. A second helicopter is bringing the male. It should land in about fifteen minutes."

"What! We have to go! We're out of time. And we've already killed the crew of the other craft, they'll know! We have to go now! We can't take the chance."

Milt turned and was about to give the order to his men as Morgan caught his arm and pulled him back around to face him. "Milt. This is worth the risk. The girl won't live without the male. They are a linked pair. She'll let herself die."

Morgan watched the other man; who was still looking doubtful. "She can do it. Force herself to die. She almost did it on the way here. And without the male we have nothing to force her to help us. She's not human and I doubt we could coerce her to help no matter what we did to her. We have absolutely nothing she wants except her mate. We have to have the other one or it's all for nothing, Milt. To save the life of her mate, the girl would do anything. Give us anything we want. We have to wait. And the crew had orders to keep radio silence. Hopefully that will help get the other craft onto the ground, but if we need to we can shoot it down with an EMP blast once it gets close and then just pick through the wreckage for the pieces and take those."

The other man looked confused so Morgan helped fill in the gaps for him. "The pieces of the other vampire, Milt. They come back together. That's why they ended up bringing him along instead of killing him there like they planned. They couldn't find a way to kill him. He regenerates too quickly. He wouldn't die."

Milt smiled. Morgan laughed. The two men got busy, making plans for a warm welcome.

Milt, Dr. Morgan, and four other high-ranking members of The Order watched the security screen inside the radar truck. A man who stank of Cuban cigars and vodka sat in front of a panel full to bursting with electronics and military-grade technology as he watched a radar screen showing the track of the approaching helicopter, but the nearby rack of security camera displays kept grabbing everyone's attention.

It showed the inside of the transport truck which held the female vampire, Jane Miller. One camera showed the inside of the truck and a large metal box, still securely shut and locked. Another camera showed the inside of that same box where they could see the girl's pale face. She was still secure in the wires and she was still smiling.

"Why is she smiling?" asked Ivan, the man in charge of this whole operation.

"Because she's communicating with her mate telepathically in the other helicopter. She's probably telling him that the men who carried her here are dead."

"Will he tell them about the attack?" Ivan asked, raising his voice, suddenly alarmed.

Morgan waved a reassuring hand back and forth, smiling as he brushed the man's concerns away. "No. Of course not, Ivan. The male knows this development is to his advantage. He'll probably rally his strength and make a break for it once the plane goes down. We'll need to be ready for him. The men will need to move very quickly and use deadly force. He'll be weakened but the men will still need to take him apart as soon as possible if he's not already in pieces. He's going to be far too dangerous to let stay in one piece till we get him to Atlanta."

An older gentleman wearing a finely tailored suit started laughing. "This is some really crazy shit."

"Yes, Mr. Keats. But if we are successful, we may just become immortal," Morgan said happily. "It doesn't get any crazier than that."

The men shared a look among themselves, a hungry, determined look, salted liberally with suspicion. Everyone suspected the double cross. Over the past four days, The Order's iron clad (unbreakable and eternal) vows of service and secrecy had become worth less and less until it was down to who can help who NOW. It was no way to run a secret organization.

"Something must be wrong," hissed the squat man at the radar screen in a thick British drawl. "They're coming in too fast."

"Fire the EMP gun!" one of the men named Ivan ordered. "Bring them down as soon as they're within range! And have the snipers open fire as well!"

Orders were relayed and men started to rush around to carry out those orders—but then the power went out on everything. Every battery and power source, even wrist watches and cell phones went dead. The big diesel engines of the semis went completely quiet and the lights dimmed, leaving the field in ominous eerie darkness as everyone paused in mid stride to look around. Even the inferred scopes on the sniper rifles of the men concealed in the clearing held went dead.

Everyone poured out of the trucks and the handful of other vehicles parked there in the field and looked around in confusion. A grey foggy mist formed around their position. Men started to panic. Out near the tree line one of the men cried out. Men began to gather in front of the trucks trying to organize and find out what was happening and what to do next. A number of those watched the five men who emerged from the radar truck, hoping for orders.

"What is this, Morgan! Is it the vampire?" asked Ivan.

"No. This can't be the vampires. They don't have this kind of power. That I know of, there's only one person on earth that could do this. It must be the Black Witch."

Milt swore in German, then darted a terrified glance at Morgan who was smiling. "Why are you smiling, you idiot? We're all about to die, you fool!"

Morgan laughed. "Don't you think it's funny that she killed the power first? How on *earth* did she know to do that? Now we can't even set off the bombs in the truck and kill the vampire. That was our hostage ploy. Our ace in the hole if the shit hit the fan." Morgan laughed and shook his head.

"No, we can still threaten to destroy the girl if she attacks!" Ivan countered vehemently.

"No, we can't," Morgan answered calmly. "The bombs are wired with electronic switches. Unless someone wants to stand there and shoot them with a gun, but that might not work with the new style plastic explosives. It's such stable and reliable stuff. Unfortunate."

Overhead the other helicopter began its decent toward the far end of the field. Ivan pulled his side arm and pointed it at Morgan's head.

"You stupid bastard, we should have left after we had the girl. You've killed us all." He pulled the trigger.

The hammer came down and made a dull "click" noise. Ivan's thick brow drew down in anger; he squeezed again and again. Click. Click. Click.

Morgan laughed. "Sorry, Ivan. Apparently she does not intend to let us go quietly into the night. No doubt the witch wants to play with us a bit first."

Morgan's hand shot out and plunged a blade into Ivan's chest, right into his heart. He stepped back to watch. Ivan looked down at the blade in shocked surprise. He dropped the useless gun from his hands and pulled the handle jutting from his chest, releasing a fount of red with it.

No one objected or cried out to the stabbing. The men and women who'd gathered around these five men, hoping for answers or orders to follow, now broke away, each one making their own decision about what to do next.

"Well, at least we know the knives still work," Morgan said cheerfully and laughed as he walked away from Ivan and a horrified Milt, wiping blood off his hand onto his already bloody white lab coat.

Command had broken down completely. Men and women ran in every direction wildly, but as the next five minutes passed, they settled into one of five camps.

The Fighters: A dozen grim-faced men formed up a defense line, stripping down to the minimum for better ease of movement, bearing knives and encouraging one another with joking male banter as they prepared to face death on their feet and with a blade.

The Runners: They were a rapidly vanishing breed as most of these took flight in the first few seconds, but occasionally another person would break (mentally) and make a run for the mist at the edge of the clearing. Everyone who entered the gray mist screamed and then went silent. No one knew if they got through or not, but it didn't sound good.

The Quitters: A group of eight men and one woman had already dropped to their knees and placed their hands behind their heads in waiting surrender.

The Moles: A good number of desperate souls hid like children playing hide and seek, some in the weeds and scrub in the field, pulling dirt over themselves to hide in the earth or crawling up underneath the long semi trailers and hiding in the wheel wells and underpinnings.

And last, but by no means the least, The Lovers: Two men and two women slipped into one of the trailers and started to passionately end their time on planet Earth doing something fun.

Morgan was firmly a part of the "mole" faction and had picked himself an excellent hiding spot that was out of the way but still gave him a wonderful vantage point so he could satisfy his insatiable curiosity and "watch the show." He was on top of one of the tall black semi trailers lying flat on his stomach, slid up right to the edge so he could see down and observe the action until Jane came for him.

He had no illusions that he'd get away, but he had at least doffed his bloody lab coat and sprayed himself down with something that might help mask his smell a touch. Might give him another minute or two he figured. Who knows. He might just make it. Stranger things than that had happened tonight.

Dr. Everet Tanner

Over the Wall

"MADAM SECRETARY, ARE you sure about this?" Special Agent Grimes asked for the fourth time.

"Just do it, Grimes, and stop complaining."

Hillary walked away to join the crowd assembled just on the other side of the "red line" beyond the reach of the curse on metal around the wall. They were far enough away to be no threat to anyone who came to investigate the "welcome wagon" as they were calling Dr. Tanner.

Agent Grimes and another agent raised the twenty foot tall wooden ladder, leaned it against the wall, and handed Dr. Tanner his "equipment." He had a white flag, complete with a nice wooden pole to wave it around on. He had a hand-written letter they wanted him to drop off first, from Hillary to King Cornelius. He had a new notepad and a new pack of (all plastic) black magic markers that he could use to write messages and toss down to anyone who came to his side of the wall.

Also in his bag of tricks was a bone horn. A real live, honest to goodness German bone horn that had been "appropriated" from where it sat on a shelf in the home that General Thompson had occupied as his HQ. The horn had been living out its days peacefully as a curious knick knack in a glass case, but now in this time of need, it was called back into active duty, so to speak, and it hung by its original deer hide strap slung around the neck of Dr. Tanner.

He also carried a rope, just in case he wanted to drop down the other side and meet whoever came to see him face to face. Grimes advised against the rope but said it was his skin to do with as he chose. His other supplies were of a more personal nature, sunglasses (it was damn bright out tonight) and a pocket full of cashews that he'd jacked from the same house the horn came from.

He also had a tall bottle of Bush beer still chilled from the freezer of the same house, which he was saving for when he got to the top of the ladder. He brought the beer for a number of reasons. Just in case they set him on fire he figured he could at least sling cold beer on himself. And of course the General's beer would help him not to get dry mouth as he enjoyed the General's cashews. And surely there was a "general" rule somewhere that clearly required beer be involved when doing something this stupid. Three good reasons made the cold glass bottle of beer the most valuable piece of equipment in his canvas bag of tricks as he manned up the ladder to wave a flag, blow a horn, and pitch down notes to the people who had just hung a new sun in the sky.

There was a flat seat rigged at the top of the ladder for him to sit down on and Dr. Tanner carefully maneuvered himself into a sitting position and then looked out over the wall and into the Kingdom of Amen Hale. It didn't look like he'd have any problems attracting someone's attention. Two nearby groups had already spotted him on his ladder perch, high up on the wall, and were approaching at a run. It looked as if there were a number of these groups, about five men in each, patrolling the entire perimeter of the wall.

Everet grabbed a handful of cashews and chewed as he reached for the letter. The two groups of angry men arrived at the base of the wall at the same time, and he pitched the letter at them. The men on the ground picked up the letter, then sent a runner dashing off down the drive with the letter in hand.

"Hello down there!" Dr. Tanner called amiably to the men far below, smiling, relaxed, and still wearing his shades. "Mrs. Clinton asked me to drop off her letter, and I'd love to come down and talk to you guys about that thing!" He pointed to the glowing ball of fire in the sky. "My name is Dr. Everet Tanner and I'm an astrophysicist. I really need to let you guys know that the sun you put into the sky will probably destroy the Earth if you're not real careful with it. Any chance I could come down and talk to Lord David?"

He watched as the men below conferred then looked up at him. "Hey, is that a Seminoles' jersey?" one of the men called up.

"Hell yeah!" Everet called back.

In short order, Dr. Everet Tanner had lowered himself down the other side of the wall and into a welcome nest of FSU fans and one angry UF fan who suggested they kill him, hide the body, and take his beer. Fortunately for Everet, they went with plan A and marched him down the drive to speak with King Cornelius.

Cornelius

———◆———

The Patriots Curse

HILLARY'S LETTER HAD been surprising, right from the first three hand written words, nice and large, right at the top:

Emma was right.

The letter went on to say that the United States had indeed been betrayed and that people within the government itself were involved. Hillary begged forgiveness for both herself, the President, and the United States for its part in the attack on the limo yesterday and for the attack on the vampires' crypt that had just taken place. She said that the helicopters which carried Jane and Dan away had landed in a field outside Atlanta and that Black Rain was already there and that she had secured the area.

Hillary's letter went on to say that the group who orchestrated this attack had taken over key communication systems and sent out false orders and that the entire country was in a temporary state of crisis as a result of this security breach. She said she couldn't say more in a letter but that the President himself would actually be holding a live news conference at two thirty a.m. and would address the nation with the news tonight before anyone could stop or change what was happening.

Cornelius read that line more than once. Things sounded bad. Very bad indeed for the President to be holding a news conference at two thirty in the morning.

Hillary ended her letter with an unusual invitation.

I know you don't have television reception within Amen Hale. I invite you to come out and watch the broadcast with me, live, as it happens. I've set up my own tent by the Gateway just beyond the limit of the curse on the wall.

I assure you, there will be no more treachery. Any future surprises will not be on my orders or the President's. Until a thorough investigation is completed, the President has stripped General Thompson of his command and placed me in charge of all military activities outside your walls and any and all dealings with your Kingdom. He feels he can trust me, even though he doesn't like me. It's hard to explain what's happening in D.C. right now, Cornelius, but America has more than enough people to fight with inside her own government right now. We need peace with Amen Hale. Come out and watch with me tonight, it's not every day you get to see Senators and Congressmen charged with High Treason on live, un-censored television.

I hope Dr. Tanner has explained how dangerous David's sun is to our planet. Everet looks like an idiot, but he knows what he's talking about. Please don't get us all killed. Billions of people will die if David loses control.

One last thing, we also have cameras set up, monitoring the situation in At-lanta from a very respectable distance. You're welcome to see that live feed as well if that interests you.

Cornelius couldn't resist the offer and he was dying to hear the news again. Believer, however, advised against the trip, saying that Rain had instructed them to stay within Amen Hale until she returned. Ryan said he would go himself, even if no one else went, to see where Rain was and make sure she was safe. Cornelius sided with Ryan, so they made preparations.

David and Dana stayed behind in case Rain chose to open one of the gateways and return that way, and Lucius asked to stay by the crypt as well, to guard Dan's body and keep it safe for his Queen. Sky was so nervous that Ryan asked her to stay inside with Cathryn, Mary, and Emma to "keep them safe," but it was more the other way around.

Cornelius brought only ten guards from Amen Hale, and none of those carried weapons. It wouldn't be guns or knives that would keep them safe as they visited; protection would be provided by the cloud men and the tiny, olive-skinned girl in the red and gray dress who scowled as she walked beside her adopted father. Bethany's little hand held his as they trudged down the cobbled drive, bathed in the warm yellow light from above.

The people in Amen Hale were affectionately calling it *"The Star of David,"*, glad for its protection and revealing light. People outside the walls had names for it too: *The Fallen Star, Abaddon, The Midnight Sun, The All-Seeing Eye* were just a few of its labels.

But the yellow rays did not brighten the mood of the group. Believer and Sky Dragon were somber and Ryan was in a state of impatient disgust. Impatient because he wanted to be there five minutes ago, disgust because they were about to trust people who had already attacked them twice.

The grim procession would have trudged the whole way from the house to the gateway arch in silence if it hadn't been for Dr. Everet Tanner, who was oblivious to the dark mood. Cornelius was returning him to the other side of the wall despite his repeated requests to "'hang out" and "stay for a while." Dr. Tanner was one of those terminally cheerful souls, cursed with the inability to shut up, complicated by insatiable curiosity, the entire condition further aggravated by a lack of tact. He started the trip to the wall by pestering King Cornelius and Bethany until Bethany asked Cornelius if she could eat him. Everet quickly moved on to Ryan who interrupted his very first question with a question of his own.

"Do you believe in God?" Ryan asked, to which Everet replied in the negative. Ryan patted him on the shoulder and said, "Don't worry, Everet, atheism's a temporary condition. You'll see things differently once you're dead. Which may be soon."

Everet decided to move on. He tried Believer, pestering with questions until Believer rumbled, "Dr. Tanner, shut up."

Everet held his peace for a minute and a half, then he moved on to Sky Dragon, who simply tried to keep his responses to Everet's questions as brief and empty as possible, not really giving him any real answers at all.

About fifteen questions deep, Everet stepped in it again. "So your ability to feel, is it the same as a human's?" Everet was writing in his notepad with his stinky black magic markers as he asked his questions.

"I've never been human so how could I possibly answer your question?" Again, Sky Dragon answered with a non-answer.

"How's your sense of taste and your digestive system work?"

"I can taste. And I can swallow."

"Excellent! How often do you have bowel movements and have to urinate?"

"Dr. Tanner, I don't eat. So why would my bowels ever need to move?"

"Whata weirdo," Bethany's sweet little voice complained. She turned back and gave Everet a dirty look.

"What?" asked Sky Dragon, his eye ridges going up inquiringly.

"That guy asking if you need to take a dump or not, when *he's* the one with diarrhea of the mouth!"

Ryan laughed, Everet finally shut up, but now Sky Dragon had to ask a question of his own. "Bethame, what does 'diarrhea of the mouth' mean?"

"When someone is too stupid to know that they should shut up, and they just keep on talking and talking even though everyone around them just wants them to shut up! That, My Dragon, is diarrhea of the mouth." Bethany liked it when Sky Dragon asked her questions about words and slang or anything else for that matter. It made her feel smart. Which was why Sky Dragon asked her questions in the first place.

"Is there any way to cure Dr. Tanner of this—diarrhea of the mouth?" he asked.

"You'll have to eat him, My Dragon, and that way he can see if you have a digestive system and find out all he needs to know about your *movements* when you crap him out." She was smiling now, which was what Sky Dragon was hoping for, and as an added bonus so was everyone else, except Dr. Tanner of course and Believer, who still frowned.

Sky Dragon and Bethany had agreed during an earlier conversation to a slight alteration in their names (just between them). He called her "Bethame" and she called him "My Dragon." Bethany had asked him if he would be "her" dragon. Sky Dragon had taken her request very seriously and answered that he would, but only if she consented to be his own, personal little princess because what self-respecting dragon went around without a princess to lock away in towers so he could eat the brave knights who came to rescue her? Bethany agreed, but only after Sky Dragon reluctantly agreed to hold the knights down and let her kill them, and then they could eat them together. Sky Dragon and Bethany had become a Dragon and his Princess from that moment on.

Once they arrived at the wall, Bethany ignored the mirror table and went straight to the Gateway Arch which opened of its own accord as she approached without her having to do anything, like an automatic door at a grocery store, complete with a little hissing noise as the air between the two openings moved around.

As soon as the door opened, the guards they'd brought moved into shielding positions around them. Waiting to meet them outside the other Gateway Arch was Hillary, standing apart from her own security that waited nearby, unhappily. She began to thank them for coming but was interrupted by Ryan.

"Whatever, lady, just do what you promised for a change and take me where I can see my sister."

Hillary nodded, not surprised by the cold reception. "Of course. Right this way."

She led them to a nearby tent that had been arranged to receive not just their party but a large number of others as well. The ten men they brought from Amen Hale moved with Cornelius and the others, constantly positioning their bodies around them like human shields as they watched for danger.

Inside the tent was a large projection screen, showing a live image of a podium at the Press Room in the White House. A second smaller screen was positioned just off to the side, and the group from Amen Hale drifted over and stopped before the smaller screen. The low res image was obviously taken from a great distance. There was a weedy field, with two soldiers guarding a bunch of prisoners tied up and lying on the ground while a third man was kneeling in front of Rain. Rain had her black dress on so she was easily identified.

"Sorry, but we don't have sound to go with the picture," explained an over-weight balding man in a grey suit standing right by the screen.

They watched as Rain cut her hand and then smeared what looked like her own blood across the forehead of the soldier kneeling in front of her.

"Do you have another camera angle? It's quite grainy," asked Cornelius.

"Yes sir, but the second camera is trained on the vampire; she's still feeding."

In front of the man was a control board. He pushed a button and the picture changed, showing a distant shot of four semis with their black trailers parked side by side. On the roof of one of these trailers stood a naked woman with milk white skin and raven black hair and glowing red eyes, sucking on the neck of a tall man who hung limp in her grasp. The camera zoomed in and they watched as Jane dropped the body, wiped her mouth with the back of her hand and smiled. She said something that they couldn't hear, then she was gone, vanished.

The fat, bald man pushed another button and the screen flipped back to the first camera again, which showed Rain talking to Jane now. Jane was still naked. She stood in the midst of the bound prisoners and soldiers and spoke to Rain, apparently unbothered by her own nudity.

"Five minutes till the start of the Presidential address," a voice on a sound system announced and others around the tents began to drift in and take their seats before the larger screen. Mindful men in suits and dour looking military officers of rank sat in the folding chairs further toward the back to give their guests from Amen Hale plenty of space to move about and not feel crowded or threatened.

"Jane certainly seems uninhibited," said Cornelius. "I wonder if she will stay nude from now on. Now that she's risen she may not see an advantage in clothing."

"Jane wouldn't walk around naked," Ryan argued. He made a grim face and scratched his head. "I hope," he added.

"No," Believer answered firmly. "I doubt she's had an opportunity to obtain clothing since her abduction. Remember, she was stolen away from her bedchamber in the crypt. I believe she was nude when they took her."

Bethany wasn't getting excited about the naked lady on the screen, but there was something that had her smiling. "Look at all those prisoners! She must have thirty or forty people." Bethany was already getting glassy eyed. "I hope they're all food."

"Bethany," Believer nudged her gently to get her attention, and she looked up into his glowing red eyes. "Do not lose yourself in blood lust, little one, keep your magic at the ready and stay alert. You are the most powerful of us here, and I hate to ask it of you, but we need you to be ready to protect us."

"Yes sir," Bethany answered Believer. She took a deep breath, cast a quick evil eye at the suits and soldiers before turning back to the screen where Rain was doing something with Jane.

"What the hell?" Bethany said. "Is Rain letting her drink her blood?" Jane had dropped to her knees and they watched as Rain held her hand over Jane's mouth.

"Can't you zoom in any closer than this?" asked Ryan as he crowded the screen.

The tech started to push buttons and they lost the picture for a minute. When it came back onto the screen they saw that things had quickly gone from bad to terrible; Jane had grabbed ahold of Rain's hand and was sucking it while at the same time Rain was glowing! Bright light beamed through her dress and from her face and hands and feet and her hair blew around like she stood in a gale force wind. Her power was getting completely out of control like it had when she'd been in the Cathedral Hall earlier that night. Believer had been there to grab her to help her calm down, but he wasn't there now. They watched as the three soldiers in the field near Rain and Jane shielded their eyes and tried to run away only to collapse on the ground before they got clear, passed out or dead. The bound prisoners all thrashed about or tried to inch away with their eyes squeezed shut like terrified, blind worms, fleeing from the blinding white light.

"NO!" Believer bellowed, making everyone jump when on the screen it looked like the vampire attacked, pulling Rain closer, up against her body as she continued to suck blood from her hand.

They watched wordlessly as Rain struggled, pushing against Jane's hold on her arm, looking terrified. Her body began to glow white, brighter and brighter, even as her struggles slowed—then she gasped and the entire screen went white.

"She cannot die, Believer. She will return to us, my son." Cornelius's voice was tight as he offered what encouragement he could.

Bethany was holding Ryan's hand with one of her tiny hands and had her other arm wrapped part way around Believer's huge leg, trying to comfort them both and herself. Behind them, Hillary and the crowd who were gathered to watch the President's address were respectfully silent.

They'd all been watching the screen and now they were watching their guests to see what their reaction would be. Hillary was feeling exceedingly self-satisfied. So many people had argued against bringing Cornelius and his people out here that she'd almost given in. But this had worked out better than she could have imagined. Now these crazy people would know that the U.S. had nothing to do with Black Rain's death, *if* for some reason she did not return. They'd seen it with their own eyes, as it happened. And as an added bonus, they all now saw for themselves just how dangerous the vampires were. She watched and broke down every word that these people and "creatures" said, gleaning through the conversation for what it would mean to her, her command, and her country.

"Jane killed my sister." Ryan's voice was empty and sad for both of them. "I know that Rain will come back, but she'll be different. She always is after she dies. And Jane's gone psycho. If she can't get control of herself she'll have to be—locked up. Rain will probably do it herself once she comes back, but doing it will hurt her."

A rumbling noise came from Believer preceding his angry words. "What is wrong with the picture!?" he complained, sounding irritated and emotional. "Why is the screen still white?" He loomed menacingly over the man at the control panel who was frantically pressing buttons and twisting knobs with no results.

"There's something wrong with the feed!" the fat man squeaked. "The optics in the cameras must have been damaged in the flash of light, when she—" He clipped the words off and resumed playing with his buttons. "We'll have more drones in position soon, and the satellite will come into alignment in forty minutes."

Hillary approached her guests, looking respectfully sympathetic, but sounding businesslike. On the big projection screen the President was approaching the podium.

"I'm sorry, King Cornelius, I'm sure you'll want to return now?" Hillary suggested and even put a hand out directing them away. Cornelius reached out and elegantly took her hand and surprised her as he bent over and kissed her hand.

"Dear lady, I believe we shall stay." He gave her a tight smile, his eyes reflected brightly with unshed tears. "I need to see this for myself." He gestured to the screen and the president. "Unless you intend to rescind your invitation? Another betrayal is not a way to assure us of a change of policy." Cornelius smiled.

They watched the interview along with the others in the tent. Hearing the news as it was given to all from the mouth of The President of the United States of America. First, he announced a state of emergency, stating that he was enacting certain powers reserved for times of extreme crisis to ensure the continuity of government. A wave of murmured dissent and alarm rose from the bureaucrats, government officials, and even the high ranking military officers seated in their unstable folding chairs.

But then the President went on to tell *why* he was taking such grave actions. He revealed the existence of a secret organization know as "The Order" that had poisoned the will of the Nation and violated the trust of the American people for years. He then accused the members of The Order of High Treason. After that introduction he started to tell the juicy stuff.

He actually began by revealing a number of things that The Order had done in the distant, and not so distant past. Some things that happened fifty years ago and some things much more recently. Kennedy's assassination made the list, no surprise there, but the list went on and on. After adding such a mountain of crimes that no one in their right mind could justify their actions or stand on their side, he revealed that The Order had been behind the attack on the motorcade carrying the teens from the drug study.

He went on to say that The Order was responsible for a second attack on Amen Hale that happened earlier in the evening. He did not give details about the attack or the vampires other than saying it had also cost American soldiers their lives.

Activity kept happening around the President as he spoke, people leaning in to whisper to him or walking behind him in the line of the camera (which they would never do by accident). It created an atmosphere of ongoing activity and momentum and made everything that much more real and frightening.

And then the perp walk started. A few went on camera "live" walking up to the podium to confess their involvement, but most had given prerecorded video depositions. There was one living ex-President (Carter), two former Vice Presidents, senior staffers, senators, congressmen, aids, lobbyists, and a number of officers in the military.

After announcing the most sensational names himself, the President allowed one of his staff to come up and go down a long list of other names, people who were wanted for Grand Treason. They were instructed to turn themselves in immediately and that anyone who aided or harbored them would be charged to the fullest extent of the law. The names included a number famous Americans and a handful of actors.

The time had flown by and people had drifted closer and closer to the screen, the watching group from Amen Hale blending almost tightly with all the disbelieving, dumbstruck faces of those around them. Everyone watched as America changed before their very eyes, but then the light of the yellow sun began to fade, which made everyone turn their eyes to the sky and then back toward Amen Hale.

Black Rain

Feeding the Beast

BULL, THE LEADER of the spec ops team that attacked the crypt, Tiger, a huge black soldier, and a smaller Mexican man they called Spider begged me for mercy and agreed to take my mark and become my servants. They were quite desperate to find some way to avoid my displeasure. They wanted a chance to die a *clean death*. They'd seen my version of an *unclean death* and wanted to avoid it at any price, even if it cost their lives or souls. I was not interested in their souls, but the rest I claimed.

The mark I gave them was nothing exotic but it was very visible; each of them now had one eye that I made solid black like mine, along with their magically binding vow to obey my every order without question. The three survivors became mine, but the fourth man I left behind to tell my family where I'd gone so they wouldn't worry about me while I was away.

He had refused my mark, too scared it would endanger his immortal soul. I told him that I would never willingly take someone away from God, but he still refused. I respected his stand, so I was merciful. We worked out an arrangement that was good for both of us and I'd gone about my way with the other three men who had shown that they were so very good at carrying out their orders. Now they could carry out mine.

I created a bag, like the one they tried to melt Dan's body in, and crawled inside. The soldiers then carried me out to the second waiting helicopter inside the bag. My men told those in charge that Dan was inside the bag, and we followed after the first helicopter that had carried Jane away. And as soon as we were close to Jane we took over the aircraft.

When I saw the lights in the field down below where they kept Jane I willed their power and batteries to die and also cursed their weapons so nothing would explode (no bullets, rockets, or other explosives). The only thing that would work in that field would be teeth and blades and magic.

Before we landed I cast a circle of mist far around the field to keep any of these men from escaping and to keep out other people who didn't have anything to do with the attack on Amen Hale. I didn't want to kill innocents if I could help it.

As I walked away from the helicopter, my three new soldiers deployed about me like my own little army, wielding knives instead of guns. We stopped briefly at the other helicopter where my men were surprised to find that the rest of their group had been shot and murdered. (Betrayed.)

I let the three men with me take a few minutes to investigate the helicopter and see to their fallen friends. I could tell they loved these men that they'd fought beside and trusted with their lives who knew how many times. They wept. They cursed. I watched. My midnight black eyes drank in the sight. Death and love always fascinated and attracted me and it waited for me around every corner and revealed itself to me in unusual ways.

This scene helped remind me what I was. A Murderer. The Black Witch. The lighter of the Black Candle. The bane of that which I loved, and it was time to kill another person I loved. It was time to go and tell Jane that Dan was dead, and then watch her die in front of my eyes.

I readied my soul, but not by making it numb so I that I could not feel, but by weeping as I came. I didn't want to rob Jane of seeing me suffer. I was filthy, covered in blood and grime, my hair and the tattered remains of my dress waving about in the currents of my power as our little group moved toward the semi trucks and other vehicles on the far side of the clearing.

Before I reached the trucks, a line of a dozen men formed up in front of us, all holding knives. One man even flourished about with a sword. Beyond the line of men who were ready to fight I saw another line formed up, ready to surrender. They were already on their knees with their hands clasped behind their heads. On the way here I'd contemplated many different horrors to pour out on these people who had dared to attack us, but finally I rejected all of it over the needs of my family.

I willed the hands and feet of the dozen men before me to fall off (severed at wrist and ankle) and watched as the line of men collapsed in a wash of squirting red liquid and shouts of surprise and pain. Quickly, I healed the men, new pink flesh closing over the stumps so they wouldn't bleed to death and be wasted. I lingered, forced to stop and stare at the horror by some odd sense of obligation. I'd done this, I should see what I'd wrought and make it a part of me. So I did.

The mass of writhing, cursing, horrified bodies flailed about, rolling around on top of a pile of their own severed hands and feet. Such powerful emotions showed on the faces of these strong men made instantly impotent and pathetically helpless. Two men started to scuttle away on their stumps and were herded back into the group by the men I'd brought with me. I ordered Spider to gag and bind my handicapped captives.

"Make sure they do not kill themselves. We only eat live food," I said as I walked away. We stopped at the row of men and women who had chosen to surrender. They all wore street clothes, no camo or combat fatigues, but they all looked fit and able bodied. Ex soldiers. Hard people. Tough.

"Displease me in any way and I will make you wish you stood with them tonight." They glanced toward the writhing quadruple amputees and back toward me, a look of pure horror on their faces.

I wondered what *they* saw. What were they thinking as they gazed upon me? My solid black eyes, my filthy shredded black dress, my crazy living hair. The thoughts of the terrified woman directly in front of me opened to my mind, but I couldn't understand a word as she was thinking in French. Understanding came as my will opened her words to my mind.

"*Oh God, she's looking right at me! Should I look down!? Should I look away!?*" She looked down at the ground. "*She's still looking at me! No! Please God, don't let me die here, let me get back to Lauren and Anna!*"

I pushed further into her mind, willing an image of Lauren to surface. A vision came (or a memory actually) of an angry eleven-year-old girl with raven black hair, complaining bitterly in French that the meat in the spaghetti sauce was ground turkey and not ground beef. I watched the woman before me now, trying to reason with her (slightly overweight) child and attempt to explain that she needed to eat better so she could lose some weight. The spoiled child threw the plate against the wall and stomped off to bed. This had been the last time she'd seen her daughter. With the memory came a bitter taste in my mouth and a tightness in my gut of regret and loss that came with the memory.

"Wha-a-at are you d-d-doing to me?" the woman stuttered out, head still down.

"I'm looking at your children. I imagine Lauren is asleep right now, safe and sound in her bed for the night."

Her head snapped up, eyes staring, her face momentarily shocked blank by this newfound terror until the dam broke and the begging began. "Please! Please! Please! Please! Don't hurt my children! Do anything you want to me but *Please!* Leave them in their beds! Let them live!"

We had an attentive audience. The other eight who had chosen "surrender" were watching and listening, as were the soldiers I'd brought with me.

"You know. That sounds like such a reasonable request," I told her. "And even though you murdered my loved ones *in their beds*," I hissed, "I plan on letting your Lauren and your Anna live and rest peacefully tonight. But know this, you cannot hide what you are because you are a woman or because you are a mother. *I am both.*" My eyes hardened and my voice growled out, "You are a murdering, black-hearted bitch, who deserves to burn in hell for what you have done tonight! Any mercy you may receive, *you do not deserve!*"

I ordered Tiger, the huge black soldier, to move those who had surrendered over with the cripples and marched on. I could feel Jane nearby and walked toward the trailer I knew she was in. Bull, the leader of the unfortunate group I'd drafted into my service, ran before me and made himself useful, opening the doors of the black semi.

With a thought, I floated into the air and landed lightly inside the truck. It was very dark inside the trailer, so I willed light to exist in the room, and there was light, not coming from any source but it was there all the same.

In the exact center of the huge trailer was a massive black box made out of steel. It looked custom made to hold a vampire. Actually, it looked like it could hold Superman himself. It was one hell of an iron box.

"Hello, Rain." I heard Jane's sweet musical voice from within the box, the noise making its way out of thin slits cut into the side, probably designed to let in air.

My heart shriveled within me at hearing the happy sound. I couldn't lie to her but I fought the wild urge to run away and not tell her that her Dan was dead. I stood there, frozen with hate for what I was, and what I was about to do. As soon as I told her he was gone, she would die. I knew it.

"*Please*," I whispered in the quiet of my mind and squeezed my eyes tight as the weight of murder pushed down on me like the weight of all creation. I did not want her to die!

"Rain?" Jane's voice called.

"*Please!*" I prayed this one word to myself because I did not know what else to pray. What could I possibly ask for? Dan was dead and gone, I'd felt his spirit go. I opened my mouth but closed it again. I couldn't tell her. I couldn't!

"*Please!*" I prayed to myself one last time; I just didn't know what else to pray. I started to cry.

"Rain, are you all right? What's wrong?" her voice called to me from the box as I cried. "Are you worried about Dan? He's alive. After you fixed his body he came here. Dan's soul is where it belongs, inside me. When we get back home he'll collect his body again, but for now, all of Dan is inside me."

"What?" I heard myself say.

"Don't worry about Dan. He's fine. He's alive and here with me now."

"What—did you—just say?" I tried to make sense of the words.

"Dan says he's very, very sorry, Rain. He should have stopped long enough to let you know what he was doing before he left his body behind, but he just had to come to me. Is his body in a safe place?"

I managed a rough "yes." My mind reeled, my skin heated. Nauseous and dizzy, I leaned against the side of the trailer for a minute, then I staggered to the back and puked.

"Mistress, what would you like me to do?" asked Bull as he climbed into the trailer with me.

"Go and guard the prisoners. Leave me be," I ordered as I used a torn shred of my dress to wipe bitter stomach acid vomit from my mouth.

He jumped down and obeyed instantly. My nerves were shot, my vision was blurry, and my mental state felt egg shell fragile. I knelt there at the back of the trailer and breathed, letting my mind rest.

Dan was alive. Jane was alive. They were both alive. I hadn't killed them after all. I hadn't lied. I'd promised to keep them safe and I had.

"So. How are we doing out there?" Jane's voice rose from inside of the box again. She sounded conversational. "Is it a horrifying bloodbath? How many of them have you already killed?"

"None," I said. My voice was a quiet, hoarse whisper.

"Why?" her voice growled darkly.

I banished the disgusting aftertaste of vomit from my mouth and throat before it made me dry heave. "Wasteful," I heard my mouth say, but my mind was still fogged and torn.

"Wasteful?" Jane asked, her voice had lost it's growl and now sounded curious.

"Food."

"Oh," she said, calm again. "Rain, could you let us out? I feel like I'm blind, talking to you and only hearing your voice and not seeing your face. You don't sound so good. Let me out so I can see you."

I willed the metal box to dissolve into dust, which revealed Jane, sitting on the floor of the trailer surrounded by shredded metal wires they must have used to tie her up with. She was totally nude but she was covered in dust now and it was all over floor. With a thought, the dust, the metal wires on the ground at her feet, all the grime and filth on both our bodies, including the last shreds of my dress, and the other little odds and ends around the trailer vanished into oblivion.

It was just Jane and me facing each other in a bare empty metal trailer. We were both completely naked. She rose gracefully to her feet and walked over to me. She studied me, starting at my toes and ending at my eyes, seeing "me" and all the other things that meant for her. Jane looked much the same as she did the last time I'd seen her before she died, but somehow she was more solid now. She was complete. Finished. Beautiful. She slowly closed the last few steps between us and hugged me, her naked flesh was cooling pressed against my hot skin.

"It's okay now. Dan and I are both fine. You saved us. You came in time and you saved us. Thank you, Rain." She leaned back far enough to see my face and still hold me in the circle of her arms as she studied my face. "When you said 'wasteful' and 'food' I heard something else in your voice. You weren't just talking about me and Dan, were you? What's happened? Are there more vampires now in Amen Hale?"

"No," I said.

Jane's brow crinkled in thought. Her head ticked to the side and I could tell she was having a conversation inside her head with Dan. Just seeing this made me relax. Dan really was inside her right now, talking to her. Dan was safe and with his Jane. Jane laughed, sounding wicked, and I knew she was teasing Dan about something embarrassing, probably us being naked together. I was right.

"Dan's having a hard time concentrating with both of us standing here naked. Especially with you touching me naked. Dan can feel everything I can feel inside my body and he is getting a little—distracted." She laughed again, the musical noise of her voice echoing inside the empty trailer like a psychedelic sound effect in a disco club.

Jane's wicked smile became positively sinful. She closed her eyes as she listened to Dan's words in her head, and I was pulled into staring at her full, blood red lips. She kept her eyes closed and actually held me closer and rubbed herself and her perfect breasts against mine and laughed with mischievous delight as she tortured her beloved with our bodies.

But Dan wasn't the only one getting aroused by her touch. I thought about Emma's kiss and her flesh and breasts pressed up against mine, and I felt my own skin flush like fire with the heated memory.

Jane's hands released me clumsily and she actually fell backwards and landed on her bottom with a little smack of flesh meeting metal floor. She looked up at me, stunned, surprised, and confused. And was that *fear* on her face?

"*What THE HELL was that!*?" Jane shouted, and the power of her voice boomed inside the empty trailer, but it didn't make me flinch.

This was the only time I'd ever seen her fall or trip or look anything less than completely graceful, and for some reason, looking at her spread out clumsily on the floor made the witch inside me rise up like a dark hungry animal. Dark passions and wild desires surged through me as I looked at her sitting there naked. I felt like a lion seeing a wounded gazelle out on the savannah. Usually, it was too swift to be prey so it avoided notice, *but not now.*

The amazing smooth feel of her skin against mine was still fresh in my mind. I *saw* Jane in a whole new way. Emma loved her, and so did I. Emma wanted her, and I realized—*so did I.* Jane was, of all creatures, most beautiful. Could we have her? Would Emma be angry if I asked? What would Believer say? What would Dan say? Could I do it? Could WE do it? SHOULD WE DO IT!?

Wait a minute.

Did I really even want to do it? I mean *COME ON!* I didn't even know what IT! was when it was women doing IT! My concentration slipped and more of my pent up power slipped free and my hair (which had gone quiet and still) surged to life and flailed around me. The light that I'd created inside the trailer changed from a soft white to a color a shade darker, more tinged with red as if altered by my mood alone.

Jane's eyes continued to get wider and wider as I stepped up to where she sat on the metal floor. As I got close, she leaned back to see my eyes and get some distance, but I just kept going until I straddled her. That surprised her. I stood with one foot on each side of her hips as Jane looked up at my body with an odd expression on her face. Disbelief? Confusion? Disgust? Longing? I couldn't tell. I wondered if having Dan inside her was making it difficult for her to look away from me.

"But you don't like girls." Jane made a face. "Or you didn't like girls!"

"Kiss me," I breathed, my voice dark and hungry. She looked so surprised I had to laugh. My own wicked laugh carried magic into the air around me like a shivering sigh.

"Rain. Not my thing, girl. I don't swing like that. Not in *that* way. And anyway, I'm married."

I let more of myself out and the walls of the trailer above and below us shimmered like a mirage and my body began to glow. Beneath me, I felt Jane shiver between my feet. The Black Witch rose and I did not fight the feeling of passion and wildness that thrilled through my soul; this was so much better than the other part of being her, the part that murdered.

"Rain, stop it!" Jane shouted at me from the floor. She sounded scared and that reached through everything.

I wiped the smile off my face and pulled in my power to a more bearable level, but I couldn't take the heat from my eyes as I looked at her lying below me, and I could not remove the longing from my voice as I spoke. "I'll make you the same deal that Emma made me. Kiss me just one time, and if you don't like it, I won't ask again."

Outside the trailer the noise of jets, lots of jets, tore through the sky. After the sound died down Jane spoke again. "You kissed Emma?" she asked, serious now.

"Yes."

"But Emma doesn't touch people," Jane said with cold certainty. "And she definitely doesn't like people touching her. Other than me," she added reluctantly. "Did you *make* her kiss you?"

"More like the other way around. I don't know if I even had a choice now that I think about it." I sighed, not a pissed sigh, but a happy one. "Emma's a witch now. I think she used her magic on me, but I don't care. I'm glad I'm bewitched."

"Screw that!" Jane growled out fiercely.

I was about to be a smart ass and say "if you insist," but before I could open my mouth the noise of jets and helicopters rumbled again outside the trailer, and below me Jane vanished. I looked up to find her standing at the mouth of the trailer, staring at me with a satisfied smile.

I thought about how that must feel. Always being faster than everyone else. It probably made her very self-assured and confident. Like nothing could touch her. I willed myself to move, but not like her, by walking fast, I just thought about standing beside her and I was there, not doing anything sinister, just standing there beside her looking out the back of the trailer with a little smile on my face as I watched her reaction out of the corner of my eye.

Jane frowned, but she didn't try to vanish again. "If you're through showing off, tell me what the hell's going on around here? I take a day for a little dirt nap with my hhhuusssbbbaanndd," she stretched the word out, "and when I wake up, everyone's gone buck ass wild and turned inside out."

I laughed, not a sexed up laugh, just a laugh.

Jane gave me the evil eye. "What's so *damn funny?*" she asked irritably.

Jane had always been so cool and controlled, almost unshakeable. This irritated, stumbling, shivering, *weak* Jane—was *endearing*. Hadn't I just had to ride in, like her knight in shining armor and save her ass? Jane looked completely beside herself and I knew that Dan was trying to talk to her. I was probably the only person on earth who could make her feel vulnerable.

I answered her question. "Jane, I'm laughing because you're cute when you're frazzled. And it's good to have you back. And you're right. Emma did turn inside out. Turning inside out is exactly what it takes to become a witch. Everything hidden, the dark desires on the inside, must come out."

Jane looked at me for a minute, studying my face again, putting it all together. "So when Emma became a witch, she told everyone she was gay?"

Right then, Bull ran up to the back of the trailer and shouted up to me, "Mistress, a helicopter is about to land in the field. It's an Army copter. What do you want us to do?"

I closed my eyes and spoke out loud so Jane could hear me, and I willed my words to reach the men inside the helicopter. *"I gave fair warning. These men attacked Amen Hale. All of the men in this field are mine. Their flesh and blood is mine. Don't land or you'll join them. Black is my color and my name is Black Rain. So mote it be."*

"Go back and keep an eye on the prisoners," I ordered.

Bull left.

"Their flesh and blood is yours?" Jane asked with one eyebrow cocked high.

"Like you said, Jane, things have changed since you died. Bethany is the Red Witch and her powers have grown and changed. She must have death and sacrifice to live. If she does not have sacrifice, she dies. It's that simple. And you and Dan need blood. And recently, I think," I shrugged, "pretty sure anyway, that I have a taste for flesh, along with other hungers which I didn't even know I had." I let my gaze slip down her naked body and I swear that Jane would have blushed if she could have. Or covered herself up, but there was nothing around to use.

"You know Dan can hear every word you're saying to me and all the ho-ish moves you keep tryin' on me. Emma was always discreet about how she felt; she just dropped a hint every now and then—but you've just come rip snorting wild out of the gay girl closet, haven't ya!?" Jane kept her disapproving gaze hard on me.

"I'm sorry! But I'm a witch, and sometimes I can't help it. I have feelings and sometimes they're hard to control. And Dan already knows what I'm doing and he's right here with you. And in my defense, you did rub your boobs all over me, and if that don't get a gay girl going I don't know what will, so include some blame for yourself in this. You wanted to torture Dan and I simply offered to help." I laughed again at the look on her face but her look turned mean fast.

"I'm not sharing Dan with anyone. Not you or Emma." Jane said it coldly.

"Fine with me. I don't want him. And I'm sure that's fine with Emma. Other than Believer, I find that I do not like men. I think my miserable experience while I lived inside Rain Marie ruined me on human males. No offense, Dan. I don't mind you being inside Jane, but it's her that I want to touch. If you don't want us, or if Dan doesn't feel comfortable in sharing your love with us, we'll understand. But if we can have you, and if you'll have us, we want you."

"We?" Jane asked, then answered her own question. "You and Emma both want me."

Jane's head twitched to the side. "Yeah right!" she muttered, talking to Dan in her head.

"What did Dan say?" I asked, curious.

Jane kept laying the stink eye on me as she answered me. "He's inside my head laughing his ass off, saying how before we died everything in Amen Hale was so *prim* and *proper* and *high brow*." Her voice colored the appropriate words mockingly. "He thinks when we get back it'll be a scene straight out of Caligula. People running around everywhere, butt naked, orgies going on in every room!"

"I'd have to ask Believer if he'd allow it first. But if Dan would let you, and if Believer would let me, Emma and I would love to have an orgy with you, Jane."

Jane laughed, then I laughed, and I knew that somewhere inside her head her Dan laughed. (Hell, he probably would have peed on himself if he had a body of his own). The night sky overhead came alive with noise as jets made another pass and the circling helicopters zoomed in for another look-see before heading off again.

"Dan is more forgiving than I am, and he doesn't care that those soldiers that you have are still alive, but there is one person here who made this personal." Jane's eyes started to glow red. "Please tell me that Dr. Morgan is still alive?"

"Not sure. There were two guys who looked like doctors in the—"

"Helicopter." Jane finished my sentence for me, her impatience getting the better of her. "No. This guy didn't die in the helicopter," Jane said, smiling now. "So he's still hiding out there somewhere." Jane vanished.

I hopped down to the ground, still wearing nothing but my skin, but it felt like it was time for the dress again. Instantly, the familiar wrapping of my calling encircled my flesh. My skin still had some leftover glow from my power spill inside the trailer and my hair and my black dress waved about lazily as I walked over to my people, all gathered together in front of the semis.

My three black-eyed men had things well in hand and organized. They'd secured a few more prisoners and bound them hand and foot with plastic ties and laid them with the rest. I was surprised to see that four of them were nude.

"What's up with the naked ones?" I asked.

"Found these four in one of the trucks, having sex. They said it was a better way to die than trying to fight you. Probably the smartest four people out here if you asked me." Spider pointed to another couple of prisoners that I hadn't noticed before. "These four we found hiding, ma'am. Probably a bunch more out there."

"Spider. I know you're trying, but call me Mistress and get comfortable with it or I'll have to let you go, and you don't want that."

He fell to his knees begging, "Mistress forgive me!"

"Shut up," I ordered. He stiffened as I reached over to his belt and drew out his knife. I was surprised to find that the entire thing was plastic. It still looked sharp, and I drug it across the palm of my hand without much thought.

"Oww!" I yelped and dropped the knife. My soldiers and the bound and gagged prisoners all stared as I reached over to the petrified Hispanic man still on his knees and wiped my bleeding palm across his forehead, then cradled my hurt and bleeding hand to my chest as I chanted:

"Protection I give as I give you my blood
To enter the mist that I made from above.
Go now and gather and bring here to me
the ones who have fled from their destiny."

I explained to him that there were a number of people, passed out, lying in the mist that ringed the field. I wanted him to bring them in. Amen Hale would need all the flesh it could get in the days and weeks to come and I didn't want to miss any of these people who had earned the right to join us for dinner. We had quite a haul already, thirty-seven, tied and trussed up with more to come.

"What the hell is this, Rain?" I turned at the sound of Jane's sweet musical voice to find her pointing down to the writhing line of amputees. "That's just nasty." She crinkled her perfect nose as she eyed them with disgust. She was still naked and bright red blood trailed from the corner of her mouth and ran down her neck and a splotch was smeared darkly across the perfect ivory skin of her stomach with another matching mark on her arm.

I could make out the bloody red pattern of a hand print left behind on her white flesh, as if Dr. Morgan just wanted to wave good-bye. The blood was fresh and wet, glistening damply in the silver moonlight, but the blood was not what made me hold my breath. The way she stood there, back arched, pushing out her perfect breasts, the dark triangle of hair hiding still more that I wanted to see but couldn't—I got lost looking at her body like *everyone* else in the clearing, stunned to *stupid* by her beauty.

Jane ignored us all, like the only smart kid in a special ed class, until her eyes fell on the pile of hands and feet and she made a horrified face. She actually looked shocked. "Damn! You're saving the scraps!" she shouted.

The mutilated men had been bound with plastic ties and gagged with the rest of the prisoners, and someone had neatly stacked the pile of the severed appendages, but the pile of parts was so *freakin' huge*! I walked over to the mound of flesh a bit freaked out myself. It had to be three feet high!

"Shit! That can't be right! There were only twelve of them." I scratched my head with my good hand. "Hmm. Two feet on each guy—and there's twelve guys—that'd be twenty-four feet—and I suppose twenty-four hands which would be—"

"That's forty-eight severed limbs, you freak." Jane gave me a sideways glance with a grimace. "Rain, you give me the willies sometimes. I don't remember you being this damn scary."

I smiled at her and had my midnight black eyes twinkle at her. She shook her head and did not smile.

"So, did you have a pleasant time with Dr. Morgan?"

"He was tasty for an asshole."

I laughed and she finally smiled back at me, looking more beautiful than ever. I looked at her body and the hunger for her rose within me again. I held up my bloody hand without even thinking about it and finally I had her attention in the same way she had mine.

Her smiled faded, her face smoothed, becoming calm and unreadable and her eyes never left my hand as I took another slow motion step in her direction. She reminded me of a predator as it watched its prey. I knew this was probably a very bad idea and would most likely get me killed, but I wanted to touch her, and this was probably my last chance before we went home. I went with it.

"I had to cast a spell and needed some blood," I explained as I took another slow step toward her. "And I wouldn't want to waste it. But—" I stopped and frowned. "You're probably already full from eating Morgan."

I turned away shyly, giving her my back. I felt a slight breeze move my hair, and I knew she was right behind me. I looked down to hide my smile, but I couldn't hide the shiver that ran through me. I knew I'd never be able to pull the wool over on Jane in any normal situation, but her brain was so scrambled by the sight and smell of my blood she was practically like a drunk chick at a rave, easily manipulated into a compromising situation. Did I feel guilty about using my blood for a chance to touch her? Yes.

But my guilty conscience went deaf when I heard Jane's voice whisper right by my ear, "*You're right. I wouldn't want to waste it.*" My sense of unease grew along with my excitement. She sounded hungry.

"Will you be careful with me? *Can you* be careful?" She still stood behind me as I whispered the words, but I know she heard me.

"All I can do is try." She sounded calm but my heart rate went up all the same.

I turned my head and spoke to her over my shoulder. I could barely see her through the screen of my hair. "Hold still then. And don't move. Let me do it."

She nodded and I turned to face her. She was still naked and covered with blood, but my eyes stayed on her face, her eyes, and her lips. Her lips were so red against the white ivory of her skin, the red stood out and demanded to be seen, the lips to be touched. Jets roared by overhead again but I ignored them as I moved my hand toward her face. She began to reach out with her own hands to take my hand in hers but I stopped her.

"No," I said. "Put your hands down. Let me do it." I froze, and she froze.

I pulled my hand back just an inch and stopped and waited, until she lowered her hands back down to her sides. The corners of Jane's mouth turned up, which made me wonder how much she suspected of what I was about to do, and why I was doing it. She kept her hands at her sides as she lowered herself gracefully onto her knees and tilted her face upwards.

She didn't open her mouth wide and show off her teeth, but she parted her lips alluringly. Her red eyes grew brighter as I angled my hand over her mouth so the blood from my palm would channel down to my index finger. I had to remind myself to breathe; the combination of fear and excitement was intoxicating to the point that my vision began to narrow and my power began to escape. I was as deaf to the screams of those around me as I was to the thundering noise of jets high over head. My hair flailed about and my body began to glow as the world shrank down to me and her.

When the fist drop of blood reached the tip of my finger, I touched it to the bow of Jane's upper lip and watched her tremble. I traced down the curve and then across the taut flesh of her full bottom lip and up the other side again, barely touching her cool skin as I left a wet shining trail of blood in my passing. I noticed that my own blood looked gold and not red as it welled up, fresh from my cut and trailed down my finger, but as soon as it passed from my glowing skin into Jane's mouth it became red again.

Jane licked her lips, her bright red tongue collecting the golden red coin I'd offered up for a chance to touch her. She leaned forward just enough to take my fingers into her mouth and suck the blood off them, and I gasped as my whole frame trembled. She sucked and worked her tongue between my fingers and ran her cool tongue down my arm and I felt her body shake.

NO! She was growling! NOT GOOD! And then her hand was on my hand, pressing it against her mouth as she sucked the blood straight from my body. She stood and her other arm pulled me in up against her naked body while she fed. My heart felt as if it would leap from my chest as I reached out blindly with my free hand to push her away but my hand found her breasts. The trembling and the fear and the excitement were too much and my body responded in a way I didn't even know I was building toward.

Orgasm. My knees quit working as it took me.

I remembered a flash of light. And then I was staring up at the night sky. I felt dreamlike and weightless as I floated in water and stared up at the stars dotting the night sky.

Was I in water? I felt below me and felt—nothing. Alarmed, I turned my head to find that I was floating in the air a foot above the ground. Jets buzzed overhead again, their deafening roar making me wince but also forcing me from my dream-like malaise.

I floated upright and looked around me. Everyone was lying flat on the ground, and for a horrified second I thought for sure I'd killed all of them, but then I saw Jane move weakly. I dropped to the ground, crawled over, and gathered her into my arms.

"Jane! Jane! Can you hear me? Jane!" I cried and shook her. Streaks of white had shot through her midnight black hair. I shouted her name again, "Jane!" and her eyes flicked open.

Her eyes had changed color; the dark red iris in the center was the same, but the bright purple and lilac had faded to a much lighter and paler shade leaving the outside edge almost white. It made her appear constantly surprised. And of course she glowed.

I held her half in my lap, her head resting against my chest as I began to cry. What had I done now? What had I done to her? Had I hurt her or her Dan? Jane lifted her head and looked around, seeing the mess I'd made.

"Next time, I'll be the one who asks *you* to be careful with *me*." Her voice sounded strange. Soft. Un-Jane like.

"I'm so sorry, Jane." I pulled her back into me and cried and wept into her white streaked hair. It looked like I'd killed everyone except for Jane, and I had no idea what I'd done to her, how much I'd hurt her. All of these men could die and I would not care a whit. Jane was the only one here who mattered, the only one here whom I loved!

"I'm so sorry." I wept into her hair.

"Rain. I am whole. Dan and I are both alive. But we will never be the same again."

"Oh my God! What did I do to you?" I squeezed my eyes shut, dreading her answer as I fought with myself to stay calm and not repeat my mistake. I'd ruined them. And for what? I'd destroyed their lives because I was horny! How unbelievably selfish is that!? I had destroyed them just because I wanted to touch Jane. I was made to kill and destroy that which I loved, and what humans couldn't accomplish, I'd managed to do all on my own. I cried, tears rolling down my cheeks.

"Please don't cry," Jane said.

I felt cool hands holding me, and I realized that somehow I'd switched places with her. I opened my eyes and stared up at Jane. Now I was the one in her arms, my head resting against the cool flesh of her bare chest as I looked up at her. She was smiling as she ran her careful hands through the waving mass of my unruly black hair that always had a life of its own (which made it "challenging" to deal with).

I heard other sounds. Other people moving around. Good. Off at the edge of the clearing I saw Spider staggering toward us bringing two new prisoners.

"Jane, what's happened to you? What have I done now?" I asked her.

She was smiling as she answered me, but something in her voice still sounded like *loss* in a way I could not describe. "Just a few minutes ago, Dan and I were complete, all by ourselves. We needed no one but each other and had all that we thought the world had to offer. We could not imagine anything that we could not find in each other's arms and in the sweet taste of the blood of men. But now our lives would be forever in shadow without you."

Jane leaned closer to me, staring into my eyes, and it was as if I could see not just her but also Dan within her as she spoke to me. "Where you live, we will live. Where you go, we also will go. You have bound us to you forever. We are yours."

I worked up enough moisture in my mouth to croak out, "But why?"

"Because when all we had was darkness, we thought it beautiful and were satisfied. Because when we tasted the blood of man, we thought it wonderful and were content. But now that we have seen your light, darkness is not enough for us. And now that we have tasted the blood of a god, what is the blood of man compared to that? Dan said that if you'll let us drink from you, he'll let me be with you and Emma."

Jane arched a snow white eyebrow, blasted white by my power, and added her own disclaimer to the offer. "I'm still feeling weird about the whole thing though, but Dan's actually looking forward to it. I'm going to need to go slow. Dan likes girls, so he's fine with it and it feels right to him, even inside my body, but I'm going to need some—*help*." She frowned.

I was horrified on so many levels it was hard to sort it all out, but I started on the sex stuff. "Shit, Jane! What a mess!" I covered my face with my hands and shook my head.

"What?" she asked.

"You don't have to sleep with me to have my blood dammit!" I shouted from behind my hands, too ashamed to let her see me. "You don't have to sleep with me if you don't want to. I'm not going to rape you! And this wasn't your fault. It's all my goddamn fault! My stupid goddamn fault! I broke you, and now I have to deal with it, and all the bullshit that comes with dealing with it!"

Jane's cold, powerful hands pried my hands away from my tear streaked face and she kissed me! At first I fought against her and tried to turn away, but she was stronger than me and held me firm and just kept kissing me.

Finally I stopped fighting against her and went limp, but she kept kissing me. Her lips were the smoothest thing that had ever touched my lips. It was like kissing living satin, and her mouth and tongue were both cool and refreshing to my warm, parched mouth. She tasted sweet, not sickly sweet, but wonderfully sweet, and she smelled like her magic, the wonderful smell of roses.

Something changed in the way she moved; her kisses no longer confident and demanding but gentle and—experimental. It was confusing and I wondered what had happened and turned away, and she growled! It wasn't loud, but I stiffened and turned back to her. I let her have her way with my mouth. I couldn't stop her, and I really didn't want to.

I finally let go and kissed her back and pulled her close to me with my arms, and it was as if this was what she'd been waiting for because she slowed and finally pulled back enough to look at me. She looked a little confused herself. Her head cocked a fraction to the side as she spoke with Dan. I didn't have any idea what I looked like but I felt half out of my mind. I waited for a whole minute or longer, which must have been at least a ten minute conversation for them. Finally Jane looked down at me and blinked.

"Your lips are blue." She blinked again. "Oh. They've been blue since you died and came back. Since you burned," she answered her own question. That was weird, but I had some questions of my own.

"So what did you and Dan talk about for so long?" I asked.

Both of her snow white eyebrows came up. "Dan's weirded out because he liked it. He feels dirty. He's worried about Believer. He just kissed you and you belong to Believer. But he liked it. And he was weirded out by other things."

"Jane. Did Dan just kiss me using your body or did you kiss me and bring Dan along for the ride?" I was beginning to get creeped out thinking that Dan had just kissed me using Jane as a shell. I didn't want another man kissing me, even if he did live inside a girl's body that I loved. But it wasn't just the body that I wanted, I wanted both the girl and her body. I had an icky feeling.

"Dan had to help me get started. I couldn't do it," Jane confessed.

I made a face and sat up, but then froze. "Wait! If he started, who was kissing me at the end?"

Jane looked away, out at the others who were starting to come to life, waking up with their new white hairdos. "I was," Jane said, still looking away.

I thought about changing her hair back to black and it darkened, but only a little at the ends, like my power was less effective on her than others. I remembered that Jane had once passed right through a shield of magic I'd made while the same shield had stopped Dan cold. Maybe Jane had some natural resistance to magic.

But she'd just drunk my blood. I called on that part of me that was still inside her and pushed my will at her again and this time her hair and her eyebrows changed back to their natural beautiful black and her eyes changed back to their original shade of violet and lilac.

Jane reached up to her hair and pulled it around to look at it. She disappeared and reappeared standing beside me. I looked up at her from the ground where I sat.

"Oh. Hmm. Rain. You missed a spot," she said, looking down the line of her body at her snow white pubic hair.

"Do you want it black again?" I asked her. "Or I could remove it altogether. The hair I mean. Shave you with magic." Awkward! Awkward! *Aaaawkwaaard!* The word chimed in my head like a musical spell but my eyes stayed locked on her crotch.

"What?" Jane looked embarrassed. "Shave? Down there?" Her head tilted to the side, conferring with Dan and as I looked up at her, I noticed that her armpits had hair also; it wasn't big and bushy, and it was *white* which made it less noticeable, but she was definitely overdue for some quality time with the razor or a jam jar filled with hot wax or something.

"What is it?" she asked, having seen something in my face. Maybe my eyebrows went up or something?

"Jane hon. When's the last time you shaved your pits?"

A horrified expression sprang onto her face. She vanished. I heard a tearing noise nearby and some muffled cries. Jane reappeared wearing a white button up shirt she'd snatched off of some poor guy; she hadn't bothered to button it, as the buttons were all gone, so her perfect breasts still showed. And she hadn't bothered to grab herself some pants, so she was still standing before me nude (except for her shy and self conscience pits, which were nicely concealed).

I didn't laugh but I did smile. "It's okay, Jane. You've been a busy girl. You probably haven't had a chance to shave since days before you became a vampire. I take it you don't like the arm pit hair." She growled. "Fine," I said.

I called on my blood inside her again to work my magic within her body and her armpit hair, what was on her legs, arms, and every white wisp of pubic hair vanished. I only had a second to admire the view before she vanished again. Another muffled scream, female this time, and Jane reappeared, this time wearing some girl's jeans. She twitched, moving her hips around then reached down and pulled at the fabric around the crotch to try and get comfortable.

"This feels weird," she complained, uncomfortable with the feel of coarse denim rubbing against sensitive flesh.

"And it looks weird too," I agreed. "And it won't do for a Queen of Amen Hale," I said with bold certainty, which made her look at me and stop fidgeting.

The shirt and pants she had on vanished as did the blood and grime she'd gotten on her since the last time I'd cleaned her up. I shaped a beautiful red dress onto her body that flowed like water down her curves while still looking elegant and regal. With a thought, I styled her hair and then I formed a necklace to place around her neck. It had dime-sized diamonds and sapphires with a black crystal skull set in the center, and I made the two eyes of the skull into glowing pinpoints of red light which made the whole thing look terrifying and beautiful. It wasn't a huge piece so it wasn't overpowering. I didn't want anything to distract from what she was. Jane was a Queen.

She turned and looked at me, giving me the full weight of her stare. I stared back and let her look down into me. I could see why Emma loved her. Even before she became a vampire she'd been stunning, when she was just Jane, reading her book in the waiting room of the doctor's office. I wasn't surprised that my brother had fallen for her. And now I'd fallen in love with her too.

Bull took a cautious step closer and fell to his knees beside me, and I pulled my eyes away from Jane. I looked around. Bull had recovered and was functioning again, as was Spider, who'd been farther away when I lost it. I saw the big black soldier named Tiger a short distance away, flat on the ground, dead or out cold. And I did hear a number of the prisoners making muffled sounds against their gags, so some of them were awake and alive as well.

"Mistress, what happened?" Bull asked me hesitantly. He'd been patiently waiting for an opportune moment to speak.

I opened my mouth to lie and say "nothing" or "none of your business" or even "fuck off" but what popped out was—"I had an orgasm." My hand flew up to my mouth as I looked into his surprised face and I felt the heat in my face flare as if my head were a struck match!

I looked down at the ground and away from everyone and tried to breathe. Air wouldn't come. I tried again and again, my mouth opening and closing like a fish out of water. Jane struck me on the back! A gasping breath of air moved down into my burning lungs! Another breath! Another.

The red faded from my vision, leaving me dazed and confused. I felt weird. Little dots floated across my eyes like fireflies gliding across the field—we were in a field, out in the woods at night. I wondered suddenly if I'd see the white rabbit with his wristwatch. Rabbits lived in places like this. Maybe he was out there hiding in the grass right now. I wondered what else was here. Perhaps there were fairies or even a unicorn and—

"Rain? Rain, are you all right?" Jane's voice was so pretty. Such a pretty voice. "Can you hear me?" A cool hand patted my check. She turned my head to face her. "You back with us now?" she asked.

I blinked as my eyes refocused on her, then on my surroundings as she let me go. I was surprised to see all the people until my brain filled in the gaps that had vanished while I daydreamed.

"Rain, why the hell did you tell him the truth? And what the hell just happened to you?" Jane was studying my odd reactions like a scientist fascinated by a new species of beetle.

"I tried to lie," I confessed.

"So?"

"Witches can't lie."

"Oh." She raised an eyebrow. "And the rest?"

"I'm mad." I looked at her and shrugged. "I would say something else but I can't lie."

"Well, that makes sense." She nodded. "So you went nuts when you became a witch?" she asked.

"Yes. And no. And both." It was the only right answer I could think to give. I wanted to go home. I was suddenly very tired and I wanted Believer. I wanted familiar. I wanted all my sisters around me. I wanted my mother and I wanted Amen Hale.

"Bull, get ready, we're going home." I pushed out my will and filled all those around me with life and energy and they woke, groaning and mumbling against their gags and bindings. I noticed that my hand still had a red gash from the knife I'd slashed it with and was still bleeding a little. It was a deep cut. I was about to heal it myself but stopped myself and held my hand out to the side.

"Jane," I said, and she was there, kneeling and holding my hand, licking the blood off and closing up the cut with her magic as she licked my palm. I worked as she fed.

I called forth an arch of stone and two columns broke the surface of the weedy earth a short distance away. The two stone pillars emerged from the earth ten feet apart but the columns bent toward each other and joined forming a perfect archway ten feet wide and eight feet high. I thought of a high place on the inside garden wall that would be safe to use and I shaped an arch like a carving with my mind, set only an inch deep into the wall but the perfect match to the arch I'd made here.

The way prepared, I opened the gate.

Black Rain

What Should Not Be

AS SOON AS it opened, brilliant light poured out and lit the shadowed field around us with a strange yellow glow. Jane released my hand and appeared beside me, looking out the gateway.

"That's not sunlight. What happened in Amen Hale?"

"Beats me," I said.

Through the opening we could see crowds of people milling about and a huge group of people gathered around the crypt in the center of the walled inner garden. In the crowd by the crypt I could also make out two people with burning crowns on their heads. David and Dana. The whole land looked otherworldly, other than the fact that it was after two a.m. and it should have been night, there were other things that made it seem *off*.

The color of the light was different, a more yellow shade. And the angle of the light was different, creating shadows in ways the sun never would. I also felt waves of magic coming through the open gateway like heat pouring out of an open oven that cooked something wonderful. It was warming and wonderful and frightening and comforting all at once. It was home.

People on the other side of the arch had started to notice us, shouting and pointing, sending up the hue and cry. Thankfully those who came running stopped on the Amen Hale side and didn't pass through the gate but gathered just beyond, waiting to welcome us home.

Lucius and five of his guards did step through to our side, but Lucius didn't go to me this time. He was like a blind man who had finally received his sight as he stared at Jane. He walked to her and fell to his knees before her.

"Forgive me, my Queen," he whispered.

It was only then that I noticed Dan. He'd retrieved his body and come through the gateway without me even seeing him do it. He stood behind Jane silently while she played her hands through Lucius's hair and looked him over, like a prize horse, inspecting his black hand, new eyes, and other features.

Dan was like a silent marble statue as he stood behind her. His head turned and he looked at me, giving me a small, polite smile. I wondered if he thought I was mad with him about the kiss he'd started. I wasn't. He had no shirt or shoes on but he'd found some black high water pants that were way too small for him. They looked like the pants that had been on the soldier I'd left behind to carry my message.

With a thought I changed his pants into a shimmering, velvety black material that hugged his lean form. I also added some magic fabric underwear to help hold things in place which seemed necessary with the form-fitting pants. Now that I'd been with Believer and been exposed to other *things*, I was starting to take things like his *thing* into consideration. I wondered for a second how guys ever put up with something hanging outside and constantly in the way of everything like that. I gave myself a shake and moved on.

I shaped a long-sleeved open black jacket that left his amazing chest exposed and I cleaned him up and did his hair as well, to make him presentable beside his Queen. I resisted the urge to add a pair of black boots to finish the look. For some reason, footwear seemed inappropriate for vampires. I hadn't made Jane any shoes either.

"Thank you, Rain," Jane spoke but Dan nodded his head.

"You're welcome, Dan." I gave him a smile.

More people were gathering in Amen Hale. It was time to go, and I was tired, but there were still things to do here so I tried to speed things up.

"Bull, give me your knife," I ordered. He rushed over and handed me his plastic blade. I walked to the five guardsmen that Lucius had brought with him. I slashed my palm again, but I didn't cry out this time, I'd been ready for the pain. I held the knife back behind me and felt hands take it as I walked toward the terrified guardsmen Lucius had brought from my new home.

"Be calm, my people. You are of Hale and so you are mine. Now hold still." I raised my bleeding hand and rubbed it across the foreheads of each of the five men then chanted my spell:

"Protection I give, to pass through the mist.
Go now and gather, the ones who are hid.
Go now and gather, and bring here to me
The ones who have fled from their destiny."

"Spider!" I called. He'd just handed off a new prisoner to Tiger and was about to head back for another, but he came running at my call and fell to his knees before me.

"Yes, Mistress." He kept his eyes on the ground.

"Use these men in your search. We will leave this place very soon. I want to be done here. Now take these men, command them, and serve me," I ordered.

"Yes, Mistress!" He sprang to his feet, then turned to the men I'd marked. He commanded them crisply to follow and marched off to obey me. The men from Amen Hale obeyed, although they looked terrified and confused with all that was happening and by this strange soldier with his one blackened eye, but they followed and went with it.

I held my bleeding hand out to the side. "Dan," I called, and he was on his knees, holding my hand. I called my power, but just into the blood of my cut hand, and my palm glowed brightly as if I held a small radiant bit of a star in the palm of my hand. My blood turned to gold as it welled up from within me and pooled in my cupped hand like a handful of molten metal.

The humans were shielding their eyes, peeking between the cracks in their fingers to see or just to stay on their feet in the presence of my power, but soon the light dimmed away as Dan drank the blood and healed the cut, sealing the brightness within me behind the veil of my flesh once again. As soon as he finished, he released my hand and fell backward into Jane's arms, apparently drunk on my blood.

"What the hell are you doing!?" Mary shouted as she stomped through the arch with David and Dana at her sides. "What the hell is he doing to you, Rain? Are you letting the vampires bite on you already! Shit! It figures. They just woke up and you're already letting them eat you. Have they killed you yet?" As usual, Mary was worried I'd been hurt which was like her.

She went quiet as she looked at me as if she'd finally found her eyes and was surprised by what she saw. She noticed that the men in the clearing around me had white hair and they all glowed faintly. The prisoners and my soldiers. They seemed to creep Mary out as she gazed around at the bleached out throng. She didn't even blink as she eyed the amputees, but she was scared. I could see the fear on her face.

"Don't be afraid. Touch me, Mary."

She took a step back and shrank in on herself. Dana cringed too and moved close to David. I sighed. I did not need more drama so I cheated. I closed my eyes and held my arms out, waiting patiently for her to come to me. I knew she would. She had to. This was what she did now. I didn't have long to wait. My arms wrapped around her as I felt hers wrap around me.

I gave Mary some time. Everyone around me was still and quiet as I held her. I looked around me, at the people looking back. They all seemed so deferential and grave as they patiently waited on the happenings of my life. As if the things they saw and the events they witnessed and just being in my presence were important to them in ways I didn't understand.

It was quiet here in our weedy field, but I did hear voices on the Amen Hale side of the gateway as others arrived and asked the questions that others had asked before them.

"What's happening in there?"

"Is the Princess all right?"

"Is that the vampires with them?"

"Where in the world are they?"

"Is anyone hurt?"

"Look at their hair."

"What are they doing with all those prisoners?"

I listened. After a couple of minutes Mary stepped out of my embrace but she kept a firm hold on my arm.

"You're tired, Rain. You need to sleep. Get this shit done so we can go home."

"Yes, Mary." I leaned against her, as if by mentioning how tired I was she'd sapped the last crumbs of my strength. She had to help hold me up.

Lucius ordered his men in Amen Hale to start moving the prisoners through the gate, and Mary gave up her hold on my arm to David and Dana and went to help in the hunt for living hidden treasures. Mary pointed them out while Jane and Dan collected and carried and men near me bound and gagged the terrified captives.

David and Dana brought me up to speed on what was happening in Amen Hale since I left while they held me upright. They told me that Cornelius, Believer,

Sky Dragon, and Bethany were out front by the gate, talking with the government about the attack on the vampires and other things.

Then David told me about the new sun he'd set in the sky and how the government was so afraid that it would destroy the Earth. I told David I was proud of him, and he did seem quiet pleased with himself, until I cautioned him about the use of his power. I told him that he needed to be careful with the Earth and not flaunt or abuse his power or he would attract unwanted attention—which would be bad for all of us.

"What kind of unwanted attention would *you* be scared of? Aliens?" he said jokingly, but my answer sobered him up the way it needed to.

"No, David. If you're not careful you *will* attract the attention of God Almighty. Use power carefully, and never forget for a second that the Earth is his and all those in it, even the ugly people. They are all pieces of his soul."

"David!" Dana yelled at him. "Go put that damn light out before God gets pissed off and gets out of bed to do it himself!"

David looked shaken; the cockiness that had been there only a moment before was so utterly banished it was as if it had never existed at all. I didn't need to ask if he believed in God. David was Jewish, and apparently he had no great desire to encounter the Lord of Hosts tonight.

"Here, take her." He handed his half of my weight over to Dana (who was much stronger than she looked) and dashed back through the gateway. I watched as he ran about twenty paces past the arch of the gateway into the yellow light of his newborn sun and slid to a stop in the center of the boulevard made by the masses of people pressing in on each side, awaiting our return.

He thrust one arm up above his head and all the heads of those lining the way looked up, watching. I could not see the sky, but I watched as the light beyond the portal dimmed and dimmed, until the moonlit glow on this side matched that of the other. David rushed back through and resumed his post with Dana to keep me on my feet.

After another five minutes I called off the hunt. I was about to pass out and we had to go. They'd found another twelve men and women which brought the total taken alive up to sixty-six. The last of the prisoners were carried through and we were finally ready to leave.

David and Dana walked out arm in arm first, looking beautiful with their flaming crowns on their heads. Next came Dan and Jane looking so beautiful the people of Amen Hale stared in wonder at the newly risen Queen of the Damned and her tall handsome Prince of Darkness, the first (and only) vampires. I was the last one through the arch and before I left I undid the magic I'd called into being.

I banished the encircling ring of mist and the curse I'd placed within this field that kept technology from working here, and then we left and I closed the arch behind us and willed the standing stone arch I'd called from the dirt in the field to crumble away.

Mary and Lucius walked with me, making sure I didn't fall and I watched as the people on each side of us fell to their knees as I passed by. Not all of them, but many. I studied the faces. Some old, some young, some just small children.

And in that moment I saw it, all the pieces of the puzzle finally snapped into place and I had to confront the finished picture. When all I saw were smaller pieces, isolated events, and scattered images here and there I'd been able to ignore what was obviously happening. But I couldn't do it any longer. They were kneeling to me, but not as they did for Cornelius and Cathryn; this was different. They were not kneeling to a Queen—this was more.

They were worshiping me. These people were worshiping *me*. They were praying to *me*.

My memory flashed back to something I'd done just a few minutes ago. I'd prayed to myself again. And again, somehow, I'd answered my own prayer. And all I'd said this time was "*please*" because I didn't even know what to pray for, but it had worked all the same. And something else—something else pulled at my memory—there was something else! Jane had said it! What was it? What!? I commanded it from my memory and it snapped forth.

"*The blood of a god.*" A god?

I remembered her saying that they were mine. Jane and Dan were *mine*. Did that mean that they would worship me too? But I wasn't a god! I wasn't! Was I? What was I?

My angry voice answered my question within my mind. "A murderer! A Black Witch! A scrap of a soul left behind by a desperate, frightened girl who wasn't strong enough to do her own killing. She couldn't bring herself to do it, so she made me, and had me do her dirty work for her, and then she forced me into killing her and taking her place."

I opened my eyes. I was on my knees in the grass. I couldn't recall when I'd closed my eyes and I didn't remember dropping to my knees here in the cool grass, but I was on my knees. I was getting used to missing little pieces of time and movement, so I didn't even worry about it or how long I'd been on the ground.

Mary was still with me, kneeling in the grass with me. Her eyes were closed and she still had both arms wrapped around my arm like a lifeline as she knelt with me. Lucius had let go of my other hand but he was nearby, keeping the sea of staring faces from crashing in and burying me. They were all around me. Staring. Their eyes needing.

I looked back at them and wondered if they had any idea what it was that they worshiped and to what kind of creature it was they prayed. Did they even know what they prostrated themselves before and offered themselves to? I wasn't even human. Not even a complete soul. I was a discard. A Frankensteined horror. Nothing but shadows gathered from the dark corners of a desperate girl's mind, given life one minute and forced to kill the next.

I did not deserve worship! I was a murderer and a monster! I wanted to scream at them and tell then "NO!" but I didn't. I wanted to tell them to "STOP!" but I couldn't. Hadn't I just prayed to myself? Wasn't I just as guilty as all of these people? What right did I have praying to me? What the hell was *I* thinking let alone all these people? I should end it before it went any further, before it got worse.

"At least I know what I am," I said to myself, so quietly no one except the vampires could have heard me, but Mary was holding my hand and she didn't need to hear, she knew.

"Then tell them, Rain. Tell them, and let them decide for themselves. It's free will. If they want to worship you then that is their choice. Most of them were Wiccan anyway, so now they would be Pagans. Just tell them and let them choose."

"But it's wrong, Mary." I shook my head. "It's horrible. God is better than me. He will not fail them and I will. I'm a bad choice. A horrible choice. They are pieces of His soul for crap's sake! And I am nothing but scraps and shadows and pain."

Mary reached out and held my chin gently with one hand and made me look at her face. Her green eyes glowed with power as she stared into me. "I chose to burn with you. And if they choose the same then let them burn with us. And if they want to, let them love you and worship you and praise you and pray to you and serve you, if that makes them happy. Just tell them what you are so they'll know and then just be who you are and let us be what we are. I've made my choice, Rain."

She stared into my soul with her glowing green eyes, and I'm sure she could feel me begin to pull back.

I looked down, away from her eyes because I couldn't do it. I would not do it. I didn't want to become a false god.

Mary spoke two words: "*Please, Rain.*"

A chill went through me from head to toe and I looked up and studied Mary's face to see what had changed and right away, I knew. She was praying to me.

As I watched, the first tears spilled over the edge of her bottom lids and glided down her beautiful cheeks. This was wrong. All of it. In a thousand ways, for a million reasons.

"*Please, Rain!*" she prayed the second time.

Some prayers should not be answered I thought within myself.

But then she prayed again, "*Please!*"

It felt as if time itself stopped while I looked at her, my best friend in the whole world. My Mary. My Sister. Her right eye partially hidden by the fall of bright green hair, already wet with her tears. Her bottom lip trembled along with the world and all those within it.

"Please let me be enough for her. For them. For me," I prayed to myself.

"*So mote it be,*" Mary prayed.

"So mote it be," I breathed.

Believer

---◆---

Home Is Where the Heart Is

CORNELIUS AND HIS people rushed out from under the tent so they could see the sky and watch as the last of the sun David had created winked out of existence letting darkness reclaim the night sky over Amen Hale and Jacksonville, Florida. Cheers rose up from the soldiers and others outside the gate where the sun was seen as a threat and a danger.

Looking up and not seeing the yellow star in the night sky was startling. An odd type of sensory shock visited those who'd spent time beneath the Faux Sun. The nighttime landscape seemed crisp and flat as eyes adjusted to the moon's borrowed light after walking for hours in a world bathed with radiant yellow. An odd feeling of loss settled into people in Jacksonville who were sensitive to such things.

The magic that had fallen down upon the land like rain for hours was gone. Over the next few weeks, dark moods, feelings of loss, sadness, and melancholy would be confronted by large doses of alcohol, drugs, and antidepressants with varying degrees of success.

"We must go," announced Cornelius.

After a very brief farewell and a commitment to speak again soon, the group left and marched back through the gateway into Amen Hale where a grim faced King was received by Byron the House Steward.

"Your Highness, Princess Rain has returned. She's opened a gateway in the garden and she's brought the vampires home with her. She's also captured a large number of enemy soldiers."

Cornelius and his group stiffened at the news, and Believer's eyes glowed a hotter red. Jane was here, in Amen Hale.

"Is she still naked?" Bethany asked.

"Who?" Byron asked.

"Jane," Ryan supplied.

Byron shrugged. "No, Lord Ryan."

Another man in the crowd answered, "She's wearing a red dress."

"How is Princess Rain?" asked Believer, his voice rumbling dangerously.

The same man answered, "My Lord, your wife is on her feet, but she seems weak and unwell. Princess Mary and Lucius were—"

The man continued talking but Believer was already gone. He moved past some, between others, and through the rest, his body gliding by without difficulty as his cloudy form flew down the path toward the house and his wife. Others on the path saw little more than his glowing red eyes in the darkness before a breeze and a damp cloud passed by that smelled like spring rain and tasted like a summer storm for the few who'd been about to scream and caught a mouthful as he swished by.

Believer stopped at the steps and the doorman was about to admit him into Amen Hall when their attention was drawn to the side of the house where a girl's voice was crying out.

"Help! Help! Please help us! Someone please help us!"

The doorman went to the edge of the porch and looked down to see who was yelling. Whoever it was was hidden in shadows up against the house behind the bushes. Believer did not hesitate; he glided over the side of the porch and down into the shadows where a young blonde woman who had only a bra on her top knelt over another form, hidden in shadows. The girl on her knees rose up and shouted again.

"Please! Someone help us!"

"Lizzy?" Believer said, recognizing the voice and the girl.

Lizzy's head whipped around. "Believer! Help us!" she screamed. "Izzy got upset that the sun went away and she ran away from me! She's hurt herself and needs to be fixed! Please help us, Believer!" she begged as she cried.

Believer had moved closer while she spoke. He could see that Lizzy had torn her shirt into shreds and wrapped them around Izzy's wrists. They were already soaked with blood. Without another word he gathered the fallen girl into his arms and stood. He looked toward the house, then back the way he'd come, trying to decide which way to go for help. And then he was moving, gliding back the way he'd just come toward Bethany.

"Stand clear!" he bellowed like thunder as he charged ahead, so others on the path wouldn't run into the physically "solid" girl he held in his arms.

His brother had been walking with Bethany on his shoulders and was already on his knees, letting her hop down to the ground, having heard his shouts. The group gathered around as Believer laid Izzy on the cobbled stone drive before them.

"Lizzy told me that she became upset when the Star of David left the sky. She ran away and has done herself harm in her troubled state of mind. Lizzy found her."

"Hush!" Bethany ordered, kneeling over the quiet form; she placed a hand on Lizzy's head and grunted.

"What's happening here?" asked a musical voice at the same instant a chill rose in the humans and demi-humans alike.

Cornelius, Bethany, Ryan, Sky Dragon, Believer, and the guards that stood about all looked up to see Jane and Dan standing nearby. They were dressed wonderfully (definitely not naked) and made no aggressive movements, but what alarmed everyone was their eyes that glowed red with an ominous light in the darkness.

"I smell blood," Jane said.

Believer rumbled! The noise was coming from his whole massive form and not his mouth. His own eyes flashed a brilliant defiant red and the air itself vibrated with static electricity as Believer, Sky Dragon, and the ten guards took up defensive positions around Izzy and the others along with Byron and the few men he had with him.

There was a silent awkward moment between the two groups. The two vampires stood motionless like stones, holding hands.

Ryan broke the silence. "Hi Jane. Dan." He scratched his head. "We got a situation here. She's hurt and she's our friend. It's probably hard for you to be here right now, you know, with her hurt and bleeding and all. Why don't you guys go wait at the house while we try to help her? All right?" He spoke calmly and even delivered a convincing smile at the end.

Jane's head tilted to the side then. Ryan and the others watched them for a second then Jane and Dan (at the same time) took three identical, robot like steps back, away from the group, as if to show that they meant no harm but they did not go to the house.

"Hey guys, she's already dead," Bethany said.

"Izzy!," Believer rumbled in frustrated anguish, looking stricken as a huge frown split his face from side to side.

"Oh no." Ryan knelt down beside her.

"Blessed Be, not one of the new twins!" said one of the guards, and soon his voice mingled with others around him, all saddened at the loss.

"Izzy!" a girl screamed.

They looked up to see Lizzy, Izzy's other half running down the cobbled drive toward them as fast as she could. Her crazed tear-streaked face looking half mad with grief and dread. Everyone braced for the horrible scene that was about to unfold, but then Believer moved forward and grabbed Lizzy (though she struggled to get away) and drew her inside himself. He walked off the path, speaking quietly to the girl he now held inside his form. As he walked away the soft comforting rumble of his voice faded away with him.

"Well," Cornelius said, relieved, "that worked out better than I'd expected." He turned to Bethany. "Bethany my dear, can you bring her back?"

Bethany shrugged. "It takes a life to save a life, Father, and I'd need to do it quickly if its going to work. I could use that guy we were saving for my birthday tomorrow. I don't mind killing him for her, but she better be more careful with this next life." Bethany gave the dead girl a threatening glare.

"Bethany," Jane spoke from where she stood, still a safe distance away from everyone. "We have plenty of prisoners you can use. We brought a bunch of men with us." Jane smiled. "Would you like me to fetch you one?"

Her voice sounded so pleasant and sweet that Bethany smiled and laughed with delight; her own laugh (though happy) was spiked with a just a touch of her own dark power and it mingled with Jane's magic that already hung, thick in the air, like a floral perfume. The two powers met and seemed to like each other as they mixed and mingled, and for a moment the air filled with a heady blend of fear, darkness, death, and other unsettling things. The humans and demi-humans present became quite uncomfortable until it faded to a bearable chill.

"Other than a man to kill, do you need anything else?" Jane asked.

Bethany nodded politely. "Yes, ma'am. I need my blade. It's in a wooden box in my room, unless my maid has taken it to the kitchen to have it sharpened."

"We'll be right back."

Jane and Dan vanished and soon returned with Bethany's blade and a struggling quadruple amputee. Bethany had them cut a pentagram into the flower bed beside the drive and they used some landscape torches to light the five points of a hastily shaped pentagram.

Bethany had Believer release Lizzy because she said her blood in the spell would help bring Izzy back and Lizzy was more than willing to give her blood to help. And so it was done, right there in the flowers on the side of the drive with almost a hundred people gathered around at just after three a.m. in the early morning hours.

Sky Dragon held the man upright while Bethany did her worst and called up the power out of his blood and death and pain and rage and sin. She cut Lizzy's wrist and added that blood to her spell and raised Izzy up, alive once again and completely healed. The people rejoiced and gathered around the twins, some welcoming her back while others were more serious and proffered sterner advice to Izzy, but most were too overjoyed to have her back and alive to worry with censure.

After the initial exuberance Cornelius quieted the crowd and had Izzy stand before him. He kissed her bloody forehead and then stared into her eyes as he spoke to her. "Why did you cut yourself, Izzy? Surely it's not because you are a prisoner because you're free now. And you're not alone anymore; you have Lizzy and the Queen and myself and so many others who care about you and love you. Do you want to leave us?"

"No!" Izzy shouted.

"Are you unhappy here? Or did someone hurt you?"

"No," Izzy said again. Firmly.

"They why did you do it, Izzy?" Cornelius's voice was kind, not angry. "Tell me why?"

Izzy started picking at her shirt sleeve nervously and looked down, avoiding Cornelius's gaze. "No reason. I didn't have a reason. I don't know why I did it. I just did it." She looked back at him, almost defiantly.

Cornelius placed a hand on his chin and tapped his pursed lips with a finger as he thought. He eyed her, his finger tap, tap, taping. The finger froze, mid tap, as he thought of something.

"Izzy, I believe you when you say that you don't know why you did this, but tell me, what part of this did you enjoy?"

"Enjoy?" Izzy looked confused by the question.

Cornelius nodded. "Yes, what part of this did you enjoy? Did you enjoy the attention of everyone coming to look for you and finding you?"

"No!" Izzy shouted. She looked mortified as her eyes scanned the crowd of faces that were following every word of the disturbingly personal conversation. She shook her head and again said "no."

Cornelius nodded again. "Did you do it because you wanted to die and leave us?"

She paused and actually looked thoughtful before shaking her head in the smallest of movements and finally saying, "No. Not yet."

"Hmm." Cornelius's hand went back to his chin for a moment before he fired again. "Did you enjoy the feel of the knife cutting your skin?"

Izzy looked up, met his eyes for only a second, and looked down again. She didn't answer yes or no.

"Did you enjoy seeing yourself bleed? Watching it?"

Her eyes flicked up for another glance but again she said nothing. She did not say a word.

"Izzy, look at me now," Cornelius ordered, his voice taking on a tone of command.

Her eyes rose to meet his. "In Amen Hale we do not hide what we are or what we need or what we desire, even if those desires are not understood or seem horrible to others, but you need help. If you want to bleed or be cut, or feel the need to be hurt, then come to me or the Queen. We will bleed you or cut you or hurt you if you need it. And if you truly decide that you must die, them come to me, and that I will do myself. But *do not* raise a hand against someone that I love again. Don't you realize, silly girl, that you are part of our family now, and I do not allow my children to be hurt? Even by themselves. Amen Hale is mine. And you are mine. Now I will have your promise, my child, that if you feel the need to see your own blood or to feel a blade against your skin you will come to me or the Queen and not lay your own hand against one that I love again."

Izzy looked surprised and embarrassed as she looked at the crowd, silently listening to every word. She stepped closer to Cornelius and whispered shyly. "The Queen would really—cut me?" She rubbed her wrists as she spoke without noticing what she was doing. "I would, won't," she twitched. "Would the queen, I mean, if I needed—it?" She looked over at Lizzy who just nodded to her encouragingly.

"Yes." Cornelius did not whisper but spoke loud enough for everyone to hear. "Your Queen will cut you and bleed you and hurt you in any way that you need to be hurt, Izzy. But you must swear to never hurt yourself again. Come to the Queen if you need to, but swear to me right now, that you will not hurt yourself again."

Silence. Everyone listened, even the crickets ended their leg scratching racket as an *unnatural* quiet settled upon Amen Hale.

"I swear," Izzy said it quietly but her words carried in an odd way.

"I hear your promise, as does Amen Hale itself, and I bind you, Izzy, by the magic of this Kingdom and by the blood that we have shed to bring you back and by your oath you have now freely given. So mote it be!" Cornelius finished loudly.

"So mote it be!" Those gathered around echoed his words sincerely.

Believer rushed to the house while they still celebrated, getting ahead of the crowd. The doorman opened the door for him and he was up the steps and through the outer hall quickly but stopped as he entered the Cathedral Hall.

She was on the other side of the room, sitting down in one of the fainting chairs that rested against the wall. Her head was down. She hadn't seen him enter the hall and he took the moment to look at her. He liked to look at her and study her so that he could love her more and know her better. She was a truly complicated creature and changed often and in unexpected ways.

Believer smiled as he studied his wife and her surroundings. She had a book in her lap that she was writing in. The pen in her hand made delicate moves as she carefully formed her letters and words. Mary sat on the floor at the foot of her chair, wrapped around one of her legs and on the other leg was Emma, attached like a lamprey on a shark. Both Emma and Mary had their eyes closed.

Rain set the pen down and leaned up enough for Believer to see her face; she'd been crying as she was writing. She seemed to consider what she'd written, looking it over one last time before setting it on a pedestal beside the chair that looked as if it was made to hold this particular book.

She looked up, saw him, and froze.

Believer watched as Mary moved without opening her eyes. She stood and pulled Emma up with her and the two girls walked away. Others were coming in and the room started to fill with those who'd been outside with Izzy and Lizzy. Believer moved and went to her.

"Carry me. I can't walk, my love." Her voice was just a whisper.

Wordlessly, he gathered her from the chair, up into the cradling bed of his arms. He moved through the growing crowd and toward the stairs. They were headed up the stairs, toward their new bedroom when Bethany shouted up at them from the landing.

"Rain!"

Believer looked down at the woman in his arms. "Just let me kiss her goodnight, love," she whispered.

The pounding of little feet on the stair soon revealed the little girl attached to them, and Believer lowered Rain down to her face so she could see her. Bethany's face and hair were still drenched in blood and she smelled of blood and death.

"You okay?" Bethany reached out and touched Rain's face with her bloody hand leaving a red smudge. "Did you die today? We saw Jane bite you on TV, and then the camera broke and everything went white. Did you die again?"

"No, Jane didn't kill me, honey, but I almost killed her." Bethany's bloody eyebrows rose and Rain smiled at her. "Have I told you today that you're beautiful?"

"No," Bethany said, her angel smile showing bright white in the red mask.

"You are. My little angel. Goodnight, Princess." She pulled Bethany close enough to kiss her bloody cheek and then Believer lifted her up and walked the last few steps to their new bedroom.

The room had been prepared with some key differences. The bed itself was ten feet long and eight feet wide. Craftsmen had been working on it all day. It had a water tight, sealed frame and a mattress that had a waterproof lining. The sheets were comfortable and there were towels and fresh dry blankets on the dresser by the bed.

Bethany followed them to their room and as Believer passed into the room and was turning to shut the door, Rain caught a glimpse of her left eye and a little black hair, peeking in after her. Believer had noticed her too and stopped just short of closing the door. He opened the door.

"Come to bed, little one," he said and Bethany stepped into view and stood in the doorway.

"You're tired though." She looked guilty for troubling them and then looked down at herself and frowned. "And I'm all bloody."

Believer repositioned Rain, holding her with one arm, and reached down and gathered Bethany up into his other arm and closed the door with a foot, as he was out of arms. He walked to the big bed, turned around and sat down on the foot of the bed and laid back, onto his back, with both bodies balanced on his front as he eased himself into the center of the big mattress.

"Is this how you sleep, Rain? You lie on Believer like a great big pillow?" Bethany asked. She was cuddled up next to Rain comfortably, quite happy already. Her bloody cheek stuck wetly to the side of Rain's.

Rain kept her eyes closed and sounded half asleep as she answered, "No, honey, we sleep inside the cloud, not outside." She gave Bethany an encouraging squeeze. "Don't be scared. It's wonderful inside Believer. It's like floating in a cloud, only better, because it's warm and safe and you're surrounded by someone who loves you. And the best part is when he hugs you."

"Really?"

"Really."

They began to sink down, down into the cloud until they were inside and floating, rolling gray and white clouds above and below and all around. Weightless. Warm. Surrounded completely by the embracing presence of Believer's rolling clouds. Bethany had been holding her breath, but now she breathed in and giggled like a little girl. Which was what she was, and sometimes wanted to be, like now.

"He smells good."

"Umm. I know."

"This is cool."

"Hmmmmm." Rain made a sleepy noise.

Bethany wasn't sleepy at all. She was still all hyped up on the power of her magic and the lingering buzz of the blood on her skin. But Rain was gone. Bethany lay there for a few minutes in silence, not wanting to disturb, just glad to be where she was. She knew that Sky Dragon didn't sleep, and neither did Believer, so he had to be awake, but she didn't want to speak and wake Rain up so she tried to lie still and entertain herself with her brain.

Bethany wondered if this was what a gummy bear felt like when someone swallowed one whole. She imagined she was inside Believer's stomach floating around like a big Red Witch gummy bear, "blood flavored." She fought not to giggle. She wondered if Believer could hear inside his clouds and finally decided to experiment to see if he could.

"Believer?" she whispered so quietly the sound was barely more than a parting of lips with no noise at all. He wouldn't have heard or noticed, but he'd been waiting for her to speak, listening carefully. Patiently.

"Yes, Bethany?" Her body vibrated as the sound came from the clouds all around her and then traveled up toward his head and out, not loud, but soft and comforting.

"Thank you for letting me spend the night," she whispered, still as quiet as a mouse.

"You're welcome, Bethany."

"Believer?"

"Yes, Bethany?"

"I love you," she whispered.

"I love you too, Bethany." She didn't see the smile on his cloudy face. But it was there.

"Em." A tiny unhappy sound.

"What's wrong, little one?"

"That's better." The little voice was happy again.

Believer's smiled returned. His wife wasn't the only complicated woman in his life, but this mystery had been easier than most to unravel. "You don't like it when I call you Bethany, do you?"

"Everyone calls me Bethany. It's not special."

"What would you like me to call you then?" Of course he already knew, but he'd been watching his brother, the way he asked her questions that he already knew the answers to, just to move the conversation along or just to make her smile.

"Little one," came the shy reply. "If that's okay."

"Then you shall be *my* 'little one'." Believer was secretly overjoyed. He'd witnessed his brother's special bond with the child and was surprised, almost shocked as he thought on it, that he'd been envious. He'd watched them together and wondered if his form was too frightening or too ephemeral for her to be at ease in his presence.

"Did you want to give me a new name also, a special name, just between us?"

"Oh no, I'd never change your name because you're Rain's 'Believer' and I'm your 'little one'." She yawned and stretched. "And I love you. And I love Sky Dragon, *he's my dragon*," she added in a sing song way. "And I love Rain and Mary and Emma and Cathryn and Cornelius and Mr. Bryant and Mrs. Bryant," her voice was beginning to slur, "and, and I love Sky and Ryan, and I love, I love—"

"David and Dana," supplied Believer helpfully.

"Yeah. And Dana and Byron and Jane. Jane too. And, an—"

Believer picked up the recitation. "And Lucius. You love him too. And Lizzy. You love her. And Izzy of course, you love her. And—" Believer kept up the list of names, his perfect memory coming in handy as he went from servant and kitchen staff to guards and gardeners, and then he stopped.

A little wheezing noise was coming from Bethany as she breathed in and out. Believer listened to the delicate noise. It blended wonderfully with Rain's deep relaxed breaths. Believer did not sleep, so these periods of rest he used for other purposes. He enjoyed taking time to admire his wife. How wonderful she was. He also took time to consider his existence. Sleep was a time to think, digest the events of the day, and to enjoy being alone with the one he loved, all to himself.

But he did not mind having Bethany here. He considered this feeling, of having his wife with him, here in bed, and *his* little one. He wondered if this was what it felt like to be a man, a real, *live,* flesh and blood man, who had his wife and "little one" in bed with him. He wondered if his experience was less, the same, or possibly even better.

He was not human, and he did not have a flesh and blood body, so there were things he could not do, but there were so many other things that he could do that flesh and blood could not. And he had witnessed, even in his brief existence, that many husbands and wives did not have happiness or love or passion together.

After some thought he concluded that his experience was superior to the human version. He preferred what he had over the other. He considered this and realized that this revelation pleased him.

"I am pleased I was made as I am. I am pleased that I am a cloud and not a man. I am pleased with my life. I love what I have been given." Believer did not pray, per se, so much as he shared. He felt within himself that connective cord that tied him to Sky and he let her feel his newfound joy in his existence. He let it wash down the cord binding his soul to hers and let her feel how happy and satisfied and how grateful he was.

Then he tried something new; he pressed his thoughts down the connective link and thought to her, "I love you, my Sky."

After just a minute, "I love you too, Believer. And I am very proud of you," came back.

Believer was still as he listened to the peaceful sounds of his wife's even breathing and the delicate wheeze of his little one.

Cathryn

Putting the House to Bed

STILL WEARING HER blue night shift Cathryn slipped out into the
long hall and was pleased to see a tall shadowy figure standing guard. His
glowing red eyes watched her approach.

"Good evening, Sky Dragon, is everyone abed for the night yet?"

"Everyone is abed except the vampires. They are using that room." He pointed
to a nearby door. "There was no longer a bed in the crypt and Jane said she wanted a regular room if possible. I placed them there. They went to their room, had
vigorous sex for about an hour, took a quick shower, and then knocked on their
parents' door. While they waited for their parents to come out they walked to Rain

and Believer's room and sniffed at the door. The vampires and their parents walked downstairs about five minutes ago, all wearing bath robes."

Cathryn listened to the detailed account and nodded. "Where are the girls?"

"Bethany went to bed with Rain and Believer and Emma is in Mary's room."

"Did Emma and Mary have sex?"

He shook his head. "They were already asleep in Mary's room when I took up my post here in the hall. I do not think so. My Sky, Ryan, Dana, and her David are all asleep, and Izzy and Lizzy are both asleep as well. Cornelius had them placed in one of the guest rooms as well so Izzy would be closer to you." Sky Dragon paused, as if unsure about his next words. "Queen Cathryn, did King Cornelius tell you about the promise he made to Izzy on your behalf?"

"Yes. He did." That had been an interesting conversation.

"Why would she need to hurt herself in this manner? Is it the result of her mistreatment at the mental institution she was housed at? I fail to see why she would want to cut herself."

Cathryn sighed. "Who knows. She's been this way for a very long time; her wrists are scarred with many cuts from years of cutting. I'm sure some of it has to do with mental illness that predated her incarceration, but whatever the reason, with this spell Cornelius has cast upon her she will be coming to me soon, and I'll have to prepare a place to hurt her."

"A place?" He made it a question.

"Yes. One room that will be set aside for the purpose of cutting, bondage, and giving pain. A place that she can see and know that it is used for that purpose and that purpose alone. Just knowing the room is there and that I will take her into it when she needs it will be reassuring. Calming."

"It sounds as if you have done this before." Sky Dragon looked surprised.

Cathryn smiled. "I have an open mind, an experimental nature, and a broad palate of desires that interest me. But what I plan on doing with Izzy is necessary and a duty. And I have never done cutting before, but I will have to learn, and I'll have to do it well because if I don't Izzy will go to Cornelius and ask him to give what he promised." She left unsaid what that was, but Sky Dragon had been there. He'd heard.

"Was there no other way to help her?" asked Sky Dragon crisply.

Cathryn blinked. Surprised. Sky Dragon was angry. "Yes. There was one other way. Cornelius told me he considered it for a moment before doing as he did. I assure you, Sky Dragon, Cornelius chose the more merciful, though more bloody path for Izzy. He could have imprisoned her. Confined her for her own protection as they had in the institution where she was before she came here."

Sky Dragon became more animated as he spoke, gesturing with his hands and his head and long neck. "But it would be different *here* than what she experienced in that horrible place, Queen Cathryn! She would not be abused or humiliated here. And Lizzy would still be with her. I'm sure she would want to stay with Izzy so she would still have a constant companion even in her confinement. Surely that would work. And it would be far less cruel than continually cutting her!"

Sky Dragon seemed to realize that his voice had gone from his usual buttery-smooth conversational tone to something bitter and stinging. He stepped back, his long neck pulled in tight, leaving his head on his shoulders. He seemed about to speak, opening his long reptilian mouth but stopped, once, twice, three times, unable to speak or to know what to say.

While Sky Dragon wallowed in his condition Cathryn kept her face absolutely blank and did not spare him. He'd earned his discomfort fair and square so she waited and let events determine themselves. Finally Sky Dragon went to his knees there in the hall, head bowed down.

"I find that I have sinned against you, Queen Cathryn. I should not have spoken disrespectfully. I should not have assumed that my judgment of this situation with Izzy was correct, and yours incorrect, or mine merciful, and yours cruel. I'm not even human, and I esteemed my own judgment superior to that of yours and King Cornelius's as you judged one of your own kind." Sky Dragon stopped speaking and kept his head down.

"What would you have me do with you, Sky Dragon?" Cathryn asked him, trying to be careful to let him create his own way out for both of them. "Should I go to your older brother to see what he thinks should be done, or should I speak to your Sky, or should I judge you myself and this can remain between the two of us?"

Sky Dragon kept his head down as he spoke. "Queen Cathryn, please judge me yourself. I will submit to any punishment you deem appropriate, but then, when it's done, please let me be forgiven and allowed to continue to serve you. I like my life very much and I do not want to lose what I have been given."

"So mote it be. Look at me, Sky Dragon." Cathryn waited until he raised his head and she could stare into his face. "Before I judge you or set your punishment I want you to answer a question. Don't answer quickly. I want you to apply every bit of that amazing mind your Sky has blessed you with and consider my question *very* carefully before you give me your answer. Are you ready?" He nodded.

"Knowing what we know of her, and having seen what we've all seen, and from the time you yourself have spent speaking with the twins, what do you think Izzy would have done if we locked her up?"

Sky Dragon did as she asked and after about four minutes he finally spoke. "She would have felt betrayed. Every kindness would have been seen as a trap and a lie no matter how sincere. She would kill herself. You were right, Queen Cathryn. Please, prepare your place and give her what she needs so she might live and be free. I like the twins. They're fun."

Cathryn's "calm face" almost shattered into a million pieces. Her voice began to betray her as she spoke. "Here is my judgment, Sky Dragon. I judge that you are a far better friend to the twins and of a purer heart for having spoken to me of your concerns than the others in Amen Hale who even now are turning in their beds, worried with the same troubling thoughts, but will be too timid to do as you have done."

Cathryn took a breath, held it, and breathed it out, letting it carry away some of her pent up emotions. "Now, as for your punishment. Go downstairs and write into the book of shadows the account of the spell that Cornelius called forth, the concerns that gripped your own heart, and the reasons that I have provided so that all Amen Hale may know that what we do is not a thing of evil, but of love. And as for forgiving you," Cathryn kissed him on the tip of his dragon snout and smiled at his surprise as his eye ridges went up.

"There is nothing to forgive, silly Dragon. You are not a guest, a servant, or a bondman like Lucius, you are family. Whether you choose to call me 'Queen Cathryn' or not is totally up to you, and I'll still call you Sky Dragon in front of others, but to me you will always be a son, just like Believer. Next time you have a concern come to me and ask me or Cornelius. We both love you."

Sky Dragon stood and Cathryn offered her hand, and Sky Dragon gave her his arm. They walked down the hall.

"You have too many daughters anyway."

Cathryn laughed. She was glad she'd decided to *put the house to bed* before she herself went to bed. Cathryn was always surprised at the things that still needed doing in the last hours of the night. She'd gotten in three hours of sleep earlier that evening while she and Mary held a sleeping Emma so she wasn't completely exhausted.

When they reached the foot of the stairs she patted his hand. "Thank you, Sky Dragon. It's a blessing to have you keeping an eye on all of the people we love."

He dipped his head on his long neck in a small bow and walked off toward the Cathedral Hall to find the Book of Shadows and do his penance. Cathryn let him go and stayed at the foot of the stairs looking out at the Entry Hall. Putting the house to bed was done a room at a time, the upstairs hall had surprised her but this room looked less mysterious.

Two men were busy cleaning the floors, the hum of the machines they pushed about on the white marble floor the only noise in the room. They were paying particular attention to the bloody smudges that Bethany had tracked through the house before going to bed and fouling the carpet all the way up the stairs and down the hall with her bloody footprints. With Bethany being bathed in blood on a regular basis, it would probably be best to change the carpet out to tile or wood flooring soon. Putting white carpet on the stairs and upstairs hall had not been one of her best decorating choices.

Satisfied with the Entry Hall, Cathryn went through the downstairs, the Green Room, the Library, the smaller private dining rooms, and the Cathedral Hall where Sky Dragon stood before the Book of Shadows, considering his words. Cathryn slipped into the kitchen. It was busy, about ten women and one man were baking, getting ready for breakfast.

She went to the correct cabinet and grabbed a plate herself and a fresh cinnamon roll from the sheet, just out of the oven, and a cup of tea then headed out toward the garden. She looked around and spotted the couple and their parents, who hadn't been anywhere in the house, sitting at the metal table in the center of the garden. As she approached the group she noticed that Jane and Dan's eyes were glowing red. They each had an odd looking clay pot in front of them.

"Hello, Queen Cathryn." Mr. Miller greeted her warmly but looked uncomfortable as he pulled and adjusted his bathrobe. "We're a little underdressed out here. Hope you don't mind that we're out here in our bathrobes."

Cathryn smiled and did an elegant curtsy, still holding her plate and bun in one hand and her saucer and cup of tea in the other. "I appear to be the one out of fashion, Mr. Miller. May I in my nighty join your robed table?" she asked.

They all stared at her as if she'd done something special, but she hadn't, at least she didn't think she had. "Yes. Please do," Jane answered in her musical voice as her parents continued to stare.

Cathryn sat down at the end of the bench between them and took a sip of her tea. "It's a beautiful night out," Cathryn began, and they all shared welcoming small talk for a minute before Cathryn realized with a little start that she was being a very poor host. The Millers had no drinks or rolls or even a light for the table. She wished she'd thought to bring a servant with her.

"Please bring me a servant," she said out loud.

"Were you talking to me?" asked Mr. Miller.

"Oh my. No," Cathryn said, surprised at herself, and it showed on her face clearly. "Sorry. Forgive me."

"Are you all right?" asked Mrs. Miller.

"Yes. Just surprised. Speaking thoughts and words unbidden is not one of my usual, peculiarities." She took a sip of her tea, her eyes looking wild and troubled for a second while she resettled herself.

"Who were you talking to Queen Cathryn?" Jane asked.

"Honestly, I'm not quite sure myself, Jane. I think I was talking to Amen Hale, but I may have been talking to myself. The Kingdom seems very sensitive to my needs of late."

"Does Amen Hale talk back to you when you talk to it?" Jane politely inquired about the half that made her sound less insane.

"Not yet," Cathryn replied and took a bite out of her pastry as the four others shared surprised looks. "It's a new thing. Cornelius spoke to Amen Hale last night and was answered. And it keeps bringing me things I want or need. Like gifts. But enough about me and enough small talk, how are you four doing? I'm so sorry about what happened." She looked at Jane and Dan. "Please forgive us for not protecting you better. This was a horrible way to begin your eternity."

"There is nothing to forgive," Jane assured her and Dan nodded as well. "It's wonderful to sit here at this table with my Dan and my parents and not have to worry about some stupid soldier trying to kill us. We're all going to watch the sunrise together. I never even did that while I was human." She looked over at her mother.

"You know I tried! You would never get out of bed," Mrs. Miller replied. "You and that body pillow of yours."

Dan growled, looking upset for some reason and Jane laughed, the musical sound so beautiful that her parents and Cathryn all stopped and listened as she and Dan had a quick silent conversation apparently about Jane's body length pillow. Jane patiently explained the joke and they all were able to share in the laughter.

Jane's father asked a more serious question. "Are we really safe from the soldiers here?" Mr. Miller looked toward the garden wall and the darkness beyond it.

"From the U.S. government, it seems we most certainly are, but not from others," Cathryn answered.

"Amen Hale heard you, Queen Cathryn," Jane said and pointed back toward the house.

Two servants were already halfway up the path. Four sets of eyes turned to regard Cathryn. Cathryn busied herself with her roll and tea and pretended not to notice their stares while the servants set two place setting before the Millers, complete with candles to light the table, and a platter laden with a variety of fresh buns and pastries. They were asked their drink preference, and Mr. and Mrs. Miller both chose orange juice.

The two servants did not place anything before the vampires or ask their drink preference and wordlessly refilled Cathryn's cup of tea. One servant departed back toward the house while the other took up a position about ten steps away, his eyes watching carefully for any need they may have. Cathryn looked toward the east; the sky was still a solid blanket of night but soon the first burn of the rising sun would begin.

"As you're about to watch the sun rise, I take it that sunlight doesn't harm you?" Cathryn guessed.

Jane and Dan both smiled. "We won't burst into ash if that's what you mean, but we will shine. Dan and I have never seen ourselves in direct sunlight. We're quite curious to see the rest of what we've become."

Jane gave Dan an annoyed look. "All right already," she grumbled and picked up the clay jar in front of her and tipped it up and up and up, the beautiful milk white neck swallowing and swallowing. She set the jar down and licked her teeth clean of blood and swallowed once again then leaned toward Dan. There was some blood on her face and on the sides of her mouth, and Dan held her head with both hands while he licked the blood off her face. Still holding her head he kissed her then pulled back enough to stare into her eyes.

"Okay, you were right. It's still edible," Jane said sullenly, frowning as she said the words. Dan growled and Jane lowered her eyes, submissively. "All right," she said, and after another second she said, "Please."

Dan vanished in a little gust of wind.

"Where did—" Jane's father began but stopped as Dan reappeared in his chair followed by another small gust of wind, not enough to blow out the candles on the table but enough to feel against the skin. The small breeze raised goose bumps on Cathryn's flesh. Dan placed a second clay jar in front of his wife and another in front of himself.

"You should have eaten that first jar while it was hot like Dan did instead of letting it sit and get cold. It would have tasted better," Jane's mother scolded gently, sounding like every other mother in spite of the otherness of her children.

"Yeah, yeah." Jane sounded just like every other annoyed teenager.

"Why don't you like the taste of your blood anymore, honey? What's wrong?" asked Mr. Miller.

Dan tapped her new jar of blood, but Jane tried to distract him and rubbed up against him like a cat, slipping her hand inside his robe to play with his chest as she laughed wickedly.

"Please, Jane, drink your blood and tell us what's happened," her mother pleaded.

Dan opened his jar, then reached over and opened Jane's, leaving the clay lids on the table. He picked up his own jar and looked at Jane but she still wasn't reaching for her own.

Cathryn raised her cup of tea. "It's only tea, but it will serve. A toast then. Here's to starting your eternity with your true love by your side. And to watching the sun rise for the first time on 'forever' with your family."

Jane's parents joined in the obvious coercion attempt, each lifting their glasses and making their own toasts. Dan used his fingernail and some blood he dipped out from his jar as ink to write his toast on a napkin which he handed to Mr. Miller for him to read.

They finished their toasts and all together, a cup of tea, two glasses of OJ, and a jar of blood went into the air as they stared at her.

Jane sighed, picked up her jar of blood, and raised it up to meet the others, making a toast of her own. "Here's to sneaky witch Queens, to my overly freaked out parents, and to my pestering and loving husband, and to Rain, because the sun may rise in the east and set in the west, but it *lives* in her blood."